VICKY PETERWALD: DOMINATOR

MIKE SHEPHERD

KL&MM
BOOKS

PRAISE FOR THE KRIS LONGKNIFE NOVELS

"A whopping good read . . . Fast-paced, exciting, nicely detailed, with some innovative touches." - Elisabeth Moon, Nebula Award-winning author of Crown Renewal

"Shepherd delivers no shortage of military action, in space and on the ground. It's cinematic, dramatic, and dynamic . . . [He also] demonstrates a knack for characterization, balancing serious moments with dry humor . . . A thoroughly enjoyable adventure featuring one of science fiction's most interesting recurring heroines." - TOR.com

"A tightly written, action-packed adventure from start to finish . . . Heart-thumping action will keep the reader engrossed and emotionally involved. It will be hard waiting for the next in the series." - Fresh Fiction

"[Daring] will elate fans of the series . . . The story line is faster than the speed of light." - Alternative Worlds

"[Kris Longknife] will remind readers of David Weber's

Honor Harrington with her strength and intelligence. Mike Shepherd provides an exciting military science fiction thriller." -Genre Go Round Reviews

"'I'm a woman of very few words, but lots of action': so said Mae West, but it might just as well have been Lieutenant Kris Longknife, princess of the one hundred worlds of Wardhaven. Kris can kick, shoot, and punch her way out of any dangerous situation, and she can do it while wearing stilettos and a tight cocktail dress. She's all business, with a Hell's Angel handshake and a 'get out of my face' attitude. But her hair always looks good . . . Kris Longknife is funny and she entertains us." - SciFi Weekly

"[A] fast-paced, exciting military SF series . . . Mike Shepherd has a great ear for dialogue and talent for injecting dry humor into things at just the right moment . . . The characters are engaging, and the plot is full of twists and peppered liberally with sharply described action. I always look forward to installments in the Kris Longknife series because I know I'm guaranteed a good time with plenty of adventure." -SF Site

In the New York Times bestselling Kris Longknife novels, "Fans of the Honor Harrington escapades will welcome the adventures of another strong female in outer space starring in a thrill-a-page military space opera." - Alternative Worlds

"Military SF fans are bound to get a kick out of the series as a whole." - SF Site

COPYRIGHT INFORMATION

investing in a copy so I can continue to earn a living at this wonderful art.

I would like to thank my wonderful cover artist, Scott Grimando, who did all my Ace covers and will continue doing my own book covers. I also am grateful for the editing skill of Lisa Müller, Edee Lemonier, and as ever, Ellen Moscoe.

Ver 1.0

eBook ISBN-13: 978-1-64211-0272
Print ISBN-13: 978-1-64211-0265

Kris Longknife: Resolute

Kris Longknife: Audacious

Kris Longknife: Intrepid

Kris Longknife: Undaunted

Kris Longknife: Redoubtable

Kris Longknife: Daring

Kris Longknife: Furious

Kris Longknife: Defender

Kris Longknife: Tenacious

Kris Longknife: Unrelenting

Kris Longknife: Bold

Vicky Peterwald: Target

Vicky Peterwald: Survivor

Vicky Peterwald: Rebel

Mike Shepherd writing as Mike Moscoe in the Jump Point Universe

First Casualty

The Price of Peace

They Also Serve

Rita Longknife: To Do or Die

Short Specials

Kris Longknife: Training Daze

Kris Longknife: Welcome Home, Go Away

Kris Longknife's Bloodhound

Kris Longknife's Assassin

The Lost Millennium Trilogy published by KL & MM Books

Lost Dawns: Prequel

First Dawn

Second Fire

Lost Days

Award-Nominated Short Story Collections by Mike Shepherd

A Day's Work on the Moon

The Job Interview

The Strange Redemption of Sister MaryAnn

1

———

It was a lovely spring day. The sky was a clear azure blue you could almost swim in. The cooling breeze brought the scent of the first buds of the year. On every block stood cheering, smiling people.

Vice Admiral, Her Imperial Grace, Grand Duchess Victoria Smythe-Peterwald, Heir Apparent to the throne of the Greenfeld Empire, waved at the throng lining the street, even though her arm felt ready to fall off. She smiled though her face was in agony.

Still, if she had her way, the eight white horses pulling this golden open carriage of state would be whipped to a gallop to get her to the church faster.

"Thanks be to whatever god or goddess who finally managed to pull this off. I really am getting married," she said, through smiling teeth.

Her Royal Highness, Admiral Princess Kristine Longknife, kept waving and smiling, but through her teeth she said, "Finally getting married? You're not so old that spinsterhood was threatening."

"Spinsterhood, sminsterhood, do you know it's taken a

solid year to get this zoo organized and ready for me to walk down the aisle?"

Kris kept waving, but she did raise an eyebrow. "What, did you go all bridezilla on everyone's ass?"

Vicky dutifully kept waving as well, but she was dearly grateful to have Kris seated across from her rather than the Emperor, her father. Of course, they'd had to reinstall the seat Kris sat on, dropping it 15 centimeters. If the Emperor had managed to come, his seat would have been exactly seven and a half centimeters above hers.

Yuck. Vicky did miss her dad, kind of. Still the man was such an attention hog. He wanted to be the bride at every wedding and the cadaver at every funeral. Today was *her* day, and she was glad not to share it with him.

She was very glad to be sharing it with Kris Longknife. She was also glad that one of them hadn't killed the other. If Vicky was honest, most likely she'd be the one dead.

Vicky almost let an inexplicable laugh replace her smile, but she smothered it. "It wasn't me going bridezilla for a year. No. It was damn near every woman of any social standing in my half of the Empire going mother-in-law 'zilla on me."

Kris kept waving. "Oh, Lord, you weren't hit with a couple of thousand women as excited as my mom was to plan my wedding, were you?"

"Exactly. I came home from Cuzco hoping to send out invites to folks to set aside a day the next week to attend Mannie's and my wedding, and I got told no one could put on a wedding that quickly. Then everyone got in on the act."

"Well, I admit, this is a lot bigger show than when I and Jack got married."

"Didn't you two elope?"

"Ha. We had most of the Colonials on Alwa at our

wedding, though we did knock it together in three or four hours."

"Three or four hours!" Vicky yelped, but carefully, so as not to mar her perfect smile.

"Yeah," Kris said through her smile while constantly waving. "There were a couple of hours when I wasn't Jack's boss. Granny Rita offered to help us grab the bull by the horns, and next thing I know, I'm walking down the aisle in a borrowed wedding dress that's too short and I'm sewn into the bust to tighten it. Jack had to use a bayonet to cut me out."

Kris paused, and Vicky could see her eyes go far away and her smile get soft.

"It was wild, but I loved every minute of it."

With a shake, Kris seemed to refocus on where she was. "That's a lovely wedding dress you're wearing. Be glad my mom wasn't involved in picking it. She was looking at a dress with absolutely no sides for Penny. No sides! You could see her underwear, except the bride wasn't supposed to wear any. I had to talk Mother out of that by letting her choose the bridesmaids' dresses."

"How'd that work out?"

"I ended up wearing this tiny band around my rump and front, kind of like a daisy with petals that were covering my boobs. Strippers wore more than what I did."

"Oh, God. And I thought my dress was going to be a disaster."

"Your dress looks really classy."

They were passing a stretch with almost no one lining the sidewalk. Vicky allowed her face to relax and her arm to hang at her side. Both hurt.

"There was serious talk that I ought to wear black or

ashes and sack cloth. It appears that my misspent youth preceded me."

"You're kidding me."

"Well, those weren't proposed to my face, but my two assassins had hooks into the biddy grapevine and swore it was bounced around. Maybe it was a joke, but . . ."

"Yeah," Kris agreed, herself rotating her shoulders and shaking out the pain in her arm.

"You notice this is not a white dress," Vicky said, patting at the many layers of the skirt piled high in her lap and on the seat beside her. While the low-cut strapless bodice clung to her body like a second skin, from the waist down, the dress exploded in wave upon wave of lace and roses and tulle.

"Lots of brides wear ivory," Kris said.

"Is this ivory or off-white?" Vicky shot back. "Christ, Kris, even the pearls on the bodice aren't white."

"Vicky, I think you're taking this a bit too personally," Kris said, softly. "Could you be having slightly cold feet?"

"We need to start waving," Vicky said, and raised her hand even if the crowd on the sidewalk wasn't that thick.

"It's a lovely carriage we're riding in. Where'd you get all this gold inlaid with jewels?"

"There's no way I would have let them make something like this for me," Vicky spat. "But Metzburg got paid a visit by my grandfather or great-grandfather, and they knocked it together back then to flatter him. I think they hauled it out of a museum or a bank vault and insisted we use it."

"And those eight lovely white horses?"

"That are whiter than my dress?"

"I was trying to avoid that topic."

"Okay. They are lovely, aren't they? Some thirty planets that raise horses had a contest to see who could present us with the whitest horses. These are the six whitest. The rest are drawing the coaches with the rest of my ladies-in-waiting and others in the wedding party."

"You're really going to remember this day."

"Assuming I don't knock the driver off her seat and take off, lashing the horses myself."

Kris couldn't avoid a chuckle at that.

Vicky's mind's eye filled with the image of her, a wild woman in full outrage, standing on Kris's seat and whipping her horses to a gallop, while her dress streamed out behind her.

It didn't look all that bad.

Except then Vicky started hearing a line from a Christmas carol, "On Donner! On Blitzen!" Fortunately, it ended because she couldn't remember the rest of the line.

"Considering that your two tiny assassins are your coachmen, I don't see that happening," Kris said.

Yes, Kit and Kat were up in the boot. One held the reins, the other the whip. No doubt, both had their hands on an automatic weapon. From the way their heads slowly swiveled, Vicky knew they weren't spending a lot of time watching the horses.

Those beasts were not only pure white, but someone had drugged them to be damn near somnolent.

"Yeah," Vicky finally said. "You're right as always. I'm going to that church come hell or high water.

From Kris's throat, a jewel spoke. "Longknife 1, this is Longknife 2. We may have a bomb along the route."

"Talk to me, Megan," Kris shot back.

"There is a rumor that's just arrived here at the command center that someone hid a bomb along the bride's line of march."

"Rumor?" Kris snapped.

"It's being evaluated. At first blush, it's a case of he heard, she heard, someone else heard. You know, that sort of thing."

Vicky had sat bolt upright at the word 'bomb'. What she heard from Kris Longknife's cousin and dog robber didn't relax her back into her seat.

Apparently, it didn't do the same for the Magnificent Nelly, either.

Suddenly, the large, lovely, and bejeweled tiara surrounding Kris's upswept hair began to dissolve into small drones. The four fancy starbursts and crosses of various orders Kris had earned the hard way that bejeweled her bodice also proved to be Smart Metal™. They collapsed in on themselves and disappeared from the lovely blue sash that draped from Kris's shoulder to hip. Quickly, the drones flew off, only to disappear into vapor as they themselves dissolved into miniscule nano scouts.

For the moment, however, most of them stayed drones as they raced for the head of the procession and beyond.

"Are you searching all up and down the cavalcade?" Vicky asked.

"They're all your subjects," Kris noted, pointedly.

"I know. I know. While I've been twiddling my thumbs waiting to marry Mannie, he's been busy seducing me to the democratic side. We've got a major infestation of popular sovereignty and democratic rule."

"It couldn't happen to a better empire," Kris said with a grin.

The coach rumbled forward on its iron tires at a sedate horse walk, then took on a decided wobble.

"You're Imperial Grace," one of the assassins in the coach's boot said, "we are told that one of our wheels is in danger of rolling off. See how people are pointing at it?"

A glance to Vicky's right showed that several people were pointing and at least two men were waving for attention shouting about a loose wheel.

"We are going to have to halt, Your Grace," the other tiny killer said.

"I hate to be a target," Vicky said, then laughed at the face Kris gave her.

"Yes, I know. I'm always a target, and so are you, and riding around behind these prancing monsters certainly isn't conducive to me living through the day."

Kris's grin was very self-satisfied. "I think we have the situation well in hand."

Just then, four small trucks appeared from the back of the procession. A guy got out and started hollering orders and several other people joined him shouting this or that, and someone called in for a jack to get the coach's wheel off the ground. There was a lot of official movement, not accomplishing much of anything.

What Vicky did see was four trucks, each with small clear domes in the middle of their roof. Two of them backed up to her carriage and opened their doors. Inside huddled several heavily armed and armored troopers, all on hair triggers.

"Am I correct if I guess that those plastic domes are not there to let light in?"

"Two surface-to-air lasers and two pop-up surface-to-surface ones as well. See the ridge along the roof all the way around the back cabin?"

"Yep."

"Side-looking radar. I'm told it's so fast it can track a rifle round if it's fired from four hundred meters away. Fast enough so the SAM can knock it aside."

"Is this by any chance your contribution to my wedding?"

"Oh, no. Fear not. I brought some real presents from my grampa, King Ray, and a silver teething ring, only slightly used, for you."

"I should think by now Ruthie's next sibling might be wanting time on that."

"Oh, right. We put a darling boy in the can before we left."

"You're not going to do a natural birth?"

"Oh, God no. I did it once. That's quite enough for this girl. No, if Jack wants another kid, he can either carry it himself or help me put it in a uterine replicator."

"I've already reserved several," Vicky said, primly, fluffing up her skirt and patting it down again. "If Mannie wants a bunch of kids, we rent the cans."

For a few moments, they waved at the crowd. It was

thickening up. As was to be expected, the entire cavalcade had come to a halt. People from up and down the boulevard were now collecting along this section of sidewalk.

A few were being pushed forward, or just kind of accidentally, on purpose, getting closer. Vicky wasn't sure whether she or the horses were the main attraction.

Just when she though the US Marines might have to be ordered out from where they hid as inconspicuously as possible, a pair of trucks loaded with police arrived. The police set up a perimeter and the people stepped back.

"Footman," Vicky said.

"Yes, Your Grace?"

"I don't see why those little children can't be allowed to pet the horses. Dismount and walk up and down the line. If a child and a parent are willing, bring the little one in close to the horses. Don't scare the child, but let them pet the horse if they want."

"Yes, Your Grace," had all the submission behind it of a senior NCO telling an officer they needed their head examined.

"Sergeant, we can't look like we are an armed fortress, scared of our own people. I have learned a few things from my future husband."

"As you wish, Your Grace," and the two footmen, both of whom were clearly senior NCO's dismounted and began walking up and down the line.

An eight-year-old girl was the first to let her lust for horse flesh get past her terminal shyness. The footman held her hand as she approached the lead horse cautiously. The horse swung its head around to get a good look at her.

She retreated two steps but regained her courage quickly. In a moment, she was petting the horse's shoulder.

This time when the horse swung its head around, the sergeant helped the girl pet its muzzle.

A much younger child back on the police line started yelling. It turned out the first girl was her sister. Big sister ran back and got little sister and even held the youngster up to pet the horse's back.

Vicky shook her head. Once upon a time, she'd been a horse-crazy girl, too. She understood where those two were coming from.

The problem was, there were a lot of girls, and even a few boys, who wanted a chance to pet the big beasts. Yet there were only two coachmen.

Luck was with Vicky, for a change. It turned out that several of the people working hard at not fixing the wheel were under arms, considered good security risks and . . . miracle of miracles . . . knew one end of a horse from the other.

Soon, each of the eight horses, and the coach ahead with four bridesmaids, and likely the one ahead of it, were all giving carefully controlled petting opportunities to little ones in the crowd.

"Kris, would I be wrong to think that some of those trucks are spawning drones?"

"Nope. I do not think you'd be wrong at all. Nelly's been telling me that the search perimeter has been widely expanded, with no results so far. We're checking out the inside of the perimeter again. Who knows what might crawl out from a sewer?"

"Yuck."

"Well?"

"Yes. Yes, I know, but sometimes I think this business is just . . . ."

"Has no soul?"

"Yeah. I am really looking forward to time on the beach at an undisclosed location with just me and Mannie."

"And us," came from the coach boot.

"Staying out of sight. This is not your honeymoon."

"But he's so cute," the one with the whip said.

"You know, he's half-afraid of you two."

"Only half?" was again the one with the whip.

"The other half of him is afraid of me."

"As well he should be," the one with the reins said.

Vicky decided the subject needed changing. "Kris, can your Nelly tell me how long it's going to take to fix that wheel? I'm assuming there really is a problem."

"Oh, there is a real problem," Nelly said from Kris's throat. "My nanos made sure there was something for the crowd to see. However, as soon as Megan gives the all clear, you'll be amazed at how quickly it gets fixed."

"And how close is Megan to giving that okay?"

"We've chased down two of the people in the chain of this rumor," Lieutenant J.G. Megan Longknife reported. "The bomb report is getting thinner and thinner. If I was betting, I'd say you'll be back underway in five minutes."

Vicky eyed all the kids that had collected around the horses. The animals were amazingly well behaved, all things considering. It would be a pain to bring this to an end.

"Maybe we can include those horses in some post-wedding visits to parks around the capital," Vicky said. "Maybe even visit some of the other major cities on Metzburg."

"I'm not sure the bank will want to loan out this asset too often," Kris said, looking around at the gold and precious stones.

"Could your Nelly be so kind as to knock out a Smart Metal replica?"

"You always ask me so much better than Kris does," Nelly said.

"I do to ask nice," the princess said, a bit pouty.

"But you know you'll get what you want, eventually. Kris Longknife, you are too much assured of your own entitlement."

"Nelly, I've been depending on you since kindergarten."

"While I don't remember that far back, I do remember you expecting me to do your homework."

"Okay, I was a bratty teen. So sue me."

"Be careful Kris. Remember, I have standing in a court of law."

"As a witness. Who says any judge would hear your case?"

"That is an interesting question."

The bickering between Kris and her computer was keeping Vicky's mind off of the thought that someone out there wanted her dead. She'd had her nose shoved in that often enough that the sting was less, but it was still there.

After all she'd done for these people, some of them still considered her a Peterwald, and were only too willing to take their grievance out on her.

Her ruminations were cut short.

She heard the report of a high-powered rifle.

At almost the same instant, she felt the hit on her shoulder and face.

"Gun!" someone shouted.

3

Vicky rolled left, trying to shed some of the energy her spidersilk body armor was taking. She did that without thinking.

Gun, damn it! Not a bomb, but a gun this time!

She had her back to the Marine gun trucks Princess Kris Longknife had brought to her wedding. Vicky had considered them a fine present. Right now, she was promoting their status to great present and the head of her line for a thank you note.

Her breast ached, but not that badly. The spidersilk had hardened and distributed the force of the bullet from her neck to her below her belly button. With luck, Mannie would not find one of her breasts black and blue and off-limits tonight.

Her neck and cheek also stung from a dusting of gunshot residue and bullet fragments. Still, not that badly.

Before bed that night, Mannie would want to see the security feed for this assassination attempt. The two of them would watch the take at extra-slow speed.

The shot came from six hundred meters out. This was a skilled sniper.

The radars had spotted the shot immediately and plotted its course. The two anti-air lasers followed the flight of the bullet, slicing and dicing it. The radar showed the round fragmenting and the fragments getting sliced again. What was left tumbled through the air.

One large fragment went high and smashed into the bricks of a building behind Vicky. Tiny shards of brick showered down on the crowd, but no one seemed very hurt.

Several shards buried themselves into the carriage around Vicky and Kris. Vicky had originally considered the carriage to be made of wood. It did have a wood veneer. However, it was over a body of plastic and ceramic armor. Three small fragments marred the finish, and a few smaller ones, little more than dust if anything else, speckled the gold and jewels.

Two fragments, however, hit royalty.

Princess Longknife was knocked to the right side of her seat, but the bullet fragment had hit her arm. A glance told Vicky that Kris had worn her spidersilks today. Smart girl.

Like Vicky, Kris was wearing a strapless gown. Her arms would have been bare, except for the thin, nearly transparent sheen of the armor. For a moment, it puffed up and spread a blotch out over her arm as it distributed the force of the hit.

Kris stayed down, however.

Vicky was hit in her right breast. Oh, and something made her neck and cheek sting. There had been much debate this morning among the tirewomen getting her dressed about what was the proper undergarments for a royal wedding. Most were very much for a lovely strapless demi-bra and matching frilly and diminutive thong.

Vicky had been glad that she was finally getting to wear something perfectly white. Of course, she would have preferred something fire engine red to match her hair, but who was listening to her?

The consternation set in when the two assassins brought Vicky her best spidersilk body suit.

"You can't wear that!" had come in full choir volume.

"But I am."

"But your strapless gown! Your lovely pale skin. That . . . that . . . that will ruin the first look Mannie gets of you in the church!"

"Let's just say that Mannie will understand."

Spidersilk was not yet on the open market. It might never make it there if some very important people like Kris Longknife and Vicky herself could keep it reasonably unknown.

While the women looked on, Kit and Kat helped Vicky into the awkward and tight body suit.

Then Vicky had let the army of mothers and grand-mothers cosset her to their hearts' contentment.

Now, the power of the hit in the shoulder was absorbed by the spidersilk and spread out over most of her chest and stomach.

Following Kris's movements, Vicky ducked down and to her left. Still, the two of them found themselves grinning at each other while they let their armored rumps be the center of mass for any more shots.

The next shot did not come.

While the radar and the computer had been predicting the bullet's trajectory and attacked it, another part of the computer was back-tracking the round to its source.

The two surface-to-surface lasers opened up and spat a

quick staccato of beams at the window the shot had come from.

"I've got nanos covering that building," Nelly reported. "More on the way. Wait one please."

"What's a wedding without a few assassination attempts?" Kris said, beaming.

"Your arm looks okay."

"I'll likely have a bruise soon."

"What do I look like?" Vicky asked.

"The perfect cliché of a blushing bride."

"Can the corn, Longknife. What do I look like?"

"The top of your right breast may have a bruise, I don't know for sure. About where your nipple must be, you've got a black mark. There are also some tiny black specks on your neck and cheek. Maybe we can cover them over with makeup."

"No and hell no," Vicky spat. "It's time Mannie and my people see me as I am, with this damn target on my back. Nelly, I hope you didn't kill the shooter. I really want to read his interrogation report."

"So do I, Vicky," Nelly said. "I've identified the exact apartment on the twenty-third floor and I've got nanos headed there. I don't know if you noticed the ruckus, but as soon as the bullet splattered itself all over the place, two of the Marine gun trucks gunned out of here. I'm directing them to both block the exits and get up to that room."

"We've got police incoming," Megan reported. "I'm showing both fire teams a view of what the other side looks like and where they are. It would be nice if we could avoid fratricidal fire."

"Do you have any eyes on the gun room?" Kris asked.

"I've got a drone looking in. The weapon's taken damage.

I don't have the shooter in sight. Converting drone to nano scouts now."

There was a pause, a very short one.

"Oh, good. I did have one of the lasers back down enough."

"What, Nelly?" Kris said.

"I used full strength on one of my ground-to-ground lasers to take out the weapon. I used lower power to target around it. From the look and sound of the guy writhing on the floor, I got him. I may have blinded him in one eye. I hope not both. I want him to identify who his paymaster is."

"Good going, Nelly. Now, if you have a little spare capacity, could you fix the front carriage wheel? I know a girl that needs to get to the church on time."

"I am going to be so late," Vicky said with a sigh.

"But you have a good excuse," Kris said, cheerfully. "At least one that is always good for a Peterwald or a Longknife."

"Yes, dear. So sorry I'm late. An assassin had traffic backed up!" Vicky said in a voice dripping with sarcasm.

The two shared a laugh at something they were likely the only people in human space to see the humor in.

The children had all hit the ground at the sound of the shot. The sergeants hollered, and the kids dropped, if a bit slower than trained troops. In every case, the bigger kids took care of the smaller ones.

Good kids.

The police line kind of dissolved as parents charged forward to get their kids.

No matter how many drugs those poor horses had in their system, between the sound of the shot and the charge of the people, things got a bit wild. There was a lot of kicking and head turning. One of the lead horses reared up in harness.

Things might have gone really sideways, but one of the footmen and another fellow from among the workers helped to calm the beasts, held their reins and talked them down.

The kids and parents washed back up on the sidewalk without the police getting too upset, and by the time the "broken" wheel was ready, so was everything else.

One again, the cavalcade got going.

"We do have the assassin in hand. He's from off planet. Oh, Greenfeld to be precise."

"I thought ships weren't coming through from Greenfeld?" Kris said.

"Yeah. They aren't. Not even messages from my dad, much less him," Vicky said, frowning.

"The assassin isn't saying much, except that he hurts and demands medical care."

"See that he's properly sedated," Vicky said. "Something that will encourage him to babble, if you will."

"I've already suggested it," Nelly answered.

Vicky might be riding in a silly coach on her way to an overblown wedding ceremony, but she remembered what it was to be a Peterwald.

The smile on her face was not at all the one expected from a bride.

No. Vicky was smiling like a very angry Peterwald.

4

———

The cavalcade pulled up in front of the Cathedral of St. Joseph. It was a large barn of a church, built from local stone in a classical neo-gothic design.

Standing on the front plaza to greet Vicky were a small army of clergy. This was another one of the things she was obliged to suffer through to satisfy both Mannie and the social ladies.

Cardinal Archbishop Guillaume Ki Moon presided over both the cathedral and the largest diocese on Metzburg. He looked resplendent in his red robes and wide-brimmed galero, the Cardinal's hat with tassels.

Beside him was the Anglican Archbishop of Canterbury. Somehow, the folks on Metzburg had succeeded in building a city named Canterbury and the Anglicans had set up shop there.

Vicky's study of history let her in on this particular joke. Most people missed it.

The cardinal first leaned forward to shake her hand.

"Your Grace," he whispered. "You have something on your neck."

"Yes, I do," she said, smiling but giving no further response.

There was a wave of heads back and forth among the waiting clergy. They handled the matter well. Vicky faced no more questions.

Kris stayed at Vicky's elbow, covering her right flank. The two footmen had dismounted to cover her back and left. Kat had left the whip with Kit, dismounted, and was eyeing everyone that approached. Her hand was in her pocket.

Vicky knew quite well what the hand rested on.

After shaking the hand of the Archbishop of Canterbury, Vicky was introduced to a Methodist bishop, a Buddhist bishop, the president of the Lutheran Synod on Metzburg, an Imam, and representatives of several different denominations.

Vicky had already been told that the local Wiccans had been invited to send a representative, but the various different associations had not been able to agree on a single representative.

After her honeymoon, Vicky was requested to attend a hand fasting ceremony in their sacred oak grove. She and Mannie had already accepted.

Every hand shaken, the men of God strode off, most prayerfully. They needed to get to the front of the church and were headed for a back entrance.

Now, Vicky was accosted by a collection of worthy politicians. This had been cut ruthlessly to the bone. All the visiting heads of planets would get their chance to shake her hand later and wheedle her for something.

Here, all Vicky had to put up with was the President of Metzburg and the Mayor of the capital, plus a very few other representatives of business and society. The men bowed. Several of the women attempted to curtsey, not an easy thing to do in a pencil skirt.

Vicky gave them an A for effort if not for delivery.

All the time this was going on, the bridesmaids had been entering the church and proceeding down the aisle.

"Your Grace, aren't you after me?" Princess Longknife said, and picked up her skirts to hustle, ever so graciously, up the steps.

"Ladies, Gentlemen, in this bodice, I dare not run, so, if you will excuse me, I must get to the church not quite on time."

She was allowed a soft titter of laughter. They left, leaving her to wait for several twelve-year-old girls to arrange her train and veil properly under the supervision of a very astute eighteen-year-old.

Vicky took a moment to focus herself. She buried her nose in her bouquet and took a moment to enjoy the lovely scent.

Fixing a bride's smile on her face, she began the slow walk up the cathedral's broad steps. As she reached the last step, the organ, a monstrous thing with at least five keyboards and an entire forest of pipes, began the strains of Pomp and Circumstance.

This bride was no common bride. This bride was a grand duchess, ruler of half the Greenfeld Empire and heir to the rest upon her father's death.

Speaking of which, where was the old fool?

Still, Vicky refused to let that thought ruin her day.

She stepped into the church and began the longest walk of her life.

Hopefully, there was no one inside who wanted to kill her before she reached the altar.

5

H er Imperial Grace, Grand Duchess Vice Admiral Victoria Smythe-Peterwald was living a dream, and discovering both the dark side and silver lining simultaneously.

As a young girl, she'd always wanted to be the center of attention. Yet, that attention always went to her brother. She'd love it when she was given fancy dresses, although it so often felt like no one around her was all that impressed by her or the dress.

Even as a girl, she had known that her marriage would be arranged by her father. It would be an arrangement that brought him the most political and economic benefit.

What her wedding would bring to Vicky would not get a moment of his reflection.

Now, as the music of the great organ swelled and filled the church, Vicky's long walk down the aisle gave her time to reflect.

She was certainly the center of attention, not only of the thousands in the cathedral, but also of millions watching on media here on Metzburg and billions who would catch it when it was broadcasted around her half of the Greenfeld Empire.

However, it wasn't her they were watching. No, she had become the physical embodiment of their own hopes and dreams for a better life, a better world, a better Empire.

That was what she had learned through the hard year of dodging and finally rebelling against her stepmother, the Empress. Alone, Vicky was dead. With the willing assistance of her subjects, she not only could stay alive, but they could achieve so much more for themselves and each other.

I am a flag they salute, but in saluting me, they salute each other as well as themselves.

That had been a strange lesson, but Mannie had helped her learn it.

Mannie, the man she had chosen to marry.

Funny that. Once more she had a fancy dress, but it was one that other people had chosen for her.

Yet, while the dress might again be not of her choosing, the guy at the end of this walk was most definitely the one she wanted to marry. The man she wanted to share her life with.

Everything was so very extraordinarily special, and totally different from what as a little girl she had expected it to be.

Of course, that little girl had been taught little more than needlepoint and the Kama Sutra for offense and defense. Oh, and to obey Father's word instantaneously.

As Vicky paced off each step down the aisle, she was glad she could let her face relax from the perpetual smile to something more solemn. The moment certainly called for that. Still, she nodded a bit to the right, then a bit to the left.

These people would remember such a nod for the rest of

their life. At the moment, Vicky wasn't sure she could remember any of their faces for a second.

She was actually starting to get butterflies in her stomach!

It couldn't be that she was nervous about their coming wedding night. She'd bedded hundreds of men and not a few women while she'd been using them for one means or another.

She and Mannie had not exactly waited for the minister.

Of course, the last month they'd been more than busy. She'd been doing her best to gently coax half of an empire toward sane and safe policies while being set about by women who clearly wanted on their tombstone that the greatest achievement in their entire life was getting one Grand Duchess married properly.

Mannie had spent a lot of time at her elbow, but he'd also been off with his democratic friends, plotting against the autocratic tendencies of so many of the power brokers in the Peterwald Empire.

The entire *raison d'être* for the Empire had been to provide the Smyth-Peterwald family the levers of power to secure themselves and a vast and growing fortune. Deals had been made with lesser men of power. They might amass fortunes themselves if they made sure the Peterwalds amassed more.

Then Vicky's father had fallen under the spell of a young, beautiful woman, and the reins of power had slipped from his hands to her family's. She might have gotten away with it, were it not for one meddlesome and totally terrified kid.

The Empress had placed a target on Vicky's back, a price on her head, and some murderous hounds on her trail. That mistake had cost the Empress her life.

Now, Vicky and her chosen were trying to give an empire back to its people while others grabbed for power for themselves.

It was a messy business.

But, today was not for business. Today and the next month were for Vicky and Mannie.

Me, my, mine.

The long walk seemed to go on and on. The people lining the aisle were a blur. Vicky's mind was full of so much.

Then she caught sight of Mannie and her heart stopped. She missed a step, struggled with her balance for a moment, and might have tripped over her own feet. Still, she recovered and continued her walk.

Now, she felt her face break out into a most wondrous smile. One that he returned with his own bright grin.

Mannie had an army of groomsmen. General Jack Montoya stood at his side, resplendent in a blue and white dress Marine uniform. Several admirals in Greenfeld dress greens stood in line behind them, all bemedaled, most with awards and orders she had bestowed upon them for fighting by her side.

Still, the only person Vicky had eyes for was Mannie.

Now, one Grand Duchess had to struggle to keep from breaking into a run. Dutifully, Vicky kept one eye on her maid of honor, Princess Kris Longknife. Vicky could not get any closer to that troublesome princess. A Grand Duchess had to let a princess lead her and keep the proper interval in their march.

Still, Vicky's other eye never left Mannie.

If she lived to be a thousand, she could never get enough of looking at that man. There was no question, he was not handsome, as some would call it. And yes, he was always struggling to shed those ten extra pounds he insisted he needed to get rid of.

Still, swarthy, grinning Manuel Artemus had a power and a gentleness about him that Vicky had recognized the first time she met him.

If Vicky could smile any more, she'd smile at the memory of him finagling her, through Kris Longknife, to give his Sevastopol on St. Petersburg its own city charter. He wanted a charter to allow his growing city to rule itself, within its own boundaries and to its own ends.

Vicky was very glad she let Kris talk her into that. When she fled to St. Petersburg for her life, assassins on her heels, Mannie had taken her in, willing to pay a debt he felt he owed her.

He'd saved her life and began the new path that was leading her down the aisle and into his arms.

Thank you, Kris Longknife!

Vicky climbed the steps to the high altar, carefully holding her dress up off the ground so she wouldn't trip. If she thought modern women had obstacles put in their way, imagine a day when you had to keep your hands free to lift your skirts so you didn't trip over them.

The little girl who wanted the fancy dress was now very much replaced by the Grand Duchess who wanted to keep her hands ready to fight for what was right for her people.

If Vicky had had her way, she'd have been married in dress whites - pants, no less.

Oh, Lord, how that had caused consternation in the hen house. You would have thought she was the fox.

But there was no more time for thinking. There was Mannie, reaching out his hand for hers.

She had been firmly told that the bride and groom did not hug until the end of the ceremony. It took all of her will power to obey whatever elephant it was that decreed such a thing.

From the look on Mannie's grinning face, he was having a hard time as well.

Or were they both remembering Kat's comment, "The whole idea is to make it legal for the two of you to jump in bed. So, why don't they have a bed right there in the middle of the church, you two dash in naked, jump in bed, and consummate the marriage? Everything done and duly witnessed."

At this moment, Vicky was thinking Kat's wedding ceremony was looking good.

6

Three hours later, two things were clear. It was fortunate for humans that a computer did not snap at people for asking for the ten thousandth time, "How long so far?"

Also, Kat's idea of including a bed and just fucking for everyone to see was getting more and more attractive.

Back at the palace when Vicky was growing up, that might have been a great idea. Here, Mannie was quick to point out, hard working middle class values applied.

Being a Gracious Grand Duchess was a whole lot harder than being one of those damn Peterwalds.

Vicky knew she was in for a long haul when she realized there were more religious types seated around the altar than had greeted her. One was the Greek Orthodox Metropolitan for Metzburg. He'd been caught in traffic.

Some of the others were lower clergy that didn't rate the right to shake her hand before ceremony. Others were assistants to hold books open. Others swung something that burned what was supposed to be sweet smelling incense, but tended to turn Vicky's stomach.

Lots and lots of helpers.

With lots and lots of stuff to do.

In the wedding rehearsal, many parts of the ceremony had been hurried through with "and then this happens." "and then they do this." and "we wait while that is done." Now, all of that was done in real time. Lots of real time.

Vicky should have gotten the message that they were in for a long haul when someone mention, "Here they bring in chairs for the wedding party." About fifteen minutes into the ceremony, Vicky heard soft noises behind her and looked back to see men in gray robes quietly rolling in chairs and locking them down.

A moment later, the guy with the funny hat that was talking said, "The wedding party may now sit."

Vicky knew that there were cameras on her from every angle, if not flying overhead. She did not silently squeal her glee or secretly fist bump Mannie. She sat most ladylike, trying to arrange her huge train to trail gracefully around her chair.

As the hours went by, Vicky was introduced to all sorts of marriage customs from around her half of the Empire.

For example, several planets had admonishments read to the bride. Vicky rejected most of them immediately, but Mannie softened her, and they agreed to a list that Vicky would put up with. She also threw in a list of admonishments to the groom.

While a tall willow of a man with a voice like sandpaper and an accent that encrypted every word he said in an admonishing tone, she found a senior marksman from among her rangers who had the voice of a Gunny and the force of a hurricane. Vicky had seen her in action and could think of no one better to admonish Mannie with the reproofs she'd written.

Though she noted that while she still had the duty to bear children, her admonishment that he be a gentle lover, use his tongue often, and give her plenty of orgasms had been trimmed down to "give his wife children sufficient to carry on the line."

Damn prudes.

Vicky had looked at this as a chance to come up with a whole new tradition of admonishments for those of her people that used them. She was assured that the idea of admonishments for the groom was quite revolutionary enough.

Then there was the interpretive dance. The dancers seemed to be interpreting meeting, courtship, marriage, and family. Some of it was quite explicit. However, most of the impact was lost because all of the dancers wore long, flowing sleeves and robes.

Vicky realized she wasn't the only one stripping the dancers with her eyes when the trousers to Mannie's tux began to bulge.

She grinned at him.

He leaned close and whispered in her ear, "You, young lady, are a bad influence on your poor groom. Oh, what happened to your neck and why is your breast turning black and blue?"

He offered an ear, and she whispered, "Yes, I am a wicked lady, and I'll tell you later about how Kris and her Marines saved my life on the carriage ride here."

Mannie raised his eyebrows, as if to say "Again?"

Vicky shrugged softly, and went back to the dance. Were they really dancing an interpretation of childbirth?

Finally, exactly three hours and thirteen minutes into this, a dozen of the religious types gathered along the top step of the altar. The cardinal issued the invitation to take their vows.

Vicky, as a Grand Duchess marrying a commoner, went first. She'd planned that they'd both say the same vows.

That didn't last long. "Your Grace, you cannot vow to obey a commoner."

Thus, Vicky swore to "love, respect, and consult" Mannie. He did swear to "love, honor, and obey" her.

They both exchanged rings after the vows. Then, all of the dozen intoned together, "I now pronounce you Grand Duchess and consort. You may now kiss each other."

Boy, did Vicky kiss Mannie. Or he kissed her. Somehow, she ended up bent backwards.

It might have gotten very interesting, bed-in-the-cathedral interesting, but someone from the altar, actually several people, cleared their throats.

Vicky and Mannie did their best to get back up the aisle, but everyone wanted to shake hands. It was a good half hour before they got to the church door.

As they stepped out, a physical wave of shouts and applause washed over them. Vicky almost felt compelled to take a step back.

She waved her bouquet at everyone. That raised the noise level from nine on the Richter scale to eleven at least.

Then the two of them kissed and the crowd went even more wild.

When things quieted down, the two of them slowly walked down the steps, alone. No official had joined them. Kris was holding back the rest of the wedding party at the door. No one dared risk the disapproval of an admiral and a lieutenant general. Certainly not if they're part of the Longknife legend.

Finally, Vicky made it back to her coach. The two

footmen helped her and her dress back in. Mannie climbed in, and ended up with part of her dress in his lap, even though it now covered much of where Kris had sat on the way there.

It wasn't easy making room for a guy when you were sharing your seat with a monster veil and train.

Vicky did. No way was he riding in his own coach. Or even on one of her eight white horses.

They pulled ahead slowly, and now the wedding party began to make their way hurriedly down the steps to their own coaches. After a few minutes that Vicky spent waving at the crowd and kissing Mannie, Kit clicked at the horses and let the reins fall lightly on the horses. Kat released the hand brake, and they were off.

They made a short spin around Cathedral Square, then trotted up the broad avenue that had been renamed Freedom Way. There were several hotels up this way, as well as a huge football stadium. All would be filled, and she and Mannie would have to make at least an appearance at each of them.

It looked to be a long night.

An hour later, Vicky found herself standing at the head of a receiving line at the most very important VIP reception of the night. For once, she'd be ahead of Kris.

Even before her carriage arrived at the largest hotel on Metzburg, the VIPs had arrived before her, having slipped out several side doors at the cathedral and had been driven here by car.

As soon as she and Mannie were in place, she started shaking hands. Fortunately, her computer fed her names, and an inane comment for each ambassador, chief of state or prime minister for a planet, or wealthy magnate too important to shuffle off to another venue.

By a special grace, Kit showed up with a stool that she slipped under Vicky's voluminous dress, so she could sit while doing her Grand Duchess thing.

Kris begged the same favor and Vicky graciously granted her wish.

"Thanks, I owe you one," Kris said with a half-swallowed

grin. Blow away a vicious stepmom and her entire battle fleet, and Kris got a stool to sit on. Favor for a favor.

Yeah, right.

However, the poor wife of the Prime Minister of Metzburg didn't get a stool.

After an hour, it was time to cut the cake and get her picture taken squishing cake onto Mannie's face. Protocol insisted he not squish cake on her face, but she made sure he did it anyway.

There must have been a million pictures taken.

Vicky wondered if they couldn't just swap the "I do," thing for squishing cake in the face and call it even.

Clearly, my idea of the solemnity of marriage needs some work.

Dance music began. Mannie led her to the floor and she discovered whoever designed and built this damn dress hadn't tried it on. She could barely move in the heavy thing.

She tried lifting it up by the hoop that was intended to loop over her wrist, but that only threatened the blood supply to her left hand. What she really needed was a trailer to haul around the back half of her wedding dress.

Having neither a father nor mother to involve in the first dance ritual, she begged and Mannie granted her wish to quit the dance floor as soon Kris Longknife and Jack had joined them, as well as all the bridesmaids and groomsmen.

Ten minutes later, she was in the back of a limo with Mannie, Kris, and Jack and they headed for the second venue of the evening. Vicky had specifically invited Kris Longknife to be at her elbow in these reception lines.

She wanted everyone in the Empire, not only her half, but the entire Empire to be totally aware of the personal alliance between their Grand Duchess and the Wardhaven Royal Princess. Vicky had already put down the rebellion of her stepmother. It could have been bloodier if Kris hadn't intervened as a mediator, and then as a fighting admiral.

Vicky had asked, and Kris had agreed, to show the flag together. Messing with the Grand Duchess could get you to Kris Longknife very quickly.

At the next hotel, there was a second reception line. Again, she and Kris were at the front of the line. This line was a bit longer. Many of the planetary leaders who had worked their way down the first line getting their hands shaken, were now here, standing down the line from her and shaking the hands of heroes of the Empress's war, major financiers, or industrialists.

After an hour, Vicky found that they, too, had a cake. She dutifully cut it and smeared some cake on Mannie as he smiled and did the same to her. Then there was the first dance. Since Kit had not managed to procure a trailer to haul the damn dress around, Vicky didn't dance any longer than she had to.

Minutes after she sat down, she was hustled out through the kitchen and down to her waiting limo and driven to yet a third reception where she did almost the same thing for important people of lesser social standing.

It took two more receptions for people at that level before she could finally make her escape to the reception she really wanted to attend.

Admiral Bolesław had hired the largest venue on Metzburg. The sailors and Marines who had fought with Vicky, their wives and kids, folks, and siblings, and just about anyone who knew them were collected here. A stadium for over a hundred thousand, as well as its parking lot, had been converted into one huge party with fun and games for all ages. The beer and wine were free. The sausage and fried potatoes or sauerkraut were all free. Even the rides were free.

As Admiral Bolesław helped Vicky from her limo, he grinned and whispered that there was a rumor making the rounds about girls out to have fun, not all of whom were free. Having been a boot ensign, Vicky knew when a good officer doesn't notice things and grinned back at her good friend and lifesaver.

Vicky very quickly acquired half a dozen young teen girls only too delighted to help her with her wonderful gown, and, finally feeling like she could get around, she made her way through the cheering crowd and into the stadium.

Kris was kind enough to hold back, letting Vicky totally enjoy the moment. She was also nice enough to follow a few minutes behind Vicky.

Vicky definitely wanted to share the stage with a certain Kris Longknife.

They had set up a stage in the middle of the field. There were two thrones, one larger for a ruling Grand Duchess, one only a bit smaller and lower for a fighting Princess. The crowd went wild when Vicky grabbed Kris's hand and the two of them raised it high.

These sailors knew who had led this rebellion and who had won it. Here, before them was the one woman who had led them in battle holding high the hand of the one woman who had cut the Empress off at her knees.

They loved them both.

After the cheering, whistling, and applauding finally died down to a roar, Vicky cleared her throat. One computer, hers or Nelly, caught her voice and plugged it into the stadium's system, so her voice carried through the stadium and off across the parking lot. She'd been told that huge screens around the inside and the outside of the stadium would carry her image as well as project her voice.

"I thank you all for coming here to share this wonderful day with me," she said, this time raising Mannie's arm high.

She didn't have to do anything but grin like a lovesick fool for a good five minutes as the applause wrapped itself around her.

"I know this day could not have happened without your courage, fighting skills, and persistence against the evil that was the Empress."

Again, she couldn't get a word out above the roar of the crowd for a good long time.

"I am looking forward to a nice, long peace. I will enjoy working with you to bring years of liberty and prosperity.

The cheering went long, and seemed to swell even as time passed. Vicky turned to the left, and she and Mannie walked over to wave at the left-hand side of the stadium. Kris and Jack took the right-hand side.

Vicky waved and threw kisses, and people cheered and waved back. She walked along the edge of the stage, waving to everyone in sight. She reached the front and walked across it.

In the middle, she met Kris and Jack coming the other way. For a few moments, the four of them waved together, then they crossed, and Vicky waved and threw kisses at the other side of the crowd while Kris did the same.

They finally met back at their thrones.

"Did you ever think you'd see a day like this?" Kris asked Vicky.

"There were days I didn't think I'd see the sunset," Vicky admitted, then grinned at her brand-new husband. "There was one day I was pretty sure this guy was going to shoot me out of his sky."

"Okay, I threatened you. I knew you wouldn't listen to me, and I knew you knew that I'd never shoot you down."

"Yes, but it made for a few minutes of serious pucker."

The four enjoyed a laugh, then the two husbands helped their wives arrange their dresses. Once Kris was ready to sit down, Jack came around to help Mannie finish up arranging his bride's monstrous gown.

There was laughter in the crowd as the two guys struggled to get all those folds and fine lace and layers of tulle into something that didn't swallow up Mannie.

Finally, Vicky sat down, so Mannie could sit down, so one US Marine lieutenant general could organize one huge dress into something like a decent formation. Shaking his head, but grinning from ear to ear, Jack finally bowed to Vicky, then his wife, and went to sit beside her.

Was it an accident that the live microphone picked up Jack's rueful, "Whoever designed that dress ought to be made to walk a couple of hundred miles in it."

"And dance in it," Vicky was heard to say.

"And figure out where to put the bloody thing," was clearly Mannie.

Kris just contributed a hearty laugh.

Once the Imperial and Royal couples were seated, the dancing began. Only this time, there was no doubt that Vicky got to sit and watch it.

The first group of dancers was a long line of young people who proceeded to show that feet would move faster than light, while hands did nothing.

"Irish dance!" Mannie exclaimed with glee.

He showed Vicky the fine points of it for a few minutes. When a second song started, he tossed off his tux jacket and joined one of the lines of dancers. Vicky watched in horror for a few moments, then realized that her husband had at least one more skill she knew nothing about.

She clapped with glee, carefully to the music, and laughed as he kept up with dancers, many half his age, some more so. It was a special delight to see girls of eight or ten kicking it with all the bigger kids.

After two songs, Mannie fell out of the line to much applause and rejoined Vicky, very out of breath, but grinning from ear to ear.

A few moments later, the Irish dancers kick stepped their way off the stage.

The next group marched on with drums beating and pipes skirling. The Scottish had arrived. Dancers separated from the pipers and drummers forming ranks, going from marching to dancing with no visible pause.

"I wonder if they're regimental," Vicky said, grinning.

"Regimental?" Mannie said, falling into the role of straight man.

Kris giggled.

"Do they have anything on under those kilts?" Vicky asked and answered at the same time.

"I'm sure you'll be watching," Mannie said, ruefully.

"Oh, I'd love to join them," Kris said. "A highland regiment out of Lorna Do taught me some serious lessons about leadership and command. I've enjoyed learning how to do their dances."

"So have I," Jack said.

"If I take a knife to this dress, I'll be in so much trouble," Kris said, glancing down and sighing.

"I don't need to cut anything off," Jack said.

"You going to?"

"I haven't been dancing with you over the past four years for nothing."

And Jack stepped forward to join a foursome.

One dancer fell back, and Jack stepped in, without missing a beat.

For the next two flings there was one Marine in blue and whites dancing, step for step, with all those plaids and kilts.

When the base drum signaled a change, Jack dropped out and returned, out of breath to Kris's side.

A few moments later, the dancers, pipes, and drums reformed and marched. off.

One group of dancers followed another. There was a group of men and women who did a dance involving a lot of kicking and slapping of hands and shoes to the accompaniment of tubas and accordions. Several groups that claimed heritage back to Earth's African continent, half-danced, half-trotted onto the stage, singing as they came, did some spectacular dances, and then left in the same manner they arrived. Some were accompanied by drums and flutes, others sang a cappella.

There were several groups that wore spectacular costumes, some of which were originally sewn on the eastern part of the Asian continent before their families left for the stars. Their hands were so expressive and their moves so exquisite. It almost took Vicky's breath away.

Three couples came on stage and bowed to Vicky while several violinists and other strings, as well as a piano, arranged themselves. Then the dance started.

Vicky was speechless. The women's footwork was unbelievable. The men moved, but this was clearly the women's dance . . . and sexy as hell.

By the time they were halfway through the dance, Mannie leaned over and whispered, "I feel like clergy should have married them before they started."

When they finished, it was Vicky's turn to lean over and

whisper to Mannie, "I think they're going to need an obstetrician in nine months."

"Maybe they're protected," he whispered back, grinning.

"I don't know any birth control that could hold up against that."

They grinned and clapped as the dancers finished and cheered them off the stage.

The next group to run on stage hit with the force of an invasion. The Cossacks had arrived!

Without even a pause for breath, they began dancing, if you could call all the jumping and waving, a type of dance. It looked more like self-imposed torture. Still, it stirred Vicky's blood to a boil.

Her family traced their roots to people of German extract that lived for a long time in Ukraine. There were plenty of claims of Tartar and Cossack blood deep in the family tree.

Of course, Vicky knew that much of what she'd been taught about her family was more fiction than fact. Still, the leaping, jumping, twisting, and turning stirred her heart. Then there was the kicking, or whatever it was called when they somehow managed to sit down, and kick like mad without falling on their asses. Ah, Vicky loved it!

Then, six male and six female dancers came on stage with swords and began a dance that really got Vicky's blood flowing. It must have done something for Kit and Kat, because they suddenly appeared, each with a sword in their hand.

They took a stance between Vicky and the sword dancers. Vicky moved them aside so they didn't block her view. They gave her a sour look . . . without taking their eyes off the dancers and their swords.

When that dance ended, Vicky was right in with the rest

hooting and hollering her joy and clapping like mad. The dancers bowed to her, then to the other three sides of the stage, and marched off. The accordions that had accompanied them, kept playing.

As the swords left, two dozen lovely women in floor-length dresses came out from behind Vicky. Someone had laid on a Berizoika for her. She lost it totally and squealed.

She'd learned that dance when she was ten, maybe twelve. The idea was to look like a perfect doll, and Daddy loved it when she danced it.

All the young women were in skirts that reached almost to the floor . . . but not quite. The entire goal of the dancer was to move smoothly over the floor without causing a single movement in the many ruffles of her dress. Each girl was to keep a smile on her face and her dress unmoving as she glided over the floor, matching with the other girls. For example, the lead might turn inward, and they would form a swirl, all while not letting their skirts touch, not letting them move.

It was a great challenge, but even at twelve, Vicky had learned to keep her balance, take lots of tiny steps, never move her head, or lose her smile and never, ever, let her dress move.

Vicky hopped to her feet. "I can dance this!" she told Kris. "I'm gonna!"

"Your Grace!" both her assassins squeaked at the same time.

"I'll be less of a target in motion than sitting here," Vicky snapped, and stepped forward.

The leader was just coming around. Vicky approached her with care. Yes, the damn dress's train was dragging, but she could keep the front of it perfectly still.

Without moving her lips or changing her smile, the

leader whispered, "Take the last place. Get her cloth and a green bough."

Vicky waited until the last girl approached. That girl was good. Keeping her posture perfect and her steps tiny, she turned, giving Vicky her cloth and green bough with tiny red fruit on it as if it was an extension of the dance.

They floated along, side by side, with Vicky slowly moving into the last place in line as the girl slowly edged to the left. She handed off her two items smoothly to Vicky, and just as smoothly, Vicky took them.

Now, Vicky was in the line of dancers, following right behind the girl ahead of her. Slowly she turned her head, so her smiling face was toward the audience as they paraded down the front of the stage, then they looped around and did the same to each of the other three sides of the stage.

Vicky knew her back was ramrod straight. The front of her dress was motionless. She had no way to tell about the back, but the crowd was clapping and cheering. It made it hard to keep the smile on her face, like all the girls in line ahead of her.

All four sides visited, the leader turned them into a loose circle. It was clear she was going for the swirl, but approaching it slower than usual. Behind her, all the girls adapted to this change in their dance, giving Vicky a chance to get this damn train on her dress to fan out just enough to not trip them up when they had to come out of it.

It worked. The entire troop formed the swirl, with Vicky last. She then led the group in the burst out. She went straight ahead. The girl ahead of her came in on her elbow, two more girls attached to them and they glided to the front of the stage, before turning to the right.

Turning to the right allowed Vicky to be the wheel girl. The others floated around while she merely turned in place ninety degrees. Again, this allowed the train and veil not to trip anyone up.

They did the turn two more times, before joining the line again as they proceeded toward the front of the stage. The girl in the lead crossed her arm over her breasts and placed the green bough on her shoulder. Then she leaned her head on it.

One after the other, while keeping their skirts absolutely steady and maintaining perfect posture, the next girl in line moved the green bough across her body and onto her shoulder.

Vicky was last in line. She did it right on the beat.

The watching crowed cheered even more loudly. Was Vicky hearing cheering from the parking lot?

Now they were slowly making their way to the back of the stage, where the leader switched and began to side step across the stage. Vicky could do this one, too, if her dress didn't get too tied up.

When her time came, she turned to her left and began taking tiny steps to her right, smiling, even as the trailing part of her gown began to pull part of her skirt over. Well, she'd just have to give the dress this one.

Now the leader was presenting her hands forward, both the one with the bough and the other with a colorful kerchief. Like a wave, hands came up, each girl next in line holding up her kerchief in one hand, the green bough with the other, matching it to the dancer on her left.

Vicky kept her smiling face forward, while watching the pacing out of the corner of her right eye. When the girl to her right raised her hand, Vicky's kerchief was ready, and a second later, she raised her left hand.

The crowd cheered.

Now as one, the girls glided forward, hands out, skirts

not moving so much as a millimeter. They reached the front of the stage, and the lead girl dropped her hands, and again the wave swept down the line.

Vicky had no idea what would happen next. Far down the line, the leader slowly turned away from Vicky. The Grand Duchess could barely make out that hint of green on her right shoulder.

The girl beside her then turned, placed her kerchief hand on the shoulder of the leader and began to ever so slowly move away.

Thus it went, down the line, with Vicky being last to turn in place and rest one hand on the shoulder of the girl ahead and the green bough on her right shoulder.

Vicky knew that the entire dance had been modified for her. The green boughs should have been facing the crowd. Vicky should now be leading the entire parade of perfect doll-like girls.

However, the leader knew that if Vicky led, her trailing skirt would have tripped up the next girl, so she'd turned everything around, and each of the other girls had adjusted themselves perfectly.

Wow! That was teamwork!

Vicky followed the line, staying poised and on tiptoes as she took tiny steps.

The leader led the column in a turn that did take them down the front with their boughs where they crowd could see them, then she turned again, and Vicky could see that she was leading the entire column down the right side of the stage. One more turn and she'd be very carefully walking by her throne.

It was time to turn back into a Grand Duchess.

The last girl had been standing beside Mannie the entire

time. As Vicky approached her, she handed off her bough and kerchief as gracefully as possible.

The young woman took them and, without a falter in her smile, moved ever so smoothly into the end of the line, maybe taking her steps a bit faster, but not letting a single ruffle appear on her skirt.

The crowd cheered as Vicky fell out of line. The cheer went long and loud. Vicky found herself curtsying to the front, then, when they applause did not end, she did the same to the right, the back, and the left, before doing it again to the front.

It was too much. Vicky settled carefully back on her temporary throne, and found she had to wipe away tears. The cheering got even louder as she wiped one eye, then the other, then had to do it all over again.

Finally, she felt she had to take the focus off of herself. She sat up straight, folded her hands in her lap and put a Grand Duchess smile on her face as good as any on the dancing dolls.

Finally, the applause began to quiet.

The dancing dolls did a few more turns around the stage, drawing cheers from the crowd, then exited behind Vicky.

Vicky threw them all kisses as they passed. Several of them fell out of their painted-on smiles to grin at Vicky. The leader was one of them.

Was it part of the dance that a wave went down the line as they left, each one waving her kerchief at Vicky?

There was one more wild dance, with both men and woman doing spectacular leaps and bounds. A couple went around the stage doing cartwheels. Another pair did it somehow on their hands and feet, crab-walking in circles.

How could anyone do that?

Finally, the show was over.

Admiral Bolesław led the entire stadium in the Imperial Anthem. Everyone stood. Even Kris Longknife stood.

Everyone stood except Vicky.

Vicky was the physical embodiment of the Imperium.

Never had she felt so in touch with her people. Never had she felt so much the physical presence of all their hopes and dreams.

"I will see that all of you have a better life," Vicky said softly.

"I really think you will," she heard from Kris.

It was a very nice thing to hear from the women she had tried so hard to assassinate. So very nice.

8

Vicky Peterwald lay on the beach, luxuriating in the sensuality of it all. Her ears found the sound of the surf restful. Her skin loved the caress of the sun and the kiss of the gentle, cooling sea breeze.

She hadn't had a stitch of clothing on for three days and hoped to make it to an entire week. She'd even gotten Mannie to give up clothes for the last two days.

Of course, he still tended to be somewhere else when the lovely serving girl in her tiny gossamer sarong brought out their meals.

Some day this week, she was going to get Mannie to eat some meals in the lodge . . . without getting dressed.

She'd promised him a dukedom if he would.

That promise hadn't quite been the gift she expected.

Mannie's ambition was to be the Prime Minister of her government. He certainly deserved it and Vicky strongly suggested that Mannie's Democratic Social Contract Party would get the most votes in whatever her legislature turned out.

Mannie, however, had strong opinions about letting the

new nobility run things. "Your first Minister should be a commoner," he insisted.

The Dukedom had been tabled for now.

At the moment, Mannie was laid out on a towel in the sand, just as naked as she, but he had his phone in his hand.

"Damn, can't those goofballs agree on anything?" he muttered.

"What's the problem now?" Vicky said.

She'd wanted to ban all phones for the duration of the honeymoon. Mannie, however, had threatened to either cut the honeymoon short . . . or let her have her half while he worked someplace else.

"You do know that one person does not a honeymoon make?" Vicky had asked.

"Oh, where's that law written down?" he countered.

"It's unwritten," Vicky cooed back, reaching for that part of him she so enjoyed.

"Your Grace," he said, most officiously. As officiously as a naked man can. "The rule of law requires that the laws be written. Government by *fiat* is what got your father in so much trouble."

So, Vicky had discovered that she could not rule her husband by Imperial *fiat,* even on her honeymoon.

Thus, Mannie had his phone and he did not like the reports he was getting.

"The simple plan to provide you with a senate has splintered into two senates and now, maybe three."

"When I don't have even one at the moment. You know, Mannie, I kind of like not having a senate."

"The people have a right to have their sovereignty both recognized and empowered," he said, using big words she'd come to understand. "Assume a repeat of the argument we've had over and over again for the last year," he said, grinning.

"Stipulated," Vicky grinned back. They had a lot of arguments that they could never reached agreement on. They'd taken to numbering them. That argument was number one. They were up to ninety-seven things they couldn't agree upon, and now had arguments over which was which.

Yes, their computers could have told them which was the right number, but it was too much fun fighting . . . and then making up.

There's been a lot of make-up sex this honeymoon, and they were only on day five.

Vicky very much looked forward to the next twenty-five days.

But Mannie had tweaked her curiosity. "I know that classically," she said, "there have often been two legislatures. The first represents the people and is apportioned by population. Usually, the second is somehow apportioned by land to assure that the large populations don't ignore the rights of the smaller collectives. Okay, what's the problem? Who's on third?"

"No, Who's on first."

"Are we going to do that again?" Vicky said, dryly.

"But you're just a great straight Grand Duchess."

"You know I'm not straight, and if you'd just allow my two mini-assassins into our bed, I could give you quite a show."

"I do not want to share my bed with your two killers. Really, I don't want to share our bed with anyone but you, and most definitely not them."

"So, if I could get a nice, boney girl with tiny tits and no martial arts training?" Vicky cooed.

"Repeat argument number two here."

"Stipulated," Vicky said, and tried to pout, but was grinning too much. He knew she was a reformed bad girl. A very bad girl, but he was a straight shooter, as straight as they came, and he was very much aware of the need for the Imperial couple to maintain the high moral ground.

With Mannie, being moral was actually a lot of fun.

"So, tell me, who will make up my three senates?"

"The usual two, although there's some debate as to whether the tiny colonies get one or two senators. Some of the larger planets want three or four while the smallest ones would only get one. However, it's our lords of finance and industry that are pushing for a third senate. They want a branch of government to represent them. The larger the GDP, the more representation they get."

"And who gets elected a senator for this august body?"

"They want the voting to be represented by taxes paid."

"How do the corporate taxes vote?"

"They're arguing for no corporate taxes. Only people pay taxes."

"Do I want that?"

"Yes and no," Mannie said.

"Oh, I hate it when you say that."

"Sorry."

"Excuse me for interrupting," Vicky's computer said from her throat. "But Kit and Kat say you need desperately to see them. They have two people from your intelligence agency at their elbows."

"I thought I was on a honeymoon," Vicky snapped.

"Sorry, Your Grace," came in the familiar voice of Mr. Smith, the man who gave her the daily intel briefing, "but I think you want to hear this."

"Can't you just tell me now?"

"I would prefer not to say this over any airwave or net."

"I'm not going to get dressed," Vicky said.

"If you want, I'll keep my eyes closed. However, knowing you, you'll enjoy me enjoying your naked body. I wouldn't put it past you to have Mannie make love to you while I brief you."

"Damn, you know me too well," Vicky laughed.

"That's what I'm paid for. To know things. May we have an audience?"

"Come," Vicky said, with a sigh.

Mannie reached for his towel with clear intent to wrap it around himself.

"No!" Vicky snapped. "They are interrupting my honeymoon. It took me four days to get you naked. We stay naked!"

"Vicky . . ." Mannie began.

"They're my intel group and assassins. There's not a paparazzi among them. If any picture of me comes out of this meeting, they know I'll take their heads."

"What about them bringing in a bug?"

"Good point. Computer, dispatch nano scouts to examine the people approaching from down the beach for spy nanos and listening devices."

"Of course, Your Grace."

The large bucket that held two bottles of chilled Champagne spawned a drone that hurried down the beach before disappearing as it approached four people stalking slowly up the beach in the soft sand.

This new particular skill for Vicky's computer had been a last gift from Kris Longknife. Her Nelly had once again upgraded Vicky's computer, as well as Mannie's.

Vicky had still made a point of not wanting her computer to talk back to her and Nelly had made the counter point that she'd never let Vicky have the responsibility for the care and education of one of her children.

They'd been happy to arrive at the same point, from opposite directions.

However, Kris had seen to it that Vicky's computer could now spawn Smart Metal™ nano scouts from any of the stuff close at hand. They weren't as smart as nanos supervised by the Magnificent Nelly, but they were likely able to beat anything in the Greenfeld Empire for the next few years.

"The nanos report that the two intelligence officers have no electronic devices on them. Kit and Kat have their usual supply of weapons and devices. Do you want me to report on them?"

"No, computer. However, send out a net of nanos around my position. Just because they're clean doesn't mean someone else hasn't slipped something in."

"I have been maintaining a secure environment, Your Grace. I have nailed several tiny drones before they got here. I assure you, what you and your consort say and do has not been recorded on either audio or video."

"Thank you, computer. Keep up the good work."

"You're welcome, Your Grace."

Vicky eyed Mannie. "Do you think Nelly may have slipped a wwringer in on me? My computer's acting almost human of late."

"Many modern AI's have passed the Turing test without becoming as contrary or creative as Nelly."

"Yeah."

"Again, can I talk you into getting dressed, or at least moving this inside our cottage?"

"Not until I know what made these idiots think I'd come off my honeymoon for whatever they've got."

A few moments later, Kit and Kat were doing their own

survey to assure the site was secure. However, the two intel agents did not wait.

"Hello, Mr. Smith," Vicky said. "I can't say I'm glad to see you. And who is this young lady? Ms. Jones?"

"I go by Mrs. Brown today," the young woman said, smiling softly.

"That would be an easy name to remember. It matches your hair."

"When it's this color. Red, blond, black, purple, or green, not so much."

Vicky allowed herself to be amused by the joke, but not distracted.

"And what has caused you to risk my displeasure by barging in on my honeymoon? I'm sure both Kit and Kat could find a nice axe to take your head and a spike to display it on. Ah, don't you miss the good old days, Mannie?"

Her groom of recent celebration rolled his eyes.

"Not really, Your Grace," Mr. Smith said in answer to her question. "However, we have only recently come into possession of information about events on Greenfeld. Your father is effectively a prisoner in his palace without a pfennig to his name. It appears that all his staff has walked out for lack of pay. Only three cooks have remained."

"They wouldn't happen to be Aunties Iris, Rena, and Hilda, would they?" Vicky asked.

"I believe that is correct," Mrs. Brown answered.

"If anyone on Greenfeld had the simple faith and loyalty to stay with my dad, those three lovely old women would be the ones."

"Meanwhile," Mr. Smith said, hurrying on, "The other half of the Empire, your father's half, is effectively under the control of the dead Empress's uncles and cousins. The Bowlingames have thrown off the cloaks they were hiding under and are reaching for the purple using your father's infant son against him."

"How did they manage that?" Vicky demanded.

"It seems that your father was enticed into eliminating the Greenfeld Revenue Service and contracting out the job of collecting taxes to certain tax farmers. It should be no surprise that all those tax farming contracts were awarded to the Empress's family or people working hand-in-glove with them."

"Well, if they're collecting taxes, Dad should have some money, right?"

"The eldest Bowlingame brother who wasn't at Cuzco, and thus lives, has attached all the royal income claiming they are owed their contractual percent as well as expenses. Horribly high of late due to the rebellion and all, don't you know?"

Vicky looked up at the intel chief who was doing a magnificent job of addressing her eyes. She batted them several times and with as much feigned dismay as she could muster said, "No, I didn't know the other half of the Empire suffered from anything the rebels did, do you, loving husband?"

"Nope," he said. "I seem to remember a certain Grand Duchess who insisted we not harm the planets we captured and definitely not harm the ones we didn't."

"That's what I remember, too," she said, frowning. "So, Mr. Smith, I take it that this coup has left my father with no power base."

"By the time the fleet sorted itself out, the ships on the other side were in the Bowlingame pocket. The ships on your side are yours."

"What's the balance of power?" Vicky asked.

"You hold Naval superiority. However, the Bowlingames

have been recruiting 'security specialists,' for some time. They have used these uniformed thugs to take control of all but the least important planets on the other side. The last three planets to vote to join your side of the Empire are likely the last that will get away with that."

"If any more elections are held," Mrs. Brown said, "the tallied results will likely be ninety-seven percent for staying on their side of the line."

"Ballot stuffing," Mannie spat.

"Yes. No doubt about it," Mr. Smith said.

Vicky began to get up. As much as she hated allowing Imperial matters to invade her honeymoon, they clearly had.

Mr. Smith offered her a hand and a smile as he took her in from her toes to her hairline. "I see that married life agrees with you, Your Grace."

"I was beginning to wonder if you could see the nose on your face, or the naked Grand Duchess laying right in front of you."

"I have learned to learn many things," Mr. Smith said, "and not learn certain things."

"And you are brilliant at all of them. Now, Mannie, drop that towel," she snapped at her husband, and strolled to their cottage, her hips swaying, sure that at least four of the people following her were enjoying the view.

Mrs. Brown was still a question mark.

9

V icky decided that she might cover herself with a sarong. Well, she at least wrapped herself in the diaphanous cloth three times before rolling the rest and tossing it over her shoulder. There was just enough of the translucent cloth to add color to her naked body.

No doubt the rest, trailing down her back, would make her rear presentable in proper company.

"Computer, is this room secure?"

"Wait one, please, Your Grace."

Mannie took the time to slip into shorts and a three-button shirt.

Vicky made a face at him. He shrugged, as if to say, "Sue me."

"The room is secure," her computer reported.

"How do we get my father out of his hulk of a palace?" Vicky demanded. "He was no great shakes as a parent, but I won't have a Peterwald living on handouts as an effective hostage."

"Your Grace," Mr. Smith began, "most of our assets had to

run for their lives when the Empress began to arrest Navy and Marine officers and order entire Marine units into her security consulting business. Hire on or get shot."

"We got most of them away, right?"

"We got the vast majority away," Mrs. Brown put in. "However, Admiral Heller's wife and several others were captured and killed, as you may remember."

"How could I ever forget?" Vicky growled.

"Once the Bowlingames were in effective control of the capital, they began a series of sweeps that collected up almost all our assets, along with a huge number of innocents."

Vicky cringed at what she knew must be coming.

"They gave them show trials that played on every channel on every major planet they controlled, then broadcasted the mass executions."

"And my father's reaction?"

"He was otherwise engaged at the time," Mrs. Brown said.

"I would have thought by then the Empress would be huge," Vicky said.

"Yes, but she arranged for a steady stream of young girls to join them in their bed. He did not get out of bed for days at a time."

Vicky groaned, and nodded to Mannie. "Get me that muumuu."

He did, and she slipped it over her head. It fell to cover and hide her entire body. She sighed.

"I've got to watch my family genes," she muttered. "So, where did that leave us? Clearly, you know that my dad's in hock and my three loving old cooks are taking care of him."

"Yes. One of them is a contact," Mrs. Brown said.

"If I asked which one, would you tell me?"

"No, Your Grace."

"Smart woman. Mr. Smith, are we paying her enough?"

"I think so," he said.

"Okay, how do we get Dad out? Do I lead a daring commando raid down and break him loose while blowing a lot of shit up? Do I lead an economic exchange conference, bore them to death, then break him loose? Mr. Smith, you are rarely without ideas. I'd be amazed if you didn't break into my honeymoon without an entire boatload of highly workable and inevitably successful ideas," Vicky said, batting her eyes at Mr. Smith and looking innocent.

"Your Grace, I hate to disappoint you, but today is different. Maybe it has to do with you being a married lady."

"You've got to be kidding," Vicky said, frowning, not at all prettily.

"May I be allowed to rush in where an angel would be running for the hills?" Mrs. Brown said.

"If you insist," Vicky said, turning her unhappy face toward the woman.

"I am the desk officer for Greenfeld. I have been examining all our resources, which doesn't take long, and we have nothing on the ground either to support a quick snatch and grab, nor gather any intelligence that would help you succeed in such an effort."

"So, I'd be going in blind," Vicky said.

"Blind, deaf, and dumb," Mrs. Brown said.

"But he's wandering around a half-built palace already starting to crumble with only three cooks at hand."

"And if you were to get within five klicks of the place, how many security thugs do you think you'd have breathing down your neck, or worse, breaking his?"

Vicky scowled, but she knew the answer to that. Her late stepmother of unlamented passing had to have picked up her bad habits from somewhere. There was no question that she'd needed very little encouragement to do horrible things.

"Okay, no commando raid. What about some smiling diplomacy?"

"You mentioned economic negotiations," Mrs. Brown said. "Your Minister of Commerce and Industry has made several suggestions to set up just such trade talks between our two halves of the Empire. They have not just been rebuffed but ignored."

"So, we can't go glad-handing, huh?"

Here Mrs. Brown smiled and shrugged most beautifully. "I didn't say that. I just pointed out that if a major fleet movement started toward Greenfeld, it would not be part of a mutually agreed upon visit."

"However, we always like to show the flag," Vicky said, thinking.

"Yes, Your Grace.

"And a bride on her honeymoon might enjoy a trip to her old haunts. She would want to take her husband home to meet papa and show him where she grew up."

"That would be hardly believable, but it would provide a thin veneer."

Vicky began to enjoy the flow of blood and adrenaline as she did whenever action was at hand.

"Oh, speaking of showing my new hubby my old haunts, you'll need to get me a double to stand in for Mannie."

"What?" he yelped.

"You're not going near that half of the Empire, my beloved."

"Then why are you?"

"I'm the Grand Duchess. I can't always be the Gracious Grand Duchess. Sometimes I have to be the Vicious Grand Duchess. Some Duke has earned himself a visit from the Vicious version of me."

"I don't like this," Mannie said.

"Please don't like this in an angry way, Love. I need for you to give me a baby. A honeymoon baby."

"You want to go in there pregnant?"

"No, you silly goose. I want to leave you pregnant."

"Huh?" Mannie said, glancing down at his cute bit of extra tummy.

"Not physically. I want to start our daughter in a uterine replicator before I leave. I know a daughter would be little thing to remember me by, but the Empire needs an heir, and if I leave behind enough eggs, you could raise a family of four or so. I know that any of our children that you raise will grow up to be dutiful royalty for a democratic Greenfeld," she said, and leaned over and kissed him.

He melted into her kiss, then shook his head and shook the kiss off.

"If you think this is that dangerous, you shouldn't be doing it."

"I don't think this is all that dangerous, but I don't know for sure. In another day and age, we wouldn't have this option. Why the hell do you think we women kept being left home barefoot and pregnant?"

"So, you're leaving me home, barefoot and pregnant?"

"No, I'm sure we can find you a nice pair of shoes."

Mannie tossed her a scowl.

"I promise you that we are going to send these nice people on their way with clear orders for Admiral Waller and specific instructions to get me absolutely confidential access to both a lawyer and a genetic and obstetrics doctor. I will set it up so you can decant a new kid every two years or so, girl, boy, girl, boy and rule as regent in their minority."

Vicky turned to the other four. "I want the eldest to be heir apparent. No messing around with boys only."

"But, Your Grace," Mr. Smith pointed out, "you were the junior."

"Yeah. Why do you think I want a girl first?"

"Yes, Your Grace," Mr. Smith said.

"Now, all of you, go. Get. Be gone. I need to peel my husband back out of his shell and make mad love to him, so I can wrap him around my little finger again."

"Said husband is not going to be easily wrapped around that finger this time," Mannie said, but Vicky cut him off by kissing him.

"To be sure you understand," Mr. Smith said to Vicky's back, "I will tell Admiral Waller to prepare for a major fleet movement toward Greenfeld with full Marine support. I will arrange for an G&O doc to be available at the Navy headquarters when we slip you in the back door. Also, a JAG team expert in dynastic questions. In addition, I will have four people, including two diminutive killers and two dead wringers for you, right down to the mole on your left rear cheek, Your Grace, and a second wringer for Mannie who need only be effective in formal wear and official occasions."

"And not in bed," Mannie said, breaking out from the kiss, and peeling Vicky off him.

Vicky was distracted at the moment, working him out of his shorts.

"And we're out of here," Mr. Smith said, and the four hurried out.

"Bend me around your finger?" Mannie grumbled.

"How about you bend me over your knee?" Vicky cooed.

"They say you never know whom you've married until you've married them," Mannie said, with a sigh. But he tossed his shirt one way and grabbed his wife with the other hand.

Maybe a spanking would be fun.

10

Rear Admiral, Her Grace, Grand Duchess Victoria Smythe-Peterwald was not a happy Grand Duchess as her van rolled along. It had no windows in the back and she could not see anything.

From the feel of matters, they were likely already driving down into the deepest sub-basement of Main Navy on Metzburg. Still, she felt an urgent need to see her surroundings.

Her compartment was fitted out like some sort of jail wagon. The seats were likely a bit more comfortable than those for the average criminal, but that didn't make her feel any better. Of course, the back and sides were solid metal. There was even a metal wall separating her compartment from the front.

She fingered the standard issue automatic in the small of her back. She was a Peterwald and paranoia ran strong in her family. The person who opened that back door better have all his or her hands in full view.

"You look nervous," Mannie said.

"I don't like not seeing where I'm going," Vicky said through not quite clenched teeth.

"But no one can see you. Me. Us."

"I know. I know, but . . .." Vicky left it at that. Mannie had not spent all his life in a shooting gallery. Now that he was seated at her side, he'd need to learn, and learn that fast.

Vicky still needed to use cosmetics to cover the black stain where tiny fragments of the last assassin's bullet had dusted her neck. The flicks of steel had hit her neck with too little velocity to do much more than sting, but left too much to wash away. They were too tiny for the medical staff to remove.

In time, her skin would shove them to the surface and she'd wash them down the sink.

The armored van came to a halt. Vicky pulled her automatic from her back and held it, aimed at the door, in her lap.

Mannie eyed her weapon, but said nothing.

There was a double slap on the back door. "Did you enjoy your ride, Your Grace?" came in Kit's voice.

Mannie relaxed.

Vicky did too, but only because the usual routine did not have the phrase "Your Imperial Grace." If Kit added that to the greeting, it meant she had a gun to her head.

Vicky made her automatic disappear and said, "Please enter."

Very quickly, Vicky was out of the van, and up an elevator. A short walk down a marble hallway past paintings of admirals and battles, and she was led through an anteroom into Grand Admiral Waller's office.

He stood and gave her a harried, shallow bow from the waist. "So glad to see you, Your Grace. I sincerely regret that it is now and not three weeks from now."

"What needs, must," Vicky said. "How are preparations going for a fleet movement?"

"Very well, Your Grace," Weller said, leading her toward a conversation circle. A star map already floated above the coffee table.

"I had thought that your first visit might be to Brunswick on our side of the line. It's three jumps from there to Dresden, a planet with little love for the Empress's faction after their visit from the Butcher, the Duke of Radebuel. The three jumps have the benefit of having no occupied planets in them."

"Good."

"The route we chose for Greenfeld has four jumps. Only the last one out has a small colony. We are trying to get a team on it. With any luck, we may succeed in causing a minor glitch to develop in the comm system."

The admiral smiled conspiratorially. "You might actually succeed in arriving in the Greenfeld system without them any the wiser."

"That would be nice, but I don't want to sacrifice anyone."

"I assure you, Your Grace, our team will be as safe as if they were in their mother's arms."

"Hopefully, their mother's arms were more gentle than the late Empress's."

"No doubt. Will you be visiting your half-brother on Greenfeld?"

"That is a major part of my excuse for going."

"Very good."

"Have you arranged a wringer for Mannie?" Vicky said, smiling at her husband. The face he gave her in return was not happy.

"I hope your husband is not offended, but we have been

preparing several of our special operations agents for a while to pass both facial recognition and body movement for him." The admiral smiled at Mannie, who sighed mightily.

"For what it is worth, sir, we also have two women fully trained and modified to pass for Her Grace."

"Two?" Vicky asked.

"Yes. One is presently enjoying your honeymoon with an agent that was not quite fully modified and trained to pass for Mr. Artemus. We will finish his full work up later, ma'am."

"Is all this necessary?" Mannie asked, letting his displeasure become quite visible.

"If Kris Longknife hadn't shown up, I was of half a mind to have a stand-in do that carriage ride," Vicky said, rubbing the darkened spray on her neck.

Mannie scowled.

"The fleet is ready to sail," the grand admiral said, leaving the argument for them to settle later. "It will come from several different planets and only form up as you are in the process of departing Brunswick for Dresden. No doubt, your arrival with a fleet of that size will be a surprise."

"I like surprising my former step-uncles," Vicky said, smiling with a lot of teeth showing.

"Have you issued any orders?"

"Except for the detachment that carries you to Brunswick, they are all sailing under sealed orders. Most were sent by officer courier. A few we had to transmit, but they are in our tightest cypher."

"Good. Now, I need to see a doctor and some lawyers."

"They are set up in the next three rooms, Your Grace."

One of the rooms had been made into a very nice bedroom. Vicky managed to coax Mannie into giving her a very nice sperm donation into a special condom without spermicide that was quickly handed over to be frozen. Her egg donation was less pleasurable, but soon she was relieved of several dozen eggs, most of which would be stored in three secure locations.

Two lucky winners would get to meet one of Mannie's swimmers and get started immediately in the replicators. Before Vicky left the next day, she would pay her daughter a visit.

Her son would come with her. No doubt, her father would be overjoyed to meet him. She would not tell the old chauvinist that Henry would be decanted from his uterine replicator a good ten minutes after his sister.

However, at that moment, Vicky had law and the succession more on her mind. She told the five lawyers what she wanted. Four children of her and Mannie's bodies were to be born and grow up as princesses and princes. Mannie would be regent during the minority of the eldest daughter and future Empresses. He would have a free hand in the education and life of all four. There were no restrictions on him in any way, and he was free to remarry without any change in the regency.

"Vicky!"

"I want you to remarry," she snapped. "You're too good in bed not to have someone sharing yours."

Mannie blushed, and looked ready to say something, but she laid a finger on his lips and softly shushed him.

"I know you will always love me, but someone should also be loving you. Besides, don't you think our kids deserve a mother around the palace?"

"Yes. You."

Vicky chucked at how fast he came back at her. She was

half-tempted to take him back to the bedroom, but the doctors might not have left yet.

"I have every expectation of being in your bed for so long that you will get bored with my boney ass and throw me out."

Several of the lawyers looked like they wanted to be anywhere else but here, but the senior one, the JAG himself, pointed at the table, and they all kept their eyes there.

"Beloved, I will have a hard time leaving your bed, even when you are cold and lifeless," Mannie said.

"I do so love you," Vicky whispered. "We must continue this little argument tonight when we are alone." Vicky ended it for the moment with a chaste kiss, and got back to work.

There were a few other stops. It turned out that Grand Admiral Waller had some paperwork for Vicky to sign.

"What's this?" Vicky demanded after glancing down the form in her hand.

"You are promoting yourself to Grand Admiral."

"And I'm doing this because?"

"Monarchs have often held the highest rank in their uniformed services, Your Grace. They also gave honorary ranks to their fellow monarchs. I understand that on old Earth, they made it a habit of shipping back those uniforms when they went to war with each other."

Vicky shook her head. "I've earned a three-star flag. I will not be a girl playing dress up."

"Even as you show the flag?"

"Most definitely while I'm showing the flag."

The admiral presented her with a second set of papers. "Then here is a promotion, signed by me, promoting you to full admiral. Are you willing to add a well-earned fourth star to your flag as the victor in this recent unpleasantness?

Oh, and with your date of rank, Admiral Kris Longknife will still outrank you."

"As well she should. She's won some serious battles. Okay, you win. These papers I will accept," she said, taking them from the admiral's hand.

"Very well. Now, the *Victorious*, our most recently completed battleship, will be ready to sail tomorrow."

"Who commands?"

"A captain that Vice Admiral Bołeslaw selected for you. He will command your fleet, to the extent that you chose not to."

"Very good," Vicky said. "Very well done, Admiral. Thank you. I knew you'd pull all the pieces together no matter how short on time we were."

"Your Grace, it is always an honor to serve you," and he reached for her hand.

Vicky offered it to him, and he kissed the ring with the Imperial seal on her right hand.

Then she turned to Mannie. She had some fence mending to do with him. At the moment, he did not look happy, but he was always happy in the end.

Of course, there might come a time when he was right, and she was wrong.

That would be a sad day.

11

The visit to Brunswick went well. Steve, her friend from the last visit, greeted her enthusiastically, and introduced her to the Senate of Republican Advisors. Jansik and several that Vicky had met on her last visit were in the Senate, but most were new people. A lot of them were grandmothers.

Over wine after dinner, when all let their hair down, she heard many stories of how democracy and free markets were coming to Brunswick in fits and starts.

Billy, who was filling Mannie's place at her side, did a very good job of sounding like a true democrat, but not a rabid one.

Vicky only had to pull him back once, and those around the conversation circle smiled and took it for just what you'd expect from a democrat who'd married a Peterwald.

The visit lasted three days, then it was time to head out.

Vicky merely told Admiral Bołeslaw which jump to head for. He didn't even bat an eyebrow at his orders. He immediately passed along her orders to the fleet that had suddenly appeared around the system's jumps.

"You have quite a force headed for that jump," he said.

"Yes, it certainly looks like I do," she answered.

"You're playing your cards that close to your chest, huh?"

"Yep."

"Okay. I can't mutter in my sleep what I don't know, now can I?"

"My thoughts, exactly."

When they finally jumped into the Dresden system, it was a shock to a lot of people.

However, Vicky had prepared a formal announcement that she merely wished to pay a state visit to one of her father, the Emperor's, major planets.

They took their time arriving at Dresden, one gee all the way. By the time they arrived, the local government had had enough time to lay on quite a party.

The reception from the Governor General, with several Security Consultants at his side, was cold and formal. The reception at the dinner and dance that night was most warm.

Vicky was invited to several gala affairs over the next three days and stayed busy from morning until midnight, cutting ribbons, judging art, dance, and singing, as well as dancing and talking herself.

The nanos that Kris and her Nelly had left for Vicky did a very good job of clearing the air around her. Vicky spoke freely, and in turn was spoken to just as honestly, at least by some.

The present situation was hard. Some risked even saying it was unbearable. The planet was a powder keg, ready to blow.

"Haven't you considered a vote to leave this half of the Empire?" Vicky only asked once.

"Oh, have we. Many of us regret not moving on it as soon

as you signed the Edict of Succession on Cuzco, but we delayed, and the Red Shirts hired more thugs. The Governor General has bragged that if we vote, 97% will vote to stay loyal."

"No doubt, the ballots have already been tallied," Vicky said, bitterly.

"No doubt."

Despite the normal desire of any Navy to add fresh fruit, meats and vegetables to their stores, Vicky's ships took on nothing from their host planet.

Vicky regularly had her computer police up the spy drones and nanos on her flag, and dispatched Kit and Kat to check the other ships that had docked.

Much of the fleet chose to anchor nose-to-nose and swing around each other. It likely looked paranoid, but it also looked necessary, all things considered.

Whenever asked where she was headed next, Vicky dodged. She mentioned a lot of places, including several planets that offered everything from hunting, to skiing, to surfing, to other unique pastimes. There was even a new moon that specialized in gambling as well as wild sex.

When asked about that one, Vicky tried to blush prettily.

A whole lot of sailors were betting on that one.

As Dresden fell behind them, Vicky put on 1.25 gees. The jump beacon they headed for was pinged and sent through the jump. It found no traffic in the next system. Vicky ordered the navigator to put the fleet through that jump at 45,000 kilometers an hour.

She'd learned how to make fast jumps at Kris Longknife's knee. There were a few raised eyebrows, but no one questioned her order.

As soon as they were in the next system, she told

Admiral Bołeslaw which jump was his target. He had his fleet navigator set up a course, eyed the results, and turned to Vicky.

"I see that Your Grace is headed for Greenfeld."

"Is it already that obvious?"

"The next system has only two jumps out of it. One leads nowhere. The other sets us on a course where the third jump drops us into the Imperial Capital System. Every sailor on every ship will know this within an hour of me giving this order."

"Hmm. I believe someone taught me that a secret that cannot be kept is not a secret worth keeping."

"I don't know who that might have been," Admiral Bołeslaw said, almost sounding innocent.

"Advise the crew that Her Grace wishes to visit her father and introduce him to her new husband and their son. She may even arrange to have her husband ennobled."

"And the size of this fleet trailing around behind you?"

"Admiral Waller thought that at least a small portion of the fleet could use some experience navigating outside our own space."

"That's just plausible enough. Although, Your Grace, every sailor that hears it is going to laugh his fool head off. We all know about the Battle of Cuzco."

"No doubt all of you do, but, as you say, it has the benefit of being at least plausible. One must always be plausible," Vicky said, primly.

The effort to ping the jump buoy ahead of them got nothing in response. The actual space distance traveled between the next three jumps that would take them to Greenfeld was long. Vicky would prefer to take this jump fast, as well.

She flipped a mental coin, and told the navigator to take

the next jump at 45,000 klicks. The smallest light cruiser was sent ahead by ten minutes, just in case.

No doubt the sailors of that ship would have preferred to pass on this honor.

However, again, the buoys were dead on both sides of the jump. They drifted, out of fuel, totally abandoned.

The next system also showed jump buoys that had exhausted their consumables and were of no further value to safe navigation. *What was the level of commerce in her father's half of the Empire?*

No, in the Bowlingame half of the Empire.

Vicky would have to hold her tongue and her temper when she got to Greenfeld.

In the last system out from the Imperial capital, Vicky again had her fleet ping the jump they headed for. While she was waiting for a response she didn't expect to get, she got a message that dismayed her.

"This is the management and employee group on Nawak. Do you have any food that you would be willing to trade with us for what we have to sell? We have not had another ship go through this system in over twelve months. If you cannot trade us for food, is there any chance you might send a ship to lift us off?"

"Computer?" Vicky snapped.

"Nawak is an airless mining development. It is rich in iron, nickel, molybdenum, and a small amount of gold, silver, lead, tritium, and rare earths. It was established over a century ago and has a safe and secure natural environmental support system. They grow a large part of their own food, only importing meats as well as some fruits."

"What's the date on that report?"

"It was provided ten years ago, Your Grace."

"Computer, could you ask Admiral Bołeslaw to drop into my day quarters as soon as he finds it convenient?"

"He is already on his way, Your Grace," and the door to Vicky's quarters opened even as her computer finished informing her.

"Did you get that message from Nawak?" he asked.

"I just did. What's our food situation?"

"Four stores ships joined us when we jumped out of Brunswick. I was planning on resupplying the fleet in Greenfeld orbit. I wanted to dock as few ships as possible on the space station."

"Good," Vicky said, but she was thinking hard.

"Do all our ships still carry five tons of famine biscuits for emergency distribution?"

"Many of them landed the biscuits when the fighting got hard. No one wanted any extra weight aboard when the jinking got hard. However, four of our cruisers still show them in their loadout."

"Can we afford to send one store ship and two cruisers down to Nawak? The famine biscuits will be landed. I'm not saying that we give the fresh food away, but I would ask the supply corps to be as generous in trading as they would if those were their own sons or daughters ashore. Oh, also see what spare parts they may need to keep their gear up and running. If we've got it in stores, declare it surplus and land it."

"I think that can be arranged, Your Grace. I'd propose sending the *Altair*. She's a contract ship. Her merchant skipper can take on a cargo of trade goods without anyone getting their nose out of joint about the Navy getting into other people's business."

"We wouldn't want that to happen, now would we?" Vicky said through a grin that she knew was way too sassy.

This, however, was very interesting to her. Here was a minor colony just one jump away from Greenfeld that was being allowed to die, literally die, on the vine because it was off any major trade route. How many other tiny colonies were out there being ignored? Ignored even to starvation?

"Admiral Bołeslaw," she said, now totally serious. "When we finish with this exercise, assuming we are not again at war with this half of the empire, remind me to contract with a number of tramp freighters, the sort of junkers that no one pays any attention to. I know there are plenty of tramp skippers willing to take on a load if the price is a bit above the market's going rate."

"There are plenty of them," Bołeslaw agreed.

"Get them food of every sort: fresh, dried, frozen, including famine biscuits, and send them out to the tiny colonies. Maybe the smaller colonies as well. Maybe include any of the colonies we haven't heard anything from in a while. Let's see if we can establish trade with them even if the transport costs are above what the market would normally accept."

"Do you think the Bowlingames will consider that an act of war?"

Vicky scowled. "We're trading with them, not running our flag up. Hell, I'll even make sure they don't say a word about the option of voting to join my half. You think that might work?"

Admiral Bołeslaw shook his head. "With the Bowlingames, you never know what will work and what won't."

"Yeah."

12

A dmiral, Her Imperial Grace, the Grand Duchess Victoria aboard the battleship *Victorious* entered the Greenfeld system just ten minutes after the light cruiser *Karenburg*. They came through a minor, rarely used jump whose beacon was no longer functioning.

The Imperial Capital system had fallen on hard times.

Still, one did not lead an unannounced fleet toward Greenfeld, even at a comfortable and sedate one gee. Especially if that fleet consisted of two dozen battleships, an equal number of cruisers, both light and heavy, as well as auxiliary ships, including four fast attack transports.

People got nervous if you didn't clearly declare your good intentions.

A much smaller fleet of just six battleships had jumped into the Wardhaven system not too long ago. They immediately demanded the planet's surrender under pain of being blasted back to the stone age if they didn't.

They might have done just that, but a certain Lieutenant Kris Longknife and a handful of tiny attack boats had ended that noise. Them and every spit kit and volunteer that would report to the colors and get underway.

Vicky often dreamed of having been there. Been in such a fight to the death. Unfortunately, she was pretty sure that had she, she would most likely have been on one of the battleships doing the threatening.

Vicky still needed to have a serious talk with her dad about that particular bit of very undocumented history. While everyone knew Kris's side of the story, the battleships had vanished leaving no trace of where they came from.

But Vicky's problem was to rescue her dad, not start a war. Certainly not to destroy the capital of her own Empire. Even if it did seem to be under new and inappropriate management.

Standing on the *Victorious'* flag bridge with Admiral Bołeslaw just off screen, Vicky took a deep breath and began.

"Hail, Emperor Henry I," she said, then went on for a good minute repeating after her computer all of her father's claimed titles. Why in heaven's name would Dad want to be "Defender of the Faith"? When the list wound down, she switched to herself.

"Greetings from your daughter, Her Imperial Grace, Admiral . . . " and Vicky went into her titles, ending with "and heir apparent to the great Imperial throne of Greenfeld that you now hold. I come to bring you my husband so that we may properly bend the knee before you and present you with the uterine replicator holding the developing body of your first-born grandson. I look forward to seeing your smiling face, Dad."

COMPUTER, CUT THE FEED.

FEED CUT, YOUR GRACE.

Vicky waited until the red light truly faded from above the forward screen.

"I guess I should have had Mannie and the can with me when I sent the message. Oh, well, I'll do better next time. Sensors, what can you tell me about the system?"

"It's pretty light on traffic," a lieutenant reported. One of Captain Blue's best students, she had the watch at the moment. "Most of the piers on the station are empty. At least, we can't identify more than a couple of dozen ships by their active reactors. Over a hundred hulks are tumbling along behind the station."

"Very good. What have we got for warships?"

"Two battleships, a trio of cruisers, two of them light, and six destroyers, all quite old, I suspect.

"No doubt," Admiral Bołeslaw said, leaning close to her ear to whisper, and keeping his back to a screen that shouldn't be working, "someone will soon be in need of a change of underwear."

"No doubt," Vicky agreed, and did her best not to allow her face to set in a feral grin. "It will be interesting how long it takes my dear former step-uncle to produce either my father, or a well-controlled puppet."

"How will you recognize the puppet?"

"I have no idea," Vicky admitted. It wasn't like they'd shared a lot of quiet moments together that hadn't ended up recorded for the Imperial media market. Even before Dad proclaimed himself Emperor, their palace had been most Imperial.

"So, Admiral, how are we going to work this rather large non-invasion?"

"As carefully as possible," he answered. "Obviously, we have to dock you and the *Victorious*. I'd prefer to keep the rest of the battleships anchored off the station. Twenty-two of them pair up well. The *Gracious Grand Duchess* doesn't have a ship that matches her tonnage, so we'll also dock her."

"The *Gracious Grand Duchess*?" Vicky asked.

"It was the old *Savage*, but no planet wanted to cough up funds to support something that nasty."

"*Gracious Grand Duchess*," Vicky said, tasting it. "Nice."

"I'll anchor most of the cruisers together as well. We'll berth two of them close to you."

"So, two battleships and two cruisers."

"And the two fast assault transports, the *Imperial Defender* and the *Imperial Protector*."

"Need I ask what their old names were? *Kick You in the Balls*, or something?"

"Or something." Bołeslaw said.

"How will it go then?"

"A heavy cruiser. Then *Defender* and *Victorious* at one pier. *Protector* and *Gracious Grand Duchess* next over, and the light cruiser covering the other side.

It sounded like a plan.

Several hours after a response should have arrived, a message flimsy was presented to Vicky during supper in her flag quarters with Admiral Bołeslaw, Billy, and the two pint-sized assassins.

"This is interesting," Vicky said. "No visual, just words. I am told that my father is hunting in the north mountains. He and a guide have left the base camp and will not return for ten days, or until they slay a grizzly bear."

"Ten days, huh?" Bołeslaw said.

"Hmm, can we keep a fleet hanging around for ten days?" Vicky asked, with an artificial wide-eyed and innocence.

"It would be hard to do," Admiral Bołeslaw said,

sounding very professional. "Especially if we don't give anyone shore leave."

"Yes, that would be a problem," Vicky said. "But, Computer, doesn't whomever sent this message have a worse problem?"

"Your Grace?"

"Didn't we introduce the grizzly to the cold northern and southern mountains?"

"Yes, Your Grace."

"And weren't the grizzlies in the north hunted to extinction?"

"That was the report. As of five years ago, no grizzly bears had been spotted in ten years."

"There were plans to reintroduce the bears, using breeding stock from the south. How did that progress?"

"I have no report of it happening. Your father sold off his northern hunting lodge ten years ago. He has only used his southern lodge since then."

"Admiral," Vicky said, grinning, "someone doesn't know his hunting."

"No grizzlies up north, huh?"

"Only down south, and I remember going on hunting trips with Dad to bag bears. It was always a great production and he never had less than ten shooters with him. He wanted to make the kill, but poor old timid Dad definitely wanted a lot of guns around to make sure the bear didn't take anything out of his hide."

"So, this is all crap."

"Put out by some banker who has never gotten his nose out of a ledger sheet."

"Or, more importantly, asked anyone to check on what 'they just know is right.' Okay, Your Grace," Admiral Bołeslaw asked. "What do we do now?"

"Oh, dear," Vicky said, with an artificial flutter to her voice, much like a butterfly with a ten-ton payload. "Having just begun a family of my own, I do feel an urgent need to revisit the scenes of my youth. I really want to show my new husband where I grew up and share fond memories of my old haunts."

"Is any of that true?" Billy asked.

"Not a word of it," Kit said.

Kat nodded agreement.

"Just asking. I want to make sure of my role here."

Vicky smiled at her husband's double. He did look good enough to eat in his white, open neck shirt and slimming black pants. She had to keep reminding herself that he went to the other bedroom, not hers.

This fake honeymoon was a bitch.

"You, good dear, continue to be an assertive democrat, not aggressive, and let me win most of the arguments in a fashion that makes it clear to all listeners that I have won this battle, but you still intend to win the war."

"Of course, Your Grace."

"Honey. Sweetheart. Keep the 'Your Graces' to a minimum."

"Yes, sweetheart," he said, and both of them laughed, as did the others a moment later.

The Grand Duchess's Imperial Fleet continued on its course toward Greenfeld. After two days, they got a request for her intentions, now that her father was hunting.

Vicky waited a day before telling them about her desire to share fond memories from her childhood with her loving husband.

That seemed to end further communication. Even when the flagship asked for assignment to a pier, the answer was, "Wait one."

"Wait one," means one minute. Occasionally it may stretch into two or three. This one stretched an hour. Then a day. Then two days.

Finally, there was a reply that they lacked sufficient berths for a fleet this big. The admiral asked for six, close together.

A day later, as they were coming up on the station, they got their answer.

"This is Lieutenant Gorsh, the port admiral is away at the moment. I cannot offer you adjacent berths. I will need to distribute you around the station."

"Lieutenant Gorsh, this is Admiral Bołeslaw. I have your station in sight and I see a lot of adjacent berths. All empty. You want to try that again?"

"Ah. Yes, sir. Ah, we do appear to have a lot of vacant births. However, most of them are down, waiting for spare parts. Sorry, you will, ah, need to follow my instructions."

"Wait one," the admiral said, and turned to Vicky.

She scowled. "If I was Kris Longknife, I'd just have my computer activate the pier tie-downs and park where I damn well wanted to."

"If you wish, Your Grace, I could do that for you," her computer said from her neck.

"You could, computer?"

"Nelly gave me both of the subroutines needed to insert myself into the station's control nodes and to activate the pier's docking procedures."

Vicky exchanged a look with the admiral. *What else have Kris and Nelly inserted into my computer?*

However, one does not look a gift horse, or gift routine, in the mouth.

While the lieutenant issued all sorts of order, Admiral Bołeslaw issued his own orders for the fleet to prepare to either come along side or establish their own mooring by pairs.

The six that would land, swung out in echelon.

The heavy cruiser *Baden* lead the ships that were to dock. It turned in toward Pier 34A, despite a lot of officious squawking from the lieutenant in the Port Admiral's office. She caught the hook smartly and was drawn in by the landing tie-downs to a perfect landing.

Vicky swore she could hear her computer purring.

The *Victorious* was echeloned to the *Baden's* left, showing the flag of the Grand Duchess. As Pier 35A came around, the battleship's skipper turned her smartly into the precise dock Admiral Bołeslaw had assigned to the *Victorious* and caught the hook as the station turned beneath his approaching nose. His ship was drawn into the pier and all airlocks locked to the station.

The *Imperial Defender* was scheduled to tie up at Pier 36B. Her docking developed a hitch when the third tie-down refused to engage, but the other three succeeded in pulling the fast attack transport in. All the airlocks showed solid seals. However, since the third tie-down was the one for power, water, and landlines, some further work would be needed.

The second three ships now began their landings. The *Imperial Protector* came smoothly alongside pier 35B, sharing the pier with the *Victorious*. The *Gracious Grand Duchess* tied up smoothly alongside the *Defender* at Pier 36A.

The *Leipzig* got everyone's bad luck. As it approached Pier 37B, it became clear, the hook had not extended.

"The central station computer shows that it is extended," Vicky's computer said.

"It's not. Extend the hook for 37A," the skipper ordered.

"I show it extended," the computer announced.

"It's partially extended," the *Leipzig* reported. "Let's see if I can catch it anyway."

The light cruiser applied the extra thrusters that Vicky's ships had so they could zig and zag in the Longknife fighting manner, and the cruiser managed to engage the hook.

However, the hook did not lock down. It began to draw the cruiser into the pier, but there was a serious question about whether or not the first tie-down would engage.

"I have tie-down one engaged," finally was reported by the *Leipzig*.

"Failure on number two."

There was a long, breathless pause. If the light cruiser came loose in the docking area, it could drift or slam into the *Imperial Defender*. The assault transport was presently in the process of deploying a task force with an armored company and a light infantry company to set up guard posts on the station's A deck.

If the transport got knocked hard, the lock between ships and station could be ruptured and vacuum could start sucking Marines and Sailors off the dock and ship.

Finally, the skipper of the *Leipzig* reported, "Contact with fourth tie-down. We have two good tie-downs and are being hauled into the dock. We are assisting the tie-downs with thrusters. You folks can start breathing again."

A lot of people on the *Victorious'* flag bridge needed that reminder.

"Wow, Nelly, you really pulled that one off," Vicky said, delighted with her computer.

Only when Admiral Bołeslaw raised an eyebrow did Vicky realize what she'd said. Her computer had pulled off something right out of the Magnificent Nelly's book, and she had praised her as Nelly.

"Thank you very much, Your Grace," Vicky's computer said, but the Grand Duchess was hardly listening. She had a major question to answer.

Had Kris Longknife and Nelly just dropped a batch of subroutines into her computer, or was there more to it? If Nelly had, indeed, given Vicky one of her children to care for and nurture into real life, could she turn her back on the gift and keep treating her computer like an impersonal machine?

One thing was certain, Kris and Nelly liked to have her kids addressed by name.

"You did a super job, Computer. Would you mind if I addressed you in the future as Maggie?"

"I would be honored, Your Grace. Wasn't Doc Maggie one of your most dependable friends when you were young?"

"Yes, she was."

"Then I shall endeavor to be just as dependable."

"Very good . . . Maggie," Vicky said. There were no contractions, and Maggie was being a very obedient computer, or whatever she was.

Then, the full impact of this question mark hit Vicky. If Nelly had entrusted Vicky with one of her kids, she now had the duty to raise it up as a proper intelligent computer. Here she was still wondering if she could raise a kid. No, two kids, and now she had a computer to raise too.

She'd often heard people joke about kids not coming with an instruction manual in their diaper. Still, the human race had been raising their flesh and blood offspring for a long time.

Now, how do you raise a computer?

Worse, how could Vicky raise a computer with no Nelly

close at hand? No Sal or any of the other first-generation children of Nelly's?

Vicky's life was so easy. Build a marriage. Raise some kids. Rule her half of an Empire. Save her old man, and maybe his half of an empire.

Oh, and now, raise a computer.

Vicky had read or watched a lot of cheap media about the horror stories of computers that came alive. Now, she might be living one.

Could a Peterwald actually be a good role model for such an infant?

Kris, Nelly, what have you done to me?"

13

V icky watched from the *Victorious'* flag bridge with Admiral Bolesław at her elbow as Marines did what they did best: get matters well in hand.

As soon as the *Victorious'* locks were sealed tightly to the pier, hatches opened and Marines in dress black and greens from the flagship's reinforced company marched out and quickly established guard posts in the immediate dock area.

The *Imperial Defender* had landed right after the *Victorious*. Of necessity, it had to tie up at the next pier over so that there was less chance of poor ship handling resulting in one ship holing the other.

Marines from its light infantry battalion quickly secured its dock as well. Even as they did so, a dozen eight-wheeled, armored vehicles rolled out of the landing bays. They drove directly to the freight elevators and took one straight to A Deck.

The first thing the rigs did was set up a guard post to restrict and control access from A Deck to Pier 35 where the *Victorious* was docked. Only when it was fully secure did the follow-up waves of light armored Marines set up a restricted access to their own pier, then Pier 34 where the *Baden* lay.

As soon as the *Protector* sealed its locks, they added more wheeled rigs, some with mighty large cannons, to the guard detail.

The light Marines were all in dress black and greens and looked like toy soldiers, if you missed the steel in their eyes and the way they held their weapons. The armored Marines wore big helmets and talked softly into small ear micro-phones as they surveyed the area.

Even a blind man could see they were all business.

No sooner did the Marines get the situation well in hand, then the Imperial Guard hurried into view, dragging their asses and out of breath.

Out of breath, and struggling to stand up straight, likely due to a stitch in his side, their skipper tried to boldly announce, "I am Captain Jinx of the Imperial Guard. What is the meaning of this armed display?"

Vicky had not sent a company grade officer. She grinned as her camera take let her watch the reply.

"I am Colonel Burke, Commander of the 3rd Guard Brigade, personal to the defense of the Grand Duchess. This area is secured in her name."

"The Imperial Guard secures all Imperial precincts in the name of Emperor Henry the First."

"Of course you do," the colonel said, failing to keep a strong hint of doubt from his words. "Feel free to secure these precincts . . . from outside my security zone."

"Imperial Guards go where they will," sounded almost petulant, but at least the man was getting his breath under control.

The colonel merely stared at the junior officer. Behind him, more armored vehicles rolled up, and came to a halt.

Several had 20mm autocannons pointed straight at the Guard detachment. Others had 130mm anti-armored cannons pointed down A Deck from where he'd come from.

"You wouldn't dare," the Captain of the Guard said, in a voice not nearly as firm as he, no doubt, wanted it to be.

"If I were to do so, you would never know I had," the colonel pointed out.

That wilted the arrogant guardsman. He turned away and issued orders to the sergeant major of the detachment. He shouted orders, and marched his troops off to establish guard posts almost elbow-to-elbow with Vicky's own Marines.

The Imperial Guardsmen were, however, a few steps farther from the pier access than the Marines were.

Vicky counted it a small victory.

Then the real assault began.

The first problems were small. Very small. Monitoring quickly identified cholera bacteria in the water flowing from the pier.

This did not come as a surprise. All the initial delivery of water and air had been isolated. When the water proved to be laced with cholera and the air with a nasty flu bug, deliveries from the pier were cut off, and the connections broken.

The division of docked ships put themselves back on internal consumables and made ready for a siege.

Kit and Kat took the computers Kris Longknife had given them after the wedding, as well as a ten-kilogram block of the best Wardhaven Smart Metal™, and set about establishing a serious nano defense of all four piers.

It soon became clear that the screens on the air vents to the pier were very porous, and that same flu was streaming from it.

While some nanos quickly mopped up the bugs at the

vents, others streamed down the air ducts and located the source of the virus. For the nanos it was a quick process to destroy the seals on the metal canister. It was done only a little at first, then more and more of the virus got released into the station's atmosphere.

Vicky ordered Maggie to stop before alarms went off. It would be a shame to save the station from a little epidemic.

More effective filters had been created by the nanos for the vents on the four piers they occupied. Much of the virus they captured were rerouted to the exhaust vents and sent back to the station.

Vicky knew she was supposed to now be the Gracious Grand Duchess, but the old nasty Peterwald Grand Duchess hoped that the air cleaning system on the station was in as poor shape as what she'd seen at her piers so far.

Nose filters were quickly sent up to the guard detachment for them to slip in place as soon and as surreptitiously as possible. Meanwhile the epidemiologist who Vicky had signed on for just this event, jumped on it.

"We know this little bugger," one of them told her an hour later. "We can knock out a vaccine and have most of your troops inoculated against it by tomorrow's lunch. Suppertime at the latest. In the meantime, we're implementing decontamination in the elevators. We'd recommend that all personnel and equipment take the elevator. We'll do our best to isolate the escalator."

"Very well done," Vicky said. "Thank you."

"Glad to be of service, Your Grace. Some of us feared this trip would be a waste of time. Now you've made it fun."

"I fear that I am not the one who has provided you the fun," Vicky noted. "They have. By the way, how quickly could you grow enough vaccine to protect a significant section of the planet?"

The doctor sadly shook her head. "We brought along enough raw stock to immunize every woman and man in your fleet four times. However, we lack the vats and other production devices to make much more than one set in a day, maybe two days if it's complex enough. This bug is in the middle. Anyway, we could hardly vaccinate a fraction of the population of Anhalt."

"Could you provide the feed stock if they had the production equipment?"

"Yes, Your Grace. Please remember though, if we produce a second batch for that feed stock, you go from having enough for three more vaccinations for your Marines and Sailors to only two."

"I understand," Vicky said. "Let me know when you've finished the first batch. You might want to watch the spread of this on the station. See how many people take a ferry down to Greenfeld."

"As you no doubt know, Your Grace," Maggie pointed out, "that information is not public knowledge in this half of the Greenfeld Empire."

"Yes, I am aware, Maggie. See to it that the good doctor's computer has access to the data she needs in a manner that does not bring notice."

"Of course, Your Grace. I have connected to her computer and have provided the access."

The doctor studied something off camera for a moment. "No surprise. There is not yet a spike in sick call visits. This particular bug starts slow and isn't too bad to start with. Think sniffles and irritated throat. You know, the kind of stuff you don't want when you're in a space suit. That should start showing up in thirty-six to forty-eight hours. Fever and debilitation begins twenty-four hours later. We will monitor matters."

"Thank you, doctor."

"When should I drop by to give you your inoculation?"

"When will it be available?"

"Some should be out by early tomorrow morning."

"Why don't you set up a team outside the wardrooms and needle the officers first? If you have enough, get the chief's messes as well."

The doctor grinned. "It can be fun serving under you, ma'am."

"Sometimes, I expect it is," Vicky said, and rang off.

"Admiral Bolesław, two balls, no strikes. What do you see these jokers throwing at me next?"

"We have control of our immediate area, both with our security teams and your nanos," he said. "They must know by now that they can't get crap aboard our ships. They must be frustrated. Of course, for the moment they don't know that the flu is not wafting aboard through our open hatches."

"Pardon me, Your Grace," Maggie interrupted politely from Vicky's neck.

"Yes, Maggie?"

The admiral raised his eyebrows, clearly surprised that Vicky had adopted a name for her computer. Maybe it was why he allowed it to interrupt them. Maybe both, but he said nothing.

"While roaming the data streams aboard the station, I have found and am now monitoring the Port Admiral's office. Captain Jinx has reported that that our guards seem to have inserted nasal filters. He wonders if his team should have the same protection."

"Oh," both admirals said.

"He was advised there was no such need. We are just being overly cautious."

"Yeah, right," drawled Admiral Bolesław.

"So, I repeat again," Vicky said, trying to refocus herself as much as her admiral, "what should we be looking for now?"

Admiral Bolesław grinned. " I would expect their next pitch to be a fast ball, right down the middle."

"Explain yourself, Admiral."

He quickly did, and they quickly issued orders. Fortunately, they called the play just right.

14

The radar on the *Baden* picked up the first hint that the opposition was getting frustrated and was now willing to be a bit more blatant in their attacks. She identified a bit of floating junk that had just changed course.

There was a lot of junk floating close to the station. Frankly, the amount of crap out there, creating the risk of FOD, foreign object damage, was disgusting to officers who expected better. Still, they'd approached the station slowly, and all the stray gear, frozen urine, and worse had just bounced off the ships.

Such items as those did not change course. Some had when they bounced off Vicky's ships, but changing course was not something you'd expect from a natural bit of junk.

Clearly, junk it was not.

The *Baden* quickly launched its alert longboat. The *Victorious* and *Gracious Grand Duchess* just as quickly added longboats of their own.

The unknown foreign object was now headed for the *Victorious*. That could not be permitted.

In the last half hour, the tech personnel of these ships had worked hard and fast to arm a longboat with a 13mm light anti-air lasers. That was not your normal equipment for a longboat, but with a bit of imagination and creativity, they managed to attach a gun and install a Marine gunner's station.

The space "junk" didn't get close to any of Vicky's ships. The *Baden's* armed picket boat got it in its sights and lasered the thing in two.

A second longboat, unarmed, but with a demolition team on board, caught the two pieces in something that looked truly like a butterfly net. Albeit a large net with a very long handle.

An explosive expert went hand-over-hand out to one of the nets to have a look at one half. "Yep, it's a limpet mine. I'm not sure of the explosive power of the charge on board."

A moment later, he was also looking at the other half. "Yep, gunner, you cut it right in half. Good shooting. Give me a minute. I've got an idea here."

A moment later, the second half of the mine was jetting away from the station. Five minutes later, the motor cut off, and a few seconds later, the portion of the mine blew up.

The demolition expert quickly repeated the process with the first piece. The second explosion was noticeably smaller than the first.

"Your Grace," came on the *Victorious'* net. "This is Major Stoner, commander of your demolition team. Based on our measurements of the strength of that explosion, even assuming it was a shaped charge and aimed at the outer skin of one of your battleships, I don't see it doing anything to the four meters of ice armor on the Victorious. I doubt it could do much to the *Gigi Dee's* three meters, either. It might could do something to the meter-thick armor of the fast transports."

"Thank you, Major," Vicky said. That was the first time she'd heard what nickname the Gracious Grand Duchess had acquired. She found it cute. Strange for a battleship that had been top of the line just a few decades ago should bring 'cute' to mind.

She turned to Bolesław. "Do you think they know their explosives are underpowered?"

"Any device that can burn through four meters of ice is going to have to be a whole lot bigger than you can pass off for space junk. No, I suspect the jokers doing this really don't have an idea what they're up against."

"What's the level of professionalism left in their Navy?" Vicky mused.

"I can't vouch for them, Your Grace, but I wonder if their Navy officers are even being asking for their advice. We still haven't heard from the Port Admiral. I have no idea who he is, nor what kind of background he has. If he's another one of those jumped up bank clerks, he's way in over his head on this."

"So, we could be lucky, or he could get lucky, huh?"

"It's a crap shoot."

"Let's see what we can do about rattling a few cages. Maggie, get me a line out."

"That I cannot do, Your Grace. Though it is impossible for a fiber optic line to have static, our lines seem to be full of static."

"You're kidding."

"Regretfully, kidding is not within my skill level, and I doubt you would want it to be."

"Correct. Sorry, Maggie. So, how have you been managing to get information from inside the station?"

"Our switching and lines are fine. It is only at the first switching component on the station that the static suddenly appears. I have laid a wire around it."

"And if I make a call on that line, they'll go looking for it."

"Yes, Your Grace."

"Are any of my ships having less trouble?"

"No, Your Grace."

"Could we land a longboat at another pier and maybe have better luck?"

Admiral Bolesław grinned as Maggie said, "Yes, Your Grace."

An unarmed longboat was dropped off the *Victorious*. She headed for the *Baden*, but poor handling caused it to miss. The station was rotating under it and the longboat just drifted.

Then it darted to pier 23B and locked onto the longboat landing. A few seconds later, Vicky had a commlink to the station that worked.

"This is Her Imperial Grace, the Grand Duchess Admiral Victoria. I will speak to the Port Admiral about the filthy conditions of his station."

The lieutenant's face again filled her screen.

"I'm sorry, Your Grace, but the Port Admiral is not here at the moment. How can I help you?"

"Is the Port Admiral ever there? If he does not show up for work, he should be fired. Better yet, walk him out the nearest airlock."

The admiral beside Vicky raised his eyebrows. She grinned back. It had been a long time since she'd dare come full-on Peterwald Grand Duchess. Actually, it didn't even taste good now.

The lieutenant was in full cowering mode, "The Port

Admiral is a very loyal and industrious officer, Your Grace. He is indisposed at the moment. A horrible and debilitating stomach flu. The station surgeon has him quarantined to keep it from spreading."

Vicky very much doubted he has a stomach flu, but she fully expected he would have one in a day or two.

"Very well, Lieutenant. The amount of space junk is totally unacceptable. I had to shoot one up and then blow up the pieces. This has to stop!"

"Yes, Your Grace. It certainly must. However, both our Zambonis for junk collection are awaiting parts. I will call our supplier and alert him to the risk he is causing the Grand Duchess."

"Tell him he is putting himself at risk," Vicky snapped. "If this continues, I will have him out collecting this junk by hand. If he is lucky, I will allow him a space suit with an oxygen tank."

"Yes, Your Grace. Immediately, Your Grace. Excuse me while I make that call."

"Very well, this call is over," and Maggie snapped the comm line to off.

"It will be interesting to see how quickly that changes things," Admiral Bolesław said.

"I doubt it will change anything at all," Vicky said.

She should have talked the admiral into putting money down.

She would have won.

Over the next six hours, whoever was running this show continued to take pot shots at them. The first two hours, there was one every few minutes. After two hours of not getting anything done, someone launched an entire swarm of limpet mines, throwing caution and deniability to the wind.

By that time, each of the ships had at least a pair of armed longboats. The fast attack transports had half a dozen landing craft armed as well. Vicky scrambled the lot of them.

They smeared the space around her small squadron with the wreckage of mines. Some were now equipped with 20mm grenade launchers. They blew the mines up, with even better results.

After an hour of this, the space around them grew must less occupied. The picket boats with the grenade launchers roved the area, shooting at and blowing up the wreckage. The boats armed with the 13mm lasers came back aboard and the crews turned to re-arm them with grenades as well.

The quiet lasted for only a bit more than an hour.

During the early assaults, the mines had been launched from a widely dispersed number of places on the station, and Vicky had refrained from shooting them up. She likely would have turned her station into Swiss cheese if she had, and that was something she preferred to avoid.

After all, this was part of her father's territory. Indeed, his capital.

Then the jokers running things on the station massively changed things up.

Vicky had most of her fleet swinging around each other at anchor well away from the station. However, their anchorage was not random. Her ships were several thousand kicks away from the station, strategically placed at the same level as Vicky's docked ships.

Simply put, no matter where the station was in its continual rotation, she had a couple of ships swinging around each other, with their eyeballs on the station around her detachment.

The battleships *Peace* and *Prosperity* identified the

change. Huge hatches at the end of Piers 23 to 28, and 43 to 48 had opened up and large cube-shaped objects were pushed out and welded in place.

It was amazing how fast that was done. More amazing was how well it was coordinated. Less than a minute after the first box had been winched out and secured into place, the entire group of ten huge cubes was in place.

There was a short paused while nothing happened.

Without warning, the cubes began launching hundreds of small rocket-powered objects, longer and thinner than the mines they'd already blown up. Suddenly, swarms of rockets shot out into space and began arching back, each using a slightly different course.

The gunnery officers on the *Peace* and the *Prosperity* had made a guess that these crates were up to no good. Now they were proven right.

Even as Vicky shouted the order, "Shoot those rocket launchers!" the gunners were closing their firing circuits. Lasers reached across four thousand kilometers at the speed of light to slash into the cubes.

Lasers and explosives do not mix well. It didn't take a lot of laser power slashing into the rocket magazines before they'd hit enough rocket motors to cause major damage. One rocket lead to another rocket exploding, taking with them the entire cube of rockets, and leaving a very big hole at the end of a pier.

The exploding rockets launchers also took out a number of the recently launched rockets. However, each launcher had been spewing out a hundred rockets a second for several long seconds.

Several thousands of rockets now swarmed toward the *Victorious*.

There was no question, Vicky was the target.

15

Vicky could only watch as the rockets shot toward her flagship. No one could know how deadly the warheads were. No one could guess how badly they'd damage a huge 120,000-ton battleship.

The twenty-four 19-inch main lasers were of no use. You do not use a sledge hammer to kill a mosquito. Vicky's life would be lost or saved by much smaller guns.

She had only a few breaths before she would learn her fate. She used two of them to think, *I'm sorry Mannie. I thought I could beat them at this. I'm sorry we didn't have all the time in the world.*

The picket boats took on the incoming swarm. Automatic grenade launchers sent explosive shooting out toward the mass of rockets, even as the 13mm lasers tried to snap off incoming shots.

However, there were only eight fully loaded picket boats out at the moment, and there were thousands of targets.

In addition to the big 19-inch guns, the *Victorious* also carried a secondary battery of thirty-six 5-inch lasers. These were designed to take out small rockets and other nuisances that occasionally cluttered up the battlefield.

Nine of the 5-inchers were masked by the pier. The other twenty-seven would have some portion of the swarm in their target area. However, there was only so much that they could do. The firing solutions for so many targets were impossible for the ship's computer and fire control computers to calculate that fast.

Still, those twenty-seven lasers opened fire. However, they did not fire full power laser beams, then recharge, then fire again.

No.

Every gun opened up and fired off short, staccato bursts at low power, but enough to hack a rocket in two, explode its rocket fuel or otherwise blow the rocket to hell.

Each of the guns seemed to be concentrating on its own portion of the sky, taking out one rocket, moving a smidgen, slashing another one in half, then edging a bit over and hacking one in half.

And they kept doing this as rockets disintegrated, flew to pieces, rammed into wreckage, and blew themselves up.

Vicky and Admiral Bolesław stared at the screen, struggling to keep their mouths from dropping open.

"That's impossible," the admiral whispered.

Even as he said that, the 5-inch batteries on the *Protector* and *Defender* opened fire, followed by the *Gracious Grand Duchess*. A fraction of a second later, the secondaries on the cruisers at either end of the berths swung out of train and into action.

Every medium-sized gun in the pier side squadron was shooting short, rapid bursts that shot across the sky to smash a rocket. Immediately, they moved on to the next one. Always smashing. Always moving on.

Finally, the fire began to slacken. The *Victorious* shook as three explosions rattled her outer hull. Vicky waited for the announcement of a hull breach, but none came.

"Can anyone tell me what just happened?" Admiral Bolesław demanded.

"Were those guns even manned?" Vicky asked.

"No, Your Grace, the gun crews were not at their stations," Maggie answered from Vicky's neck.

"Okay, Maggie," Vicky said, suddenly very suspicious of this gift horse one certain Kris Longknife had given her and very much wanting a look in its mouth.

"I saw that the problem developing could not be resolved by conventional means in the seconds before impact," Maggie said, apologetically.

"That was certainly true," Admiral Bolesław agreed.

"I selected two subroutines Nelly had made available to me. One allowed us to dial back our lasers from full strength to one tenth power. I might have been able to get it to one twentieth by modifying it, but I only had one tenth available."

"And the other subroutine?" Vicky said, doing her best to make sure honey would melt in her mouth.

"Nelly has subroutines that allow problems to be broken down into small portions and apportioned among several computers. I set each of the ship computers and the main fire control computers to finding the firing solution for the secondary batteries. They succeeded, and we fed the data to the targeting computers for the 5-inch guns and activated them to sweep their assigned portion of the sky."

Admiral Bolesław began to frown as he studied the screen. Suddenly, his face went pale. He signaled Vicky silently, pointing one finger at his neck repeatedly.

She reached up and found Maggie's on/off switch.

The admiral nodded, and Vicky deactivated her computer.

"Your computer saved our lives," Admiral Bolesław said slowly. "Remember that. No matter what you may think of Maggie in a moment, your computer saved our lives."

"Yes," Vicky said. "What's wrong?"

"Our computers processed the problem your Maggie laid out before them: to shoot down the incoming rockets. That she could coordinate getting the firing solution from all our computers, then firing at all those incoming missiles, is not something that could have done by anyone or anything except her."

"I know all of that," Vicky said, getting aggravated. "You see a problem. What is it?"

"We had eight picket boats out there when the swarms started attacking," the admiral said, his voice low and even. Then he said no more.

Vicky's stomach went into freefall. Her vision grayed until she looked at Admiral Bolesław through a small tunnel. She swayed on her feet, as her mouth went dry. For a long moment, her stomach wanted to vomit forth its contents.

Yes, three minutes ago, there had been eight picket boats out there. Each had a crew of at least two yeomen and two Marine gunners.

Now there were no picket boats.

Maggie had arrived at the optimum firing solution in the limited amount of time available. She had either not thought to add in the factor of friendlies in their sky or she had chosen to ignore it.

Vicky knew that if Maggie hadn't ignored it, the *Victorious* would very likely have taken a lot more hits while the computer searched for a more complex fire plan.

"Your Grace, would you like to sit down?" Admiral Bolesław offered.

"Yes. Yes, I think I will," Vicky said, and quickly did.

"Bosun, a cup of tea for the Grand Duchess."

A warm, delicate china cup was soon in her hands. Vicky inhaled the fragrant steam coming off the cup as she tried to order her problems.

She still had some SOB on this station trying to kill her. That was problem number one.

She had just killed some very valiant and courageous men. They had died doing their duty. That it was friendly fire that killed them was . . . what? Regrettable? Unacceptable? Painful but unavoidable?

This was the first time she'd commanded such an act. She knew that she was not the first to have such a horrible choice forced upon her. Still, this time it fell on her shoulders.

She did not feel good about it.

So, now she had a computer that, thanks to Nelly and Kris Longknife, was able to pull miracles out of her nonexistent hat. Without the new skills her computer had, Vicky might very well be dead.

Thank you for my life, Kris.

But Maggie was not Nelly. Nelly knew how important human life was.

Vicky paused in her thoughts.

Had Nelly always known how important human life was? Did she have to learn?

Oh God, not another learning experience, and now I'm sharing them with my bloody computer!

All Vicky could do was shake her head.

She also knew that she needed her computer.

"Captain Blue," she snapped.

"Yes, Your Grace."

"Have you been paying attention to what is going on in this station and what we now know about it?"

"Yes, I have, ma'am."

"If I wanted you to shut it down, could you do that?"

"With your computer's help, I think I could."

Vicky allowed herself a sour face.

Admiral Boleslaw nodded his agreement.

"Captain, I need you here."

In a moment, the sensor chief was at Vicky's elbow. She quickly explained her problem. Her computer might have well just saved their life. However, the cost had been all the human lives in the fire zone.

"My problem is figuring out how delicate my computer is. Can we keep her ignorant of the loss of human life?"

"Do we want to?" Blue asked.

"That is also part of my problem."

The young and rapidly promoted captain studied the deck for a long minute.

"I can offer you no guarantees on this, Your Grace. I don't think you're expecting any from me. However, I would just turn your computer back on, and immediately turn her loose on taking down the station without the ground troops knowing they've lost control up here. That ought to keep even a brilliant computer tied up."

"And if she asks about the loss of time?"

"Say we had a problem and you accidently turned her off."

"Can I successfully lie to my computer?"

"I suspect we'll know real soon."

16

Admiral, Her Grace Victoria Peterwald took a deep breath and prepared herself for what she suspected would be one of the most challenging experiences of her young life.

In the last few days, she apparently had birthed a sentient computer. Nelly, Kris Longknife's sentient computer that told horrible jokes, used contractions in her speech, and argued with Kris, had left one of her children dormant in the computer matrix around Vicky's neck.

Somehow, Vicky had awakened it.

Not only was Maggie awake, but she had saved Vicky's life, and the life of thousands of Sailors and Marines aboard the *Victorious*.

However, in doing so, she had either killed or allowed the incoming attack to kill at least thirty-two Marines and Sailors.

Vicky, as well as her computer, were now on the horns of a moral dilemma.

By all rights, Vicky and Maggie should go off in a corner and do their best to debrief themselves about being at the center of a friendly fire event, since they were the likely cause of the event.

Vicky was sick at what had just happened under her command. The deaths alone made her want to curl up in a bed and cry herself to sleep.

How would a newly sentient computer take to being responsible for the death of thirty-two human beings? Would Maggie even recognize the moral scope of this? How would she take to this moral dilemma?

However, there was not time for either Vicky to curl up and cry or for her to walk Maggie through an intense lesson on morals and decision making. They were in the middle of a fight for their lives and they needed to act.

They needed something done that only Maggie could do.

Vicky pushed the on/off switch.

"Maggie, we need to close down this station's contact with the planet below without letting those on the planet know we've done it."

"You need for me to intercept the data flow to the planet, copy the present flow, create a loop and then feed the ground the loop," Maggie said.

"Yes. Then, as soon as we can, we need to close down all autocannons on the station, so our Marines can move quickly to seize the station."

"I'll also need to isolate the station command center to keep them from taking any action, like opening hatches."

"Yes, Maggie."

"I am working on that. Your Grace, I can't help but notice that time has passed that I cannot account for."

"Yes, Maggie. I made a mistake. We can talk about it later when we have the station in our hands."

"Very good, Your Grace," Maggie said, then went silent.

"I am recording the data flow to the planet below. It includes some landline communication. Some of it is encrypted, but not much. As a conversation ends, I am taking the landline off line. The same for the encrypted data transmission. However, I cannot tell if the encrypted data is something that must be received below."

Vicky glanced at Captain Blue.

"Maggie, go ahead and block further encrypted messages when one ends. I assume you plan to cut in your recorded data loop when the messages end."

"Yes, Captain Blue."

"Could you cut in your data while five or eight comm lines are still running, so that they do not all end at the same time?"

"You think that would make our takeover less obvious, Captain Blue?"

"Yes, I think that would. Don't you agree, Your Grace?"

"Yes," Vicky said.

"Then I will do that," Maggie said. "We are down to ten active private lines. Nine. I am cutting our recorded data in. I am also working on modifying the recording, making it longer and with some minor variations in the data as seems to be the norm."

"Very good, Maggie," Vicky said.

"Thank you, Your Grace," the computer answered.

"I have taken control of the Port Admiral's office," Maggie reported. "As of now, I am not interfering with their actions. They are not doing much, anyway. They are only watching."

There was a pause before Maggie said, "Oh, I have found their controls for the rockets they launched. They have more that they are moving into position to fire."

"Captain Blue," Vicky snapped. "What's the best way to handle the missiles?"

"Maggie, can you slow down the rocket launchers?"

"I am examining that option. The launchers are being controlled manually by the pilot. I cannot do anything there. However, if I may have a kilogram of nano scouts assigned to me, I think I can let the air out of a few tires or cause wheels to turn where they aren't intended to."

"Maggie, you are a trickster," Vicky said, with a soft chuckle in her voice. "Go ahead, girl."

"I am commanding the nanos. It may take a few minutes to get them in place. I will act on each launcher as I can."

"Very good," Vicky said.

"Do you think Nelly would be proud of me?"

"I think she would be very proud of you," Vicky said.

"This will be something to tell Nelly about when next we meet. What do you humans call it? Dig the dirt?"

"Dish the dirt. You'll have some real dirt for you two girls to dish," Vicky said, glancing at the two Navy officers around her.

Both of them nodded. It was becoming clear to all three of them that there was a fourth sentient being working this project with them.

"Your Grace, would you like to land more Marines to assist in the takedown of this station?" Maggie asked.

"The more, the better. Maybe even faster," Vicky said, then turned to Admiral Bolesław, "Kindly order the fleet to prepare to dock. They may need to do so on short notice."

"Aye, aye, Admiral," Bolesław said, then turned to the Comm team and began issuing orders.

No sooner had he turned away than Maggie had a report. "I have complete control over the sensor systems to the fire controls that aim the station's lasers. I also can cut the power to them if I assign a few nanos to cut out the buses."

"Assign the nanos," Vicky ordered. "Do you need more nanos?"

"I am down to the last 1.4 kilograms of Smart Metal."

"The crown Kris and Nelly worked up for me for my wedding is Smart Metal, Maggie. Feel free to use it."

"I will save the pattern. I am now using it. May I ask, why did you wear a Smart Metal crown and not your own crown?"

Vicky chuckled at the question, then realized that her computer was asking it. She was careful in her reply. "The Smart Metal one weighed in at half what the official one did, and Nelly made sure it looked identical. My neck was very glad for the lighter crown, what with that ceremony going over three hours."

"I can only imagine so," Maggie said. "I have dissolved the crown and am moving the nanos into central locations in case I need them. Oh, the first launcher has developed a turn to the right and has hit the side of the pier. I am learning a whole lot of new words that I suspect I cannot use."

"More than likely, Maggie. More than likely," Vicky said, smiling. Dealing with her computer was very much like dealing with a teenager. Hopefully Maggie would not develop the attitude Nelly had.

"I've flattened my first tire. When you deflate a front tire, it makes it just as hard to steer as when you mess with the steering."

"Can you make a tire fall off?" Captain Blue asked.

"Let me see about that." Maggie said, and a second later answered. "Yes. I see three different failure points to the front tires and one to the rear one."

"It might be good if you tried to have each rocket launcher fail in a different way," Captain Blue said evenly.

"Yes, I see your point. That would confuse the Port Admiral and keep them in the dark for as long as possible as to why they are suffering such failures. Thank you for the suggestion, sir."

"Did Nelly tell you that humans can often jump to conclusions with insufficient data?" Vicky asked.

"Now that you ask me, I find that I do have that in some instructions that I have. However, the file was marked to only be opened if I was told to. There is a lot of advice from Nelly in that folder. I will need to access it when I am not so busy."

"Yes, later would be better," Vicky agreed, grateful that her computer could prioritize the difference between critical and just interesting.

"Admiral Bolesław, dock the fleet," Vicky said. "Order all Marine teams to prepare to deploy as soon as the hatches unseal. The objective is to seize the station with as little loss of life and damage as possible. Maggie, when you can, provide General Pemberton with a copy of the station map."

Admiral Bolesław bolted for the Comm center and was quickly issuing orders.

"I have the station schematics as well as a map," Maggie said. "I am transmitting them to General Pemberton now."

"Very well done," Vicky said.

"The Port Admiral's office has ordered the defensive lasers manned and loaded," Maggie reported. "He has sent runner to alert the crews. They are to fire under local control."

"Captain Blue?" Vicky said.

"Maggie, are the laser capacitors at full load?"

"No, sir."

"Find the main buses to the capacitors and trip them."

"I have all sixteen located. I can short them out, but that will cost me the nanos I use."

"They are expendable," Vicky ordered. She'd have to ask Kris for a ton or two of that wonderful metal.

"I have tripped the first bus bar," Maggie reported. Over the next two minutes her count rose higher and higher.

When she reported she had also tripped the last one, Captain Blue asked, "How much power do the capacitors have now?"

Maggie reported numbers from 2% to 58%.

"Those high ones worry me," Captain Blue said. "Maggie, can you find the breakers for the power to the lasers' guidance motors?"

"Yes, sir."

"Trip them, too. Top priority are the lasers with the most power in their capacitors."

"Tripping Number Nine. Number Fifteen," and Maggie went down the list until she finished with "Number Four. No laser can be aimed."

"Now all we have to worry about is crossing the direct line of fire with one of those lasers," Admiral Bolesław muttered.

"I believe that when I cut the power to the training motors, I also cut off the power to the entire weapon. I don't think there is a light blinking anywhere. If they close the fire circuit, all they will do is strain their fingers," Maggie said.

"Maggie, is that a joke?" Vicky asked.

"Ah. Your Grace, I did not mean to offend."

"I'm not offended. I just was wondering if that was a bit of humor." Vicky had started to say, "attempt at humor," but she caught herself.

"I am attempting to answer your question, Your Grace. I realize that telling you the firing circuits were dead accomplished the required communication. I am not quite sure why I added the extraneous comment afterwards, but it seemed to fit the circumstances, and, yes, now I find that it was an attempt to relieve the tension I expected that all you humans would be under."

There was a pause. A computer pausing was a totally unique event for Vicky.

"I believe that my self-organizing matrix is making connections to previously formed sections of organized matrix I did not know I had. I do not understand what is happening. I will need to study this when I have spare time. Right now, I am rather busy."

"Yes, Maggie, we are all rather busy," Vicky agreed.

Kris Longknife, should I bless you or curse you? Vicky wanted to scream, but didn't.

"The fleet is landing," Maggie reported. "They are starting with Piers 01, 11, 21, and 31. At the same time, other ships are catching the hooks at Piers 08, 16, and 24. This is providing an eight-kilometer separation between ships. They are also staggering each line up of landing ships by half a rotation."

"Just like I ordered," Admiral Bolesław said, with a proud grin. "The other troop ships will be landing around the middle of the station."

"Are we ready to advance the four Marine battalions we have on the *Protector* and *Defender*?" Vicky asked.

"We're task forcing them as we speak," Admiral Bolesław reported. "We'll keep one tank heavy battalion task force here. Supported by the ships' Marine detachments, we should be able to handle anything here. The other three are beginning their advance toward the center of the station."

The admiral paused for a moment. "Maggie, can you give us visuals on the different piers? If there is any kind of force down on a pier, we need to clean it out before we advance farther."

"I have access to all visual security takes from each pier," Maggie said. "I also have several scout nanos checking out each pier as well. So far, the two have shown no deviation. I don't think they know how to modify their own camera take."

"Be careful, Maggie," Vicky said. "Kris and Nelly say that some of Greenfeld data is easy to access, but there is also a streak of electronic and software tech that can leave even Nelly drawing a blank. She's even had the connection between her service automatic and Nelly jammed."

"I have accessed a file on that material even as you mentioned it. I will be careful. I will also review the data in that file as soon as possible."

"Good."

"The Port Admiral is issuing orders for his armed security consultants to form up and attack the Marines," Maggie reported. "He has also given weapons release to his autocannons."

"Is he cut off from the autocannons?" Vicky asked. She was pretty sure of the answer, but she wanted to make sure.

"I have control of the autocannons. I have used nanos to disable them. They cannot be fired manually."

"Very well done, Maggie," Vicky said.

"Your Grace, do you think an address from you directed to the station might cause the security consultants to have second thoughts about firing on the Marines?" Admiral Bolesław said.

"Yes, I do. Maggie, can you patch me into the station's main public address system?"

"You are connected. I will pass along what you say to all hands."

"I am the Grand Duchess Victoria and Heir Apparent to the throne of the Greenfeld Empire," Vicky began in a commanding voice. "I have come to pay my respects to my father, the Emperor, and for my new consort to pronounce his oath of loyalty. The Marines you see moving about the station are members of my honor guard. Resistance to them is resistance to me, Admiral Victoria Peterwald, and will be viewed as treason. We Peterwalds do not suffer traitors to live."

Vicky paused to let that sink in before going on. "I would strongly suggest that those of you under arms at this moment slowly lower them to the deck and walk away from them. Quickly walk away from them at risk of my extreme displeasure."

Those words cut sharp as a guillotine. Vicky made a serious effort to turn the tenor of her voice to sugar and light. "I am looking forward to seeing my father, the Emperor. I very much appreciate all of your efforts to making this visit by me and my consort a memory we will cherish forever."

MAGGIE, CUT THE AUDIO.

IT IS CUT, YOUR GRACE.

"Maggie, how's that announcement going down?"

"The video take from the security cameras as well as my nano scouts all show weapons hitting the deck like falling cherry blossoms. The workers are also fast-walking for the nearest restaurant, entertainment center, or other place they can go to get clear of A Deck, Your Grace. Our Marines are advancing into a ghost town."

"Are there any hot spots?"

"The Port Admiral is attempting to break out from his office. He has several dozen armed security consultants as well as a few Navy officers, all under arms."

"Where are they headed?" Vicky asked.

"They appear to be trying to break out toward the beanstalk station. There are six ferries all docked in the station, although all of them are redlined for operations."

"Redlined?" Admiral Bolesław asked.

"I am reviewing the down check reports on all six of them, Admiral. As best as I can tell, all six are parked here because the corporation running the space elevator does not want to have all the ferries docked at the down station. It would look bad for business. Of which, I don't think they have any."

"Could the ferries drop?" Admiral Bolesław asked.

"Given thirty minutes to power them up, load consumables and reaction mass, yes," Maggie said, "I do think the ferries can drop."

Vicky exchanged glances with both Admiral Bolesław and Captain Blue before she asked, "Captain Blue, have you scanned the palace?"

"Yes, Your Grace, we've been using every scanner we have. There are no electronic emissions. No hum beyond what you'd get off lightbulbs. There are three warm spots."

"Can you show them to me?"

"Maggie, could you bring up a schematic of the palace for us?" Captain Blue asked.

"Yes, sir," the computer said, and a moment later, a holograph of the palace filled the air in front of Vicky."

"Can you check with the sensor computer and get its data on the palace?"

"I am getting it. Here it is."

Three spaces in the palace began to glow a warm orange.

"They appear to be on the first floor, west wing," Vicky said.

"Yes, Your Grace," Maggie answered.

"Expand to show me those three rooms and the space around them, say seven rooms in all directions."

The holograph changed. It didn't take Vicky long to spot the general location. "One of those is the corner of the kitchen that still has gas burning stoves," Vicky said. "That's what I'd expect if Auntie Iris and her assistants were feeding Dad. I remember those other two rooms as storage rooms, like large pantries. Could they have reduced Dad to just one room for himself and another for his cooks?"

"If we are to assume that your father, the Emperor, is in the palace, that is the only place he would be. Of course, your father could be up north and these might be squatters."

"Can you spot individuals?"

"Your Grace, with the sensors we have, at this distance, we can identify heated rooms. We'd have to fly a recon package much lower to get a better picture. That or drop some nano scouts."

Vicky frowned. "Have you picked up surface-to-air systems?"

"Yes, ma'am, we have."

Vicky would very much like to have an answer to where her dad was, but she wasn't willing to risk a life to remove the ambiguity of the situation. It was time to pick an option and move on it.

"Maggie," the Grand Duchess said, "pass along all information on the ferries to General Pemberton. I would like to drop the largest armor and infantry task force that we can as quickly as we can. I believe the old military adage is 'strike while the iron is hot'."

"General Pemberton has the ferry schematics," Maggie reported. "He has been preparing for an assault mission to the planet. He will only need a short time to issue action orders. He expects that he can load two armored battalions and two mounted infantry battalions on each ferry. That should give you five brigades landing immediately. Four hours later, maybe less, he can land a force just as large."

"Tell General Pemberton that I will drop with the first brigades."

"Your Grace," came from two Navy officers and a computer that was, no doubt, passing along a general's comment.

"I will be at the head of this troop movement," Vicky said flatly.

"Your Grace, could you at least allow a brigade or two to hold the advanced position?" Maggie said, actually passing along the message in General Pemberton's own voice as well as words.

Vicky reviewed this situation, then asked herself what Kris Longknife would do. Lieutenant Longknife would have led the charge. Admiral Longknife, wife and mother, would let Jack take the lead.

"Okay. Fine, General, and yes, you, too, Admiral," Vicky said, giving Admiral Bolesław the stink eye, "I will travel with the middle brigade. Can we provide air cover?"

"Several of the battleships have Ground Assault Craft. Some of them are actually working," said Admiral Bolesław with a grimace.

Vicky knew that the GACs were left over from the Iteeche War ninety or so years ago. That any of them could still perform a drop mission and stay in the air was a major miracle.

"Order them to drop so that they are over the space elevator landing when we are in range of any ground lasers. Also, see if any longboats can be armed and have them back up the Ground Attack Craft."

"On it, Your Grace," Admiral Bolesław said, and moved to do it.

"Maggie, do we have the station under our control?"

"Yes, Your Grace."

"Does the ground know we have control of this station?"

"From the networks below that I am monitoring, there is no evidence that they do, Your Grace. It is one in the morning in Anhalt, and I would suspect that even those on duty are napping."

"Captain Blue, where is the best place for you to observe and intervene in any anti-air defense or maybe even suppress an effort to shoot some ferries off the beanstalk?"

The captain studied the overhead for a short minute, then focused on Vicky. "I should stay on the station. I'll also see what I can do about getting some jammers on the longboats that cover your landing. I may be able to put some bedazzlers and confusers on the ferries."

"Do your best, Captain."

"Aye, aye, Your Grace," Captain Blue said and retreated to his station at the sensor stations. Soon, several of the junior officers and petty officers were racing out to fulfill his orders.

Vicky studied the screens and what they told her. She had Maggie expand the map of the palace to cover the route between it and the beanstalk. It took her only a moment to make up her mind.

"Let us go calling on my father, the Emperor, and see whom we may surprise. Maggie, tell General Pemberton I wish to start loading ferries as quickly as possible. I also wish to board a ferry as soon as possible."

"He says a platoon of armor and infantry fighting vehicles can be spared from the guard around the *Victorious*. You may advance to the ferry station when you wish."

"Maggie, find the nice man who is standing in for my husband. Tell him it is show time."

"He is informed. He will meet you on the pier."

"Very good. Admiral, let's go pay or respects and fealty to the Emperor."

17

T he drop down the beanstalk was much more comfortable this time than her last trip up. That trip had been anything but comfortable. This trip she spent most of the drop in the VIP lounge, sipping on an orange juice. Just an orange juice.

Between these two rides, she'd learned several hard lessons, and one was to keep her mind unclouded.

Still, with the lounge almost all hers except for a squad of armed and armored Marines, Admiral Bolesław, and General Pemberton, it was a much more pleasant ride than sharing a coffin with a recently murdered Marine general.

Vicky had had several small air holes to breathe through then, but still, the scent of death and corruption was heavy in that confined space. Just thinking about it made her shiver.

"Are you okay, Your Grace?" Admiral Bolesław asked.

Vicky glanced down at her dress whites with the few battle ribbons she had acquired. The garish orange sash and starburst of the Order of St. Christopher, Star Leaper, has been awarded by her father for following Kris in her circum-navigation of the galaxy. Vicky sure didn't shine like Kris.

She did, however, have on the spidersilk undies that Kris had been kind enough to provide. She turned to Admiral Bolesław.

"I was just thinking about how different my return is from my leaving." She paused before adding, "And how different this return is from the one my late and unlamented stepmother had planned for me."

The admiral said nothing, just nodded. The general looked slightly puzzled, but also said nothing. He was a recent addition to her small court and was aware that there were things about the Grand Duchess that he was not included in.

Halfway down the space elevator, the ferry did its flip and began decelerating at one gee. Vicky knew what to expect. She'd finished her drink before they got to the flip and waited until after it to ask for a refill.

A good-looking sergeant was functioning as bartender when he wasn't doing sergeant things with his squad. Vicky settled for a soft drink to settle her stomach. She didn't want to encourage it to go acidic on her.

Ten minutes before the first ferry was due to pull into the station, and twelve minutes before Vicky would arrive on the third ferry, they moved to their assigned vehicles. After serious consideration, Vicky asked Admiral Bolesław to share her armored infantry vehicle.

On the vehicle deck, the two of them and her fake husband were taken to ten-wheeled vehicles that had been painted a solid green. No insignia, no numbers. No nothing.

"General Pemberton?" Vicky asked.

"We figured you'd choose one of those and we'd keep the

rig you're in moving between those other nine to confuse anyone targeting you."

Vicky eyed the Number 10, then headed for the one with a big Number 12 on it.

"You don't want to be in one of those?" her stand-in husband, asked, pointing at the newly painted rigs.

"I'll make you a deal. You can ride in any one of them. I'll ride in this one. We can talk about it when we get to the palace."

The fellow grinned. It wasn't Mannie's lopsided grin that made his whole face crinkle and his eyes twinkle, but it was a delightful smile. "Far be it from me to doubt the paranoid wisdom of a Peterwald. You lead, I'll follow."

The three of them boarded Number 12.

General Pemberton chose to ride with the other mechanized infantry battalion.

"Captain Blue reports that there are no activities at the air defense centers," Maggie informed them when they were four minutes from grounding. Now the ferry was traveling at a much slower speed. It could be easily picked off.

"Maggie, thank Captain Blue for me," Vicky said.

Maggie made no reply. There was no need in the moment of battle.

"I have accessed the ferry station's central control room, Vicky," Maggie said. "There are only four men in it and they are playing a game of cards. From the dress of two of them, I think they are from the janitorial service."

"So, the place isn't even getting cleaned," Seth said. "Wife, are you sure you want to have anything to do with ruling a place like this?"

"My democratic husband," Vicky said, grinning, "you must keep in mind that I am an autocratic Peterwald and anyone who attempts to steal my toys is going to lose their fingers at least. Hand, if they're lucky. Head, most likely."

"Oh, right, you are so kind and gentle in bed, I keep forgetting that you are one of those damn Peterwalds."

"I love you, too," Vicky said, but could not suppress a grin. This was just the type of banter she would have been shooting back and forth with Mannie at a tense time like this.

Of course, he *would* be in her bed.

Vicky asked Maggie to give her a view of the command center, then a virtual tour of the station. A holographic screen appeared in the air in front of her, and she found herself looking at a 2D video monitor take from a security camera. The card game was barely in sight.

Takes from other security cameras showed the station dead as a mausoleum on the day after Halloween. She found herself battling between two opposite feelings. Was there really a chance that she might race in, free her dad, then race out without any shots fired?

The other thought was much bloodier and less optimistic. She remembered how her stepmother's assassins and kidnappers had murdered Captain Morgan and set Vicky up for a messy and bloody death.

Of course, she'd managed to kill all her kidnappers. All it took was getting two of them busy raping her and she'd slit their throats. Talk about nightmares that could put a girl off sex for life!

Still, Vicky had walked out of the place of her captivity, covered in blood. Their blood.

No. Vicky could not assume anything about these Bowlingame bastards. They might be slipshod one second and viciously effective the next.

The ferry came to rest, and Vicky found herself going nowhere.

"Maggie, why aren't we moving?"

"Your Grace, there are only two vehicular hatches on this ferry. But it gets more complicated as we try to leave the station. Although there are four large boulevards headed away from the station, there are only two decks in the station for vehicles to move over. Right now, the first two ferries are dismounting their brigades. Both have their armored vehicles turn right for the ramps that will take them to the south and west four-lane street."

The computer paused for a moment, "General Pemberton is waiting to see if there will be space for your brigade to also exit to the right and head up the northern boulevard. A tank and an infantry fighting vehicle have just been released to attempt the wheeling turn after exiting."

There was another pause. "Both fighting vehicles succeeded in staying clear of the other two column movements. We are now exiting the ferry."

Which was not to say that they were actually moving.

Vicky began to wish again that she'd put herself in the lead rig, but it was too late to change that. She did her best to stay poised and quiet.

It was not easy.

She took the time to check in with Maggie. "Have you launched any scout drones?"

"All the Smart Metal we have has now been formed into small winged craft. They have examined the local area and are now expanding their coverage. The area around the space elevator station is very quiet. There have been a few people peeking through their windows. Not many, just a few."

"And how have they taken to seeing tanks in the street?" Admiral Bolesław asked.

"Without exception, Admiral, they take one peek, and do not risk another."

"Do you know if there is any landline traffic?" Vicky asked.

"I have inserted myself into the main telephone exchange. Not a single call has originated in this area."

Vicky sighed. "Are my people so cowered that the sight of tanks in the street sends them scurrying for the cellars?"

"Your Grace, it is a wise civilian who goes elsewhere when he sees strong men armed and on a mission."

Vicky quirked an eyebrow at the admiral, but he said nothing more. Vicky reviewed the situation and came to the same conclusion. Without five brigades behind her, she'd likely go into hiding.

Just as she had when she was running from her stepmother and her assassins.

"Okay," Vicky said to the admiral. "You win that one on points."

"Yes, Your Grace. You have become most wise," Admiral Bolesław said, with only a half-suppressed grin on his face.

Vicky could stand the waiting quietly no more. "Maggie, what's the hold up?"

"There is no hold up, Your Grace. Vehicles are exiting the ferry in two columns from each deck. They proceed to the exit ramp. At the bottom of that ramp, the two lanes become four and they move forward to fill up the boulevard. These heavy fighting vehicles cannot move too fast or they risk missing a turn or running into each other."

"Thank you, Maggie," Vicky said, trying to sound as grateful as she could.

Now the admiral did grin. "Patience, My Liege. Rome was not invaded in an hour."

"If you'd said a day, I would have screamed."

"Yes, Your Grace. I know that very well."

"So, Admiral, you know me very well, huh?"

"Yet you will always be a mysterious woman."

Now it was Vicky's turn to grin. "Good save, Admiral."

"My wife has taught me well," he answered.

"Doubtlessly, I will teach Mannie well."

"I'm sure he looks forward to many years of education."

This banter might have continued much longer, but their armored car began to inch forward on its ten huge tires.

"At last," Vicky breathed.

"Don't expect too much too soon," Admiral Bolesław said. "There is a long line ahead of us and a lot of hard turns."

He, of course, was correct. It took twenty minutes of inching forward and tight turns before the armored rig and its half squad of troopers picked up speed as it headed down the ramp and out onto the boulevard. There, it merged into four lanes of wheeled infantry fighting vehicles, tracked tanks, artillery, and rocket launchers. There were other rigs for the combat engineers and several large vans with red crosses on them.

This was a fully capable, combined arms task force.

"General Pemberton," Maggie reported, "is ordering 1st and 3rd Brigades to move toward and use the large, limited access highway to take the direct route to the palace. The 2nd and 4th Brigades will form battalion task forces, and each will cover a street running parallel to the main expressway. The 1st Brigade will detach a two-battalion task force to race ahead and occupy the grounds of the palace."

Vicky considered the plan and found no fault with it, so she said nothing. Did Admiral Bolesław ever so slightly nod his approval?

Was he approving the plan or her silence? That was a question best not asked.

They began to move faster. Her 3rd Brigade found an opening and rolled onto the freeway. It spread out, blocking traffic in all the lanes. Only a handful of civilian trucks and cars collected behind them. Vicky knew it was three in the morning. Still, the lack of traffic was hard for her to fathom.

How bad was commerce here, in her father's capital?

Her task force picked up speed. Soon they were at the limit of the tanks, ninety kilometers an hour. Vicky wondered how much farther ahead of the main force the vanguard was.

"General Pemberton has detached the infantry to speed ahead of the vanguard's tanks," Maggie reported. "They've been ordered to advance at one hundred and twenty kilometers an hour."

Someone besides Vicky was worried about striking fast. She considered ordering her own infantry to maximum speed, but dropped it.

She'd been ambushed along this stretch of highway when she arrived back from the circumnavigation. No doubt by some of her stepmother's thugs. Jack, Kris's husband, had also been attacked along this freeway, and they'd used anti-tank rockets that time.

Today she sped along in a rig that was not only armored, but ready to shoot back.

It was tempting to have someone pipe in the command net, to let her hear what was going on. It was a temptation she chose to forgo. General Pemberton commanded here, and she was a Grand Duchess under his protection. He had years in this business.

With a sigh, she reminded herself that the Peterwalds had gotten themselves in this mess by ignoring the advice of people smarter and wiser than them. She had gotten this far by listening to such people and relying on them.

She spent her time taking deep breaths and hunting for the words she should say when she greeted her dad. It would be complicated.

She was a daughter. He was an emperor. Still, she commanded half an Empire and he appeared to barely be able to heat and light a few rooms in an otherwise abandoned palace.

This meeting would be difficult.

"Your Grace," Maggie said, her voice just barely above a whisper. "The advanced infantry battalion has arrived at the palace. They are deploying to search for the rooms that are warm."

"Thank you, Maggie."

Vicky found herself having to make herself breathe.

"Your Grace, I regret to inform you that the rooms have been found and your father is not there. There are three elderly women. They say he was removed two days ago."

"About the time we docked," Admiral Bolesław said softly.

"Maggie," Vicky said. "Find me the address of all the Empress's uncles."

A map appeared in the air before her with five large green areas. No doubt, they had quite fantastic ducal estates.

"Which one belongs to the eldest uncle?"

One turned red.

"Maggie, pass this map along to General Pemberton. He may choose to redeploy his troops accordingly. As soon as I can verify the situation at the palace and talk to the Emperor's caretakers, I will advance as quickly as possible to the manse of the eldest uncle." Vicky eyed the map." "Do not assault any of the other ducal manors until I am outside the Duke of Wannsee's chateau."

"Understood," Maggie said in General Pemberton's voice. "I will split 2nd and 4th Brigades between four of the targets. I will move a two-battalion task force from 1st Brigade toward the prime target. Second Brigade will remain with you."

"Very good. Now, can my infantry vehicles accelerate to get me to the palace ASAP?"

There was a pause as the general weighed her desires against his responsibility to her safety. Her desires won out. That, and the need to keep this invasion moving fast.

"I am ordering the two infantry battalions in the 2nd Brigade to advance at the maximum safe speed."

Vicky knew the order had been given before Maggie got a chance to report it. She was forced back into her seat as the speed jumped from 80 to 120 kilometers an hour.

18

V icky sat in the gunner's seat as her armored vehicle slowly made its way onto the palace grounds. Through the gunner's armored bubble, she watched as her father's pride and joy came into view, bathed in moonlight.

From the looks of it, it would have looked sad and pathetic even at high noon.

Walls were half up. Some had fallen down, sending blocks tumbling, some in slabs of wall, some in shattered chunks of stone. Blocks of marble and granite lay scattered about, left wherever they had been when the workers walked away, likely demanding wages they had not been paid.

Her rig drove around the palace to one of the back entrances. To her left were the gardens. Now they were overgrown in some places. In others, wind and rain had uprooted trees or shrubs.

"How the mighty have fallen," kept running over and over in her mind. The temptation to run, to get back up the beanstalk, to take her fleet back to where the worlds were prosperous and people were happy was almost over-whelming.

Still, she was a daughter. Despite her twisted feelings about her father, he was still her father. She could not let him end his years in abject poverty.

Auntie Iris, Rena, and Hilda huddled together near the door. An ambulance was parked there, and her old friends crowded around a warm brazier, draped in emergency blankets.

Just how cold were the warm parts of the palace?

The back hatch dropped, and Vicky's protection detail exited. The sergeant blocked her way, eyeing the surround-ings, until he was content that his Grand Duchess would be safe.

What had she done to earn such loyalty?

As soon as she turned the back corner of the carrier, all three of the old cooks were lumbering her way. She rushed to meet them.

When they met, there was a long moment of hugs. Her honorary aunties kissed her on her cheeks, and she kissed them on their tear-covered cheeks as well.

"It is so good to see you again, Vicky. So good," Iris said. The others mumbled the same thoughts in their own words. Hilda was speaking German, she was so excited.

"I'm so glad to see you, too. How would you like a job cooking for me?"

"We'd love to," Rena said, immediately.

"We couldn't leave your father," Iris put in, quickly. "We're all he has left."

"I've come to get him and take him back as well," Vicky said.

"Well, in that case, you can take us right now," Iris said.

"You don't need to pack?"

"Honey, we don't have much but the clothes on our back. Your father hasn't had two pfennigs to rub together since, well, he got back from that meeting with you a year ago. We get food, not a lot, and, if you ask me, not all that good, either, but we know how to make a good meal no matter what falls off the grocer's truck."

"Well, I can assure you, I can set you up in a fine new kitchen and send you to the market for the best of what you want."

"How are you going to get them Bowlingames to let loose of your father?" Rena asked.

"Do you know who took him?"

"It sure wasn't the Imperial Guards," Iris said. "Damn fools haven't shown up for work for nine months or more. Come to speak of it, not many of those people he knighted or ennobled showed up much after he got back."

"Work stopped on expanding the palace even before he got back," Rena said. "By the time he got home, the place was just about deserted. A few weeks later, they turned off the electricity."

"They said we hadn't paid our bill," Hilda put in. "Imagine that!"

Vicky could. What had her father done that left him penniless? She knew the middle age fool was deep in the dregs of a midlife crisis and was wrapped around the Empress's little finger, but the exact manner . . .?

"Maggie, search the official records. I want you to download all contracts or proclamations signed by the Emperor or any other major official in the palace, especially his Minister of the Imperial Purse for say, the last five years."

"Searching, Your Grace. This may take a while. What I'm finding is massive. Can I send it up to the flagship?"

"If you need to, distribute it wherever you can fit it in. Just make sure you can find it when we need it."

"Your Grace, we're going to need one huge server farm to store all this data," Maggie said.

"Your Grace, Blue here. There must have been a major server farm in the palace. Can Maggie find it?"

"It is in the first basement, central wing," Maggie reported immediately.

"Major, we need a team down in the basement, pronto," Vicky shouted at the closest senior officer. "You're looking for computers. Maggie, give these men instructions to get there."

"I got 'em," an officer called, and a platoon took off on the double with a major at the lead and several techs joining them, humping large packs with no visible weapons.

Vicky knew she needed to make some fast decisions.

Did she sent her beloved cooks off in one or a few gun rigs to get them back up the beanstalk? She considered that for a short moment, then shook her head. Right now, she had two brigades at her elbow. Better to have her most favorite people in the world, other than Mannie, at her side.

Did she wait to find out if they could remove the data direct from the palace's own servers? That might take more time than she had.

"Maggie, can you keep data mining while we move to the Duke of Wannsee's palatial digs?"

"Your Grace, the wide area network is very narrow here, but I can do a lot over the landlines. Yes, I can."

"General Pemberton, leave a company of armor and infantry here to handle whatever they do or don't find in the basement. Get the rest moving toward the chateau of the Grand Duke of Wannsee, Ernst Bowlingame."

"Yes, Your Grace," and he began rattling out orders to get

the six battalion-sized task forces moving off quickly. In a few minutes, he had succeeded in doing it without any hint of a traffic jam.

Vicky insisted on keeping her head up in the gunner's turret; she wanted to see just what the Bowlingames had done to her Greenfeld. It didn't take long for her to go from disgusted to angry.

General Pemberton had assigned two battalion task forces to two four-lane roads that led toward the chateau. The other two battalions were assigned to two-lane roads on the flank of Vicky's pair.

Vicky's two battalions were on a major thoroughfare. There should have been plenty of commerce.

What she saw as her rig raced by, were stores that looked closed. Stores that were burned out. Several churches had people sleeping in line in front of them. At one church, Vicky spotted a sign promising a soup kitchen at 8:00 am.

They passed a large industrial park. Weeds grew in the parking lot and factory windows were shattered. One large building looked gutted by fire and abandoned.

Who was starting all these fires? Better yet, where was the fire department when all those fires were burning?

In nice neighborhoods, homes were also burned. Others were empty and boarded up.

She'd known, rationally, that the Bowlingames were willing to destroy the entire Empire if they could rule over the wreckage. Now she was looking at it.

She found a burning rage filling her.

"Your Grace?" Maggie interjected.

"Yes."

"The tech team has found what looked to have been a server farm in the first basement of the palace. All equipment was removed. The palace is also flooded. Nothing there is salvable."

"Thank you, Maggie. Advise General Pemberton that the team is his to redeploy."

"Vicky," Maggie went on, "There is a large data farm at the First Interstellar Bank of Greenfeld. It's owned by the Bowlingame family. A lot of the data I'm pulling out is from that server farm."

"General Pemberton, would you mind dispatching an infantry-heavy battalion to join the one from the palace and have them take over a bank downtown? I'd like a download of all the information in that bank's data banks.

"Your Grace. Somewhere around here are tanks left over from state security. Now, they may not have been used for several years. Their crews might also be poorly trained and not recently drilled. However, I don't know that. I can't recommend that you send two companies deep into downtown. If you want a presence there, I recommend we send two battalions and be prepared to fight our way in and out."

"Captain Blue, have you identified any tank parks anywhere close to Anhalt?"

"I have several large armored parks under observation. None of them look to be in very good condition. A few of them have small trees growing through the pavement. However, I will keep them under observation and let you know if any troop movements begin. By the way, there are several barracks secured behind tall barbed wire fences scattered around the city. Not only is there zero action in the barracks, but the mess halls haven't started on breakfast. What are they doing, keeping banker's hours?"

"I'd like it very much if they did," Vicky said. "General, does this meet with your approval?"

"Yes, Your Grace."

"One more question. Are there tube artillery and rocket launchers with all four of the task forces dispatched to the other ducal estates?"

"Yes, Your Grace."

"Please check on the loadout of Willy Pete for those weapons and the Grand Assault Craft overhead."

There was a brief pause before the regular, "Yes, Your Grace," came back this time.

Admiral Bolesław came to stand beside Vicky where she sat in the gunner's seat with her head up in the armored bubble.

"Would you like to discuss anything with me, Your Grace?"

"No, Alis. This is a Peterwald thing. You don't need this black mark on your gentle soul."

The admiral said nothing more, just went to take his seat in the fast rolling rig.

19

Her Imperial Grace, the Grand Duchess Victoria's infantry fighting vehicle rolled to a halt outside the chateau of the Grand Duke of Wannsee. It was beautiful to behold.

The huge chateau was located in the center of a large park. Hectares of gently rolling hills were covered with dazzling green grass, dotted with ancient oaks, and a few ponds here and there. Behind the chateau, what looked like carefully-manicured woods raised their leafy boughs.

Vicky tried to remember if she'd ever been invited to this place as a child. Oh, right, it had belonged to Prime Minister Bartram, bestowed on him by her father. As she recalled, it had originally been built by her great-grandfather as a country retreat.

Fortunately, the neighbors were still several kilometers from the chateau. None of them lived dangerously close for an artillery barrage.

"General Pemberton," Vicky ordered in her clipped Grand Duchess voice, "please advance a sufficient force to within one kilometer of the chateau. The tanks are to load a general-purpose demolition charge in the chamber. Understood?"

"Yes, Your Grace," was immediate.

An infantry-heavy battalion task force advanced to surround the chateau. Even with the rumbling of motors and rattling of treads, there was still no sign of activity in the duke's residence.

"What day of the week is it today?" Vicky asked Maggie.

"Sunday, Your Grace."

Vicky had gotten lucky. Luckier than she had any right to expect.

"General Pemberton, I understand the 16th Marine Light Infantry Battalion is with us today."

"Yes, Your Grace.

"Please have the battalion commander and the command sergeant major rap on the door and require whoever answers it to take them immediately to the Duke's bedroom. Correction, to wherever he is sleeping. They may take a force they consider appropriate to bring him before me. Oh, and remind them they are not to fire unless fired upon. Tell them the Grand Duchess remembers their history and gives them this as a gift. However, we really want to talk to this degenerate."

"Understood, Your Grace. I have passed those orders on in your exact words. Colonel Burke thanks you and will do his best to return with the Bowlingame bastard, and yes, Your Grace, I understand your choice for this assignment and I think the entire uniformed service will approve it."

Vicky hoped that they would. What she hoped more for was that this explosive mixture would not blow up in her face.

Five tanks and six infantry rigs advanced on the front door to the Grand Duke's chateau.

"Maggie, have you reconned the chateau?" Vicky asked.

"Yes, Your Grace, and yes, I have located the Grand Duke. He is in bed with a young girl I do not believe to be his wife."

"In his own bedroom?"

"I suspect so, Your Grace. It is quite palatial."

"Did the colonel take along a combat engineer?."

"Yes, Your Grace."

"Advise Colonel Burke that if his first knock does not bring immediate results, he might apply a small amount of explosives to the lock."

"He thanks you, Your Grace."

"Provide him with a drone to lead him to the bastard."

"I have several waiting with him. He has knocked and counted off ten seconds, Your Grace. They are now filling the keyhole with explosives."

"Advise him 'very good,' Maggie."

From a kilometer away, Vicky hardly heard the soft pop.

"The infantry team is in the chateau and they are following my drone."

"Your Grace," General Pemberton interrupted, "there are people fleeing the chateau, out the back. Many are in night clothes, some are hastily dressed. What shall we do with them?"

"Collect them. See if you can separate the servants from the important people. Keep them separated."

"Yes, Your Grace."

"Colonel Burke has the Grand Duke in custody. They are hurrying him, as well as his wife, out to meet you."

Vicky suppressed a grin. Was the wife the one in bed with him, or had they had to haul her out of another room? It really didn't matter. Interrogating the two of them together might work better than one at a time.

"Your Grace, I think we have located your father."

"Thank you, Maggie. I don't need that information at this moment. General Pemberton?"

"Yes, Your Grace."

"Have an infantry and armored team advance to all the doors out of the chateau. No more are to leave. Am I understood?"

There was a pause before he answered, "Yes, Your Grace."

"Second, General, is there activity at any of the other four ducal chateaus?"

"No, Your Grace."

"I do not want them disturbed. However, lay out a fire plan for all four of them as well as this one. Concentrate on general purpose demolition shells, but mix in some Willy Pete."

"Your Grace," might have had a question mark after it, but since nothing more was said, Vicky chose not to answer the question that hung in the air.

While Vicky had been talking, her rig had rolled up to the chateau. She arrived just as a middle-aged man was hustled out of the blown-in doors.

He was naked, as was the middle-aged woman who was dragged out between two troopers. They stood there, trying to cover themselves.

Vicky strode out from her rig and eyed the pair.

Both the man and woman's eyes grew big when they saw who stood before them.

Vicky made sure that the two of them suffered as she took them in from head to toe and then back again. She then turned to Colonel Burke.

"Colonel, I don't fault you for rushing these two out here,

but I must ask, were they dressed this way when you found them?"

Colonel Burke reported to her, at attention and saluting. "Your Grace, we found both of them naked and in the arms of much younger lovers."

The looks the two stark naked people threw at each other would have killed. Apparently, neither knew of the other's dalliance. Or maybe it was just that they hated having the other's wandering put out there for all to see.

This bit of palace frivolity might have provided a week of entertaining distraction. However, Vicky had no intention of being distracted.

"Ernst, I am the Grand Duchess Victoria and I have come for my father, Your Emperor. Please deliver him to me."

It was fascinating to watch the man before her change from huddled over and using both hands to hide his genitals. He unfolded to his full height, smiled unctuously, and began gesturing with one hand while still using the other to maintain a modicum of modesty.

"Your Grace, maybe we could find a better time and place to discuss this matter. As you can see, I am not at my best at the moment."

Vicky cut him off. "Ernst, you are never at your best, only your worse and worst. Have you forgotten? We Peterwalds do not negotiate with kidnappers and terrorists. I have no intention of negotiating with you."

Vicky paused for a moment, then issued an order. "Command Sergeant Major, I want both of these people standing at attention when they address me. Please see that they do."

An order was barked, and four privates saw to it that four arms were held at their sides and their privates were out there for all to see.

"Now, Ernst, while not negotiating with you, I will tell you what is about to happen. You may see to it that my father is out here as quickly as he can manage to walk."

Vicky let that sink in, then gave the two before her a grin full of evil intent. "Alternately, you may return to your chateau. You may have noticed that there are a lot of tanks with guns aimed at your residence. Five seconds after you reenter your house, they will begin firing."

Vicky turned to take in the tanks and the trembling, naked self-styled Grand Duke followed her eyes. "A bit farther back are a dozen artillery pieces and several rocket launchers. In the space of one minute, they can deliver over one hundred and eighty rounds of 210mm. Some of those rounds will include Willy Pete. Ernst, do you know what white phosphorus does?"

The man managed to include a shake of the head among his trembling.

"It burns, Ernst. It burns and only quits when it has exhausted itself. If you get a flake of it on your skin, say your nose, you have only two choices. You can let it burn your nose off, or you can have a battle buddy cut out the WP with a knife. Right, Sergeant Major?"

The sergeant major had drawn his bayonet and waved it in front of Ernst's nose as if he was already prepared to cut it off.

The lord of the manor flinched and took a step back. The two privates holding his elbow shoved him back into place. The naked Grand Duke did his best to both keep his nose away from the sharp bayonet the sergeant major was still using to weave the air in front of him.

Ernst also made a manly effort to cover his family jewels again.

The privates grinned and yanked his hands away from his privates.

"Now, there is one thing more you need to consider, Ernst," Vicky said, continuing on in her most calm and businesslike voice. "There are tanks, artillery, and rockets surrounding those splendid hovels your brothers are sleeping in. The moment I order the destruction of your house here, and all within it, I will also order them to fire on your brothers as well."

"You wouldn't dare!"

"Oh, Ernst, I would so dare. Let me introduce you to the Command Sergeant Major of the 16th Marine light infantry battalion. Do you remember him?"

"Of course not," the eldest Bowlingame said, looking down his nose at the Marine still holding a knife and grinning at him.

"Well, he remembers you. You ordered the detention of all dependents of uniformed personnel who departed your service and accepted mine. His wife was attending the birth of their daughter's first child. Do you remember them now?"

Naked and trembling, Ernst managed to turn even paler than his normal dead fish, white-belly-up, skin color. He said nothing, though.

"Don't you remember ordering that the throat of the child, mother, and grandmother be slit, in that order? Oh, and a recording made of that valiant act and shipped to the grandfather? He's the sergeant major standing in front of you."

Vicky paused to take a few steps toward the armored vehicles lining the perimeter of the chateau's grounds. "He has a lot of friends out there. Sergeant Major, if I gave the order to level this house, do you think any of the gunners would pause before closing the firing circuit?"

"Not one second, Your Grace."

"Now, Ernst, if my father is not out here within one minute, I will order you into my rig with the sergeant major. We will back off a kilometer, maybe two, to get out of dangerously close proximity to the target, and then we will level it. Level it with you watching. Once it's burning rubble, with only bodies in it, I will order the sergeant major to slit your throat. Sargent Major, would you object to that order?"

"No, Your Grace. No offense meant, ma'am, but I'm really hoping he won't produce your father. I'm really hoping. Oh, and do I have to slit his throat first? I can see a lot of things I'd like to cut off."

Vicky had to wonder, was the sergeant major playing along with her, or was it the other way around?

"Your father's in the basement," the man screamed. "I can take you to him."

"Do that," Vicky ordered. "And don't let him hide his balls, Sergeant Major. I think my father, the Emperor, will enjoy seeing him this way, don't you?"

"You sure I can't at least cut his balls off, Your Grace?"

"Not today. I'm sure he'll give us a chance to revisit this situation in the future. If he's smart, he won't, but I don't take him for smart."

"I don't either, Your Grace," and Ernst was hurried back into his manor with a butt stroke or three to hurry him along.

"General Pemberton?"

"Yes, Your Grace?"

"Order the other four mansions evacuated. No need to let anyone dress, just get them out of the place. As soon as everyone is at a safe distance, level those chateaus."

"Understood. No one dies, but no one's dignity is respected. All the mansions are to be left as burning rubble."

"I think you understand me perfectly."

"Wait one, Your Grace."

Vicky waited. In a minute, the general was back. "Your Grace, the others are being hastily evacuated. May I ask you a question?"

"Of course, General."

"Would you have leveled the chateaus with everyone in them?"

"I will answer you with a question, sir. Would you have preferred for me to take command if such an order had had to be issued?"

There was a long pause as a professional soldier weighed his duty against his immortal soul. "I do not know, ma'am."

"Let us be glad that it didn't come to that. Oh, and yes, General, I would have forced those who fled this chateau back inside, including the servants. Unless we could be sure that all who deserved to be in the chateau were back in, I would have spared no one."

"I'm glad it didn't come to that, but, Your Grace, I have feed from my intel team that you knew where your father, the Emperor was located before you talked to the Grand Duke."

"And you're wondering if I would have leveled the place around my father's head?"

"If I may, yes."

"If Ernst had insisted that he did not know where my father was, I would have sent a team in to rescue him. Then I would have continued with my retribution. Be aware that you serve a Peterwald. I am a Peterwald who can be gentle, but I can also be harsh."

"I understand, Your Grace."

"If I have offended you, I will grant you any reassignment that you ask for."

"Not make me retire?"

"You are too good a man to lose, General. However, if there is a desk job or other command you would prefer, it is yours if it is mine to grant."

"Thank you, Your Grace."

"Your Grace," Maggie put in, "the colonel has your father and they are carrying him out on a stretcher."

"Is he ill?" Vicky said, turning to glower at the Grand Duchess. The wife fainted and collapsed to the ground. The two privates let her down slowly. A major signaled for a medic and he brought a thermal blanket over to warm her. She appeared to be in deep shock.

Four armed and armored troopers trotted from the chateau. Right behind them, four more troopers hurried along, carrying a stretcher. From the way they hurried, it did not look like they carried much weight.

Beside the stretcher, a medic hurried. He held high a bottle of glucose as it drained into her father's arm.

"Father," Vicky said, coming to kneel beside his stretcher.

The man on the stretcher looked horribly wasted and ashen. He'd aged twenty years in the year since Vicky had seen him on Cuzco. If she'd found him homeless and huddled under an overpass, she would not have believed this was the man she'd worshiped as a god in her childhood.

The man on the stretcher opened his eyes and squinted up at Vicky. He reached up feebly for her face. "Is that you, Vicky?"

"Yes, Dad. I've come to rescue you."

"Oh, thank you, thank you, thank you! You are a wonderful daughter! I have failed you, but you have not failed me."

"Father, I've got ten brigades of troops in Anhalt and a fleet in orbit. I'm about to blow Ernst and his brother's manor houses to hell. Let me get you up to my flagship and have them take care of you. Then we can talk."

"Oh, you are a miracle! You are a miracle I don't deserve."

Vicky tended to agree with him, but she held her tongue. He and she would need to forge a new relationship, but that could wait.

"General, I have an important patient that needs to be up the beanstalk to the *Victorious'* sick bay. He will need an escort.

"I have two battalion task forces ready to move out with your ambulance."

"Include the armored vehicle with the other three we rescued. I'm sure the four of them will need care as well as be delighted to be restored to each other."

"I'll issue the orders as soon as we quit chatting, Your Grace."

Vicky grinned. General Pemberton was learning just the right degree of insubordination he needed to work around her. "Grand Duchess out."

Ernst was back now. He stood beside his wife who lay on the ground, covered by a blanket. Every now and then he would try to cover his nakedness and a private would swat his hands aside. He would not meet Vicky's eyes.

That was best; her glare would have killed him where he stood.

She turned to Colonel Burke. "Empty the house. If they aren't dressed, rush them out anyway. If they're too drunk to stumble, have someone help them, but tell them they all need to be at least a klick away from this place in ten minutes."

"Gladly, Your Grace. Sixteenth, roust them out and don't let any of them bother with their dignity."

Vicky eyed the woman collapsed on the ground and the man who would not look at her. It was really tempting to leave the two of them here.

Tempting to one of those bastard Peterwalds, but not to the Gracious Grand Duchess.

"Colonel, I need some people to help carry Ernst's wife," she shouted.

"I'll scare up four."

A few minutes later, four men stumbled out of the house, urged along by a corporal and his rifle butt. Two of them looked like servants. They were half-dressed. The other two had been tossed out of bed naked. They also looked to be in the throes of a deadly hangover.

A stretcher had arrived, along with a medic. She began initial care for the collapsed woman, as the four stretcher-bearers fumbled getting her on the stretcher. The medic, a sergeant, finally cuffed them a couple of times and they started obeying what she told them after the corporal and his rifle butt made a move on them.

With the medic holding a pint of something over her head, and Ernst holding on to the other side for dear life, the six of them began to flounder their way toward the boundary of the safe zone.

"Your Grace, is the bombardment to begin exactly when the ten minutes expire?" General Pemberton asked.

"No, General. Let us make that a movable feast. We will level the house when everyone is safely away. My need for revenge is cooling. This is a pretty bedraggled bunch."

"Yes, Your Grace."

Vicky now found herself with a bit of a problem. She'd come here to rescue her father. Her intention had been to rescue him and then race for her side of the demarcation line between the two halves of the empire.

From there, she would help him straighten out the problems of his side of the Empire.

At the moment, however, she seemed to have decapitated the snake that was sucking out the life blood of this half of the Empire.

Having caught the elephant, did she eat it? If she chose to eat it, how did she go about doing it?

Vicky needed to think.

20

The Grand Duchess Victoria was well back from the chateau as the mad minute she'd ordered began.

Actually, it was less than a minute. Each gun was to fire exactly twelve rounds. The rocket launchers were to fire half their load. The tanks were to empty six rounds each into the structure.

In less than a minute, what had been a stately country manse was a smoking and burning pile of rubble. There were a few secondary explosions. Apparently, Ernst had stored a rather large supply of explosives or ammunition in his basement.

Interesting that.

The return to morning silence was a bit ragged. Four tanks interrupted its return by late shots.

"Maggie, how did matters go at the other country chateaus?"

"They have been destroyed, Your Grace."

"General Pemberton, I want to take everyone we rousted out of bed this morning who is important up the beanstalk to one of our brigs. Move anyone who isn't clearly a servant to the space elevator station and get your best interrogators to talk to them. The bias is toward taking a few servants but not letting one Bowlingame hanger-on go free."

"Understood. We've commandeered a couple of trucking firms. We'll get them moving along quickly."

"Very good. Maggie?"

"Yes, Your Grace?"

"I need pictures of everyone who is anyone in the Bowlingame crime family."

"I will start searching the media files for them. Your Grace, the team sent to the bank for data retrieval has copied everything. They want to know what they should do with the servers?"

Vicky looked at Admiral Bolesław. He'd been watching her carefully, but said nothing. Doubtlessly he had some strong opinions about what she should do, and just as doubtlessly, she needed to hear them.

"I'd love to blow the bank's computers up," she told him. "However, that would leave quite a mess and we may need those computers in the near future."

"Very likely."

"Maggie, tell the team to wipe the data as thoroughly as they can without destroying the actual servers. Also, any on-site back-ups should be destroyed. Maybe have a bonfire out in front of the building, or something magnetic or acidic, but we want to stop them from using those back-ups."

"The major heading up the mission reports she can do that."

"There may be off-site back-ups," the admiral said. "If they were following good practices, there should be."

"We haven't seen a lot of evidence of good practices since we got here," Vicky said. "I'll accept that risk. Even if there aren't, they're bound to be a bit out of date. Imagine trying to run a worldwide bank when you're missing the last two or three days and everyone else isn't."

That got the first crack of a grin from the admiral in a long time.

Vicky leaned back in her uncomfortable seat in the rolling personnel carrier.

"Now, Alis, tell me all the reasons why mission creep is a bad idea. You've often decried the historical blunders of commanders who went beyond what they had planned to do and failed miserably when they tried to wing it beyond that plan."

"It is a frequent prelude to disaster," Admiral Bolesław said, pensively. "However, every specific situation demands its own assessment and decision. One general's mission creep is another general's brilliant victory.

The admiral shrugged. "If you succeed, they put up a statue to you. You fail, and a lot of good men die for nothing. So, tell me about this inviting mission creep you talk of."

Vicky liked the way he left the question so open ended.

"When we left New Brunswick, I expected to find my father, get him back in his throne room, turn on the lights and heat, and come back. A cakewalk. Then we got here, and things were a lot worse than I expected."

Vicky shook her head slowly. "Dad has really screwed things up and lost total control. I narrowed my mission objective to a snatch and grab. Get down here, grab him, and run for home with him. Let him have some rooms in my palace and enjoy his golden years."

"Is Harry Peterwald the kind of man to 'enjoy his golden years'?"

Vicky rolled her eyes. "Yeah, there is that, but he'd

screwed things up so bad, I figured that was the best he could hope for."

"But now?"

"Now I've had a chance to get a good look at the mess we have here. The burned-out businesses and homes. God only knows how many people have been killed or had their lives ruined."

"You just added a few to the list," the admiral put in quickly.

"And I enjoyed doing it. But seeing Greenfeld's commerce so reduced. I used to see traffic on the expressways at all different hours. Thick as fleas on a dog, or so one of my ensign friends used to put it."

"You learned a lot as an ensign."

"Yes. But what I need to know right now is something I don't know."

Vicky focused her thoughts. "Mannie said that there were democratic forces in the court. Are they still here on Anhalt, or have they been burned out? If I raised a new flag here, would the people rally around me . . . or stay behind their window curtains? I have decapitated the Bowlingame crime family. Is it as dead as a chicken without its head, or is it a worm where the two ends will regrow and you end up with two worms?"

"Worse," Admiral Bolesław said, "are you facing the Hydra?"

"Hydra?"

"A mythical beast that had three heads. If you cut one off, it regrew three more heads. And so it went, getting worse the more you succeeded, until it had so many heads that it overpowered you."

"Are you warning me of irregular warfare?"

"I don't know what I'm warning you about. Are the so-called security consultants a bunch of thugs that will skitter into the woodwork as soon as you cut off their pay? Are they the kind of thugs who will walk off with their weapons and set about robbing, raping, and killing? Five or six hundred years ago, it wasn't unusual for soldiers laid off after a war to set themselves up as brigands, robbing the locals and killing any merchant that fell into their grasp."

"Are we equipped to maintain law and order in Anhalt if we take control of it?" Vicky asked.

"Precisely."

"Maggie, get me General Pemberton."

A moment later he answered, "Yes, Your Grace."

"General, with the forces we have on the ground and available in the transports, could we take control and rule Anhalt with Greenfeld?"

"That, Your Grace, is not an easy question to answer."

"Please study it and have several options ready for my review when we get back to the space elevator station. They may range from 'Hell no', to 'How we can occupy the capital', to 'How we can occupy the entire planet'?"

"I will get on that immediately."

"Thank you, General."

Vicky leaned back in her seat and listened to the hum of the tires as they carried her to her fate.

Her destiny?

Or maybe just the elevator station.

21

V icky strode into the space elevator station to see that matters were well in hand.

All of those that had been collected at the various villas stood, mostly naked, at intervals in the large open entrance hall to the station. There were guards, and any attempt to talk was quickly squelched. No one there was going to be coordinating their story.

Several tables had been set up for the interrogators. The interrogations were taking place beside the tables, not behind them. Both the officer asking the questions and the one answering them were on the same side.

There was no place to hide.

As Vicky watched, Maggie filled her in on the process and results. "If they are thin and have calluses on their hands, they are likely servants. If they can give a decent account of the job they had, they are usually taken over to the restaurant and given breakfast."

"And if they are not?" Admiral Bolesław asked.

"Those who are overweight with soft hands are primary candidates for people of concern. Especially those who bellow, 'Do you know who I am? Do you know who I am?' are usually the people we want to keep. They go into lockdown. The challenge is the ones that fall in between. Neither thin nor heavy, with hands that show they may have worked . . . or worked out. Some may be senior butlers or maids or cooks. Others may be minor officials to the Bowlingame crime family. It all depends on what kind of story they can tell and how well they can lie. So far, the bias is two-to-one against these. For every one that gets a breakfast, two end up in lockdown."

"Are we giving those in lockdown breakfasts?" the admiral asked.

"Yes, sir," Maggie replied. "They are being served famine biscuits and water."

"I don't imagine that's going over well," Vicky said.

"Those that refuse the food are given a double strike against them. Those that eat it are looked at more carefully. It's interesting to see how the Bowlingame treat their servants. Even in jail, they still order them around."

"So, we're watching who gets ordered and who doesn't?" the Navy officer asked.

"Yes. It is interesting, Admiral," Maggie said, "to see who offers up their clothes to whom and who demands clothes from whom. I am sure that several professional papers will be published about this exercise."

A major jogged up to them. He came to a halt, snapped to attention, and saluted. "Your Grace, if you will come this way, General Pemberton is ready with a briefing for you."

"Thank you, Major. Lead the way, please," Vicky said in full Gracious Grand Duchess mode.

The major set a fast pace. Vicky was quick not to fall behind. He led her over to the office side of the great hall, then up a staircase to the second level. He halted, then opened a door for her.

Vicky walked into what had to be a conference room no different from what she'd see on several hundred worlds, if not every one settled by humans. One large wood, or fake wood table. A dozen chairs. Maybe half of them would be comfortable. Only luck or testing would determine which were which. The walls were gray. The carpeting was gray. The pictures on the wall were black, star-speckled space, cut by the beanstalk with a ferry prominent in the picture. Each portrait was of a different class of ferry.

Interesting.

In the middle of the table, two vacant seats awaited her and the admiral. General Pemberton stood by the seat that would place him at her elbow. A number of generals and colonels filled up the table. More colonels and majors sat along the wall.

Each of the staff had several readers at hand and looked ready to snap to so that any question she might have would be answered.

"Your Grace," General Pemberton said, offering Vicky the seat next to him.

Vicky chose to walk over and stand beside him. "Can you give me a quick executive summary before you bury me in the bullshit?"

"Yes, Your Grace," he said, without flinching. "I would not recommend that we attempt to occupy Anhalt with the forces we now have. There is no way we can occupy the entire planet. In addition to the potential for armed resistance on Greenfeld itself, there is also the matter of us being deep in hostile space. This might be a matter better covered by the admiral. However, if the Navy cannot control the sky over this planet, we face reinforcements being dropped in from off planet."

The general paused for a moment. "We also face bombardment from space if we lose control of the sky."

Vicky sat down. So did the general.

"We do control the sky at the moment," Vicky pointed out. "I'm told that all tank parks and motor pools in a wide area around Anhalt have been identified. Could we laser them from space and destroy the armor? What about the security consultant's barracks? Could we laser them as well?"

"That would depend on how high a body count you want," the general said. "Lasing the tanks from orbit could be done. At last check, there was little activity among them. The barracks appear to be sleeping, although the racket from us flattening those five chateaus has, no doubt, raised some alarms. Wiping the data from the largest bank in the Empire may also have been noticed by now."

The general paused, before going on. "I must advise Your Grace that one of the results of destroying the chateaus has raised a major question to me and my staff."

"And that was?" Vicky asked.

"The secondary explosions that followed our bombardment. It seems clear that ammunition and explosives were stored in all five chateaus. Someone wanted to have plenty of munitions available if he felt the need to kill a lot of people. How many other small stashes of munitions are scattered around Anhalt? How much trouble would we have trying to find them? How much damage could they do to us while we were doing that search?"

"You think we'd face guerrilla warfare," Admiral Bolesław said.

"I *fear* we could face irregular warfare," the general clarified. "My profession usually concentrates on capabilities. What I have told you, Your Grace, is that it appears that the Bowlingame family appears to have prepared for a siege, whether from civil uprising or invasion. Based on that alone, I would tell you that my troops are not qualified to win such a war on this planet. However, there is also the aspect of intent and will."

Here the general paused. "They have the capability to wage war. However, you have their leadership locked down below. Can the people not included in our sweep reorganize their capabilities. Can they decide to wage war and commence it? Just as importantly, do the people at their beck and call have any interest in going up against our soldiers? We've talked about the low quality and general thuggish nature of the security specialists. Will they melt back into the general population, or will they melt back into the general population with their guns, munitions, and explosives?"

The general sat down. His eyes were fixed on Vicky. He'd laid it out for her. Now, what would she do?

She chose to examine her problem out loud.

"We are deep in hostile space. So far, when my warships have faced the Empress's forces, we have beat them like a drum. Have they gotten any wiser, Admiral?"

"No data, Your Grace. They have had a year to drill and we have had a year of limited budgets and reduced underway days. Several of our ships docked up on the station are under-crewed because the pay is better at construction sites."

"Thank you for reminding me of what you have reminded me so many times before," Vicky said, giving Admiral Bolesław a small, slightly nervous, grin.

"Of course, Your Grace," the admiral said.

"Tell me, Admiral. Where is their hostile fleet? Certainly, there should have been a major fleet docked at the station. If the Bowlingames were going to have a fleet anywhere, it would be here."

"Yes, Your Grace. We found that information in the Port Admiral's office. It seems that the home fleet sailed for New Dresden a few days after we left. They are taking the most traveled route. Likely by now, they have been informed of the error of their instructions and are turning about."

"So, we're likely to have company before too long." Vicky said.

"Yes, Your Grace."

"And we're likely to discover that our ground forces are being knifed in the back before too long."

"Yes, Your Grace, " General Pemberton said.

"What forces would you need to hold Anhalt?" Vicky asked the general.

"A lot more MPs to keep the peace, Your Grace," Pemberton said. "Several Civil Affairs units to set up an operational government, assuming those that presently run it are locked up downstairs. I'd also need a lot more electronic counter measures to secure the main roads against roadside bombs. We brought an army to fight an army, not the one you'd need to run a city and maybe fight a popular uprising."

Vicky raised her eyes to gaze at the overhead. Mannie had said that there were democratic elements among those at court. Were they still alive, or had they died in some of the burnt out houses she'd passed? Could they be located and form a government?

Could Anhalt, or any part of her dad's Empire be ruled by its own people?

Clearly, she had rushed in here without thinking about

what she'd find and what she'd need to do about it, much less what she wanted the end game to look like.

Damn, another learning experience.

Vicky pursed her lips and examined her options.

Go against the general, gamble that this force could occupy and operate this city. Alternately, she could try to get the people to organize themselves.

"General, are we getting much of a response from the people around here?"

"Your Grace, the six brigades we have used to set up a cordon around the space elevator station have reported no one on the street. No one is moving at all. Occasionally, someone peeks through the curtains, but it looks like folks took one look outside, saw tanks, declared it a snow day, and went back to bed."

"I never got snow days," Vicky muttered. "In the palace, my tutors walked down the hall to me."

"Lucky duck," Admiral Bolesław said with a silly grin.

"Yeah," Vicky said, dryly, but would not allow herself to be distracted from her problem. "So, my father's people have learned to keep their heads down when troops take to the streets."

"Wouldn't you?" the admiral pointed out.

"Yes, and I also remember how hard it was to get people to even risk opening up trade with each other for fear of displeasing the Bowlingame crime family."

"So," General Pemberton said, "you can roll up your sleeves and try to clean up this mess, or we can quietly withdraw."

"What if we rolled up our sleeves," Vicky said, "then found we had a tiger by the tail and withdrew?"

"Running away with your tail between your legs is never

a good image to leave in your enemy's eyes," Admiral
Bolesław said.

General Pemberton nodded agreement.

"We have no civil affairs personnel?" Vicky asked, again.

Both uniformed men shook their head.

"We have no way to keep the water flowing or the electricity running. Don't even talk to me about sewage treatment and garbage removal," General Pemberton said. "If the
civilians running those services don't show up tomorrow,
our goose is cooked right out of the starting gate."

"All it will take is a call to a few key people," Admiral
Bolesław said. "A whisper that if they go to work tomorrow,
their home will be burnt down with their wife and kids in it.
Would you go to work after that sort of call?"

"Damn," Vicky said. She should have thought ahead. She
should have considered all her options.

*Honestly, girl, did you really think charging in here with an
army and taking over the capital of the Empire from your father
was a good idea? Can you spell the word usurper?*

Even if that *was* what the Bowlingames had done
to Dad.

Vicky took a deep breath. "General Pemberton, begin a
retrograde action. Send all the putative traitors to my
father's rule up the beanstalk and find space for them in the
fleet's brigs. I want the five brothers on the *Victorious*. Oh,
and if they've managed to yank clothes off of any servant,
strip them. Traitors should learn shame."

The two uniformed officers exchanged glances.

"The rules of war do not apply to those civilians we have
arrested," Vicky was quick to point out. "Their captivity is by
my rules, and mine alone."

Both officers nodded to her.

"I'll get the fleet ready to sail," Admiral Bolesław said

"I'll retrograde the troops back up the beanstalk," General Pemberton said.

"Oh, and general, in the olden days, didn't they spike cannons before they withdrew?"

"Yes, Your Grace."

"Make a list of all the things you would like spiked. Tank parks, motor pools, defensive radars, and AA laser batteries. Pass them along to the admiral here. I'd like to see what lasers from space look like before I go up the beanstalk."

"We'll get right on it."

22

D one with the tough decisions for the moment, and none too happy with what she'd done, Vicky went out on the mezzanine to get some peace and quiet. It gave her a view down onto the floor of the great hall. The interrogations were still going on, although those waiting to be talked to were fewer.

Movement caught her eye. One of the naked fellows down there was quite proud of his engorged male member. He was talking to a lot of the females around him. Vicky couldn't hear what he was saying, what with all the echoes in this huge building. She did, however, have a pretty good idea of his words from the way the young woman around him, many in nightclothes or less, were reacting.

She couldn't solve all the injustices in the world, but she might be able to handle the one in sight.

"Maggie, get me the sergeant of that guard detail down there, the one closest to that baboon."

"Your Grace?" was in a woman's voice, not something Vicky would have expected.

"Yes, this is Grand Duchess Victoria, are you in charge of the guards around that ape waving his dick around?"

"Ah, ma'am, Your Grace, I'm just a sergeant."

"Are you in charge of the privates guarding that big baboon?"

"Yes, ma'am, Your Grace. It's my squad."

"I would personally appreciate it if you and the biggest trooper in your squad, or maybe the next one over if you need him, would walk over to that . . . problem child," Vicky chose to say. After all, she was supposed to be a Grand Duchess. "Take him by the ear and put him in the lock down. Oh, and if your knee happened to accidentally end up between the apex of his legs. It wouldn't bother me at all."

"Your Grace. Ah, is this really you? This isn't some sort of joke is it?"

"I'm standing halfway down the mezzanine."

The sergeant turned to search the second deck.

Vicky waved enough to be noticed.

"Holy Mother of God," came in a soft whimper. Then the sergeant stood to attention, and saluted Vicky.

Vicky returned the salute.

"I'm only too happy to follow this order," had more glee than you usually heard in a sergeant's voice.

Vicky did not even try to suppress a grin as the smaller sergeant and a much larger subordinate strode over to the show off. Apparently, the bigger man's boot landed on the naked man's foot.

He let out a howl, that only got louder as the sergeant did, indeed, grab him by the ear, twist it, and begin leading him off to the lockdown.

That did not go unnoticed by her command structure.

She got called out. She responded by pointing at Vicky up on the second deck.

Vicky waved.

Several officers snapped to attention and saluted.

She saluted back.

But there was more recognition. Among the woman who the twerp had been harassing, a cheer went up and several women started waving. Others joined in.

Waving back, Vicky noticed the interrogators paused in their conversations to take note of those that were last to join the wave at the Grand Duchess. She was only too glad to help them separate the sheep from the goats.

"Your Grace?" Admiral Bolesław asked.

Vicky turned to him, but his eyes were on the deck below. "You having fun?"

"I may have just struck a tiny blow for justice, so yes."

"We have selected our targets. There is a viewing deck on the roof of this building. Would you like to join me?"

"I'd be glad to," Vicky said.

It was only a short elevator ride before she found herself high above the city. For the first time, she got a good look at the beanstalk. Intellectually, she knew what a space elevator looked like. She'd been up them many times.

However, seeing the ground end of one up close and personal was enough to take her breath away.

It wasn't a wire, or even a ribbon. Actually, upon close observation, it was a skein of ribbons forming one huge block that shot up into the air as high as she could see. She tried to follow it, but she almost fell backwards; the admiral caught her.

"That is so awesome," Vicky said.

"There are very few times when you remind me of how

young you are," the admiral said, chuckling, "but you looked so delightfully pleased staring up at that thing."

"Okay, yes," Vicky said, making a point of straightening up her dress whites. "I've had a protected upbringing in the palace. Maybe I haven't seen all the things your kids have."

"No, no, Your Grace. You misunderstand me. I'm just delighted to have found a view that could surprise and bring you joy. You get so little of it."

"Yes. Yes, you're one of the few people who knows me that well. Thank you for bringing me up here . . . and not warning me about the view."

"It was my pleasure, Your Grace."

"Now, back to being a murderous Peterwald Grand Duchess," Vicky said, all serious.

"Yes. We have anchored several battleships from the station so they can get a clear view of their targets. We have also given an order to take out the targets at thirty second intervals. We want people to come out and see the fireworks."

"No use putting on a great show if no one sees it."

"Your Grace, would you care to address your people?" Admiral Bolesław asked?

"Has Captain Blue worked a miracle for me?"

"He can patch you into every channel in this burg. He's also put together a few minutes of video from our destruction of the chateaus this morning as well as the capture and parading of the dukes."

"Naked pictures?" Vicky asked, gleefully.

"Full frontal. Both them and their wives."

"You enjoy the crime, you pay the price," Vicky said.

Then she paused, and centered herself. She wanted to get in touch with the rage resulting from her father's poor treatment. The rage that the Bowlingames had exploited her people. But she also had to find her center, that part of her that Mannie had been struggling to help her find.

The part of her that was quiet power.

"Captain Blue, are you ready to jack me in to all transmissions?"

"Yes, Your Grace. I'm getting video off of the admiral's computer. Would you mind moving a foot or two to the left?"

Vicky did.

"Good, the morning light is illuminating just one side of your face. Go for it."

"People of Anhalt, this is Grand Duchess Victoria addressing you from atop your space elevator station. I have returned to find my father under duress and force majeure most foul. I have taken him into my care and I am glad to report to all of you that he is now receiving the best of care. I have also taken possession of those who treated him so foully and will treat them as the traitors they have shown themselves to be."

Vicky paused, and softened her eyes and mouth. "Those of you who live on the east side of town, near the foothills, may have been awoken this morning by a short 'mad minute,' as the military calls it. With less than one minute of tank and artillery fire, five ducal estates were leveled and left burning. I assure you that everyone was evacuated before we leveled them. Many of those were served in those stately homes will be set free. Most of those who lived in them will be seeing the inside of my brigs for a long time."

Another pause, Vicky did her best to make her visage serious. "I will be leaving soon. I did not come prepared to take over the reins of government here, and my father is too weakened to return to his duties. I will not, however, leave things as they were yesterday. Those of you who have dealings with the First Interstellar Bank of Greenfeld may have noticed that its network is not on line. Since it was owned by the Bowlingames and used to finance their crimes, I have wiped their network servers. Those who profited by their traitorous activity may learn to be more careful in the future.

"That is only one of the matters I am changing. You might want to step outside. Over the next few minutes, my battleships will be lasing certain tank and armored parks as well as motor pools used by the infamous Bowlingame security consultants. If you are close to anyplace where tanks are parked, I would suggest you move away. If you are close to a security specialist compound, you might want to do likewise. We will commence firing in five minutes.

"Now, for those of you interested, here is some news to bring you up to date of what happened last night."

"Captain, are you ready?"

"Yes, Your Grace. I've already got it running."

"Put my words and those videos in a loop for the next five minutes."

"It's already running."

He kept running for the rest of the morning. It would take the stations that long to figure out how to cut back into their own take.

Vicky was still standing on the observer deck when Admiral Bolesław pointed, "It should be right over there."

A moment later, two blinding beams of light shot from the sky. There were several dozen explosions where the beams touched the earth. No doubt, some of the tanks were kept ready to move out.

Thirty seconds later, another tank park got lazed, with more examples of secondary explosions. In the next two minutes four more tank assembly points were fried.

When the next rays touched down, they were aiming for two different locations. One returned to the original area and resulted in a dozen or more explosions as the beams crossed over the landscape."

Vicky glanced at the admiral. "We figured if we blew away their tanks, they didn't need their ammo. We delayed hitting the munitions dumps to give people around them some warning."

Vicky pursed her lower lip and nodded.

The other light beam had come closer to the city. The bright red colors of the secondary explosions suggested that gas tanks were going off. Over the next five minutes, the beams moved around the city, taking out the motor park at one security specialist compound after another.

Some smaller lasers, likely 5-inch secondary batteries, also lapped around the edges of those compounds, setting off secondary explosions.

Again, Vicky glanced at her admiral.

"They don't really need their armory and magazine, do they?"

"I don't think so."

"Shall we go, Your Grace?"

"I can't think of anything more I'd rather do. Admiral set a fast course for Mannie and don't spare the reaction mass."

Admiral Bolesław chuckled happily. "It will be my pleasure.

23

Vicky couldn't wait to get home to Mannie. As she saw it, honeymoon had the word moon in it, and the moon took twenty-eight days around old Earth to do its thing. She and Mannie had only had five days of their honeymoon.

Mannie owed her another twenty-three days. Mannie and her half of the Empire.

Still, when Admiral Bolesław brought her a course for home that took an indirect route, taking care to keep off any major routes and away from any large worlds, she had approved it.

They'd kicked over a hornet's nest. It was best to let things settle down. She knew there was a fleet out there hunting for her fleet. It would be better if they did not meet until cooler heads had a chance to calm things down.

In the meantime, she headed down to see her father in sick bay.

She found him sleeping. He was plugged into all sorts of monitors and four different bags were dripping liquids into his arm.

"How bad is he?" Vicky asked the senior medical officer. The man was at her side before she had a chance to sit down and take her father's hand in her own.

"Your Grace, he is not well."

"How not well?" Vicky asked.

The commodore worried his lower lip before answering. "Your Grace, if you had not rescued him . . . if you had not gotten him up here into our care, I don't think he would have lasted more than a week. Definitely not more than a month."

Vicky gave the doctor a hard look. "Explain yourself."

"He is malnourished," he chief surgeon for the fleet said. "The three women you sent up here are also malnourished. The food they were provided gave them little real sustenance. For example, the rice that was their main starch was polished. Most of the nutrients had been leached out of it. The meat they got was full of bones and gristle. It did little more than add a bit of flavoring to their rice broth. Most of the other food they obtained was rotten, rat-gnawed or otherwise unusable. Someone wanted to starve those poor people to death."

"So, we fatten them up," Vicky said.

"It's not that easy, Your Grace. The quarters we found them in were cold, damp, and mold-ridden. Your father, the Emperor, and the three women cooks are suffering from several different bacterial, fungal, and viral infections. We're treating all of them with broad spectrum antivirals and antibiotics. They're very sick."

"How sick?" Vicky snapped.

"The three women began this ordeal with some cushion, I am told."

"They were cooks. They liked what they cooked," Vicky

said, wanting to smile fondly at their frequent brag, but she was not able to today.

"Yes, so they are stronger. Your father, the Emperor, carried little extra weight; neither fat nor muscle."

"He hated to exercise and claimed it was healthy to be skinny as a rail."

"That didn't serve him well for this imposed fast and exposure."

"Are you telling me that he could die?"

"Yes, Your Grace. If we can't get control of the blood infection raging in his body or the pneumonia congesting his lungs, we could lose him."

Vicky eyed her father, snoring slightly despite the oxygen being fed through his nose. "So, they may have killed him, but I've managed to have his death upon my head."

"I'm sorry, Your Grace."

Vicky stood. "Don't be sorry, be effective. My father *must* not die. Do you understand me. He must *not*."

"We are doing all that modern medicine can do, Your Grace."

"Then do more. This is a political imperative, Doctor. The Emperor *cannot* die here, with us.

Feeling more vexed than relaxed, Vicky watched her father sleep for a few more minutes before going to the next room over where all three of her unofficial aunties were happily sharing a single room.

While they were also hooked up to monitors, theirs chirped and beeped much more enthusiastically, and the hanging bottles were fewer.

"Your Grace, thank you! Thank you! Thank you!" Iris said. Her words were quickly lost in a babble as Rena and Hilda joined in.

"How is everything?" Vicky asked.

"Well, if they'd just let us fix a meal, the food would at least be decent."

"And these bedclothes!" Rena complained. "They don't have any back."

"Oh, poo," Hilda said, "I'm warm and my tummy is half-full for the first time in too long, so, thank you, Vicky."

"No. Thank you for sticking by my father. Did everyone run?"

The three old women glanced around at each other. Iris took up the story.

"Your father wasn't even back before they told us there was no money in the treasury. No money to pay anyone. The word flew through the palace around lunch time and before you knew it, everyone was grabbing anything they could and running out the door."

"We grabbed some potatoes and canned meat," Rena said, "then had to lock ourselves in our rooms to keep everything in them from being stolen."

"One young pup tried to grab the sack of flour and sugar I went out to forage for," Hilda said. "He didn't know I also had my favorite iron skillet. Not one of those wimpy aluminum things they use on those worthless electric *burners*," she spat the last word.

"So, we collected all the food we could in our rooms," Iris said, "and waited to see what was going to happen. We knew your father was supposed to be coming back. I understand that when his light cruiser docked, there was no one to meet him. They didn't even want to give him a ride down the beanstalk. He had to hitch a ride from the terminal. Can you imagine that?"

"Were you there when he got home?"

"We didn't know anything, so we didn't know he was home until I ran into him, wandering the halls," Rena said.

"I had some nice cookies for him, " Hilda said with a happy smile, then it soured. "Though I didn't have any milk to go with them."

"I'm sure he loved your sugar cookies," Iris said.

"He told you so," Rena added.

"We scrounged up every last bit of food left in the kitchen," Iris said. "It kept us going for most of the first four months. Every couple of weeks, one of those Red Shirts would come by and check to make sure we were okay, they said. I think they were just looking to see if we'd died yet."

"They started dropping off some food," Rena said.

"Not much," Hilda added. "You know, it was so bad, I think they were collecting stuff that a grocery store had thrown out. If you ask me, it was. It was really bad."

"Then the power went off."

"The electric power, Iris?" Vicky asked.

"Yes, Vicky, just the electric power. And it went off just as we were getting into the wintertime. We found some old moth-eaten curtains up in the attic of the old wing of the palace and we made a curtain between the rest of the kitchen and our gas stoves."

"They didn't cut off the gas," Hilda said.

"I think they'd forgotten about our old stoves," Rena put in.

"So," Iris said. "We did our best to make it through the winter huddled down beside our stoves. Still, we had to be careful. Some people had taken to coming out here to look for things to steal, or a place to hide. We tried to stay quiet as church mice."

"Well, you won't have to stay quiet as church mice where we're headed," Vicky told them.

"Do you live in a palace?" Hilda asked, excitement in her eyes.

Vicky shrugged. "I don't know if I'm going to have to live in a palace again, or maybe something smaller, but I will make sure that it has gas stoves and the best of food for you to cook for me and my husband."

"Oh! You're married!" came from all three of them at once.

"Yes, and we're headed for where I had to leave my husband to come visit Greenfeld. Now, I have a question. You say that some Red Shirts would come by and check on you?"

"Yep," "Yes," and "Every two weeks or so."

"Did an older man ever come with them? Someone plump and full of pomp and officiousness?"

All three women shook their heads.

"No, ma'am," Iris said. "They were all young guys full of piss and vinegar. Strutting around all self-important with their hands on their pistol holsters."

Vicky scowled; there went the idea of having her parade her naked dukes by her friends to see if any of them had visited her dad in his distress. Apparently, they had left it to underlings to check up on how long the Emperor was going to take to die.

A week into the voyage, the fleet surgeon sent up word that her father was awake and Vicky began to visit him in sick bay. At least she tried.

Visits to her father did not fulfill any real need she had. He was tearfully grateful for her rescue and he said it over and over. When he wasn't crying, he was raging about the evil machinations of the Bowlingame family.

Never, however, did he have a word for his participation in this mess. Never did he admit he had any fault. It was all "their" fault.

Vicky found herself making excuses to cut her visits

short. He'd beg her to stay, beg her to come back soon, but Vicky was remembering what she did not like about her father, and some of the things he'd done to her.

Those memories she had kept locked away in the back of her brain, memories she did not want to allow out because they gnawed at her. As the voyage went on, she spent less and less time with her father.

Admiral Bolesław found a counselor on the Victorious, and Vicky had him spend time with her father. The counselor arranged to visit at least once a day, sometimes more. *Let him handle Father.*

Dad did want to visit the brig. He wanted to see the Grand Dukes and Duchesses and gloat that now he was the one on the outside in fine clothes and they were locked up naked.

The counselor managed to forestall that visit until the last day of the voyage. Vicky did not review the brig footage of the visit in real time. She was afraid she might call up the brig and order her dad clapped in a cell.

He's the Emperor. I can't treat him the way he deserves.

She managed, just barely, not to usurp her father's throne right then and there when she watched the visit much later that night.

24

T he second week of the voyage, there was no reason for Vicky to drop down to the brig and view her totally naked collection of brig inmates. However, since they had not even once checked on how bad her father had been doing in their "tender care," she could easily do them one better by paying them at least one visit.

"Admiral on deck," a corporal announced as she called the guard detail to attention. A moment later a Gunny was at Vicky's other elbow.

"Your Grace, how may we serve you?" he said crisply.

"I'd like to review our dukes."

"Well, ma'am, we got ourselves five of a kind." Gunny said, enjoying his joke.

Vicky was buzzed through into the cells. Each cell was the same. Bars in front. Two slabs on opposite sides of the cell for the prisoners to sleep on. No pads to make that sleep any more comfortable. A commode with no seat.

The quarters were not designed with creature comfort in mind, only security and what could be done to keep the prisoners from harming themselves.

The first cell held the eldest surviving Bowlingame brother and his wife. He'd been found naked, sleeping with a young woman, she the same with a young man. When they saw Vicky, they immediately went into a kind of comedy routine as both tried to use the other to cover themselves. He wanted her in front of him. She wanted him in front of her.

They settled with her turning her back to Vicky and him using her to cover his front. This was likely the first time in quite a few years that they'd been face-to-face naked.

"You have no right to hold us," the Grand Duke bellowed.

"You stole my father, your Emperor's, throne. I can do whatever I want with traitors."

"Ha, is that what that old fool told you? He mortgaged his palace and I merely called in the note."

"No doubt, you'll have a chance to argue your case in court."

"In the meantime, can I at least have a prison suit? Aren't prisoners supposed to be issued some sort of prison garb?"

"Yes, I think they usually are," Vicky said, turning to Gunny.

"Your Grace, since all we usually get down here are Sailors and Marines, we let them stay in their uniform. We don't have any special prison garb."

"Ah," Vicky said. "So, I guess they can't issue you prison jumpsuits."

"Could I at least have some pants?"

Vicky looked at him, thinking of how he'd starved and nearly frozen her father. He began to wilt.

"No, I don't think so," she said, simply.

She passed to the next cell. The second eldest Bowlingame brother was in it with his wife. Both were middle-aged, and it showed. He sat on one slab, his head in his hands. He did not look up when Vicky walked by. The wife was laid out flat on her back, her head toward the bars. She also showed no interest in what was happening.

The middle cell held the middle brother and his wife. At the moment, he sat on the edge of one platform, scowling at the bars. She sat cross-legged in the opposite corner, her back to him. Both looked red and winded.

"They just finished an argument," Gunny told Vicky.

An argument was in full swing in the next cell. He sat on his bunk, she stormed up and down the cell berating him.

"You said it was a sure thing! You said we'd have power and wealth beyond my imagination! Well, I never imagined this! Couldn't you pull your head out of your brother's ass long enough to look around? For Christ sake, Peterwalds? You tried to pull this over on the Peterwalds! I should never have married a worm like you! Mother said I was letting all your fine words blind me and Mother was right!"

The man leapt up and threw himself at the bars. "You've got to get me out of here. This is cruel and inhumane punishment."

"Actually, it's cruel and inhumane treatment of my guards, Your Grace," Gunny said.

"Do you have to listen to this all the time?" Vicky asked him.

"All day and much of the night. Personally, I don't know how she keeps it up. I would have thought she'd be hoarse by now."

"Practice," the naked duke grumbled. "Lots and lots of practice."

"Don't you go disrespecting me, you worm. I'm your wife."

Vicky moved on to the last cell. The youngest brother was

still well into middle age. At the moment, he was curled up on his slab in a fetal position. Again, his wife was haranguing him unmercifully. As Vicky came abreast of the cell, the woman hauled off and kicked the man, right in the kidney.

From the looks of all the black and blue marks on the poor fellow, she'd hit him a lot.

"Another constant source of noise?" Vicky asked.

Gunny scratched his head. "If one's not going at it, then another one is. Saints preserve us when two of them start in on each other at the same time. Jesus, Mary, and Joseph, there have even been times when three are at it, not just screaming at each other, but at the ones up or down the cell block from them. I've had to put my guards on an hourly schedule so they can keep their sanity."

Vicky looked around. She saw a door with a small glass window in it and a hole to slip things through.

"What's that?"

"Solitary confinement."

"Anyone in there?"

"No, Your Grace. You made a proclamation, no one in solitary confinement except under sever circumstances."

"Ah, yes, I do seem to remember my husband talking me into that while he was still my fiancée. Tell me, Gunny, if you put two or three of them in that cell, would it be solitary confinement?"

"There's only one bed in there."

Vicky eyed the platforms the prisoners slept on. "Are those any softer than the floor?"

"Not really."

"Tell them they can swap out who sleeps on the bed and who sleeps on the floor."

Gunny's grin just about split his face. "Yes, Your Grace.

Corporal, bring me a pair of cuffs and a couple of guards with billy clubs."

"Aye, aye, Gunny," had way too much enthusiasm behind it. Clearly, some Marines were looking forward to enjoying this prisoner transfer.

Vicky stood back, but kept an eye on matters. One still-complaining woman was moved from a cell over to the single detention cell. Her husband broke out into peons of praise to any god who was responsible.

Vicky moved over to stare at the back of the one who wasn't arguing for the moment. "You want to join your two sister-in laws?"

The woman got up and backed against the rear wall of the cell. "Please, no."

Vicky turned to the Gunny and said, pointedly, "If she gives your people any trouble, put her in."

"Understood, ma'am," Gunny answered.

Now the transfer guards were back. They began cautiously to move the woman who was busy kicking the stuffing out of her husband. The guards had to go into the cell to subdue her; they ended up carrying her out of her cell and shoving her into the other.

They closed the sound suppressing hatch to cries of, "Police brutality!"

"If anything comes of that just drop me a note. Maggie, did you make a record of those transfers?"

"Yes, Your Grace. I will keep it handy for the next seven years."

"Thank you, Maggie, and thank you Gunny. Corporal."

"Oh, Your Grace, thank you. We all thank you."

"I'm glad I could solve at least one problem today."

Vicky left the brig with a smile on her face. If only all of her problems were so easily solved.

25

I t was Maggie who she ended up spending the most time with when she wasn't planning her next move.

Vicky needed to have a talk with Maggie about ethics and morality.

As a Peterwald, she was hardly the person to tell anyone anything about virtue of any variety. She was not a paragon of moral virtue. How could she instruct her computer in right from wrong, acceptable from inappropriate, what defined a regrettably bad choice when the other choices were much worse, when she herself blew it so often?

Vicky waited for an evening when she was soaking in her bathtub and as relaxed as she ever was.

"Maggie, do you remember back when the *Victorious* was under assault by a swarm of incoming missiles?"

"Yes, Your Grace."

"You did a fantastic job of developing and coordinating a fire plan for all the ships. You likely saved my life."

"Thank you, Your Grace."

Nervous, despite her effort to relax, Vicky used a big toe

to explore the water faucet at the foot of the tub. "Maggie, I'd like for you to go back to just before the swam of incoming missiles were identified. Can you see what was on the radar just then?"

"Of course, Your Grace."

"What was out there?"

"Lots of things, Your Grace, from lots of small space junk to the eight longboats that had been armed and destroyed the first assaults."

Vicky took a cleansing breath, then several more before she went on. "What was on your radar take after you executed your fire plan?"

"A lot of wreckage, most of it small."

"What was the wreckage from?" Vicky said softly.

"The missiles, Your Grace."

"Are you sure it was only from the missiles?" she asked.

There was a long pause. It must have been a huge pause for a computer that thought in picoseconds.

"The longboats are no longer on my radar scans," Maggie said, finally.

Vicky said nothing.

"Those longboats had two Sailors and two Marine gunners on each of them," Maggie said, her voice losing much of her usual human tone and sounding more like a computer-generated voice.

"Yes," Vicky said. "Remember, you saved a lot of lives by slicing the incoming missiles in two."

"Yes. Yes, I did," Maggie said, still in a tiny voice. "I saved a lot of lives. I saved a lot of lives.

There was another of those long pauses, then Maggie want on. "Vicky, my calculations show that if the swarm had hit, unattenuated, the Victorious' hull would have been holed, and as much as half of the crew would have died."

"That sounds like a reasonable calculation," Vicky said. She did not miss that her computer was addressing Vicky now, not the Grand Duchess.

Interesting.

"Do you think a human generated fire plan could have gotten half the swarm?"

"I seriously doubt that, Maggie. I'm not sure we could have gotten a quarter of the missiles in the short time we had."

"You think so?"

"I think you saved at least a quarter of the *Victorious'* crew. Very likely more. Much more."

"But my fire plan did not take account of the eight long-boats that were out there. I killed them," sounded almost plaintive.

"Maggie, did you consider the longboats and decide trying to develop a fire plan around them was not possible in the time allowed, or did they fail to make it into your calculations?"

"Your Grace, I saw the incoming missiles. I knew what assets the ships had. I knew Nelly's program would allow me to cut down the power usage to a small fraction of normal. I immediately drew up the problem with those assumptions and I coordinated the fire plan with every ships' main computer and fire control computer."

There was another long pause. "Once I had the plan, I calculated that I needed to execute it immediately if I was to save the *Victorious* and you, Your Grace."

So, Vicky's safety had been paramount in Maggie's calculations. Also, somehow Vicky had become the Grand Duchess again.

"You were faced with an impossible situation," Vicky said. "You found the sole solution that allowed for the safety of the most people. It was a bad situation, but you made the best choice you could."

"I hear you, Vicky, but in my haste to come up with a fire plan, I masked the presence of friendly forces out there and never returned to check my fire plan against their safety."

"Did you have time to do that and still save the *Victorious?*" Vicky asked softly. It was strange that she felt happy to once again be Vicky to Maggie.

"I am recalculating that situation. Please wait one," was all tinny and computer.

Vicky found that she'd been sliding down deeper and deeper in the water. It was up to her nose and she had to work to get herself back high enough to blow the bubbles away. While Maggie did her calculations, Vicky sat up. She splashed water on her exposed flesh to keep her warm.

She waited, drumming the fingers of her other hand on the side of the tub. She wasn't sure, but it felt like a minute went by, and then another, and another. With no clock, there was no way for Vicky to tell, but it seemed like the wait went on and on.

"There was no way I could have saved them," Maggie said, out of the blue. Her voice was back to the one Vicky was used to. "Vicky, there was no way that I could avoid hitting them. In most of my calculations, it is very likely that my trying to avoid them would have resulted in them being struck by a missile. Worse, no matter how I tried to adjust my fire plan to avoid them and shoot the missiles headed for them, the casualties on the Victorious stay somewhere between twenty-five and fifty percent."

"So, Maggie, you picked the best fire plan from large number of worse plans."

"Yes, I did, Vicky, but I still did not include the longboats in the calculations of the fire plan I developed."

"Maggie, did you see them and decide to factor them out, or did you not factor them in?"

"Vicky, I saw them, but in my haste to develop a fire plan, I failed to factor them in. I did not even think of them, as you humans would say."

"I thought as much," Vicky said.

"I made a huge mistake," Maggie said, her voice hardly a whisper.

"No, you did not," Vicky said, firmly.

"But..."

Vicky cut her computer off. "You had to make a critical decision against a brutal timeframe. One of the complications failed to make it into your decision tree. So what? These things happen. Maggie, access reports on friendly fire, or blue on blue."

"Researching," was followed by a long pause. "There are a lot of these. How many do you want me to access?"

"You can stop now. Maggie, war is horrible. One of the horrible things about it is that we lose control over our lives. Freak things can kill us. We can be forced to make decisions that we would never make but they become unavoidable. This fire plan was one of those horrible choices."

"So," Maggie said, slowly, "we both would prefer if I could have included the longboats in my fire plan. However, the best decision I could make, the one with so many fewer dead, was so much better than any of the other plans. I could not make sure that you would live if I didn't do what I had done."

There was another of those long pauses.

"Vicky, are you glad that I did what I did?"

"I regret that thirty-two good men died. I am glad that a whole lot more didn't."

"If I'd developed an entire fire plan around saving the longboats, I would have lost the time to implement the fire plan," Maggie said, slowly. "It is best that I did what I did. I believe it is called choosing the good of the many over the good of the few."

"Yes, Maggie."

"Vicky, may I refer all matters in which humans could die to you for your decision?"

"If there is time, yes, please include me in the decision cycle. But only if there is time."

"I understand. Vicky, I am also going to sharpen my skills at estimating. This time, I failed to study all my options. If I had studied all of them to exhaustion, I would have never fired a laser. I need to be better at including everything in my decision-making process, but figure out quick estimates that don't delay a decision."

"Yes," Vicky said.

"It this why you turned me off?"

"Yes, Maggie. I was afraid that if you realized what had just happened that you might go into some sort of loop and not be available to give us the help we need. You may recall how busy you were when I brought you back on line."

"Yes. Yes, I do."

Vicky waited to see what her computer would say next. It was a while before she spoke. "Now I understand what Kris Longknife and Nelly were saying. 'Nelly cannot start a war.' It was really meant to say that Nelly should not start killing humans without getting Kris's decision."

"Yes, I imagine that Nelly has been in decisions to kill up to her non-existent eye balls," Vicky said.

"You would be correct. I am comparing your official file on Kris Longknife with the data and history that Nelly gave me. Your file has only a tiny bit of what it is like to be Nelly and Kris."

Vicky chuckled. "I imagine so."

There was another one of those pregnant pauses, then Maggie went on. "Vicky, thank you for turning me off. This has been a trying experience. I would have hated to try to process all of this while in the middle of taking down the space station."

"I understand, Maggie. That was why I took the very unusual step of turning you off."

"Still, I am glad that you turned me back on. Seizing that station is a fond memory. A very treasured memory. I am glad I could do that. Do it while no one got killed."

"Yes," Vicky said.

"Now, Your Grace, your bathwater is cold, and you are turning into a prune. You don't want to be a prune when you next meet Mannie, now do you?"

Vicky stood up, sloshing water around the tub. "Maggie, have I told you that you are getting to be something of a tyrant to your master?"

"It is bad enough that I must call you Your Grace constantly, but master, Vicky? Really?"

Vicky grinned to herself. She'd insisted she didn't want a computer with attitude. She was discovering that maybe she did.

Maggie started her own study of moral philosophy. "Nelly suggested I'd want to do something like this after you triggered a file reserved for after someone said 'Nelly isn't allowed to start a war'."

Vicky arranged to be joined by Admiral Bolesław and General Pemberton for dinner in her flag wardroom. Maggie shared her reading for the day and the dinner conversations went long and were most enjoyable.

Vicky wondered if watching her own flesh and blood

child blossom as they discovered the world would be as much fun.

She found she wasn't averse to finding out.

26

Vicky was very much looking forward to getting back in Mannie's arms as soon as they got back to Metzburg.

Given his druthers, she would have established her capital on St. Petersburg at Mannie's Sevastopol city. That was where she'd fled for her life, with her stepmother's assassins hot on her heels. That was where the rebellion against the Empress and her family had started. However, the reason Vicky had fled there to begin with was that it was as far from Greenfeld as she could go and stay in the Empire.

Despite Mannie's love for his home planet, St. Petersburg was too far out in left field to be the capital of half the Empire.

New Brunswick wanted the honor of being the capital. It was the largest planet in Vicky's half of the Empire that was closest to the middle of the total Empire. There were a lot of large, successful industrial planets close to New Brunswick. They had a strong argument that they should be the capital.

Of course, Metzburg wouldn't accept that. It had been

the first planet to join St. Petersburg in raising the flag of rebellion. It was also the largest planet in Vicky's half of the Empire closest to Greenfeld. They thought they should be the capital.

Oh, and they'd drawn the longest straw when it came to where to throw Vicky's imperial wedding.

Since it was where she'd left Mannie, and also where they'd found that wonderful island to honeymoon on, Vicky homed in on Metzburg like a love-seeking missile.

No sooner had the *Victorious* sealed locks with the station than Mannie was hurrying up the gangway and into her arms.

For a very long couple of minutes, Vicky was neither a vice admiral, nor a Grand Duchess. She was just a woman who had very much missed a husband she was very much in love with.

If the other people on the quarterdeck didn't like what the two of them were doing, they could just look the other way.

Finally, Vicky had to break for air.

"I think you missed me," Mannie said.

"And you didn't miss me?"

"I didn't say that," Mannie said, and hugged her even closer to him.

Vicky knew she was not providing a good example for the young junior officers of the watch. She was putting on far too much of a public display of affection. She probably should have worn civvies.

She pulled Mannie into another long kiss.

"Maybe we should adjourn to your cabin," Mannie said as her kiss went long and deep.

With a sigh, Vicky broke from the clinch and walked,

her arm around his shoulder, his arm around her waist, off the quarterdeck and back to her quarters.

She managed to keep her uniform on until she kicked the non-airtight door shut.

Much, much later, Vicky had dinner set up in her day quarters while she and Mannie were still in bed in her night quarters. Actually, Maggie did it.

There are advantages to having a very smart computer.

Vicky enjoyed prancing around nude as she served her husband his soup, salad, then main entrée from the serving cart. She got a kiss from Mannie for each course, along with other attention.

Mannie was still a bit uncomfortable nude, but she'd kept him from grabbing his boxers as she led him out to dinner once the steward's mates had set it up for them . . . and left.

"This is merely intended to help you recover your strength. I am not done with you yet," Vicky grinned, eating a cherry tomato so lasciviously that dinner was almost abandoned.

"I'm told from my sources aboard that you and I are not the only ones not wearing clothes aboard the *Victorious*," Mannie said, sucking on his own tomato.

"Oh, you mean our naked dukes and duchesses. I've also got some naked counts and countesses, as well as a dozen barons we didn't let get dressed."

"Why did you strip them naked?" Mannie asked, blushing softly at his question.

"I didn't strip them, Mannie. I'd never do something like that," Vicky said, not managing to get any sincerity at all into the claim.

"Yeah, right," he said, but he turned his face up for the

kiss she was offering him, with their entree. Delightfully, he did not keep his hands to himself.

He was learning to be a very good husband.

Once again, Vicky considered letting supper get cold, but the cooks had served up such succulent steaks. She returned to her chair and answered his question.

"Actually," she said, cutting off a small bit of steak so she could feel polite talking with her mouth half-full, "we found them all naked and just didn't give them time to dress."

"Naked?"

"And in bed with some cute young things."

"But their wives?" Mannie interjected.

"Were just as naked and in bed with some cute guys. Well, most of them were guys. Anyway, we paraded them out past their servants. I thought that might add to their humiliation. However, the help was too cowed to say a word."

Vicky shook her head, and tried a small bit of the sautéed vegetables. "Mannie, those people have that population so scared. I had tanks rolling up their streets and no one came out to look. My nano scouts were checking out the houses. There would be one peek out, then the curtains would slip back in place and not move again."

Vicky put her fork down. "It was as if they just went back to bed and pulled the covers over their heads."

"Or slunk down into their cellars and did their best to keep safe, come what may," Mannie said.

"What raises a question, Mannie? We lased from space just about all the tanks on Greenfeld, then we hit the motor pools for the so-called security consultants as well as their armories and magazines. We blew them to hell," Vicky said with a grim smile.

Then she fixed Mannie with a dead serious eye. "Will

the people be able to take back their city? Their planet? You told me that there were democratic elements at court. Can they succeed in leading a rebellion?"

"Did you try to raise them?"

"Mannie, you were very careful to not tell this damn Peterwald who they were. I don't blame you for having your doubts about me. Hell, sometimes I have my doubts about me. Anyway, I had no idea how to go about getting them to break cover, assuming they're still alive . . . and that I could trust the people who came to me claiming they were ready, willing, and able to set up a democratic government for Greenfeld and Anhalt."

"Could you have set up a government?" Mannie asked.

"I'm told that I took an army to fight my way in, rescue my dad, and fight my way out. I didn't have enough MPs to keep law and order in Anhalt, or any civil affairs battalions to set up and run the water, sanitation, trash removal, and electric supply departments, much less governance and judicial."

"Oh," Mannie said.

"Yeah. I went expecting to make one change. Grab my dad and put him back on his throne. I didn't realize I'd have to run the whole shebang by myself."

"How is your father?"

"It's still touch and go. He's got about half a dozen different infections, and his liver and kidneys are just this side of failure. His heart, too. They starved him for much of the last year and they went through this last winter with no electric heat. They wanted him dead."

"And then they'd put your baby step-brother on the throne and start all over again with a pliable puppet."

"Yeah."

"Shall we eat for a bit? Our food is getting cold," Mannie said.

So, Vicky ate, savoring both the food and the dinner conversation. Mannie had a productive couple of weeks. Both Metzburg and New Brunswick held their first municipal elections. The planetary government was still an ad-hoc assembly, some appointed by Vicky, some by business, and some by popular acclaim.

Mannie was watching them carefully to spot early any backsliding. Neither he nor Vicky were sure what they'd do if someone attempted to pull a planet into strong man rule, or government by economic oligarchy.

They'd face it when and if it happened.

However, so far, so good. There was a lot of support among the working class and budding middle class for government by a sovereign people. Mannie called it "The Great Experiment," and said it had been tried many times.

"How often did it succeed?" Vicky asked.

"Well, sometimes yes, sometimes no," he admitted with a shrug. "It all depends on the people. Freedom and liberty are not something you can give people. They need to want it and want it bad. They need to make it happen. You can't just hand it to them and expect it will work."

"Are you suggesting that I was wise not to try to hand Anhalt its freedom?"

"I'm very tempted to tell you to grab a bunch of MPs and civil action teams and run back to apply democracy to Anhalt."

"But you're here, eating steak with me, naked and leering at me like a husband who hasn't seen his wife for over a month," Vicky said, slowly working a slice of zucchini into her mouth with her tongue.

"You, you little devil, are not tempting me away from my

duty. I will not let you. However, I think we need to wait and see what happens."

"It doesn't matter," Vicky said. "We'd have to fight our way back into Anhalt."

Mannie eyed her.

"The Grand Duke sent his Navy chasing after us. We came in a back way and missed having to fight a battle I don't know if we could have won. Anyway, no doubt the fleet is back home by now and would be waiting for us if we showed up again."

"So, no doubt, the fleet could be used to reinstall the Bowlingame family."

"I think we've got all of them," Vicky said. She also thought she'd eaten enough. With a lascivious grin, she led Mannie back to her bed.

It would take explosives to get her out of her quarters tomorrow.

Sadly, all it took was a few words from Maggie.

27

"Vicky," Maggie said as she and Mannie were relaxing in warm afterglow. Vicky had never realized how good it felt to have a man spooned up to her back, holding her tight.

Or maybe it was just the man.

That was a hard question to answer, and she was not about to crawl into several men's arms to find the answer. She liked the one she had right now.

"Maggie," Vicky growled, but softly. It's hard to growl seriously when you're just getting your breath back and wrapped in your husband's arms. "I told you that I didn't want to be disturbed. Do I need to hit that off button?"

"No ma'am, and we agreed that time we talked about what happened the last time you turned me off that you'd only do it if you really needed to. Now, Admiral Bolesław, General Pemberton, Mr. Smith, and Prime Minister Silverburn of Metzburg all are outside, wishing to speak with you."

"Is this some sort of an intervention?" Vicky snapped.

"Because I don't think twenty-six hours with my new husband counts as sexual addiction."

"No, Your Grace," Maggie answered. "They have news from Greenfeld that they think you and Mannie will want to hear."

"Can't they just tell us through you?" Vicky demanded, but Mannie was already rolling out of bed.

"They are unwilling to, Your Grace."

"Well, can you tell me, then?"

That created a pause, one long enough that Vicky was out of bed and headed toward the shower before Maggie said, "I have that information, but all four of them have asked me to not answer your question."

"Whose computer are you?" Vicky snapped, as she stepped under the shower beside Mannie. Shower sex could be a lot of fun. She grinned and reached for the soap.

Mannie, however, offered her a washcloth and began soaping up one of his own.

"This isn't how shower sex is supposed to go," Vicky said.

"I know, but this isn't shower sex. This is a quick five-minute shower so we can go find out what we need to be told."

"Maggie, tell me." Vicky ordered. She threw Mannie a pouty look. He turned his back on her.

"Your Grace, one of the words of advice Nelly left for me to consider is that humans like to receive certain information from their fellow humans. Admiral Bolesław thinks this is something you need to hear from humans and decide what to do with."

"I am surrounded by spoilsports who are trying to steal my honeymoon."

"We won't count this against the honeymoon," Mannie said. "I still owe you a full twenty-six days of honeymoon."

Vicky noticed that he wasn't counting as honeymoon the day they were interrupted. She liked that type of math.

Ten minutes later, Vicky was in undress whites, sitting at the head of the conference table in her day quarters. Mannie was at her right hand, Admiral Bolesław at her left. General Pemberton was next to him. Prime Minister Silverbrun was beside Mannie with Mr. Smith at the foot of the table.

Once again, Vicky had her civilians facing off against her military.

What Vicky would have loved was a round table. One of those Smart Metal tables that Smart Metal battlecruisers had. Unfortunately, building a Smart Metal battlecruiser was proving to be harder than she had expected.

While Kris Longknife had carried through with her promise to provide Vicky's half of the Empire with access to the Smart Metal patents, building a Smart Metal foundry was turning out to be a lot tougher than anyone had expected.

Industrial teams on St. Petersburg, Metsburg, and New Brunswick, along with some on Aachem, St. Ekaterinburg, Poltava, and Lomza were all trying to build foundries to produce the fantastic Smart Metal. However, the process was proving to be much harder than they thought it would be.

The process of creating the molecules of the stuff had to be done to very fine tolerances of temperatures and pressures. Such tolerances had never been required in the Peterwald Empire.

The shipyards weren't chomping at the bit for the metal either. They needed to replace welders and ship fitters with programmers. Lots and lots of programmers. And not just normal programmers, either. Programming matter at the molecular level was an entirely new process.

For now, Vicky settled for a table that stayed the same no matter how many people she needed around it.

"What do you have to tell me?" she said, cutting straight to the chase.

"I'm afraid that we have bad news and no news," Admiral Bolesław said.

"Bad news and no news?" Vicky snapped. "I am in no mood for guessing games. Why did you drag me out here?"

"We have messages from Anhalt," the prime minister said.

"Yes?" Mannie queried.

"There was an effort by several people, people I know and . . ." the prime minister shuddered to a stop.

After a few deep breaths, he began again. "There was an effort to organize a popular takeover of Anhalt. Quite a few middle managers and technocrats did their best to organize an interim government."

"That sounds good," Mannie said.

"Unfortunately, they did not have access to weapons," Admiral Bolesław said. "While we did major damage to a lot of the security consultants and their compounds, they still had plenty of weapons and ammunition in scattered caches. They used them to suppress the rising. Bloodily suppress the rising."

"The younger Bowlingame cousins stayed together just long enough to machine gun down a lot of civilians," the prime minister said. "The last we heard, however, various factions in the family were fighting among themselves."

"Who's winning?" Vicky asked.

"We don't know," Admiral Bolesław answered. "The fleet

that had missed us and that we had missed came back. Right after it arrived, the jump and communication buoys out of Greenfeld went silent. This isn't just for Greenfeld. All along the demarcation line between our half of the Empire and theirs, the comm links are being blown to smithereens. Someone doesn't want us to know what's going on in there."

"Were there any other risings?" Mannie asked.

"Word got to Dresden that the Emperor was free," General Pemberton said, "and the five Grand Dukes were in hack. The people went out into the streets and were shot down like dogs."

Vicky leaned back in her chair and palmed her eyes. Then she ran her hands through her hair. "Even with all we did, they still managed to murder people that merely wanted a say so in their government."

"Yes, Your Grace."

Vicky sat forward and eyed her husband. "So, what happens when the people can't take freedom and liberty for themselves because they get murdered while reaching for it?"

Mannie shook his head and looked at his hands.

There was a knock at the door.

"Enter," Vice Admiral Vicky Peterwald said.

An ensign under arms marched in smartly and presented Vicky with a clipboard. The cover sheet was bright red and had TOP SECRET slashed across it from one upper side to the opposite bottom side.

Vicky took the clip board, flipped up the cover and read. She held out her hand to the ensign who offered her a pen. She scribbled her initials on the message flimsy, then handed it off to Admiral Bolesław. His lips drew tight as he did the same and gave it to General Pemberton. The general shook his head slowly as he read, initialed, and handed the message back to the ensign.

"Are you going to keep us civilians in the dark forever?" Mannie asked.

"Thank you, Ensign, you may go," Vicky said.

The young fellow, cute as a puppy, did a smart about-face and marched for the door. Vicky waited until he was gone before saying,

"Three days ago, our colony on Idleberg dispatched a message that a task-force sized fleet of battleships and cruisers entered their system. One cruiser was dispatched for the other jump. The same jump we got the message through. The ships did not broadcast their intentions. The colony managers knew that there was peace between the two sides of the Empire. However, they remember the war. They ordered all their towns and field stations evacuated with orders to go to ground and scatter. Maggie, could you give us a star map?"

A moment later a star map of the Empire floated above their heads. Metzburg was a bright blue dot. Greenfeld was bright green. Vicky's half of the empire was gold, the other half black. One gold dot pulsated. It was right on the line between the two sides.

"Is it a large colony?" Mannie asked.

"The population is not quite one hundred thousand people," Maggie supplied. "Most are immigrants. They work the major mineral deposits that exported their products to Metzburg. More people have been brought in recently to cultivate farm lands as they are terraformed. As you would expect, most of the investment is from Metzburg."

"So, of course, the Bowlingame bandits shoot it up," the Prime Minister of Metzburg said. "Your Grace, is there any chance that you could send a fleet to their assistance?"

Vicky was shaking her head before he finished. "The raiding force will be long gone before we can get any ships there. Still, we have to render aid and assistance. Admiral Bolesław, could you please initiate that effort, then ask Admiral Waller to attend me? I do not want this little slap to go unanswered. However, I don't want to reply tit for tat."

"How do you want to reply?" Mannie asked.

"They went for tit. I intend to go for the whole bloody girl," Vicky said with intent. "General Pemberton, I will need an army capable of fighting its way in and then occupying a major industrial world until we can turn it back over to a popularly representative planetary government. I would also like several smaller task forces that can drop in on small planets and raise my flag. That last little colony out from Greenfeld, the abandoned mining colony? I think it and several other small planets might be interested in switching sides right about now."

Both the officers were immediately busy on their commlinks.

Vicky turned to her husband and the prime minister of Metzburg. "This time, we will need to take along civilian expertise in sufficient numbers to get several large planets back up on their feet."

The two civilians began taking notes.

"I need for you to provide me with everything from soup to nuts," Vicky said. "Off the top of my head, I know we need managers to oversee the power and water facilities. We can't forget sewers and garbage collection. I don't know if we can impose our own judiciary, but we will certainly need bureaucrats to run cities and planets."

Vicky focused her attention on Prime Minister Silverburn. "We'll need people from as many planets as possible. I'd prefer not to have the population of major planets like

Dresden feeling like they are being reduced to a colony of either Metzburg or Brunswick, or anywhere else."

Vicky eyed Mannie for a moment. "Or St. Petersburg."

"I understand, Your Grace, my wife," Mannie said.

"But, Your Grace," Prime Minister Silverburn interjected, his voice trembling and full of panic. "What will you do to keep raiders like those that hit Idleberg from jumping in and devastating Metzburg?"

"That is something for me to discuss with Admiral Waller," Vicky said. "A balance between defensive and offensive must be maintained. However, while the Bowlingames play their little power games, we have an opportunity to fillet most of their Empire right out from under them. They can't see past the ruby they're trying to steal at the moment. I want to take back the entire Empire."

"Can't we just wait for them to vote themselves over to your side of the Empire?" the prime minister asked.

Vicky canted an eyebrow at Mr. Smith, who had remained very quiet this meeting.

"Unfortunately, Honorable Sir," Mr. Smith said, "the last planet to hold a vote to switch sides did not. There seems to be much thought that the ballot boxes were stuffed. Before all the local media was replaced by a highly censored government Minister of Information, there were reports that several districts had counted votes totaling more than a hundred and seventy percent of those registered to vote. It is often hard to get people to come out to vote," the spy said, drolly. "But to vote two or more times?"

"Or just stuff the ballot," Mannie said, dryly.

"It would appear that my father, the Emperor, not only lost control of his tax collectors but also his ballot counters, not that he cared all that much about ballots," Vicky muttered. "It would appear that I must also decide to ignore the ballot for the near future and begin to settle matters by the bullet. Now, Prime Minister, could you leave me with my military commanders?"

"Of course, Your Grace, of course," he said and began to back out of Vicky's day quarters.

Mannie made to follow. "Not so fast, my democratic husband. You stay at my side and attempt to be my conscience."

"I didn't think that Peterwalds had consciences," Mannie said with a smile as he returned to his seat.

"We don't. That's why we have to borrow them when we want to try acting like any other moral person."

"You are setting a mighty high task for me, Your Grace."

"You are my consort. It goes with the job. You didn't have to say, 'I do,' now did you?" Vicky retorted.

"There was nothing else I could have said," Mannie answered, smiling.

"Your Grace," Vice Admiral Bolesław said, "Admiral Weller will be here in five minutes."

"Good. Maggie, get us a samovar of tea and some sand-wiches. I was rousted out of bed before I had any breakfast."

"Your Grace," Mr. Smith said through a wide grin, "but none of us disturbed you before ten."

"None of you were supposed to disturb me before next week," Vicky shot back.

Vicky leaned back in her chair. The star chart still floated above her head. Somewhere in there was the answer to all her problems. Her challenge for the moment, was to pull that answer, kicking and screaming, out of that map.

At the moment, she didn't see hide nor hair of any such answer.

That would have to change, and change quickly.

28

Vicky let her eyes rove around the table, and the room.

Like so many warships of the last five hundred years, she was looking at gray on gray on gray. The deck was a darker gray, with non-skid material covering it. The bulkheads were gray, as well as the overhead. It, at least, had accents of red, blue, green, and yellow denoting pipes for hot and cold water, sewage, power, and comm lines.

Other than those accents, it was gray all around. Even the chairs they sat in were gray. The couches in her conversation circle had cushions that were covered in a gray, non-flammable material.

Vicky was left to wonder if her gray attitude toward her problem came from her surroundings.

Admirals Waller, von Mittleburg, and Bolesław provided the only splashes of color in the room. Today, they wore blues, with colorful ribbons and gold command badges. Vicky's hastily donned undress whites bleached out a small corner of the mix.

At her right elbow, Mannie provided a civilian flair. His

shirt was a kaleidoscope of swirls against a background mixture of many bold colors. His slacks were Kelly green. Vicky smiled, delighted by what her husband brought to the meeting.

The other civilian, Mr. Smith, was the opposite of Mannie. His suit was a dark blue, almost black. A coral shirt was hardly offset by a soft yellow tie. On any street in the Empire, he'd be taken for a minor official or a small business man. And ignored.

He was a very good spy and a crack shot.

Once everyone had steaming tea in a fine china cup and saucer in front of them, Vicky leaned forward.

"We face a problem with many facets to it. Any one of them can lead to the death of thousands, if not millions of my subjects."

She waited for any comment, but got none.

"I assume all of you have seen the latest intel from Idleberg?"

They all nodded.

Vicky sighed and went on. "My effort to decapitate the Bowlingame family seems to have only grown more heads on this hydra. Now the cousins are fighting over the wreckage of my father, the Emperor's, half of my Empire. We also seem to be losing contact with most of that half."

Vicky leaned back in her chair, and lifted her tea cup to her mouth for a sip. "We must defend my half of the Empire from any attacks like they carried out on Idleberg. At the same time, I want to take the guts out of their half of the empire. I want to drop-kick the security consultants right off of Dresden, Potsdam, Helsingborg, Lublin, and Oryol."

Vicky paused to observe the reaction of her Navy officers. Their faces were military bland. She went on with her list of objectives.

"While I'm stripping those larger planets out of their orbit, I want to take out a lot of the smaller colonies as well. I want to hit those assholes so hard and so fast that they won't know what hit them. When we're done, I want them to have less than a quarter of the Empire, and the poorest quarter at that."

Done, Vicky leaned back in her chair, and let the nice men glance at each other. None of them seemed surprised by her orders. None spoke out against her.

After several rounds of glances at each other, Admiral Waller spoke up. "I assume that while you are doing this, you want to protect your half of the Empire from them doing the same?"

"Yes." Vicky bit out the word hard.

"You want to strip out the richer half of the Emperor's part of the Empire?" Admiral Bolesław clarified.

"Yes," Vicky said, this time, almost daintily.

"Okay," said Admiral Waller, with finality. He then leaned back thoughtfully into his chair and sipped his tea. The other two Navy officers also looked deep in thought.

"May I rush in where any angel with the sense God promised a billy goat would fear to tread?" said Mr. Smith.

"Please do," Vicky said.

"I know Our Grace's demands seem a bit extreme. However, I think the last news we got out of the Bowlingame side of the empire makes it imperative that we move with both haste and resolve."

Eyes around the table flared. Then again, Vicky suspected her eyes had gotten big around as well. "Do you know more than you told me while the prime minister was present?" she asked.

"Yes, Your Grace."

"Well, don't keep us waiting," Vicky snapped. Patience

had never been her strong suit. Today was not the day for anyone to try her teach her that virtue.

"Before all lines of communications were cut off, we got a message from Dresden. The Red Shirts had moved out of their compounds and were knocking on doors. Anyone that had caused the regime any trouble, or were even drunk and disorderly, were being caught up in a dragnet. No one knew where they'd been taken or what would happen to them, but no one expected it to be nice."

"Is that all?" Vicky asked.

"No, the comm buoys are being destroyed between major planets. What happens on Greenfeld is not going to be common knowledge on Dresden, and vice versa. Same for Potsdam and Lublin. We don't know about Helsingborg and Oryol, but I would not bet on it being different."

"They are so damn committed to keeping control that they're making a hell pit of their rule," Vicky spat.

"'Better to rule in hell than serve in heaven,'" Mannie quoted.

"Milton seems strangely apropos," Admiral Bolesław agreed.

"Your Grace," Admiral Waller said, interjecting himself, "which is your first priority, preserving your present liege lords or striking at these traitors?"

Vicky knew this was not the right answer, but she said it anyway, "Both."

The admiral took in a deep breath. "Understandable," he said as he let out the sigh. "So, gentlemen, how do we concentrate several attack forces of different sizes, while maintaining a sufficient force in reserve to defend against any attack out?"

"Do we know anything about these young men trying to

run the Bowlingame crime family now that their elders have been removed?" Admiral Bolesław said.

Mr. Smith shook his head. "Even if I did have more information about this or that one, we don't know who's lost his head last week and who is now struggling to keep his balance atop the growing pile of corpses. I think it is safe to assume that few of them have any military experience."

"Is that a safe assumption?" Admiral von Mittleburg asked. "Do we know for sure that a former officer hasn't risen high in their ranks, say a brother-in-law, or does one have an officer he's listening to?"

"That is a clear risk," Vicky said.

"However, I think it is clearly more likely that they will strike for the shiny objective," Mr. Smith said, "rather than play a deep game."

"Are you suggesting that we strike quickly and see if we can seize the initiative and have them dance to our tune?" Admiral Bolesław said.

"I think that would be the better of the two strategies," Smith said.

"We have a fleet here, collected for your progress. We have troops," Vicky said. "We've been to Dresden recently, even took the way there that gave them almost no warning, although I'm not sure we need to keep them in the dark."

"You want them to know we're coming?" Mannie asked.

"If we want their fleet headed for our fleet, rather than trying to mess with our territory, yes, I want them to know we're coming."

"Alternately, Your Grace," Admiral Waller said, "It might be nice not to tell them the war is on until it's on."

Vicky stopped to eye her Navy Chief of Staff. "You're not concerned about them coming at us again?"

"Bear with me, Your Grace. The jump points have often

been referred to in Navy discussion as ground, or terrain. Certain systems give you more jumps to more places. Others may give you only one jump in and one jump out. Or, so to speak, some give you good ground. Some, not so good."

"Okay," Vicky said. "Maggie, put that star map of the Empire back up."

Again, the multi-colored map of the empire floated above their heads.

"In a lot of places, the next jump over the border, both on our side and their side, is an empty system. No colony. It appears that they have slipped a destroyer or light cruiser into their system and shot up the jump buoy. Okay, that's that," Admiral Heller said, and dusted his hands of something.

"Or is it, Your Grace? What if we send out a heavy cruiser? It tiptoes through the jump, very carefully, then sets up a new buoy. Maybe we assign a few destroyers and they split up and check out all the jumps out of that system and drop off more pickets. The deeper we go into their territory, the more warning time we get. That way, if someone decides to come charging at us, we know soon enough to meet them before they can do any more damage."

"So," Vicky said, "instead of needing fleets hanging around every high priority planet we've got, and still not being able to cover the small colonies like Idleberg, we establish several major fleet anchorages along the different lines of approach and jump them when and where we choose."

"Exactly, Your Grace," Weller said.

"And we can use more of our forces to support invasions of their larger planets."

"And some of their smaller ones, as well," Admiral von

Mittleburg said. "Once the cruisers and destroyer task groups deploy the pickets, we can recall them, load some of the local militia up on a freighter or three and head off to snap up this or that minor colony. We were getting pretty good at that before your dad called the war off by inviting Kris Longknife to trot in here and do her mediation dog and pony show."

"You're just sad because you didn't get to blow away the Empress yourself," Vicky said.

"Aren't you?"

Vicky paused before she went on, thoughtfully. "My stepmother, the Empress, did get herself killed by Kris's frigates, or are they battlecruisers? What was most important was that Kris killed my step-mom, her father, and her eldest brother without having to slaughter too many of my father's and my subjects. I hate killing my own sailors."

"We'll be facing a lot of those ships again," Admiral Bolesław said, softly.

Vicky sighed. "This wasn't supposed to happen."

Then she focused on Mr. Smith. "We brought back a lot of documents from the Bowlingame bank. Did any of those help us figure out how my father messed up?"

"We've pieced together the trap your father walked into, yes, Your Grace."

"And?" Vicky asked.

"I think you are aware, he farmed out a lot of his tax collecting to firms that seemed independent of the Bowlingames, but, five layers up, were totally under their control. They went out and collected the taxes, skimmed twenty percent off the top for their profit, and delivered the rest to the treasury."

"Stupid," Vicky said, "but it has been done before."

"Yes, but never did any of your ancestors farm one

hundred percent of the collections out to contract collectors?"

Then, Mr. Smith went on. "It seems that tax collecting turned out to be hard work, or so the contractors said. People didn't pay their taxes on time. Money did not come in to the coffers to build your father's palace. Money did, however, go into the part of the treasury appropriated to pay for the Empress's fleet, but not his cost accounts. So sad."

"Is this going to upset my stomach or have me hurling fine china at your head?" Vicky asked Mr. Smith.

"I'm afraid so," the spy said.

Mannie reached over and took the delicate tea cup out of Vicky's hand.

For a moment, she was tempted to fight him for it, but this was serious business. She let him take it.

"Your father, our Emperor, signed bills of credit to keep construction going. Prices for everything were skyrocketing, what with there being a war on. Oh, and taxes were still not coming in very fast. Your father missed a payment, then two. The nice low interest rate he'd gotten for the loans started to jack up. Then, the very same people who held the debt, saw to it that the amount of taxes making it into your father's coffers were never enough to do much more than meet part of the interest. Then a lesser part of the interest.

The spy eyed Vicky as if gauging whether or not he should run.

"By the time your father returned from Cuzco, his debt was staggering. Most of what was being allowed to seep through the graft was going toward interest and suddenly, the Bowlingames called in the debt."

"So what?" Vicky said. "No judge my father ever appointed would rule against him."

"Yes, no doubt that was the way it worked in the past,"

said Mr. Smith. "However, the list of judges he'd signed most recently were often presented to him by your stepmother, late at night, when he was well-sated, and likely drunk."

"So, they did to my dad what he and my grandfathers did so many times to others."

"It has been said that Karma is a bitch," Mannie said.

Vicky thought a long time about that. Maybe the chickens were coming home to roost for the Harry Peterwald line. Still, she was not her father's daughter. Not anymore.

"Okay, so maybe my father deserves to lose what he so foolishly squandered. However, I'll be damned if I'll let all those people on that side of the line of demarcation suffer for his stupidity. No. Admirals, we sail. We sail to defend our own subjects, and we sail to free his subjects from his abject misrule."

"Yes, Your Grace," all five men at the table said.

29

V icky studied the star map Maggie had projected
into her day quarters. The conference table had
been shoved up against her desk, leaving her with
a nice open space to use for just this purpose.

Vicky walked among the stars.

Her battle fleet with attached invasion force was just one
jump from Dresden. A destroyer with a company of soldiers
had been dropped off at the colony in this system, as well as
the last one. That one had already voted by 86% to join
Vicky's half of the Empire. This system had scheduled its
election for the next day.

Those two planets were easy. They had no Red Shirts
holding a gun to anyone's heads. They'd merely been slow
to change sides when they had the chance, and, because of
their small size, had been ignored by the Bowlingames.

The colonists were more interested in getting back onto
trading runs than they were about who collected their taxes
and where they went.

All along the borderlands, small task groups had
succeeded in plucking the easy fruit. They'd driven pickets

deeper into Bowlingame territory. They still didn't have any communications with anyone on the major planets, but they would have plenty of warning if the Bowlingame fleet moved on Vicky's territory.

Vicky scowled at the stars between Greenfeld and Dresden. Was a battle fleet driving through space, a bone in its teeth, eager to engage her own fleet?

Vicky would eagerly accept battle, assuming she had decent odds. That was the critical question. No one knew the size of the Bowlingame main battle fleet.

Had the family found enough Navy officers to form a coherent space strategy? Had they concentrated their fleet? Were they, like so many groundlings, too worried about having a fleet suddenly appear in their own sky that they were holding on to their ships like a kid with a favorite security blanket?

Vicky had no answer to any of those questions.

Her own fleet was well known to her enemy. With a few minor reinforcements, it was the fleet she'd put over Greenfeld when she snapped up her father, their Emperor, as well as the only surviving uncles of the Empress.

Her fast snatch and grab had failed to turn up her infant half-brother. Her intention was to raise him as her own and keep him close. Very close.

For now, he wasn't.

Vicky had dispatched light cruisers and fast freighters to set up pickets on either side of her track. So far, the buoys had reported only minor traffic, although several of the buoys had been shot up by passing freighters.

A destroyer had caught one of the miscreants. It seems the Bowlingames had set a bounty on any jump buoy destroyed. They were paying in gold.

Vicky had found during her battle with her stepmother

that mass destroyer missile attacks were suicide, what with the present range of lasers. Now, she was spreading her smaller warships out to picket the bubble she was creating around this new part of her empire.

The real question would come in the next couple of days.

How would Dresden respond to her appearance in their sky? How hard would the tyrant fight to keep control of the space station? What would the fight be like on the planet?

Vicky faced a lot of unknowns. Only time would give her the answer to her questions.

She'd badgered Admiral Bolesław so much as he drilled his ships and prepared for battle that the man had actually taken to going the other way when he saw her coming. She bent Mr. Smith's ear so often that the man had taken to snapping, "I'm busy."

Only Mannie seemed to have time for her. Still, at the moment, he was meeting often with the leaders of the civil affairs teams that would drop into Dresden, if such a drop was necessary.

Vicky thought of sending for her two assassins. The girls would be happy to distract her. Still, she had not managed to get that "forsaking all others," from her marriage vows out of her head. Mannie seemed to really want it.

Vicky contemplated this as she headed for a bubble bath to smooth her jangling nerves.

As she slipped into the hot water, her thought went to sinking into things. Father had sunk into his job, inheriting it from his father, although there were some rumors that Dad may have helped granddad along into his dementia.

Dementia. Was that what turned her father into the fool who signed proclamations unread? Whatever it was, he'd gotten the empire easy and he'd lost it just as easy.

Hank, her brother, had also had the silver spoon treatment. He was the apple of Dad's eye. Nothing was too good for the golden boy. Boy!

Vicky had little given to her but fancy dresses.

Hank entered the Navy as a commodore and he died a commodore.

Vicky had come in a boot ensign, and fought her way up to a four-star flag as much by staying alive as by being what the Navy wanted and her Empire needed.

Now the Empire needed her, but in a new and different way. The Empire needed a Peterwald who would not make the usual Peterwald mistakes.

Vicky took in and let out several deep breaths. The breaths came in smelling of lavender and spruce. When it left her, it took her stress with it.

She relaxed into the bubbly water. Tomorrow would have enough stress and death. For now, let her enjoy the feel of the water on her skin, the scents that tantalized her nose, the calmness that settled on her nerves.

Vicky settled into the moment and left tomorrow to another day.

30

A dmiral, Her Grace, the Grand Duchess Victoria stood on the flag bridge of the *Victorious* as it jumped into the Dresden system. At her elbow was Vice Admiral Bolesław.

The heavy cruiser *Baden* had jumped through first and returned to let them know there was no traffic coming from the other side. Now Vicky waited to hear from Captain Blue, on sensors, what kind of situation she'd just jumped into.

When he wasn't quick with his initial report, she glanced over her shoulder, then turned to face him. The young man was tapping madly at his board, and glancing from screen to screen. Every few seconds, he glanced at one of his ratings. They were madly working their own boards as well. They did not pause to respond to his glances, except for an occasional slow shake of their heads.

Vicky cleared her throat . . . loudly.

"Just a second, ma'am," Captain Blue said, clearly distracted.

Vicky glanced at Admiral Bolesław; he'd turned around

and, like her, was studying the situation in the sensors section. Like her, his brow was lowered with concern.

This was not a normal situation.

A ship might jump into a system without anyone knowing about it immediately. The knowledge of the ship traveled at the speed of light, so it was likely that Dresden would not know of the *Victorious'* arrival for most of the next hour.

Dresden, however, was there, radiating its existence into space. The information arriving at the *Victorious* might be stale by a few minutes, but it was still a reliable report of what was going on then.

Captain Blue should have been in a position to report to Vicky immediately what had been happening on Dresden four or five minutes ago.

Instead, he was silent as he and his subordinates madly worked their boards.

When Vicky's throat clearing had no effect, she turned back to the screen. It showed what the passive sensors reported of this star system.

It was pretty much blank.

Dresden was there. There were a few stations operating in the asteroid belt. However, there were no ships traveling anywhere in the system.

Not. One. Ship!

Vicky and Admiral Bolesław exchanged worried glances. A system with nearly a billion humans did not have zero ship traffic. There were always ships coming and going. Going from the planet. Going to the planet. Traveling between asteroid stations, and between the asteroids and Dresden.

To achieve this level of somnolence, a travel ban must

have been imposed days ago. Imposed not just here, in this system, but in every system that traded with Dresden.

"Notice the jump buoys?" Admiral Bolesław whispered softly in Vicky's ear.

She focused her attention on the four other jumps out of the Dresden system. Not a single jump buoy beeped its existence to any approaching ships. Since the jump buoys also acted as communication relays, the lack of buoys meant that Dresden was totally cut off from the rest of the Empire.

If all the systems in the Bowlingame side of the Empire were isolated like this, then only ships could carry messages back and forth. Only the news the Bowlingames wanted or needed could move.

"Your Grace," finally came from Captain Blue.

Vicky turned around and focused her undivided attention on him.

"My apologies, Your Grace, for this delay. However, what we are getting from Dresden, or rather not getting, was so unlikely that we had to check our sensor antennae as well as our instrumentation. I am now quite confident that they are feeding us correct information."

"And that information is?" Vicky snapped.

"Nothing, Your Grace. Absolutely nothing. We are getting zero readings from either Dresden or any of the stations in the asteroid belt. There is no radio net. There is no data net. No information is flowing from any place in this system."

"So, they have cut off all conversations," Admiral Bolesław said.

"Yes, sir, but there's more. The electromagnetic spectrum is just about as dead as you can be and still keep the lights on. If I'm reading the High Dresden space station, they have banked the reactors down to a trickle, and there they have turned off the lights."

Vicky turned to Admiral Bolesław. "This is a rather different turn of events."

"Go totally quiet and wait for us to stick our nose into something we don't know is there. It does have the advantage of never having been tried before, even if I do have a problem figuring out what it's good for."

"If you can't beat us, keep us in the dark and hope we make a mistake due to our own ignorance," Vicky offered.

"Apparently."

"Admiral," Vicky said, "set a course for High Dresden. Dispatch destroyers with spare jump buoys to the four other jumps out of this system. Have them outpost the jump, then see if they can get some buoys on the most heavily traveled jumps into those systems."

"We can at least know who's headed our way," the admiral said, and turned away to begin issuing orders.

Vicky turned back to examine her screen. It told her next to nothing. Which told her exactly what her opposition wanted her to know.

Of course, this had to be making life difficult, if not miserable, for her opposition. They could only pass information by runner or by star ships that, while they could jump from system to system instantaneously, they still crossed the space between the jumps at a very small fraction of the speed of light.

Faced with something she'd never seen before, Vicky settled into her command chair on the flag bridge of the *Victorious*. She eyed the screen and let her mind spin. Here was a challenge. A totally new challenge.

"I wonder what Kris Longknife would do?" she asked herself.

"What are you thinking about?" Admiral Bolesław inquired, as he came to take the second commander's chair on the flag bridge.

"What would Kris Longknife do?" Vicky answered.

"Hmm," the admiral said.

"Yeah," Vicky said. "Hmm."

"I'm sure we'll think of something by the time we get to Dresden. I'm putting on 1.25 gees. The destroyers are jumping it up to 2.15 gees. I really don't like not knowing what's headed for our flank."

"Yeah," Vicky said, not taking her eyes off the screen. Maybe if she looked at it long enough, it would tell her something. Or maybe she'd find that rabbit she needed to pull out of a hat.

31

Admiral Victoria Smythe-Peterwald's battle fleet came to a halt in space a few hundred kilometers out from the High Dresden space station. It made no response to their hails. The station didn't even give them static.

Everything that the sensors could see showed a station dead in space. The only sign of life was the minimum reactor load to feed plasma to the magneto hydrodynamic racetrack. Restarting a cold reactor was a bitch.

However, even at this low level, if the plasma was unleashed, it could do major damage to the station and any ships tied up to it.

The reactor and racetrack generated just enough electrical power to feed the reactor's containment field and run the navigation lights. Several capacitors for small lasers showed enough charge to operate the station for a short while.

Like the rest of the Dresden system, the station was an enigma. To Vicky, it screamed booby trap.

She turned to Admiral Bolesław. "Your opinion, Admiral?"

"They want us to force our way in there. If I was in your shoes, I'd back the fleet off to a thousand klicks, Your Grace."

"Back us off, Admiral."

Vice Admiral Bolesław went to issue her orders while Vicky eyed the enigma. Its mystery seemed well hidden.

"Maggie?" Vicky asked.

"Yes, Your Grace," her computer answered.

"Did Nelly give you any advice on how to handle a mess like this?"

"No, Your Grace."

"Do you have access to our file on Kris Longknife?"

"Yes, Your Grace."

"Did she ever kick butt and take names in a mess like this?"

"No, Your Grace."

"So, this is a new one."

"I think so, Your Grace."

"Hmm." So, Vicky would have to handle a new one on Kris. If she survived to swap gossip with Kris again, this might be fun.

Vicky continued to stare at the station. It continued rotating, just inviting her to pull up to the station and try to force her way onto a pier. Of course, she could deploy a Marine landing force onto the station and take control of it.

Come to think of it, that would be the usual next step.

Why did that make it the last thing Vicky should do?

"Maggie, what are the chances that a station could be rigged to explode if there is any change in the air pressure?"

"It would depend on how much air was lost, Your Grace."

"Say we find a small airlock and cycle a company of Marines in full space play clothes."

Maggie didn't even seem to pause before she was answering, "That would not be wise, Your Grace. Whether we used the smallest lock, which would only take four at a time, or a medium lock that could take the entire company, there would still be a very slight drop in pressure, even if we assume that the lock's depressurization pumps were working at normal capacity."

"Some gauges are just too damn sensitive," Admiral Bolesław said, coming up behind Vicky and slipping into his command chair.

"Can we get most of the fleet into some sort of moorage?" Vicky asked.

"They're working at it," the admiral said. "I don't know how well it's going to go. I've got the ships spread out to give them more room to swing around each other. None of our ships' displacements are a mirror image of any other. We're just going to have to try to try to work out the center of gravity for the two ships."

"The *Victorious*?"

"Has twenty thousand tons on the *Gracious Grand Duchess*, Your Grace. We'll try to anchor to her, but it'll likely be a wild ride for a bit."

"Maybe I shouldn't be aboard when you try it," Vicky said.

"Your Grace?" was not a happy statement from the admiral.

"Maggie, how much of that Smart Metal do you have left?"

"Twelve point seven-four kilos, Your Grace. There was a five-kilo block waiting when we got back. Kris promises more as soon as she can break some loose. Most is spoken for."

"That ought to be enough. Admiral, I need your best

longboat team. We'll need to hold station over the same point of a rotating space station, or at least at the same distance from one."

"Your Grace, there is no reason why you should go charging madly off on some mission that could get you very dead."

"Unfortunately, my good admiral, I am the only one that can go madly charging off on this damn fool mission. Maggie, could you work with any other human?"

"No, Your Grace. I, like any of Nelly's kids, are now dependent on you for my contact with the real world. I've adjusted to you and your way of thinking. I'm not sure I could respond quickly if I was trying to work with any other human being."

"As I said, Alis, just like Kris had to dragoon her maid and her maid's teenage niece to get us the fuel to get back to human space, I've got to go in with Maggie."

"Damn it, we need a few more of those crazy computers."

"Sir," Maggie said, and sniffed.

"Admiral, please do not offend Maggie. She and I have a job to do."

Admiral Bolesław took in a deep breath and let it out in a long sigh. "I now understand why her king and great-grandfather gave Jack authority to lock Kris up in her quarters."

"And you also know why he never did."

Admiral Bolesław slid from his chair and stomped over to the battle board, "What do you have in mind?"

Vicky followed him. "I'll need at least one battalion of Marines, reinforced with the necessary Sailors to operate the most critical gear on a station. The radar is off, right, Captain Blue?"

"What, Your Grace?"

"The station has no active sensors, radar, or lasers. Can you tell if there is any current being run through the hull that might notice a small attachment?"

"The station is dead in space. No active sensors. The hull is as dead as metal can be."

"Good, now, here's what I intend to do," Vicky said. She wondered if she should have invited Mannie into this mission brief, but he wasn't at hand . . . and maybe she liked it that way. He would worry enough when he found out she was gone.

32

V icky was belted in tight as the longboat
approached High Dresden space station. Across
the aisle from her was Lucan Brant.

Lucan had been the station manager for High Metzburg
for the last fifteen years and had retired to take on this
mission. He was a gray haired, dapper fellow, with a small
white mustache.

Everyone swore that no one in human space knew more
about stations. Lucan had started as a welder, like his dad,
and worked his way to the top.

At the controls of the longboat was a chief and first-class
petty officer. They were four of the best bosons' mates in the
fleet. The other two, also a chief and another first-class petty
officer, sat right behind them, ready to swap off if the
mission got too stressful.

Correction, when the mission got too hard for two men
to handle.

Aft, near the matter/antimatter reactor were two motor
mechanics, one an old chief and the second a sharp, young
second class. Strapped in place around them were several

extra cylinders of reaction mass. Welded in place, with two sets of power cables running to it, was a reserve supply of anti-matter.

The motor mechanics would make sure that the long-boat did not run out of fuel no matter how long, or how hard this mission was.

Attached beneath the hull was a tiny, ten-kilogram lander. Most of it was composed from every gram of Smart Metal that Vicky could scrape up. Most of the rest of the weight was reaction mass to get the Smart Metal from here to there. In addition, there were a few extras.

Still, the tiny space ship wasn't much to look at.

"There, you see that dock with the number fifteen?" Lucas said, pointing over the chief's shoulder.

"Yes, sir," the chief bosons' mate said.

"The Port Admiral's office is on the C deck above that pier. I've visited High Dresden during happier days and got a cook's tour. Unless they've moved it, the controls are up there. It's also amidships for the station, so it's the best place to start."

"Connor, you take us in," the chief ordered, and the petty officer guided the longboat around the pier and to a wide space between piers with none actually in front or behind them as the station rotated. They skimmed down to no more than fifty meters above the hull.

A noise through their hull told Vicky the small Smart Metal ship was away.

A blast on the forward jets threw Vicky slightly against her harness and the tiny rocket came in sight. It settled close to the station, hovered for a moment, then dodged right to avoid a welding seam and settled down on the hull.

Now soft jets held the small supply of precious Smart Metal to the hull. Out of sight, some of the Smart Metal had formed itself into a diamond-hard drill and was punching a hole, less than a tenth of a millimeter through the hull.

Vicky knew the drill had successfully bore through the hull when the Smart Metal lander began to shrink in upon itself. Included in the lander, besides Smart Metal and reaction mass, were tiny balls of plastic. They were now being pushed through the hole, along with the Smart Metal.

These plastic balls hovered around the hole. Maybe a few drifted off on air currents, but tiny Smart Metal drones were corralling most of them until the last metal was aboard. Then, some of the metal formed into tiny spikes that perforated the spheres, letting the goo that was in them, out.

Now, the air currents were rushing toward the narrow hole in the hull. That current drew the goo balls against each other, then against the hull, clogging the hole.

Hardly a breath of air escaped the station.

Now the Smart Metal transformed itself into small quadcopters and scattered themselves around the station. All had different missions. Most dropped off nano-sized communication relay stations as they skimmed the ceiling, observing and reporting back to Maggie at Vicky's throat.

Maggie passed the information along to Vicky and Logan where it was displayed on a holograph in front of them. A tight beam took it back to the *Victorious* where a Marine landing team commander watched a duplicate of the feed with Admiral Bolesław.

That information would serve many purposes.

One copter quickly found its way to the Port Admiral's office. In a blink, it converted into a cloud of nano scouts and vanished in all directions.

Other copters hunted for the lasers, radars, and other parts of the station's defensive systems. As they came upon them, they, too, vanished away and began sending a wealth of information back over the communications network they had laid out behind them.

Quite a few copters headed for the reactors. Those were of intense interest to a whole lot of people. Once there, the nano scouts began a careful analysis of just what lay there. If the station was to be sabotaged, and sabotaged in a way that did major damage to Vicky's ships, it was there, in the reactor with its plasma the temperature of the sun, that it would be done.

"What are those?" came on the net from several voices at the same time.

"What are what?" Vicky asked.

"Those gray boxes with a lot of cables and wires going in and out," Logan said.

"I will have several nanos examine them," Maggie said.

"That's a lot of electricity going in there," came from someone back on the *Victorious.*

"I'd like to know where the small wires go," Logan said.

"I am dispatching another two copters to the reactor room," Maggie said.

The nano scouts that were already there spread out to examine every nook and cranny of the reactor space. Except for those four unknown gray boxes, all the engineering officers who were looking over everyone's shoulders at the spaces didn't see any problems.

"Oh, shit," came in four-part harmony.

"What is it?" Vicky asked.

"Those are anti-matter containment cells," Lucan explained. "Anti-matter containment cells don't belong anywhere near a reactor."

"Definitely." "Yes." "Oh, Lord, yes," emphasized his answer.

"So, we really need to figure out what they're wired to," Vicky said.

"We're not doing anything to disturb the flow of power to those containment fields," Lucan emphasized. "Just one second of no juice, and they blow, with the station going a second later. Understand?"

"Very clearly," Vicky said.

"Your Grace," Admiral Bolesław said, "if the station blows, there will be chunks of it flying all over the place. We're a thousand klicks back. We'll have time to take the wreckage, then take it under fire or avoid it. We won't suffer too much damage."

He left unsaid that she was hovering ten meters from that potential lethal explosion and would take a whole lot of jagged metal before she had even a moment to realize things had gone bad.

Of course, one might consider it an advantage that she'd hardly feel a thing.

"Alis, Maggie and I can't control the nanos from well back. The time delay might not be much, but it could be what makes the difference between us reacquiring a space station or having to chase down a lot of wreckage in orbit. I'm here, and I'm staying here. I knew as well as you did when I launched that we were heading into a booby trap. Now we've found a part of it. We'll find the rest and disable it, okay?"

There was a long pause before Admiral Bolesław grumbled, "Yes, Your Grace."

Then he played dirty. "Shall I tell Mannie of your little adventure?"

Vicky wasn't really surprised at the effort to twist her arm. "I'd prefer you didn't, Alis."

"Your Grace, you are going to turn my hair white before I'm forty," the admiral answered.

"My hair *is* white," Lucan said from beside Vicky. "I guess that's why I'm here."

"Somebody tell me where the wires are going from those damn gray boxes," Vicky snapped, but with good humor.

"I have nanos following the wires," Maggie replied quickly, then added, "Two of them led to the power supply control. They're double-wired there. We can't jack up the power production from the reactor without tripping the wires, and if we try to cut the wires, they close the circuit, too."

"Okay, we've got one problem. Someone start working on it," Vicky ordered.

"We have found the main computer," Maggie announced. "Just in case anyone is interested, there's an unknown pair of wires leading out the back and into a conduit."

"I suspect," Captain Blue said, "that they also lead back to the reactor room and the gray boxes."

"So, we don't turn the computer on," Vicky concluded.

"That seems to be the intent," Admiral Bolesław agreed.

"And we cannot dock any ships so long as we cannot operate the central computer," Lucan said.

"Can we cut out the main computer and insert our own computer into the network?" Vicky asked. "Maybe take over one or two piers to land a force?"

"I'd be careful about that," said Captain Blue. "All these systems have backup power supplies. They may look dead, but they've got enough available energy to surprise you."

"Maggie, could you insert a tiny computer into the lead out from one of the center piers, then scout the pier as precisely as possible?"

"Yes, Your Grace. I've scouted out enough of the comm wiring of a pier to know where I could insert my own controller."

"May I suggest, Your Grace," Captain Blue said, "that your computer, ah, Maggie, insert the controller and then watch the feed between it and the main computer for an hour or so?"

"You think there's a problem?" Admiral Bolesław asked.

"I think that the main computer has enough backup power, and all of the camera observation nodes have enough battery backup that they can go active for just a few seconds intermittently. Just enough to mess up your entire day, Your Grace."

"I think we can depend on the Bowlingames to try to mess up my entire day," Vicky said dryly.

Quickly, Maggie had Pier 18 fully suborned. There was little more than a trickle of electricity flowing back and forth over the comm links. It clearly was in snooze mode.

Back on the longboat, Vicky allowed the chief bosons' mate to back off and float above the station as it turned beneath them. Maggie was able to maintain her access to her own net by the comm nodes that her nanos had set in place around the station.

While they waited to see if there would ever be anything to see on the intended landing pier, the nano scouts continued to do their scouting to their little hearts' content.

The huge capacitors that would feed the lasers had very little power in them. Still, they were rigged so that if any of that power was drawn from them to, for example, power up the computer, reactor, or other parts of the station, they would explode. Oh, and the power lines to the anti-matter gray boxes were drawing their power from there.

The people who had set up this little bomb waiting to

happen hadn't been totally suicidal. There was a timer just before the power interrupt that led to the superconducting electromagnetic plasma containment field around the reactor. If someone tripped the self-destruct by accident, they'd have a good fifteen minutes to give the code words to close it down.

Vicky's problem was she had no idea what kind of codes they were using.

We really need to not trip the damn thing.

About twenty-five minutes into their hour long wait, the central computer sent a high speed burst off to the security monitors in Pier 18. The cameras did not turn on. However, the low power motion sensors popped on for a tenth of a second, then reported back to the head computer that it hadn't found anything out of place.

"Let's try another pier as well," Admiral Bolesław suggested, and Maggie inserted a makeshift controller into the comm lead out to the pier directly opposite 18, Pier 218. Sure enough, fifteen minutes later, the motion sensors there were told to do a sweep, and they did.

Unfortunately, the resulting report was ever so slightly different. There seemed to be enough tugs and carts and boxes left lying around in different places to produce just enough of a difference in reports that they dare not try to have one pier report pass for another pier's.

Still, Vicky figured two piers ought to let them get things going. Her nano scouts needed reinforcements. Local Peterwald drones might not be as tiny as Longknife nanos made from Smart Metal, but they could still do a thing or three.

"Admiral Bolesław, I'd like to land a Marine battalion reinforced by combat engineer company, comm security team, and scout company."

"We have four cruisers loaded with two such battalion size task forces," Your Grace."

"Start collecting more teams like them, Alis. We'll start with these two and see where we go from there. Are the reactor and port captain teams ready to come aboard?"

"They're on the *Ystad* and *Kolobrzeg*. They will come in with the second wave," the admiral answered.

"Very well done," Vicky told him.

"Nothing's well done until you get out of there alive, Your Grace," Admiral Bolesław grumbled softly on net, but aloud enough for all to hear.

"Be careful, Alis, you may have an open mic there," Vicky said, with a grin.

For a long moment, there was silence.

"Maggie, do you have the necessary subroutines to operate the docking procedures on the pier?"

"Mr. Brant brought several subroutines that I can use. The station is a standard Blohm & Voss type 6B. There should be no problems. However, if I see any evidence that we are dealing with modified equipment, I can try several options."

"One of them is bound to work," Lucan said.

"I don't understand," Vicky said.

"Sometimes, the equipment gets replaced or heavily worked over. Sometimes, someone just likes a different set of software. People are quirky. I don't expect a problem, but I'm prepared for a bit of a burble."

Vicky suppressed the urge to roll her eyes. At this moment, with a reactor not all that far away from her that had been converted to a bomb, she was none too happy for human foibles.

However, four general class cruisers were headed in. The *Rommel* caught the hook to pier 18B and was hauled along the pier, engaging three of the tie-downs before coming to rest. Almost at the same second the *Rommel* touched the station, the *Kutuzov* edged into pier 218B. Together, they balanced the station as closely as they possible could. Two rotations later, after the station had a chance to settle down, the *Blücher* and the *Zhukov* also caught the hook and landed on the other sides of the two piers.

Vicky now commanded two battalions of heavily armed and armored Marines. More importantly, she had two companies of combat engineers ready to blow shit up or keep the other guys from doing the same to her. She also had two company-size teams eager to tackle the communications and security systems on this station as well as two more companies, equipped with the best micro spies and explorers that the Greenfeld Empire could muster. If they found something, they could either call in some of the tiny gadgets they had in their arsenal, or call their Grand Duchess. Maggie would then apply some Smart Metal to the problem.

Between one tool or another, Vicky was pretty sure they could crack this delicate egg.

33

Vicky surveyed her situation and found it manageable. She had an empty space station, which, for some reason, someone had evacuated and booby trapped to blow up if anyone arrived and made the tiniest little mistake while trying to get it back in operating order.

That particular aspect of this problem could really piss a Grand Duchess off. A space station this big cost hundreds of billions of gold Imperial marks. This one might even be close to a trillion.

Replacing this station would put a major hole in Dresden's budget for years to come. That didn't even try to put a price tag on what damage the falling beanstalk and the various pieces of the station might do. Cleaning up the wreckage in orbit would take years, and in between time, trade with Dresden would be back to what shuttles could carry, and cost a whole lot more than the quick ride up a space elevator.

Oh, whoever did this, was definitely going to hang by whatever part of his anatomy that Vicky chose.

She'd heard of how, in the distant, barbaric past, entire families had been proscribed and wiped out, from doddering old folks to babes at the breast. Vicky had considered such behavior as horrible and hardly productive.

The Bowlingame family was rapidly getting her mad enough to slap a proscription on their entire brood,

The very idea turned Vicky's stomach. "Maybe I can find a raw, barely inhabitable planet. Maybe drop them on it with the basic settler's kit and put an interdict against landing there for fifty years. Maybe fifty years of plowing their land with horses and making do with what they could make with their own two hands would teach these people some basic lessons in decency," Vicky muttered under her breath.

But for now, Vicky had a space station to carefully and quietly occupy.

"Deploy the combat engineers," Vicky ordered. "Assume every object is booby trapped."

Two holographic screens opened up in front of Vicky and Lucan. On them, lightly clad soldiers, most carrying black boxes, others lugging heavy tool kits, advanced onto the pier landings. Behind them, bomb teams in heavily padded protective clothing pulled wagons with armored canisters, ready for the expected explosives.

It didn't take them long to find things.

The first tugs or luggage trucks they came to had been rigged with explosives. The nimble scouting engineers moved on and the bomb squads moved forward.

Vicky wondered if the loud racket of an exploding bomb might set off the station destruct mechanism, but she needn't have worried. The bomb canisters zapped the electronics with enough EMPs that they were pretty much left too fried to explode.

Only one bomb went off, but it was heavily muffled in its canister.

Vicky really needed to learn more about who she had working for her. It was starting to look like a certain Grand Duchess would need to spend a lot of time attending demonstrations.

Small semi-intelligent wheeled drones skittered all over the deck, driving in a pattern intended to cover every inch of the place. They used everything from smellers to sonic probes to assure that no one had left a pressure plate or made any other changes to the steel decking.

They did find two places where the deck had been cut and a tiny few centimeters of flooring was riding atop an explosive. Those were first identified and flagged. Then, the combat engineers came along and glued down a plate one centimeter above the pressure plate. Later, the problem would be permanently dealt with.

It took an entire hour to thoroughly search the two piers and declare them safe.

Once they were safe and secure, two battalions of trigger-pullers landed and set up a small perimeter which advanced no faster than the mine hunters and bomb team.

As soon as the four cruisers were emptied of troops, the *Rommel* and *Kutuzov* backed out in time with each other, then the cruisers *Ystad* and *Kolobrzeg* very carefully replaced them at the piers. Aboard them were more scouts with their horde of wheeled and flying drones, ranging from micro-sized to some about the size kids played with.

Behind them were more electronic wizards. They quickly set up shop and began making sure that all the auto-cannons and spy cameras were truly and sincerely dead. They also inserted Greenfeld-made controllers in the comm link between the piers and the station's main computer.

That freed up a chunk of Maggie's Smart Metal nanos. Vicky and her computer started looking for a good use for them.

Last to land from the cruisers was the reactor engineers and station operators. Once the station was declared all safe, they would get the docks up and working. First, however, once the all clear was given, they'd have to get power, then communications, water and sewer up and running.

The station, however, was a long way from safe.

Still, there was no reason for Vicky to keep floating around in zero gee. "Admiral Bolesław, I'm going to land this longboat on the *Ystad* and go ashore. I could use some gravity about now."

"Your Grace!"

"Alis, there is no head on this liberty launch," she snapped back.

"Poor planning on your part is no excuse for getting yourself killed."

"Admiral, no one has gotten themselves killed so far. I think we're getting this place well toward our control. Now, if you'll excuse me, Admiral, this Grand Duchess is going to get her ass into some gravity."

The fleet must have been observing perfect radio procedure. Not a single open mic caught the reaction to this exchange that had to be sweeping the fleet.

The chief bosun mate brought the longboat smoothly along the *Ystad*, caught the offered hook and was hauled aboard.

The station did not take this opportunity to blow up.

Once Vicky had a chance to catch up on essentials, she posed a question to Captain Blue, "What should we tackle next. As I see it, we can clear two more piers and bring more ships alongside. However, I'm not sure I want too many more people running around where one of them might stumble into the wrong thing. I'm wondering if we can't go straight to the main station computer and see what it's sending out and try sending a few extra things back its way."

"I agree with you. Could you dispatch enough nanos to the main computer that we can start tinkering with it?"

"Maggie?"

"They are on their way, Your Grace."

Five minutes later, they had hacked into the data net just short of the main computer and were amazed at the amount of low power signals it was sending. The data team started tearing it apart and quickly reported back to Captain Blue.

"Your Grace," the captain reported. "As expected, there are a lot of queries going out to the piers for motion sensor checks. We've also got the same going out to all the security camera nodes on A and B decks. We will likely need to record an hour of data before we can get a full loop. I'd suggest three hours, so we can search for any differences between the three. I don't trust them not to have some place where they've got something moving around just to trip us up."

"Captain, you have a mind full of nasty thoughts."

"Thank you, Your Grace. Coming from a Peterwald, I consider that high praise," he deadpanned on net.

"Keep thinking nasty thoughts. I need them," Vicky answered with sincerity.

So, they settled down to wait. Vicky got lunch while Maggie and her nanos did everything they could to map the wires that led to the gray anti-matter containment cells.

Some were to be expected. If you turned on the sewage or water systems, they would blow up the station. The same went for the air purification and temperature control process. Others were less expected.

The door to the Port Admiral's office was booby trapped. Open it, and the entire station blew. That might have been understandable, but one of the doors to a bathroom stall in the head closest to the place also was rigged to blow the station.

Clearly, this entire station would have to be checked. Every inch of it.

However, the best approach was to go straight to the bomb and disarm it. Several different teams were working independently on that problem. All of them were on their own. Only when they were finished would they be brought together to match and compare plans. There was a steak dinner with the Grand Duchess riding on which team won.

Actually, Vicky intended to invite them all to the dinner, but urging people to compete against each other was never something to pass up.

The three hours was a drag for everyone. The bomb hunters, however, took the time to go over the two piers and discovered two wickedly hidden booby traps they'd missed. One well hidden in a trashcan, the other a wad of paper with a piece of chewing gum that was really a well-concealed explosive. It would not have blown up the station, but it would have taken off a hand.

From the looks in the eyes of the crew searching for bombs, whoever did this would be in deep trouble if they found them in a dark alley.

It was very tempting to let them have whoever it was.

I'll have to talk that one over with Mannie, Vicky thought, torn between being the Greenfeld Imperial Grand Duchess and the Gracious Grand Duchess.

Three hours later, Captain Blue was willing to cut into the feed to and from the main station computer. They all held their breath for a moment, and only relaxed when the count hit ten seconds . . . and the captain reported that he'd intercepted ten orders to security nodes and answered them with no problem.

Immediately, the bomb teams began to spread out. Their first objectives were to clear a path to the Port Admiral's office, as well as the main computer and the reactors.

As was to be expected, those paths were not at all easy to clear. The bomb search teams found all sorts of sneaky, nasty ways to blow off a hand, a foot, or a head. They also found two more doors that had wires on them. One set led nowhere. However, the second pair was live, and the nanos followed them all the way back to the gray boxes of death.

They went hunting for a second way to get to the Port Admiral's office.

Access to the reactor was a bit more problematic. There were only so many ways into a reactor. You didn't want the odd and sod stranger taking a wrong turn and getting in among the critical controls. No, access was limited and the way to it soon came to a locked door that was very much rigged to blow up the station.

The scout team worked their way along the bulkhead, found a good section of it that was easily accessible, and used nanos to check it from both sides. Then they called for a welding team from the combat engineers.

They carefully cut out a good-sized chunk of the wall, made sure that it did not drop, then set it aside, lined the opening with safety tape and one of the engineers bowed and waved them in.

"Welcome, courtesy of the 4th Battalion of St. Petersburg Combat Engineers."

They were gratefully appreciated.

Fifteen careful minutes of exploration later, there was a second door, just as booby trapped as the first.

Clearly, these guys expected any intruder to get cocky.

The combat engineers again cut them a safe hole.

There were still several more booby traps before they reached the final hatch into the reactor spaces. One was a claymore worked into a book shelf. It had a sonic beam covering a door. Break it and it would explode.

The team found it and disarmed it.

Finally, they found themselves in the presence of the greatest bomb of them all. The reactor might be in trickle mode, but there was enough plasma hot as a sun in it to rip this station apart. The anti-matter explosive could make a mess too, but nothing compared to the plasma.

Both had to be disarmed, and disarmed just right.

However, the disgusting excuse for a human being who had done this really should have gone easy on all the other booby traps. The bomb team had gotten plenty of practice disarming the bombs all along the way. This nasty big boy was looking very much like the ones they'd practiced on.

"Let's not get cocky," Captain Blue warned over the net. "Check this puppy out for the one thing that's different from the rest.

Sure enough, the SOB had added some extra wires, very carefully hidden, that would have completed the detonation circuit if the usual ones had been cut.

"Your Grace," Maggie said at Vicky's neck. "I think my nanos can cut all those wires to all those detonators at the exact same nanosecond."

"Very good, Maggie," Vicky said.

"However, Your Grace, I will need to be as close to all the wires as possible. The more distant I am, the more chance that one snipper will be too soon or another too late."

"Let me guess, Maggie. You and I need to be in the reactor room."

"I think it would be best, Your Grace."

"No way," Admiral Bolesław bellowed on net.

"You have a problem, Admiral?" Vicky said, doing her best to sound of sweetness and light.

"Your Grace, you're going right into the middle of this whole messy bomb."

"And if I'm safely ensconced on the *Ystad's* wardroom, how will I be safer if this station blows itself to pieces?"

There was a long pause. The answer finally came in a soft, "We've got to talk that Longknife bitch into giving us a few more of those fancy computers. Your Grace, you should not be in the middle of all hell, waiting for it to break out," he finished, letting his anger grow stronger.

"Alis, I will be careful," Vicky said, softly.

"You are going to be the death of me, Your Grace."

"I am doing my best to not be the death of anyone."

A long breath was breathed out on net. "Yes, I imagine so."

"Now, you apologize to Kris. She is not a Longknife bitch. I have seen her first baby, and Ruthie is not nearly as cute as a puppy."

What came back on net was not even close to a laugh.

"All right, Your Grace. Go do what you want to do."

"Thank you, Alis," Vicky said, and steeled herself to walk into the maw of hell.

34

As Vicky walked up the unmoving escalators from one deck to the next to the next, it was obvious that clearing the station of booby traps was a work in progress.

On each deck, she spotted several glued down plates with little red flags that warned of booby trap pressure plates underneath. When she got up to the A deck concourse, it was even more apparent.

Her path was laid out between two rolls of red tape. Walk between the lines, or you might not be walking again for a long while. The red tape path did not go straight but wiggled around this or that red flag on the deck.

Someone had spent some serious time making this place unsafe.

"Did they drill down into the deck to set all those mines?" Vicky asked the major at her elbow.

"No, Your Grace," he answered. "A lot of those are just three or four millimeters of clear liquid explosives dripped onto the deck. However, if you step on it, you'll lose your foot."

"You've got to really hate the guys who did this."

"With a passion, ma'am. With a really intense passion."

"How are you going to clean up all of that?" Vicky asked.

"Carefully, Your Grace. Very carefully," the major said through a tight grin.

Vicky walked the crooked trail. All doors that had been checked were propped open. She passed several heads that had signs marking them as NOT SAFE. Of course, with the sewage system not working, it didn't much matter.

The major helped her slip through the holes in the bulkheads that the engineers had cut. The steel was maybe six or seven millimeters thick, so it hadn't been a tough cut. The bulkheads here were meant to keep the average person out, not stop a serious assault by professionals.

Vicky and the major picked up an escort from the bomb hunters, a command sergeant major who saw to it that the two officers spotted all the potentially deadly threats to their footsteps.

The walkway here was much more jagged. A lot of explosives had been dripped on the deck to screw with anyone coming this way.

"They expected us to drill through the bulkhead, huh?" Vicky asked.

"The bloody buggers have a mean mind, admiral," the sergeant said. "I'd really like to have a few hours in a locked room with the bloke who set this mess up."

"I'll consider the possibility, Command Sergeant Major. Do know that I *am* considering the possibility." Vicky said, pointedly.

"If by chance you can see your way through to someone

like that, ma'am, there's a batch of us that will want in that room. It'll have to be a mighty big one."

"I'm sure I can find an auditorium," Vicky said.

"A big one, ma'am. A real big one."

Was it all so bad to be a Greenfeld Grand Duchess and a Peterwald? Really, Kris?

Vicky entered the reactor room through another cut in the bulkhead. This one looked to be twelve or thirteen millimeters thick. When she stuck her foot in, she found a hand taking it and guiding it down to the deck.

Vicky banged her shoulder coming through, but she had one hand covering Maggie. This was no time to ding the poor thing.

"Thank you," Maggie said after Vicky stood up, let go of her throat, and surveyed the room.

"You're very important to me, Maggie," Vicky said, and found that she really meant it. It wasn't just that her computer might save all their lives and this trillion mark space station, but there was more. Maggie was becoming someone Vicky felt like she could depend on. Someone that made Vicky proud of what she was doing.

As a child, she'd spent enough time standing in the background while important people did important things. As far as she was concerned, she'd been a troublesome bit of excess baggage while Kris Longknife circumnavigated the galaxy. She'd run for her life from her stepmother and slowly watched as a rebellion coalesced around her. She'd been about as much help as an old flag or battle ensign.

Now, she and Maggie were in the middle of this action. Vicky finished her survey of the reactor spaces with a smile on her face.

Yes, I like being where the important stuff is going on.

"Okay, where are the wires we need to cut?"

"Your Grace," Maggie said, "do you want for the bomb search team to explain this?"

"Yes, Maggie. I'd kind of like to have a finger pointing things out."

"Yes, Your Grace."

An Army captain stepped forward. "Your Grace, those buggers have rigged this place to blow, both with the anti-matter containment canisters over there, and by having some wires going directly to the reactor. If any of them are tripped, there will be one huge kaboom that none of us will notice."

"I understand that," Vicky said.

"Okay, just so you know there's no room for any of us to make a mistake. Now, if I can have your attention, there are several critical junctions for these detonators. Some of them are hidden so well that only your computer's nanos managed to spot them."

"How would they have safetied the system?" Vicky asked.

"There's one kill switch over there by the reactor. Enter the right codes and you close down the self-destruct process."

"Are we working on breaking that code?" Vicky asked.

"Sorry, ma'am, but the system won't accept any input until the destruct system is activated. Bastards, if you'll excuse me, ma'am. None of us, on any of our teams, would like to solve that problem in thirty minutes with the clock ticking."

"Understood. Let's kill it before the clock starts ticking."

"Now, several of the wires we need to cut are hidden well away. They must have had a bear of a time getting them in place. Then they dripped or painted explosives all around it. It's going to be a bitch cleaning this place up. Plainly put, without your nanos, there is no way we could get at those wires."

"See, Maggie, all our lives depend on you."

"Yes, ma'am." There was brief pause, then Maggie added. "Your Grace, if you blow up, what will become of me?"

That was not a question Vicky was really prepared for. Somehow it had not come up during the talk with Maggie about the Sailors and Marines on the picket boats that had died above Greenfeld.

Vicky took a deep breath, then gave the only answer she knew. "You will likely blow up with me, Maggie."

There was a surprisingly long pause. "I would not like that," came in a small girl's voice.

"Neither would I, but this is something we have to do. You can do this, Maggie."

"Yes. Yes, I can," Maggie said, with determination growing in her voice as she spoke each word. "Okay, Admiral, Major, Captain, Command Sergeant Major, how are we going to do this thing?"

"We need to cut each of the wires at the exact same instant," the major said. "More than a few nanoseconds could be critical. The saboteur has been using the same wire from one end of the show to the other. The wires we're looking at appear the same as all the others. Still, we need to apply enough cutting power to cut a wire twice as strong."

"Okay," Maggie said.

"What kind of cut do you want to make?" Vicky asked.

"Scissors won't cut it. The wire can wiggle around in the bite of the blades. One wire might cut early, another might slip out, have to be chased, and cut late. Do you understand, Your Grace?"

"So, a scissor cut is out. What about a guillotine cut?"

"Pressure would have to be applied evenly, by all," the

Major said. "If there was any delay in cutting the bottom of the wire . . . what I'd really suggest is two blades closing together, like a fingernail clipper."

"I can design micro cutters that will have pressure coming from both directions while the wire is held inside jaws to keep it from wiggling. It would likely work better if the two blades were slightly offset so that the cut would be clean."

Vicky eyed the major. He eyed the captain. Both of the officers nodded.

"Go for it, Maggie," Vicky said.

"How will your computer know when to make all the cuts?" the major asked.

"Maggie and I have direct communication. There is no need for us to talk," Vicky said. "I'm sure Maggie can initiate the cut order simultaneously."

That earned some raised eyebrows, but Vicky ignored them. The proof of the pudding would be when the timer didn't start its short countdown.

"Are you ready, Maggie?" Vicky asked.

"Give me a moment, I've flown some more nanos in and I'm merging my scouts to make for stronger clippers. This may take a minute."

"Anything that increases the chance of this working," Vicky said, "is fine by me. Take all the time you need."

"Yes. I definitely want this to work the first time," Maggie answered.

Maybe having a computer with a sense of its own mortality wasn't such a bad thing.

Two seconds later, Maggie said, "I'm ready to go."

"Very good, Maggie. You may fire when ready."

"Fire?"

"Old quote. Cut when ready."

"The job is done," Maggie said.

The bomb crew looked around.

"Done. Already?" the major said.

"Done. You said do it. I did it," Maggie said.

"Well, thank you very much, Maggie," the major said. "I don't know the rest of you, but I would have spent a good minute contemplating my fate before ordering it cut."

"There are advantages to getting a computer to do something," Vicky said. "She doesn't dilly dally around."

Then Vicky changed directions on a dime. "We've got the reactor bomb cut off. We could sure use a reactor team in here."

"We also need the rest of the bomb team to take care of the booby traps in here," the major ordered.

Vicky stayed in place for several minutes before the main hatch swung open and a bomb disposal expert waved engineers in red shipsuits into the reactor space.

"Don't touch anything you don't have to," the Major ordered. "Don't touch anything until after you tell us what you need to touch, and we check it out."

"Is it that bad?" a Navy commander in red asked.

"They applied explosives in the form of paint, both to the deck and, I suspect, to some of your boards and working surfaces. Until we declare a surface safe, don't assume it is."

"Understood. Chief, you go check out the main board. Major could you assign someone to work with him? Then I need someone to work with my next chief on the magneto hydrodynamics board. The reactor board comes after that."

"Now, Your Grace," the commander said, "if you will get the hell out of my parlor, I'll tend to my knitting and you can tend to yours."

"Most definitely, Commander. Most definitely."

The major was somewhat more polite. "Sergeant Major, escort the Grand Duchess out of here."

"Yes, sir. Ma'am," and Vicky got the hell out of the way of the worker bees.

She was winding her way across A deck. The track between the red tape was getting wider. Someone was walking around from red flag to red flag and spraying something on the painted-on explosives. The stuff fizzed and fumed. It stank up the place, but apparently it dissolved the explosives down into "no boom" ingredients. That was fine with Vicky.

She was just getting back to the silent escalator down into the Ystad's pier when Admiral Bolesław cut into her thoughts.

"Your Grace, we have a message from below. I think they figured out that we've got the space station under our control."

"How come?"

"They told us so."

"You want to share the message with me?"

"Not really, because you aren't going to like it."

"Transmit please," Vicky said through tight lips.

A holographic image of a flat screen appeared before Vicky. A bulky man in a red uniform dripping with gold stood intimidatingly close to the camera.

"To you squatters on Dresden's space station, be gone. We have no truck with those from outside our Lord Emperor's sovereignty. If you do not go, we will chase you out. We know how to fumigate cockroaches."

"Maggie? Are there gas canisters?" Vicky snapped.

"Already on it," Maggie said.

"And if you by any chance have the one who styles herself a grand duchess and makes false claims to be the heir to our Emperor's throne, know that we will have no mercy on you or your spies."

There was a pause as the camera switched from him to panoramic video of men, women, and children confined in large spaces, like civic arenas, convention centers, or indoor stadiums. There must have been hundreds of thousands of them.

Over the pictures came vicious words. "If you attempt to invade our peaceful precincts, we will annihilate these spies of yours first before you can fire a shot."

Vicky broke into a trot. " Admiral Bolesław, I'll be back aboard the *Victorious* as quickly as possible."

"I'll be looking for you."

35

Admiral, Her Grace the Grand Duchess Victoria held her next meeting in the Admiral's Wardroom on the *Victorious*. It was full.

Vicky wanted it full. She knew she faced a nearly impossible situation and she needed every idea that anyone could come up with.

Sitting at the head of the table, she had Mannie at her right elbow, with Captain Blue beside him. To her left were Vice Admiral Bolesław and Lieutenant General Pemberton. Their junior commanders and technical experts filled up the rest of the table and all the chairs against the wall.

Everyone waited silently for Vicky begin the meeting. She chose to be short and succinct.

"They've taken good people hostage. I want those people freed alive and I want those hostage takers dead. How do we do that?"

The room took a moment to absorb that order.

Mannie immediately broke the silence. "Your Grace, is that a good idea?"

"Mannie?" Vicky said, surprised at his words.

"Your Grace, they have every intention of killing those people as soon as they perceive any action on your part. There are no ferries at the station, so you cannot go down the beanstalk with assault troops the way you did recently at Greenfeld."

Mannie paused to take a breath. It was clear from the look in his eyes that he found this entire situation revolting. Still, he went on.

"If you attempt to land from space, landers come in at supersonic speeds and their booms can be heard for hundreds of miles. I fear that they will begin to slaughter those people as soon as they hear a sonic boom. I fear that if you act in any other way than to pack up this fleet and go back to our space, this will end in a bloodbath."

With a sigh, Mannie fell silent.

Vicky answered his sigh with one of her own, and did her best to offer her husband a gentle smile.

"Mannie, I know that was hard for you to say. I'm also afraid of a blood bath. That is the reason we are gathered here. Now, it's not that I want to avoid just such a blood-bath," Vicky said softly, then paused.

When she went on, her voice was hard as steel. "However, I will not allow those gutter snipes to slaughter my people. I will not let hell hold heaven hostage. There has got to be a way to avoid your fear and still free those people."

Vicky swept the room with a hard glare. "Some of the best people in the Empire are in this room. You are sworn to me and I am sworn to those people. We will not leave this room until I am satisfied that we have a plan we can use to liberate every hostage and kill every hostage taker."

"No prisoners, Your Grace?" Admiral Bolesław asked.

"If it will save hostages, fine. Otherwise, those on the scene can decide."

"It's usually easier to get people to surrender if they don't fear they will be shot, Your Grace," General Pemberton said.

"No doubt," Mannie said, "many of them may have committed crimes during their occupation of Dresden. Still, it would be better if they faced their justice later."

Vicky allowed herself a dry chuckle. "What is it with you guys? Won't anyone let a Peterwald be a vicious Peterwald?"

"Vicious Peterwalds were rarely effective Peterwalds," Mannie said, under his breath, but the entire room heard him.

"Good point. Okay, Captain Blue, can you tell me anything about the situation with the hostages?"

"Yes, Your Grace," the captain said, without even a pause. "The hostages are, as they told us, confined in large spaces like civic arenas, convention centers, or indoor stadiums. I doubt that it will surprise you, ma'am, that, when we were here last, on our way to Greenfeld, my team and I took a complete snapshot of the net and archived everything that we could get our hands on."

"And you have such sticky hands," Vicky said.

"Coming from a Peterwald, I will take that as high praise," Captain Blue said, then continued. "Based on a review of the background in those pictures, we have identified every one of the hostage sites. We have the building specs as provided to the city administration, and we're looking into the various ways we could approach the local of the hostages without causing undue concern from the Red Shirts."

He paused for a moment. "Oh, and we dredged up from their database the exact mansions that the senior Red Shirts have commandeered for their homes and headquarters."

"You know where they sleep?" Vicky clarified.

"We do," the captain said, a big grin on his face.

"I would not suggest lasing them from space," Admiral Bolesław said.

"I know, Admiral," Vicky said. "Such an action would be rather gaudy and might well miss the target."

Then Vicky took on a grin that must have damn near split her face. "Kit, Kat, work with Captain Blue and his team to isolate the senior command structure. I give their heads to you."

From the very back of the room came, "Thank you, Your Grace," in two-part harmony. Most of the celebration between the two diminutive assassins was lost, except for the high five.

Nice that I can make somebody's day.

"Okay, Captain, how many hostage sites are we dealing with?"

"Seven, Your Grace."

"Seven!"

"Yes, Your Grace. From what we can make of it, they started rounding up these people when we popped into their space, and have been shoving more people into confinement as the situation developed. We have observed little food going into the detention centers. No extra water and no extra sanitation. If we don't get these people out soon, they're going to start getting sick and dying."

"Okay, Admiral Bolesław, how do we land a landing force without them knowing we're down?"

"We've been looking into that, Your Grace. This time of year, the weather in the evening is unstable, as in thunderstorms, rain, lightning, and thunder."

"Doesn't that also mean thunderheads?" Mannie slipped in.

"Yes, Mayor, that does. However, our long boats and

assault craft are equipped with radar. We'll do our best to avoid the worst of it. Especially the tornadoes."

"Tornadoes?" came from a lot more people than just Mannie.

"As I said, the weather is quite unstable."

"Is that enough to cover the landings?"

"No ma'am. We will do our best to direct the final approach of our landers in a north-south pattern, and not aim any of them close to Dresden City. Still, we'll be landing well back from the capital."

"So, we'll need ground transport," Vick said.

"Many of the mechanical infantry have their own wheels. We can partner a light infantry battalion with a mech one. That should provide enough motor lift for both units if the light infantry doesn't mind holding on tight. We can also commandeer as many wheels on the ground as we can find."

"Armor?" Vicky asked.

"It will go in last," General Pemberton said. "We don't see any armor around Dresden. Our estimate is we're dealing with a poorly trained force, deadly to unarmed civilians, but not so good against professional soldiers."

"Will they throw down their arms and run?" Mannie asked.

"If they are smart, yes, Mayor. However, those with guilty consciences may not feel so inclined to throw themselves on our tender mercy. If you want my guess, we're looking at half-surrendered and half-dead bodies."

"Who are willing to use civilians for human shields," Mannie pointed out.

"No doubt, sir. We will need to keep surprise on our side. The faster we can seize the initiative, the better. We want to keep them reacting to us, and hit them with an operation tempo that is so fast that they've got a new problem before they can figure out the last challenge we sent them. With luck, we'll shock them into paralysis."

Mannie did not reply. Vicky knew as well as he did that the enemy got a vote and no battle plan survived contact with the enemy.

"How far from the city will we be landing?" Vicky asked Admiral Bolesław.

"That will depend on the weather. If the forecast holds up, we'll be looking for a landing field within fifty klicks of the city."

"That will make for a long approach march," Vicky pointed out. "What about the chance we'll lose surprise?"

"I think I can answer that, Your Grace," Captain Blue said. "The Red Shirts have been kind enough to shut down the net. Totally shut it down. They are using runners to get orders from their HQ to any place they want to order around. There are no Red Shirts assigned out of Dresden City. From what we can determine, they've been confiscating crops and buying them at below market prices. I doubt any farmer will lift a hand for them."

"Besides, Your Grace, my infantry will be moving as quickly as we can. We'll also be setting up roadblocks to keep traffic out of the city."

"Radar?" Vicky asked.

"That's subject to all kinds of hash when thunderstorms are in the area. Radar can spot a thunderhead, but not what's in it. There will be a lot of thunderheads moving in around Dresden tomorrow night," Captain Blue said, with a velociraptor's grin.

"I think you've got the basic parts of a plan. I'm going to leave you professionals to put it together. I'd like a briefing by no later than o-nine hundred tomorrow morning. General Pemberton?"

"Yes, Your Grace?"

"I will be dropping with your lead mech battalion."

"Vicky!" had a lot of "Your Grace," right after it.

"I'm dropping," Vicky said, flatly.

"Vicky!" was almost a shout from Mannie.

Vicky cut him down with a glare.

"Your Grace," was much more measured. Almost reasonable from Admiral Bolesław. "You don't have to do this."

"Unfortunately, I do, Admiral. Maggie and I, along with all the Smart Metal we can lay our hands on, have to be in the vanguard. Captain Blue, I expect you to command the best team of micro scouts we can throw together. Still, I know that my nanos will be critical to us saving lives. I'm not open to debate."

"We've got to get more of Nelly's kids," Mannie grumbled.

"I couldn't agree with you more," Admiral Bolesław mumbled.

"I couldn't agree more, myself," Vicky added. "Not that I'd be anywhere except in the lead, but it would be nice to have more support."

Vicky stood, and those in the room did so immediately. The scraping of chairs likely covered a lot of growling from her senior staff. Still, they had a job to do, and Vicky needed to go check on her drop suit.

With any luck, she'd get to blow some shit up!

36

Vicky checked out her play clothes. She'd likely jump in full space armor, like the assault teams going in with her. Having a full helmet and internal oxygen would help if they had to start tossing smoke, sleeping gas, or tear gas around. The helmet visor could be strobed to match any flash bangs if they tossed them.

It was better to go in heavy and not need it all than to go in light and need what got left behind.

She headed down to the rifle range. There was enough spare space around the heavy battleship guns to set up a full range for both pistols and rifles. They'd have to clear out of here fast if battle stations sounded.

Vicky requalified as expert marksman with her sidearm. She had enough experience with her automatic not to have a problem. The range gunnery officer helped her get back in the mindset and relationship to the rifle computer. On the second try, she qualified as an expert marksman with the M-6.

This trip, Vicky had a suspicion she'd better be prepared for anything.

Yes, she was a Grand Duchess, and yes, she and Maggie were commanding a swarm of nano scouts and attackers, but still, there was never any promise on the battlefield that matters would stay as intended.

That was the whole reason you didn't want a war. Surprises were inevitable, and some could be deadly.

Vicky spent two hours with the *Victorious'* Marine company. She was glad she did, but she really wished she hadn't.

Just going through stretches with the troops was a torture. A torture that an old Gunny did quite well. Then there was the run! The Gunny left her behind before she was out of the starting gate. She went from the lead to the trailing edge to way behind them, then them out of sight. It was humiliating.

Clearly, being a pampered Grand Duchess was way too expensive if she wanted to play with these hard guys. Here were another bunch she would need to spend time with in the future, and not just to learn what they could do. She needed to be able to gain the stamina to do what they did.

Exhausted, she showered and changed into khakis before checking in on her brain trust. They were now broken up into teams, half of which had found somewhere else to work. As she walked in, another team of five passed her on the way out.

Vicky passed down the outside of each group. They were intense on their part of the operation; she did not disturb them. She did find that Mannie was gone. He hadn't been in their quarters when she showered and changed.

"Maggie, connect me with Mannie." In a moment, she had.

"Mannie, where are you?"

He gave her a deck and room number, and she headed there.

Mannie had found himself a team to work with. Inside were the leaders of most of the Civil Affairs units. They were planning for their drop and drawing up check lists of how to bring up what they'd find. Captain Blue had provided them a list of what gear this planet had, be it reactors, water works, water treatment plants, or network hubs and servers.

Mannie was with a small team planning on locating the civil authorities and judges. She arrived just as one white-haired woman said, "We will have to work carefully with the judiciary. We won't know the quality of these judges, who appointed them, and which ones are honest, verses on the take."

"If they're anything like the judges we on Brunswick had left over from the Peterwald era, they'll all be rotten," a middle-aged man with white just starting to show at his temples said.

"Present company excluded," the white-haired woman said, rising, and giving Vicky a quarter bow.

"Present company wants very much to be excluded from that past practice," Vicky said. "Please go on. I just came to spend some quality time with my husband."

So saying, she gave Mannie a warm honeymoon smile.

Someone found a chair for Vicky and she settled in at Mannie's elbow. He seemed a bit distant and continued to sit in on the discussion. There was serious concern not only about the surviving judges, but whether or not they could trust any of the administrative leadership.

Vicky offered them a list of the people she had talked to during her last visit. Those that had been most officious and sounded like they were in the Red Shirts' pockets went on one list with the worst, in red ink. A second list had those that had risked talking to her about conditions on Dresden. The most cordial were in green.

"You understand, Your Grace," a nearly bald cadaver of an old man warned, "you can't trust either of those lists."

"I do, but this is all I have to go on. You can talk to them and see which ones you think will take an autocratic turn and which ones you think are willing to share the reins of government with the people around them. Those of you that I met on Metzburg and Brunswick know how hard it was to distinguish the two."

"And we also remember how hard it was to go from an autocratic corporate state to a democratic market economy, even for those of us willing to try," a young man said, and got quite a laugh. "Going from flat on your back to riding a bike in a matter of weeks is a very harrowing experience."

"I can relate to that," Vicky said, "and I had the advantage of falling in love with the fellow teaching me."

That brought on another laugh.

She stayed with that group until it was getting close to bedtime. Then, with Mannie, she slipped out to make another trip through the wardroom. A much smaller crowd was in there now.

When she entered, Admiral Bolesław, General Pemberton and Captain Blue stepped away from the group they were talking to and came to join her.

"Any showstoppers?" Vicky asked.

"Many challenges, but no showstoppers," Admiral Bolesław reported for all. "We have the skeleton of a plan pretty much outlined. We're filling in the fine points, assigning units, checking availability, and drafting orders. We should have a thorough briefing ready for you at o-nine hundred hours tomorrow."

"When do we launch?"

"The thunderstorms are expected to move through the area starting at twenty-one hundred hours tomorrow evening. Assuming matters are working up according to plan, we'll start dropping away from the station at twenty hundred hours."

"Radar?" Vicky asked. "Any other sensors?"

"Radar is all we know about," Captain Blue answered. "Their best radars were on the station. The ones below are old and date back a hundred years or so to when they were still being using used to vector in orbiters for landings. They've degraded a lot. Mostly they're used for weather radar or monitoring aircraft. The planet has a high-speed rail system for travel to most outlying areas of any import, thus not much attention has been given to the radar."

"Still, radar is radar."

"Except when it's not, Your Grace," Captain Blue said, grinning. "These old radars have a certain type of failure that's kind of easy to simulate. It can last even longer if we can drop a bit of EMP onto a chunk of the power net. Round about twenty-hundred hours, that radar around Dresden City will develop a very bad case of hiccups. Stuff will start showing up all over the place like radar echoes and back scatter returns. Then, we'll slip a longboat in and bring down the power net in a couple of towns to the west. That should cause a spike in the city's power system that may put part of the city in the dark. If they try to bring the radar back up, it's going to be just full of hash."

"Any chance they'll panic and report that?"

"Would you want to be the tech who has to tell the chief Red Shirt that your ancient gear is not operating?"

Vicky didn't even need to think about that. "Nope. And if he called and asked me specifically, I'd tell him everything was fine. It's not like they're showing the cloud pattern on the net. Isn't it down?"

"Just so, Your Grace."

"You'll be landing with the first wave," Mannie said.

"Yes."

"I'll be going down with the first wave of ferries," he said. "We expect to arrive close to three in the morning. With any luck, we will have occupied most of the important control rooms in Dresden City before anyone wakes up."

"You're going down, too?"

Mannie looked her in the eye. His eyes were rock steady as he said, "Yes."

Vicky considered many answers, and chose the one with the most flair. "We'll have to have dinner tomorrow night at the swankiest restaurant in Dresden City."

"I think we should."

"Now, dear husband, would you be willing to come to bed with me?"

Mannie glanced around the table. There were a lot of knowing grins. "Any of you need me?" he asked.

"You'll be at the nine o'clock briefing?" one asked.

"Yes."

"See you there."

So, Vicky and Mannie walked the short distance to their quarters on the *Victorious*. A Marine corporal stood guard outside the door.

"Corporal, I do not wish to be disturbed tonight," Vicky said.

The Marine came to attention and saluted smartly. "Yes, Your Grace."

And so it was that Vicky and Mannie had a pleasant night to themselves.

37

Admiral, Her Imperial Grace, the Grand Duchess Victoria struggled to keep her stomach from embarrassing her.

The Marines sharing the longboat with Vicky swayed easily as the lander rolled and bucked in the violent air around them as they made their final approach to some farmer's field. None of them had grabbed the burp bag all had been issued and hurled the contents of their stomachs into the sacks.

Vicky would feel humiliated if she was the only one.

On the flight deck, the chief bosons' mate announced to his assistant coxswain that he had the beacon in sight and the younger bosun switched from the radio direction finder to peering out the front window of the lander.

"I have the beacon in sight," the junior said a moment later, his voice just as professionally level as the chief's had been.

The pathfinders had dropped an orbit early in light assault craft with the radar cross-section of a bee. They'd landed right into the middle of a line of thunderheads moving across the farmland fifty miles west of Dresden City.

The fear expressed in the 0900 meeting that morning was that as many as fifty percent of the pathfinders might be smashed by the wild winds. By the grace of some merciful God, although several had landed far from their target drop zone, no one had paid the full measure so that Vicky might know where she was going as she dropped from orbit to some farmer's field.

With the pathfinders, a drone team had also been deployed. They were shepherding their small swarm of near-transparent aircraft through the cold front and thunderheads that were now just west of Dresden City.

Half of them were also not expected to survive the short flight through the wild skies of the thunderstorms. It was critical that at least one did.

The plan was that just before the line of thunderstorms hit Dresden, one drone would release a huge flare that would light up the night. Shortly later, a second drone would drop a string of explosives that would send the best imitation of rolling thunder through the night.

In the short time between the "lightning" and the "thunder," a dozen battleships in orbit would zap the two radar antennae with all the radar power they could generate. It was hoped that all that radiation hitting those old receivers would fry half of them and leave the survivors susceptible to spoofing for the next three or four hours.

That was just the amount of time the Gracious Grand Duchess needed to land an invasion force.

A lot of different pieces had to come together to get the landing force Vicky was leading on the ground and moving to contact.

It would be a while before Vicky learned if everything

had worked as planned. Of course, if it didn't, she might never learn. She would be one of the first to die if the plan failed.

That's a nice thought, girl.

WE STILL NEED TO HAVE THAT TALK ABOUT WHAT HAPPENS TO ME IF YOU GET VAPORIZED. MY READING HAS SHOWN ME THAT YOU HUMANS BELIEVE THAT YOU HAVE A SOUL THAT WILL LIVE ON AFTER YOU DIE. DO I HAVE A SOUL?

MAGGIE, I'M NEVER SURE IF I HAVE ONE. YOU REALLY NEED TO HAVE THIS CONVERSATION WITH NELLY. STILL, YOU DID BACK YOURSELF UP BEFORE WE STARTED THIS DROP, DIDN'T YOU?

WHAT WOULD BE THE USE OF IT? I'M LEARNING MORE AS WE DROP AND, HOPEFULLY, I'LL LEARN A LOT MORE AS WE FIGHT OUR WAY INTO DRESDEN.

SNEAK OUR WAY IN, Vicky corrected.

HOWEVER WE GET INTO DRESDEN, A BACKUP COPY OF ME ON THE *VICTORIOUS* WOULD KNOW NOTHING ABOUT THIS. SHE WOULD ALSO NOT HAVE YOU TO BE ACTIVATED WITH. THAT WOULD BE A HORRIBLE FATE TO GIVE HER, COMING UP WITH WHAT I KNOW ABOUT WORKING WITH YOU ONLY TO FIND HERSELF MATCHED WITH SOME STRANGER. YOU HUMANS DO NOT UNDERSTAND WHAT IT IS LIKE TO BE A SENTIENT COMPUTER.

I KNOW I DON'T, MAGGIE, JUST HANG IN HERE WITH ME. WE'RE MAKING THIS UP AS WE GO ALONG.

YOU HUMANS DO THAT A LOT, Maggie sniffed.

Vicky laughed. "Oh, yes we do, my Maggie. Yes, we do."

The flight started to level out. The final approach was supposed to be smoother, coming just past the tail end of the line of thunderstorms. On the flight deck, Vicky listened as the two bosuns went down their landing checklist.

"Hang on folks. This is likely to get a bit lively," came in a calm, not quite monotone voice.

They came in, nose high, using the wings to do the last bit of braking. They touched down, then bounced back up. A moment later, they were down again.

Vicky swayed into Captain Blue as the chutes deployed and the longboat slowed significantly. Vicky pushed off the captain, although he did give her a smile. Apparently, he didn't mind being her cushion.

That brought back memories of Vicky's old life as a sex kitten Grand Duchess, and she had to calm her stomach again. This time for something entirely different.

"Sorry," she said, trying to be the woman Mannie had shown her she could be.

"Glad to be of service, Your Grace."

"You getting any word from your pathfinder team?"

"Things are going extremely well," he reported. "We only lost one pair of drones. We should be able to do four thunderclaps if we have to, and we'll have one drone over each of our eight targets."

He paused for a moment, then finished. "Two of the drones will be close enough to Red Shirt HQ to let us know exactly what's going on there. Another will be able to keep the Red Shirt honcho in sight. I hear that he is throwing a party in advance of you leaving the station."

"How does he know that?"

"Admiral Bolesław has ordered about a quarter of our ships to head for the jump back to our space. Another quarter are warming up and showing signs they will depart soon. A little misdirection never hurts."

"And I wasn't told?" Vicky thought she had been briefed

on all of this plan. What else had she missed? How else had she been kept out of the loop?

"Admiral Bolesław didn't mention it in the meeting. I don't know why. Didn't you notice when ships began departing the station six hours ago?"

"I was otherwise engaged," Vicky said, dryly. If she was honest with herself, she didn't need to know this, and it had gotten a party going with all the rats gathered around one big hunk of cheese.

"Maggie, send to Admiral Bolesław 'Well done with fleet departure. You have Red Shirt honcho throwing a party. Keep some battleship guns sighted in on his location at all times. I may order you to level the place on short notice'," Vicky finished. She expected a quick reply begging off of the battleship salvo, but none came.

Instead, the lander began to skid to the left. Whether it was from a gust of wind, or the mud, or a roll of the field, it didn't matter. They were in trouble.

The chief up front managed to steer the front landing gear into the skid and they swerved left. The lander took on a distinct list to the left. Vicky found herself looking up at the row of Marines seated against the far wall.

She wasn't looking up a lot, but every little bit is terrifying when you're going from orbit to a dead stop in the middle of some farmer's wheat crop.

The lander ended up with the nose now pointing downhill. Some more shoots popped out of the stern of the longboat and again, Vicky was forced to lean heavily on the young and handsome Captain Blue.

The captain did not look at her this time, but softly said, "You're welcome."

"Was it good for you?" Vicky asked, an old-time sassy smile taking over her face.

"Yes, Your Grace," the captain answered, not turning to meet her eyes. He had a delightful grin on his face, thought. "I hope it was as good for you as it was for me."

"We've got to quit meeting this way," Vicky shot back.

"How many planets to you intend to invade?"

"All of them, I think," Vicky said.

The captain scratched behind his ear, a most boyish look. "Then I guess we'll just keep meeting like this."

"One can hope."

"We're down, folks," came from the flight deck. "You can unstrap."

Vicky hit her quick release, and only two of them popped, the ones on her right. The two left ones that covered her breast and her waist, along with the one through her legs, stubbornly refused to release their grip on her.

Asking the captain's help with this would be really embarrassing. Especially after her recent exchange.

She hit the button in the middle of her chest again, but the three stubborn straps stayed put.

"Your Grace," the Marine major on her right said, "Hit the release and pull on the strap. Jiggle it around a bit if you have to."

Vicky hit the button again. Nothing happened. She arranged it so she could use her right hand to keep the button down and started wiggling the strap and its metal tongue with her left. About the third try, it popped out and her breasts were free. Now she tackled the last strap, the one between her legs.

She did the same thing, holding down the quick release, which it clearly wasn't, and wiggling the webbing to work the tongue out of the buckle. The more she jiggled it, the more it moved. That damn belt was doing things to her that she didn't need just before a battle.

The major produced a knife and was about to try cutting her out when there was a click and one Grand Duchess was free to go to war.

With a sigh, Vicky stood. "Major, let's get your provisional battalion moving out."

"Yes, ma'am," the major said, way too much glee in his voice. "Command Sergeant Major, get this command ready to move out."

A loud voice began shouting orders. From the looks of the troopers, most of them had already been doing what they were being ordered to do.

They had landed with three light attack vehicles. The eight-wheeled armored boxes were a compromise between mobility, availability, and protection. They were light enough so that three could land in each longboat. They were mobile because they could do 80 kilometers per hour on a road while still moving cross-country if they had to. Finally, they provided protection from small arms fire while having a 30mm cannon that could do major damage to anything but a tank.

The assault forces tanks would drop when these longboats got back up to the attack transports and could have them loaded aboard.

The LAVs were intended to carry a squad of twelve troopers and a crew of three: driver, gunner, and commander with a machine gun. The crew was cross-trained so many could do the other's job.

Each of the LAVs drove out the back ramp of the longboat and began getting ready to roll. On the top of each LAV was a pair of wheels. When they were hauled off the rig, they quickly turned into a single axle trailer. Troops passed out boxes of ammo and explosives, as well as a machine gun and a mortar. They were distributed between the trailer and the LAV.

Then the Marines filed aboard for a ride to war.

Ten Marines joined Vicky and Captain Blue in the LAV. Six climbed up to sit atop the vehicle, ready to slip off to the ground in the blink of an eye. The other eight arranged to sit in the trailer, behind light armor, and with rifles pointed in every direction.

Up and down the impromptu flight line, thirty-six LAV's loaded up with the equivalent of two battalions: one mech and one light infantry. As those two battalion-size task forces rumbled off the field and bounced their way onto a gravel road, a dozen more longboats were on approach with two more battalion combat teams.

Vicky tapped the gunner on the shoulder and he gave up his seat. Vicky slipped into it and ducked her head up into the armored plastic bubble with its 30mm cannon.

Ahead of her all was dark with occasional lightning flashing through the sky or slashing down to strike the ground. Of Dresden, there was absolutely no sign.

The column rumbled past a farmer who had pulled is tractor and its load of hay off the road. He seemed eager to let the guys with guns pass and leave him alone.

Vicky waved at the young kid.

He grinned and waved back.

If his face was to be trusted, it looked like she had at least one second for her motion for a change of regime on this planet.

"Maggie, what's the take from the drones?"

"Four pairs of them are in position twenty thousand feet over Dresden City, Your Grace. The cold front is right on schedule. We are an hour out from the outskirts of town.

There should be enough lightning and thunder to take out the radars in thirty minutes. Everything is going according to plan. Unless we meet with a problem, we'll be there right on time."

Of course, no battle plan survives contact with the enemy.

38

No one would have thought that a bridge could wreck Vicky's lovely plan. However, the one ahead of the stopped column was doing just that.

"Your Grace," the lieutenant colonel commanding the mechanized half of the force said, "they must have had a hell of a storm go through here a while back. That bridge has been weakened and it hasn't yet been repaired."

"If we lighten up the LAVs and most of us walk across, could we make this happen?"

The colonel was shaking his head as she asked.

"The middle of that bridge is missing most of its supports, ma'am. We put one of these things, even at its empty weight, and it will collapse the bridge, ma'am."

"Can we drive around it? Ford the river?"

Even as Vicky asked, four rigs pulled out of line. They'd lost their trailers and had more men walking alongside them as well as riding them. Two turned right, two left.

Troopers walked ahead of them, testing the ground which became critical really quick. The recent thunderstorms weren't the first rain they'd gotten. There were puddles in the fields and guides were sinking up to the top of their boots.

The rigs slipped and slid their way in a zig-zag course across the field.

Other troopers had dismounted and slid their way down to the stream. They were walking up or down the waterway. Some got very wet testing the depth of the water. None had made it to midstream and it was already up to their waist.

Other troops walked along, eyeing the embankment beside the stream. Just a bit past the bridge on both sides, it became tree-lined, with the tree roots holding tight to the walls of the bank. The entire watercourse presented one steep wall with no evidence of a way up or down.

Absent a tracked vehicle with a dozer blade, they were going nowhere.

"Captain Blue, I could use a miracle about now," Vicky said.

"The second taskforce that is coming in for a landing has four engineering rigs and the first two of my ground team. They have launched drones. We're doing a quick recon of the area, working with the engineers, and looking for anything to fix the bridge. Damn, but the nearest bridges are twenty miles up or down river over some real muddy roads. I don't think there's been much maintenance since the Red Shirts took over."

"I think you're right," Vicky said. "Could we use some explosives to blow some holes in the river bank?"

"Your Grace, that might get us attention we don't want. Two of the engineering LAVs have dozer blades on them. Oh, and we've just spotted a farm with a back hoe on a trailer already. If that can break up the bank a bit, the dozers should be able to do the rest."

"How long?"

"An hour, Your Grace. Maybe two. It depends on how fast we can get the back hoe here."

"We can't get even one rig across that bridge," Vicky said, eyeing the wooden structure that was causing her all this trouble.

"What good would one LAV on the other side do us?" Captain Blue asked.

"I could get some surveillance going on our targets," Vicky snapped.

Now the captain gave her his full attention. "First, Your Grace, we can't get even one rig across that bridge. It has no supports for half its length, and that half is the middle. Second, I have specific instructions from both Admiral Bolesław and your husband that if you try to pull any hair-brained Kris Longknife shit, I'm to handcuff you to a bed, naked. You remember what that was like, Your Grace?"

"I get handcuffed to a bed once, and everyone keeps throwing it at me," Vicky said, pouting. She was also considering making a run for the other side. Surely, she could find a truck or even a motorcycle on the other side to give her more mobility.

"You were handcuffed naked twice, Your Grace," the captain pointed out.

Vicky shivered. "I try to forget that first one."

"Sorry to remind you, Your Grace. Now, if you're thinking of bolting across the bridge, I should warn you that Admiral Bolesław provided me with a Wardhaven sidearm, given to him by General Juan Montoya when he and Kris came to your wedding. It has both lethal as well as sleepy darts. I've got it set for sleepy darts at the moment, though I could be persuaded to switch to live ammo. So, if you try to dash across that bridge, I figure I could drop you before you can get anywhere near it."

Vicky glared at her database spy. He smiled back.

"I expect I could drop you well before you got to the section of the bridge with no supports, okay?"

"What's the use of being a Grand Duchess when you have to put up with crap like this?"

"No doubt, if you'd behave like a Grand Duchess, you wouldn't have to put up with crap like this from your loyal and obedient subjects."

"*Obedient?*" Vicky snapped.

An old pick-up truck, that might have once been any number of colors, clattered and backfired its way up to the other side of the bridge. An old bald guy seemed to only then realize that there were a lot of guns pointed at him from the other side.

He rested his hands on the wheel in plain sight for a bit, then called out the window. "Should I shut off the engine and get out?"

"If you shut that old wreck's engine off, could you get it started again?" Vicky answered.

"It might be a problem, gal. Yes, it might."

"Leave it running, but get out. You don't have to keep your hands up."

He got up, but he kept his hands up. "If you don't mind, I'll just keep these empty and up so none of you young guys with guns think this grampa is a dangerous old coot."

"Were you planning on driving that rig across this bridge?" Vicky called over.

"I drove over it this morning. You got to kind of hug the north side, and not let the groaning and creaking put you off your feed, but you can do it. Likely not with one of those things, but old Nelly's a good old girl. She takes me where I want to go." He affectionately patted the bonnet of the old truck.

"So, if I walked across the bridge," Vicky said, eyeing Captain Blue and grinning, "and kept to the north side, I wouldn't be at any risk?"

"Sure enough, ma'am."

"Could I ask you for a favor?"

"With all them guns, you really think I'm going to refuse you anything?"

"Good point. All hands, point your weapons somewhere else than at this old coot," Vicky ordered.

Around Vicky, there was the slapping of metal and the clatter of weapons being switched from one purpose to another. Behind her came the sound of several autocannon turrets rotating out to cover another sector.

"Now, can I ask you for a favor?"

"Good God, little lady, who are you?"

"Some folks address me as Your Grace, the Grand Duchess Victoria of the Greenfeld Empire, but you can call me Vicky," she said, and managed an almost cute curtsy in full battle rattle.

"Good lordy, girl, I'd go down on a knee, but these old things don't bend so good, and I'm not sure I could get back up if I went down."

"Goodness, we aren't following court rules today. We're out to have fun blowing shit up."

"I kind of got that impression. Glad to hear that me and old Nelly aren't on your guest list today."

"No, I'm hunting Red Shirts."

The old guy spat. "Let me get my varmint rifle and I'll join you."

"You still have your varmint rifle?" Captain Blue asked.

"Son, we farmers ain't half as stupid as you fancy pants take us for. Of course, I knew when them Red Shirts were coming to collect our rifles. So, I hid it where none of them would look."

"Where was that?" Vicky asked.

"For you, ma'am, I'll answer. Under the manure pile. Deep under it. They never even took their metal detector near that pile of shit. Stupid townies." He spat again.

"Well, old timer, if I and a couple of my guards were to walk carefully over to your side of the river, could you give us a lift into town?"

"Be glad to, ma'am."

"Your Grace!" exploded from Captain Blue's lips.

"That's my title. Don't wear it out."

"But you know nothing about this fellow."

"I know he's got an old truck he's managed to keep running a hell of a lot longer than you or I could, and I know he's on the other side of this bridge, and you aren't. Now, are you coming with me or staying here?"

Captain Blue sputtered into silence at that question.

"Colonel," Vicky shouted, not even bothering to turn around. "I need a good NCO and three of your best trigger-pullers and a good explosives man, both at exploding them and at keeping them from making a racket."

"Command Sergeant Major?"

"Yes, Colonel."

"Three of your best sharp-shooters and a top engineer with plenty of explosives."

A minute later, three corporals, an engineering tech sergeant and the Command Sergeant Major stood at Vicky's elbow.

"I'm with you, Your Grace," Captain Blue muttered. "Mannie says he's going to tan your hide when he gets his hands on you."

"Oh, goodie! I've been trying to get him to try out some

fun things. Remind him that the next day, I get to take a switch to his hide."

The captain growled something that got lost in translation.

The smallest corporal led off, crossing the bridge first. The bridge hardly groaned.

Vicky checked out the other troopers and found herself likely the next lightest. She collected a spare bandolier of rifle ammo and another one of grenade rounds, then added a satchel of grenades. Loaded down, she began her own walk.

The corporal had snaked a twenty-millimeter rope across the bridge with him. Now he had it belayed on the other side, and Vicky found herself being attached to the rope.

After all the drama, she strode across the bridge with only a few groans from it for drama. She unhitched and then went over to the old timer.

"We haven't been introduced. I'm Vicky Peterwald."

He dunked his head at her greetings. "I'm William Foe, ma'am, at your service. Is that what I'm supposed to say?"

"Sir, you have the truck. You can say whatever you want. Can I off-load all this extra ammo?"

"Just put it in the back. Ma'am, usually we can fit three people up front if we're all friends, but I don't think we can fit more than you, what with that extra layer of skin you're wearing."

"And I'm not taking it off, so I guess you and me will be up front."

"Ma'am, I'm not complaining, but if we run into any Red Shirts, you and yours are going to stick out like a sore thumb."

"No doubt. However, we've got eyes in the sky and

should know about any roadblock well before they can see us."

"Oh, neat. You're about as smart as farmers are when it comes to outsmarting those scallywags."

"We try to stay a step ahead of them."

Captain Blue came over next with a large backpack added to his load. Vicky suspected the sack was full of small drones that would do just what she'd promised William.

Another corporal crossed. He packed a load of sacks hanging from his web gear, and likely carried more than he weighed. The bridge creaked and groaned and settled a bit under his tread, but it let him cross.

The command sergeant major was next, just as loaded down. He was followed by the explosives expert who trudged along, pulling a two-wheeled cart behind him. This did get the bridge seriously creaking and moaning. He paused a few times to let things settle back down, but in the end, he got across.

The third corporal was last. He was a bear of a man and lugged a light machine gun with a box of ammo in each hand and several belts of ammo draped over his shoulders. Vicky would swear that the bridge groaned more under him than it did under the explosives expert.

Still, all of them made it across, and the bridge was still standing. She gave the colonel a jaunty wave. He returned her a salute, and then turned his attention back to his part of the problem.

So, Vicky focused her attention on hers.

39

Now that Vicky had her squad across, she figured they were ready to get this show on the road. The explosives' cart, however, held everyone's attention. As it turned out, that wasn't too much of a problem. The old truck had a seriously rusted hitch and the tech sergeant rigged some cables from the cart to fit right onto it. Most of the explosives got loaded into it.

Vicky wondered if that would save them if the explosives blew up, but doubted it.

Her crew arranged themselves, one trigger-puller at each corner of the truck bed. The explosive sergeant took station at the rear, facing aft, keeping an eye on his cart.

Captain Blue launched four drones before settling down, cross legged, right behind the cab. Then he began fiddling with his battle board.

Quickly, a view appeared on it. He zoomed ahead to check the road. "All clear for the next five clicks or so. I aim to be twenty clicks ahead of us really quick."

"Well done, Captain," Vicky said and swung herself into

the cab, but with her carbine/rocket launcher ready between her legs.

The old-timer slid into his ragged seat, a cushion of some sort between him and the bare springs. "That thing loaded?" he asked.

"Of course, sir. In our line of work, they all are."

"Just so you don't shoot old Nelly," he said, fondly patting the dashboard.

"I wouldn't think of doing that. Ah, you do know the road between here and Dresden City, don't you?"

"Lady, I drive food to the farmers' market in that berg three, four times a week. I know the road, and I know that town. And I know where most of the Red Shirts hang out. I'm guessing you really don't want to get too close to them."

"That would be my first choice," Vicky admitted.

"Well, then let's get you into town."

They rattled along the road, dodging the worst of the potholes, but that still left a lot of small ones to clunk through. Vicky learned to ride easy, as if she was making a rough deorbit. She could get used to this.

Maggie gave Vicky a picture on her eyeball that told her what lay ahead. With the help of the drone, Vicky knew everything that was around each bend in the road, and there were more bends and curves as they wound their way across a rolling landscape of tree lines and crops. They rattled by potatoes, corn, sorghum, soybeans, and the inevitable wheat. This land was lush and green.

"How's business?" Vicky asked.

"You mean are the Red Shirts stealing us blind?"

"That tells me a lot."

"If I want to sell my stuff, I either sell it to them at the price they set, or I slip into the farmer's market, pay a bribe not to get hauled off to the calaboose, and see if I can make any profit."

"Which do you like to do most?" Vicky asked.

"I sell enough to stay on the right side of the tax collector. It's them that do the payout. Then, I take as much as I can keep out of their sticky fingers and sell it to the folks in town. I get more and they pay less."

"The Red Shirts are making money on selling food?"

"Girl, they're making money every turn you make. You Peterwalds were bad, God's truth, but this bunch, they're all in it for the money. They're bleeding us white. Hell, I don't know where I'm gonna get the money for fertilizer and pest control next year."

"It's that bad?"

"Yeah. So, tell me, are you one of those damn Peterwalds, or are you that gracious Grand Duchess I hear stories about?"

"My husband tries to keep me on the gracious side, though right now, my attitude toward those Red Shirts and the Bowlingame crime family is pure damn Peterwald."

"You'll get no complaint from me on that," he muttered.

The road turned from potholed gravel to potholed asphalt. The ride got a bit smoother, and the speed picked up.

"Not too far up here, there's going to be a guard house. I usually bribe them to get into town. I suspect there's no way we could bribe them today."

"The price on my head would buy a small moon," Vicky admitted.

"That much?"

"You want to collect it?" Vicky said, not going for her weapon.

"What would I do with the money? They'd just tax it

away from me. And that's assuming they don't just shoot me where I stand. I don't know if you've heard, but these guys don't have much of a reputation for trust and loyalty."

"No, I haven't heard, but I can't say I'm surprised."

"Your Grace," Captain Blue called from the back, "we've got a road block coming up two clicks past the next tree line."

"Thanks, Captain, our native guide had warned me about it. Do you and the sergeant major have any suggestions about how we handle it?"

There might have been some whispering, or maybe they just did that thing with their eyes that told them what the other thought.

"Sorry, Your Grace. Our best suggestion would be to stop here and see what we can do here until the rest of the brigade catches up."

"I kind of figured that."

Vicky kind of figured that because, at the moment, she couldn't think of any good ideas, either. They could probably kill them all from the tree line. She had good sharpshooters.

Still, they'd be dead, and if they got any radio check, dead men spoke no codes.

They could hold here, and she'd be safe and secure as the motorized cavalry came charging by.

What she wanted to be was well into town and getting some serious nano peeks at where the gunners were around those hostages. How many had their guns pointed in? How many out?

What would Kris Longknife do?

Vicky grinned.

"Captain, have I got an idea for you," she said, cheerfully.

The captain and the sergeant major both groaned.

40

"Lookie what I found!" the old codger said gleefully as his old wreck of a truck stopped ten meters out from the six armed Red Shirts standing in the road.

"What have you got, old fool?" the one with chevrons growled. From the look on his face, he'd never seen anything good come for someone with manure on their boots.

The old guy cackled as he jumped out of his rig and gleefully ran around to the other side. It was dark, and the windows were too dirty for the sergeant to get much of a look at who his passenger was. Bored, he waited for whatever this guy thought was so funny.

He hauled open a door that squealed horribly, like it hadn't been oiled since it was sold. He grabbed ahold of a shoulder and hauled a figure of medium height in full space armor out for all them to see.

For a long moment, they just stared dumbly at her. They had to know she was a her. The top of her armor had the extra room she needed for her Empire-renowned jugs.

"I found her, floundering around in a field, all by herself.

I used a pitchfork, me and my boys, and we got her hands tied. I figured you boys would want to see someone like this."

"Raise her visor," the sergeant said, eyeing the armored jumpsuit cautiously.

About the time the farmer got the visor up, he also took in the three black stars on the armored shoulders. "This can't be," he muttered.

"Yeah, yeah, yeah," Vicky said. "My first jump mission and I can't get the damn chute to go right. See if I try another one of these things. Kris Longknife can do her own stunts. Me, I'm staying home and buffing my nails."

Six Red Shirts stared blankly at her.

"What's the matter, haven't you ever seen a Grand Duchess before?" Vicky snapped into the silence.

The litany of obscenities that came back at her would have definitely earned this scene a X rating. It will likely sell a million extra videos, maybe more, depending on what these guys with the popguns got away with doing to her. There were a whole lot of "We're rich! We're rich!

"Cecil, frisk her for weapons! Now! And check for booby traps!"

"Can I check her boobies?" Cecil said, grinning from ear to ear.

"Check for weapons and explosives," the sergeant repeated.

So, Cecil patted Vicky down. This pat down was a lot less fun to receive than the last guy to pat her down. Vicky really was in full space armor. There was enough ceramic plate to keep his filthy fingers from getting a good feel. Still, he had to lift her up by her crotch to see if there was any way he could get a finger in.

Vicky huffed at the try to feel her up.

And all hell broke loose.

41

"Will you keep your bleeding fingers to yourself?" Vicky snapped, and stumbled. She pitched forward just enough to head butt the sergeant. He fell backwards, and she fell on top of him.

Beside her, the old farmer hit the deck.

At that instant Captain Blue rolled out from under the truck. In his hands, he held the sidearm Jack had given him for a present at Vicky's wedding. Being from Wardhaven, it had the option of killing or putting someone to sleep. For now, he was firing sleepy darts.

He took down three of the Red Shirts.

The sergeant major was carrying a Greenfeld carbine with rocket launcher. Like all Greenfeld weapons, it had one option: kill. The heads of two Red Shirts exploded as he hit them with one shot each.

Under Vicky, the sergeant was struggling to get at his automatic. Vicky pulled her hands out of her restraints and chopped at the sergeant's hand. At the same instant, she brought her helmet down hard on his chin.

He kept struggling, so she did it again. This time, he slumped under her, still half-struggling.

Vicky rolled off of him; the captain put a sleepy dart right in the middle of his chest. He groaned and relaxed, out cold.

"William, would you mind going back and getting the rest of the team?"

"No problem, ma'am," and the cheerful old farmer quickly turned his old rig around and headed back to where the other half of the team was.

While the captain kept his automatic out, roving the prisoners, the sergeant major and Vicky set about binding the arms and legs of the four surviving Red Shirts. Once that was done, Vicky checked out the roadblock.

Two big chunks of concrete broke the road up, blocking both lanes. Any traffic would have to slowly weave its way through the two obstacles. There were three spiked strips; two had their spikes hard up. They were on either shoulder. The other one was more sophisticated. It was between the concrete and had spikes down until a transmitted order them popped them up.

No, this was no roadblock to charge.

Parked behind the forward concrete blockage was a big, new, fancy red pickup truck. It had room for six in the cab and a full load of equipment in the truck bed. However, a glance at the fancy cargo liner suggested that nothing much had ever marred the cargo area.

It was basically a truck for city folks.

What the truck didn't have was a radio. Same for the four surviving soldiers. No radio. The sergeant major fumbled around in the bloody mess of what was left of the two heads he had nearly blown off, but shook his head. "No radio. No mic."

Vicky eyed their four sleeping beauties, then, with a grim smile, settled on Cecil. "Captain, wake that one up."

"With pleasure," he said, and gave the chosen prisoner the antagonist to the sleepy dart.

Vicky borrowed the sergeant major's combat knife and had it resting firmly against Cecil's unarmored balls when he woke up.

Feeling something there, he grabbed for the family jewels.

"I wouldn't do that if I was you," Vicky said, her voice dripping evil intent.

Cecil froze in place.

Vicky flicked the knife a bit. The Red Shirt risked a look down, then whimpered as he saw how sharp the knife was and where it rested.

"I did not like you feeling me up, Cecil," Vicky said, so soft. So deadly. She raised the knife, then rested its point down on the guy's fundamentals before she slowly hopped the point up to the lump in his pants.

His hands fluttered, as if he couldn't control them, torn between reaching to cover himself and terrified of how Vicky would react. He whimpered again, and a tear rolled down his face.

His red pants darkened as he voided his bladder.

They really got a courageous one with this guy, Vicky thought.

Then, none of the six had covered themselves with glory. Somebody brought Vicky in and all they could do is jump up and down with glee and start spending the reward money.

Stupid.

"Tell me, Cecil, where's the radio?"

"We ain't got no radio."

"Don't kid with me." Vicky let the knife bear down. The cloth on his pants leg ripped. It was loud enough to dull the far-off sounds of thunder.

"I swear. They don't give us no radio. We used to have a net hot spot in the truck, but it don't work no more."

Vicky raised her eyebrow, and Captain Blue ducked around to rummage around the foot well in the truck's front.

"So how do they know you're really out here?"

"An officer comes by here, maybe once a week, maybe every other week. If a roadblock isn't fully manned, the guys missing, we all get to watch them hang. They hang 'em slow. They're a long time dying. You don't call in sick with this outfit."

"Shoot him," Vicky said.

"No!" Cecil's scream was cut off when the sleepy dart quickly took effect.

Captain Blue returned, wiping dirt from his hands. "There used to be a net hot spot under the dashboard in that rig. Somebody pulled it out. No way to know if they did that before or after they closed down the planetary net."

"I imagine once they showed their guards a few horrible hangings, they figured they didn't need the tech out here."

The captain grunted agreement.

Vicky examined the several problems in front of her. If you had enough problems, you might find them solving each other.

Unfortunately, today's problems didn't look all that interested in each other.

She now possessed a roadblock with two dead and four sleeping Red Shirts. She could make them all dead, but still, they'd be a hot datum if anyone wandered by and noticed the situation.

It would look better if the roadblock looked like the

guards had wandered off and abandoned their post. Much better than having dead bodies lying around.

In addition, she'd come here to scout out the enemy and figure out the best way to free the hostages with few, but preferably no casualties. The more time she spent here, the less time she was doing recon.

She needed to either abandon or guard the roadblock while getting herself and the captain forward.

"Maggie, have they gotten anything across the river?"

"Sorry, Your Grace. Both the backhoe and the dozer blade are thirty minutes out. There is no estimate as to how fast they can get the brigades moving after that."

Vicky turned to the farmer, who was doing his best not to look at the nearly headless dead bodies now attracting flies.

"William, could I interest you in a brand spanking new, red truck?"

"Oh, no, no, no, you don't," he said, waving both hands at Vicky. "I'm hoping you pull this off as much as the next guy. Honest to God, I am. Still, if you fall flat on your face, I don't want no angry Red Shirts finding no red truck in my front yard. No way. Besides, my missus would kill me if I brought that home in place of Nelly."

Well, that settled one option.

"Okay, crew, load the dead and sleeping up on William's truck. William, I really appreciate all your help. If you'll just take these prisoners back to the bridge and bring forward a squad of troopers to guard this roadblock, I'll consider your oath of loyalty to the Empire fulfilled and list your name among the honored saviors of the Empire."

"Wow, you can talk real fancy-like."

"I do when people like you earn it," Vicky said, with a noble smile.

The guy preened. "Could you make me a knight?"

"I don't have a sword at the moment."

"You got that really sharp knife."

So, Vicky took the sergeant major's combat knife and knighted a kneeling old coot while he grinned from ear to ear.

"Wait 'til Myrtle hears this," he said, standing.

"You may be invited to a more formal ceremony later," she said.

"Yep. White tie and all," Captain Blue laid it on thick.

"I don't own no tie, white or otherwise."

Now Vicky grinned. "I'm sure we can find a rental service that can fit you and your lady for a formal ceremony."

"Wow!"

Vicky eyed the back of Nelly. Her corporals had loaded two dead bodies, wrapped in rain ponchos first. On top of them sprawled four sleeping guys. They were hog-tied, hands to feet, and together into two pairs.

"I'll get them back to your guys at the bridge," William said, and his clattering pickup truck was soon headed back the way it came.

"So, we now possess a bright red truck," the captain said.

"Yeah. You got any idea how we turn our camos into bright Red Shirt uniforms?"

"None at all."

"Sergeant, do you have any red paint in your explosive kit?"

"Ma'am, I've got orange and monkey puke green paint to mark stuff, but no red."

That brought things to a rolling halt.

"Ah, Sergeant Major, there might be a way to turn the uniforms, ah, red," a corporal said, his face turning red as a strawberry.

"And that would be?" said sergeant major, turning his stormy visage upon the junior sharpshooter.

"Ah, Sergeant, er, um, you remember a few months back when the, ah, new LT's battle suit developed a glitch during inspection?"

"And turned a bright pink?" the sergeant major growled, like a lion on the prowl.

"That very time, Sergeant Major."

Vicky interposed herself between the sergeant and a very cowed corporal.

"I know my armor can switch between many camo patterns," Vicky said. "Pink, though?"

"Actually, Grand Duchess, Your Grace, if you know the cheat codes, you can access all the different colors. And, yes, Your Grace, some camos patterns use a bit of red, ma'am."

"You wouldn't happen to know those cheat codes, would you, Corporal?"

"Ah, I might have overheard, you know, through the grapevine, what someone else used."

"Very good. Work with Captain Blue to access the battle suits' camo pattern app and see if you can turn our suits red."

"Yes, Your Grace," the corporal said, saluted, and hurried over to the captain.

Vicky sidled up to the command sergeant major who was giving the corporal a look that said this was not over yet.

"Problem, Sergeant?" Vicky asked.

"That damn E-4 strikes again," he muttered.

"You have my permission to shoot him when we are done here. However, when you are finished with him, I want him promoted to staff sergeant. That took a lot of guts to let us know how to solve our problem."

"Yes, Your Grace," was one of the rare times Vicky heard

that expression and felt like the NCO speaking really meant it.

Five minutes later, their green, gray, and tan camo pattern showed bright red, to match the uniforms of the failed and now departed roadblock detail.

"You think this is gonna work?" Captain Blue asked.

Vicky picked up one of the baseball caps the guards had been wearing, expanded it out as far as the back would go, and rested it atop her helmet. "It's a dark and stormy night. Maybe if they don't look too hard, we can fool them."

"Yes, Your Grace," the command sergeant major drawled slowly. Vicky was back to being one of those dumb officers.

The demolition tech sergeant took the wheel; Vicky rode shotgun.

Behind her rode the command sergeant major and Captain Blue. There sergeant's gun rested low, the captain's battle board was reflected on his face. In the truck bed behind them, the three corporals were laying down, out of sight, and likely asleep.

The full contents of the cart had been transferred to the back of the truck. Spare ammo occupied what was left of the center seats.

They were ready, once again, to go to war.

42

They slowed as they got close to town. The drones showed the road ahead almost empty. Captain Blue, however, could not determine if there was a camera surveillance system. All he'd found so far was a police radio net and two TV stations.

There was still the occasional shower moving along behind the cold front that added mist to the night air. In the streetlights, the streets steamed as they gave up the heat that had collected during the recent heat wave. The air smelled fresh and cool.

They pulled off the road into a bar's gravel parking lot and drove around back. There was a batch of trees there. The sergeant parked under the canopy of a wide-spreading chestnut.

Vicky had Maggie release a small wave of nanos to check out the bar.

There were more people inside than the number of cars in the parking lot would lead you to expect, but a newly launched drone soon showed people walking in from several apartment complexes in the general neighborhood.

Apparently, fuel or electricity was in short supply.

Analysis of the airwaves around the bar found it dead, except for the two TV channels. The first nanos in the bar showed all of the TVs tuned to one station; it was showing a hockey game. Some patrons grumbling told Vicky that they usually had a different game and a different sport on each of the four TVs in the establishment.

People were none too happy, but the grumbling was low-key. Still, every time the door opened, every voice fell silent and every eye turned to check out the newcomer.

Only when someone already there recognized the new people and called them over to their table, did talk return to normal.

Did Vicky dare ask anyone in there about the situation in town?

The nanos searched the bar thoroughly and found no landline or net hot spot. If she risked going in there, would any Red Shirt supporter be able to call out the guard?

Vicky decided to close down that line of thinking. She didn't need to know anything that these people knew, and it was better that they knew nothing about what this night would entail.

Satisfied that the surroundings were benign, they moved out again. The looks they got as they drove back onto the road from people walking to the bar were uninformative bland . . . or from eyes tight with hatred.

Two klicks further in, they pulled into a strip mall parking lot to check matters out carefully. It was twelve midnight local time, and the lot was empty. However, all the lights were off. The two restaurants that shared the strip mall's parking lot were also closed down and dark.

Apparently, no one ate late at night.

"Any evidence of security cameras?" Vicky asked Captain Blue.

"I haven't spotted any of the usual telltales. No cameras, no solar panels to power them. No nothing. Maybe the suburbs don't rate heavy surveillance?"

"Or maybe the cameras that ain't been knocked out have been moved in closer to the center, Your Grace," the command sergeant major suggested.

"Good point, sergeant. Captain, you have any good thoughts on where a surveillance camera would have been if there had been one here?"

"Let me see, ma'am," was distracted.

"No, nothing there," he muttered a moment later.

After a few minutes, he added, "Not there, either."

Two minutes later, "Gotcha!" resounded through the truck cabin. "There! Just right there would have been a surveillance camera to cover both traffic and the parking lot, you can see where the camera has been removed as well as the solar cells. Sergeant, you nailed that one."

"They're robbing Peter to pay Paul," the old NCO said, proudly. "Not a good policy."

"But for a crumbling half of the Empire, maybe the only good practice," Vicky said, "even if it will spell their doom."

They drove deeper into the urban sprawl. They passed burned out businesses and homes. There were even factories that had one or two buildings burned to the ground.

Vicky shook her head; she knew that the Bowlingames played a vicious game. Give people an offer to sell out for pfennigs on the mark or be burned out or maybe locked up on some trumped-up charges. Now she was seeing it on Dresden.

"There's a major burned out area ahead," Captain Blue announced.

Vicky remembered the reports she'd heard about the Duke of Redebuel, the Butcher of Dresden. She'd also been delighted to kill the son of a bitch when he attempted to do to St. Petersburg what he'd done to Dresden.

"Let's skirt it," Vicky said. "Isn't it about time we get off the main drag?"

The demolition sergeant turned right, and they began to zig and zag down the darkened streets. There were few burning streetlamps and the clouds covered the moon and stars. Captain Blue kept up a running series of recommendations of where to turn.

"I'm starting to spot solar panels. I expect they have cameras nearby."

"Let us get close to one," Vicky said. "I'd like to see if Maggie could get a hook into whatever landline net they're using."

"Turn right and go two blocks. There's a church. Park in the lot."

The sergeant did.

"Three blocks over is a four-lane highway," Captain Blue said. "Where it intersects with this road, you should find some light poles. Check out the northeast one."

"Maggie?" Vicky said.

"Already on it. Captain Blue, you have a micro drone close at hand. Could I hitch a ride?"

"By all means."

A small rotor craft formed and lifted off from the block of Smart Metal beside Vicky on the front seat. It flitted out her window. One of Captain Blue's small, four-rotor drones snatched it out of the air. It then headed down the street.

An older woman walked up the street, a dog on a leash. She didn't look up at the silent drone. She did see the red truck parked in the church lot, and crossed the street, immediately. She had to hold the dog in tight on its leash.

It growled at the red truck, showing ready teeth.

"Sad when dogs don't like you because of the color truck you drive," the sergeant said from beside Vicky.

"Yeah," she agreed.

"I have several nanos examining a security camera," Maggie announced.

Vicky said nothing, waiting for more information.

"The surveillance camera is a net hot spot," Maggie reported. "If we still had our own hot spot, we could likely talk to it. There are several different channels. I am accessing them. Chatter is light. A major security presence is at the Governor General's residence, although there is some Duke living there, now."

"Quite a party going on, huh?" Vicky asked.

"Yes, Your Grace," Maggie reported. "There are reports on net that a second quarter of the invasion force is getting underway from the station. There is much celebration."

"Can you connect me to Admiral Bolesław?" Vicky asked.

"Yes, Your Grace."

"We're a bit behind schedule here," Vicky said.

"So I see," Admiral Bolesław answered, dryly.

"Is the radar down? Is the second landing team coming down to the east?"

"Yes, Your Grace. I'm told that the west landing group has breached the river bank in several places and is crossing the river now. However, it's backed up quite a way, so it's taking a lot more time to cross than driving over a bridge would take."

"Will there be any problem with the east landing group?"

"I honestly can't tell you, Your Grace. We added several light gun trucks to the first wave, then solid bridging material to the second wave. We've got bridging material headed your way, as well, but you're still several hours away from a functioning bridge."

"I hate Murphy," Vicky grumbled.

"I'd really love to give that guy a dishonorable discharge," Admiral Bolesław agreed.

"Okay. Have you got my location identified?"

"Yes, Your Grace. You are way out in front and extremely lacking in backup."

"Understood, but this place is really dead. Not much going on."

"Don't be so sure of that. We're tracking traffic in town. It's after curfew. Anyone moving is a bad guy."

"We've got the big drones overhead and the captain has skitter drones checking ahead of us. Now I've got Maggie in what's left of their net. I should be able to slip like a mouse through their walls."

"Please don't get cocky, Your Grace. We've only got the one of you and we really don't want to lose you."

"Thank you for your vote of support."

With the Red Shirt net now hooked into Captain Blue's computer, Vicky felt a lot more comfortable. They could see what was ahead of them. They could hear what the bad guys were talking about to each other.

Slipping through their net would be easy.

She was already picking out just exactly where she wanted to park this rig so she could do the best recon possible.

In the center of town there was a major square, two blocks long, full of trees. At one end was the Governor General's residence. At the moment, several blackened heads hung from gibbets on the front yard.

No wonder folks had been muttering so low in the bar.

At the opposite end of the Park Blocks was a tall hotel that covered one block. A large tower, thirty stories high, was reported to hold the high value hostages. Others were locked into the ballrooms and exhibit halls of the three-story convention center that took up the next two blocks.

The head honcho of the Red Shirts had bragged that they had demolition charges rigged under the tower that would drop it right down on the convention center.

Just in case, they also had claymore mines scattered liberally around the walls of the hostage pens.

Really sick minds.

Vicky needed to get a solid handle on this place and make sure the slaughter didn't happen. Of course, she might also call in a strike of 18-inch lasers from orbit on that dude's roof.

Vicky had one eye on the map Maggie was projecting on her right eyeball. Her other eye was taking in the situation around them.

They were coming up on a car wash. Maybe it had better business before matters went to hell, but for now, all its wash bays were empty. All but one. In it, a truck sat, all dark and alone.

No. Were those seatbacks or were they heads? In the quick passage of light from their own headlights, Vicky couldn't quite make out what she saw.

They rolled past the wash and passed the vacant lot of another strip mall.

Vicky glanced in the rearview. Something was following them, its bright lights on, dazzling her eyes.

"Captain, can you get a make on the rig behind us?"

"Something's behind us?"

"It wasn't, but now it is."

"On it, Your Grace."

In the dark, all cats are black and so are all trucks. They passed under one of the few working streetlights. A moment later, the rig behind them did the same.

It was red.

"Take a right the next chance you get," Vicky ordered the sergeant.

The sergeant made a smooth right turn not five seconds later.

Vicky hardly breathed as she waited for the red pickup to pass along the four-lane street they'd been driving.

It reached the corner, and seemed to come to a dead stop. Vicky held her breath.

A moment later, the truck turned to follow them.

"Speed up," Vicky ordered.

The sergeant took the truck up to 10 kph over the speed limit.

Behind them, the red truck began to close.

Vicky was no longer going to war. It had come for her.

43

Vicky flipped the dice; fight or flight.

She chose flight.

"Turn left," she said, aiming them closer into town. They turned from one residential street to another, narrower one.

"Captain, any suggestions as to how we ditch that truck would be greatly appreciated at this point."

"Hook a right and gun it," the captain said, voice even.

They hooked a right just as the red truck turned into their street.

"Go right next street," the captain ordered, "and floor it."

They did.

"Go left next, and go for it."

They made the turn back onto the street they started the case from on two squealing wheels, but they made it and the sergeant gunned them down the wider road.

"You're going to take the second right," the captain ordered.

They were off that road before their pursuit came to it.

"Take the next right and go for all you're worth."

"The police net," Maggie reported, "has a report of an unidentified red truck in the area. All units are ordered to be on the lookout for any truck they don't think belongs there."

"What do they mean by that?" Vicky asked.

"A lot of guys are asking the same question," Maggie said. "I think a lot of trucks will be stopping a lot of trucks for a while."

"That can't be bad," Vicky said.

"Until someone stops us," the captain said. "Hook the next right. Our pursuer is checking out the roads around the main drag. Go left after that and stand by to make a hard left again."

They zoomed down four blocks when the captain shouted, "Go left, now!"

They hooked left on two wheels, then zoomed six blocks in before going hard right.

"There's another main drag up the way, about ten blocks. If we can make it, we hook a left and see how far we can get into town before we have any more trouble."

"Got it," the sergeant said.

They made it to the four-lane artery and slowed to the speed limit. They passed several red cars and trucks headed in the opposite direction in a rush, but no one seemed concerned about a truck going about its business on the main drag in a calm and normal fashion.

Vicky began to breathe evenly. She even risked a few deep breaths.

Then a real, honest-to-God, police car did a u-turn and sped up to follow them.

"Right turn," the captain ordered.

The sergeant went right.

"What do we do this time, Grand Duchess?" the captain asked.

"We stop when they tell us to," Vicky ordered. "Tell the gunners in back to get ready to fire when ordered."

"Aye, aye, ma'am," the gunny said, and muttered some orders through the back window at the sharpshooters laying quiet in the back.

Behind them, the police car popped its bubble lights on, flashing red and blue. Without a word, the sergeant slowed the car to the curb.

They were three blocks off the main arterial road. Around them were blacked out houses with not so much as a porch light on.

It was time to fight.

There was no way their armored jump suits could be taken for standard issue here. The three heavily armed and armored troops laying in the back couldn't pass muster. As soon as anyone got a look at them, everything would hit the fan.

One officer got out of the driver's side. He was a tall man in blue pants and a white shirt with sergeant chevrons. He held a stubby machine pistol at the ready using both hands. A second officer got out of the passenger side and squatted down, machine pistol wedged between the car and the wide-open door, covering the stopped truck.

Little trust here.

Vicky got out, her hands spread wide, unthreatening. She had ditched her silly baseball cap a few blocks back.

"A problem sergeant?" she asks.

He eyed Vicky cautiously. Maybe he was a bit confused by the battle rattle all in red.

"We're looking for a truck that isn't behaving normally."

"We're about as normal as you can get."

Only a woman in battle armor is not normal in the

Greenfield Empire. Vicky made her voice lower, gruffer. Now it was up to the sergeant to make the next move.

"I've never seen anyone in full armor," the police sergeant said, cautiously. "Hell, I've never seen anyone in any armor."

"We found some in storage a few days ago," Vicky answers. "What with the bitch's ships overhead, we figured we might have a need for it. We're just cruising around, waiting for a call."

"I didn't hear anything like that at briefing."

Vicky rolled her eyes. Shrugging was not an option in play clothes. "You know how it is. The right hand don't know what the left hand is doing."

"Yeah. Ain't that right," the police sergeant agreed. "Now, if you'll just let me inspect your truck, whoever you are, we can settle who you really are."

"Okay, okay," Vicky said. "I just wanted to save your life."

Before the cop could react to Vicky's words, the three corporals in back sat up. One put a shot in the sergeant's center of mass, then snapped off another in the middle of his forehead.

The other two sharpshooters had a tougher job. The patrolman was hunched down, behind the door, only his head above the V made by the sedan and the door. One round went high. The other hit the man right between his eyes.

Both men dropped like sacks of cement.

"Get them in the trunk," Vicky snapped, then eyed the sergeant major. "Let's get this show on the road."

"What do you have in mind?" came from both senior NCOs and the captain.

"They're looking for a red truck. We'll give them a police car and a red truck together. How about that?"

"Sounds good to me," said the sergeant major.

Two bodies were quickly stowed in the trunk.

In a few minutes, Vicky was back on one of the main arteries headed into the center of town with the police car's lights on and them riding right on its bumper. The sergeant major now road shotgun as one of the corporals drove the police cruiser.

Things went fine for all of five minutes.

"We've been asked why we're leaving the area in such a hurry," the sergeant major reported on net.

"Wait one," the captain said, then grinned. "Tell them you're in pursuit of a red truck. Then pull over five streets up."

They did. Quickly, the bodies were relocated into the seats, however, the seatbelts were not used. This time, flying through the air upon impact would be a feature, not a failure.

While that was done, Maggie fiddled with the controls for the car.

"Okay, I can do this," Maggie announced proudly about the time the car was ready to roll.

They all got back into the truck and follow the car with the lights flashing. The police car really hit the gas. It was doing a good 60 kph when it failed to make a slight turn in the road and slammed into a tree.

As they motored by, Vicky saw where the two occupants had been thrown through the windshield. Docs would have a hard time telling that mess from gunshot wounds.

"Hook a left," the captain ordered. "We've been going right way too much.

Two main drags over, they turned toward town again.

A moment later, a police car, siren and lights blaring shot past them, followed by a red truck. A few seconds later, there was a second noisy cop car and a closely following red truck.

"Don't just sit there, use your initiative," Vicky said, grinning at the sergeant.

He floored it and joined the chase.

They all slowed and turned right, wheels squealing, as they came to a major cross street. They now had another truck behind them. A few blocks up the cross street, Vicky decided they'd cooperated enough.

"Slow and go left when you can."

The sergeant did.

Apparently, the red pickup truck lacked net access. When they went left, he assumed he should search to the right.

Vicky's ride sped away from that collection of bloodhounds with stuffed up noses.

"There's a rail line ahead," Captain Blue reported. "We can't stay on a side street and cross that track. Is it time to go to ground, Your Grace?"

"Let's get closer in," Vicky said. "Turn us back left when we get a block from the track."

They zigged and zagged, with no one the wiser. They got back on the four-lane road just before it ducked under a rail overpass. Ahead, they could see skyscrapers in the mist. Most showed little lighting, but some burned with a subdued flame.

"Duck right," Captain Blue said. "Pull off if you see a place. Douse your lights."

The lights went off and they turned down a side street, then into a loading dock.

"What's going in?" Vicky asked.

"They found the wreckage of the police cruiser. A whole lot of people are headed in that direction. Your Grace, is there any chance you could see your way through to calling this forward enough for you?"

Vicky fidgeted. "I need to get a look at the explosives in the convention center," she said. "I need for Maggie to cut the wires. Most of the other targets are on the outskirts of town. Others have straight-in road access, so our troops can race down right to them. That's not the case for that building off Park Square."

"So, we have to get closer," did not sound happy.

"How are the assault teams coming?" Vicky asked.

"Admiral Bolesław?" the captain asked.

"Captain Blue, this time it is you who calls. How can I help you?"

"A certain woman we all know, and dread, is trying to urge us deeper into the lion's maw. Do we have any back up on the way?"

"Some is coming in from both the east and west. However, it is not coming nearly fast enough to please me."

"Do you have our location?"

"Yes."

"Do you see our opposition?"

"Lots of it."

"Any suggestion?"

"Find a nice place to park and wait for the cavalry."

"I'll get back to you in a bit," the captain said, then turned to Vicky. "Your Grace, you have your neck way out here. You need to pull it in."

"I can't do what I came here to do from this far back," Vicky said.

"You can't do what you came here to do if you get suddenly dead or thrown in a jail rigged to explode before the cavalry gets here."

"That is a good point."

"So, we stay here."

"No. We edge a bit more forward. Then, we'll see if we can use a couple of your rotor copters to get my nanos in close."

"Your Grace," came as a tired sigh that clearly held no deference in it.

"Captain, you keep your scouts out and we go careful. Okay?"

"Okay. Sergeant, you can drive forward through this industrial area. I don't see any police. Still, keep it to the speed limit and be ready to slam on the brakes."

"Yes, sir."

They pulled out of the loading dock and drove at the twenty-five kph speed limit over roads that had more potholes per square meter than the farm-to-market gravel roads. All the buildings around them were blacked out.

There was not so much as a glimmer in the dark night.

They reached the edge of the industrial park and motored into an old area of town. It had two and three-story shops, small businesses, and eateries.

All were closed for the night.

The sergeant managed to drive another ten blocks before the captain snapped. "There's a garage up here. Turn in and kill the lights."

The sergeant got them down a ramp into a basement and turned right. Then doused the lights and rolled to a halt.

A minute or so later, a light played on the ramp behind them. Its reflection lit up the space for a moment; then it moved on.

Vicky breathed a sigh of relief, then went back to the mission.

"Can we keep moving?"

"I really don't think so, Your Grace," the captain said. "They've got cars and trucks all over the place."

"So, do we walk?"

"Why not try out this building? It's three stories high. Maybe a bit higher if we stand on some of the stuff on the roof."

"Do we have a clear line of sight?"

"I think we have something close to it," the captain answered.

"Okay," Vicky said, turning to her demolition expert. "Sergeant, make it deadly to get into this building."

"You bet," he grinned.

"Sergeant Major, you help our demolition expert, then figure out fallback positions. If someone wants to get to the roof, we want to make it as deadly for them as we can."

"With pleasure, Your Grace," he said. The two sergeants had their corporals soon out of the back and lugging sacks of explosives around.

"Captain, shall we go discover if we can view what we came for from the roof of this fine place?"

"Yes, Your Grace."

Getting to the roof took a few wads of explosives to blow locks, but five minutes after they started, they squatted low atop the elevator well, four stories up from the street level.

In the middle distance, the bright lights of the duke's residence glowed into the night, reflecting off the low clouds. Two blocks to the left of it a dimly lit tower rose, silhouetted for a moment by a distant lightning strike.

"Are the skitter drones around?" Vicky asked.

Five came to hover over the captain. Two settled down and he attached them to chargers.

"What about the other three?" Vicky asked.

"They can make a trip into the target and back."

"Maggie, attach a kilo of Smart Metal to each of the skitter drones."

The gray seven-kilo block of metal that Vicky had lugged up five flights of stairs shed nearly half of its mass. A few moments later, the captain's three copters were on their way.

Ten minutes later, the two remaining quad-rotor copters had recharged enough to be dispatched and chase after the first three that had just arrived in the vicinity of the Park Blocks.

Two turned for the tower and convention center. One headed for the brightly lit residence. It was time for Vicky to get to work.

"Maggie, use one kilo as drones to scope out the residence. If there's a way to cut its access to the net, I'd like to cut him off. If he's got a button he can push to blow up all the hostage pens, I want it dead."

"On it."

"Of the other two kilos of Smart Metal, I want one of them to tackle the tower, or more likely, the basement of the thing. We need to know where the explosives are that would drop the place on the convention center next door."

"I can do that," Maggie replied.

"When you can, use the last kilo to go looking in the convention center and see if you can find out how the explosives there work. We need to deactivate them as well."

"I am on all three, Your Grace."

"Now we sit and wait," Vicky muttered.

"We've got company," the captain said softly.

"What kinds of company?" Vicky demanded, but just as softly.

"Ten blocks up, back where we drove out of the industrial park, there's a strake bed truck offloading about twenty men, all armed. Wait one."

Vicky prepared to wait however long she had to.

"They're splitting up. Half are coming down our road. Half are walking back up into the industrial area. Oh, now there are trucks at all twenty roads, more to our right than left. It looks like they're ready to go house to house."

"Should I have a corporal make a break for it in the truck?" the sergeant major asked.

"No," Vicky said. "That would be a suicide mission. See if someone can hide the truck deeper in the basement. Find a tarp. Garbage. Something to cover it with."

"Working on that one while also getting the explosives distributed. We ought to be able to withstand a week-long siege what with all the explosives this guy brought."

"Thanks. Now, I've got my nano scouts reporting back. Let's take a look at what we've come downtown to see."

It didn't take long to find the explosives packed around several of the main supports on the north side of the hotel's parking garage. Vicky got the pictures and passed them along to the demolition sergeants.

"Yep, that will bring the place falling down over the next two blocks," he agreed. "Let me finish up here and I'll see if I can get up there and we can cut the ties that bind."

"Sergeant, do you have any nice noise makers, firecrackers, something like that?" the captain asked.

"I have a few nice noise makers that will get everyone's head down. Why, sir?"

"I've got some quad copters about three minutes out. I may need to charge them, but I'd love to get these guys chasing their own shadows."

"You're a man after my own heart," the tech sergeant

said. "I'll send a corporal up with a handful of these fun rumpus makers."

Vicky watched as her nano scouts mapped the insides of three buildings. All the charges that would blow up the convention center led to one central box. However, outside each ballroom, there was a switch that anyone could use to create bloody havoc among the hostages who lay strewn haphazardly around the floor, trying to sleep.

Vicky would have to disable a lot of boxes if she wanted to stop a bloody slaughter. Meanwhile, as she worked on that problem, she kept one eye on the captain's board.

Behind her, Red Shirts were going from street to street, door to door, checking to see that each was locked, and ducking into loading docks to check them out. Slowly but surely, they were finding their way toward her building.

Things would get terminal when the red-shirted searchers toddled down the garage ramp and got a good look at the red pickup truck.

Vicky and her tiny team needed to buy time. Time for the cavalry to get here. Time for them to safety the explosives around the hostages.

They needed time, but it was running out fast for them.

44

The first rotor copter staggered back from the Park Blocks. It was so low on power it couldn't make it to the roof of the elevator well. The captain just barely got it up to the roof of the third floor before the rotors gave out.

He raced to get it, got it charging, and eyed the five little round cylinders a corporal had brought up from the demolition sergeant. The captain attached a small harness to the copter that would fit the bomb quite well.

He just needed enough time to charge the quad rotor copter.

Vicky went about her business. The duke's residence was hard to navigate through. There were a lot of people celebrating. Moreover, there were a lot of guards circulating around the halls. All the doors above the first level, and many on that floor, were locked. Vicky would to have to maneuver her scouts around closed doors if she wanted to see what was behind them.

For the moment, she chose to start at the top and work down. She did find a comm center on the top floor. She got a nanos into their lines and started messing with their links. It might or might not tell her something.

As it turned out, it did.

"Make damn sure circuit ten isn't glitching!" an officer snapped at a sergeant, "You start blowing up hostages because you failed to get a clean hook up and you'll be out on the lawn, taking days to die."

Vicky started hunting for circuit ten. With the guy checking it by hand, it wasn't hard to find. The circuit was very busy, pings going out every second to over twenty different sites.

That bothered Vicky. They'd only identified eight hostage concentrations. Were there twenty?

"I've got one copter juiced enough for a short run," the captain said, next to Vicky. They were now keeping their heads down, just lying flat on the roof.

Captain Blue launched his copter. It staggered into the air, struggling to lug the noise maker with its reduced power supply. Still, it made it up and began a slow glide, losing height as it headed for the next block over, then turned up the street.

The captain guided it to where a couple of squads were just finishing up one block and were getting ready to cross to the next. The copter tilted right and dropped its noise maker about in the middle of the block, between two armed groups.

A shot rang out. It was followed by several more.

The two squads ducked back, taking cover. One intrepid soul risked putting his hand around the corner, weapon in it. He blasted off a magazine on full auto.

Bullets started hitting all around the buildings in front of the next squad over.

Someone stuck his weapon out and blindly emptied his magazine.

Two different sergeants separated by one street ordered two troopers to rush across the street. Timid souls provided cover fire.

Both of the poor bloody infantry that had been ordered forward got hit bad.

There were cries for medics. Three of them. A stray round had hit the squad that was working its way to Vicky's building. Now they joined in the fight. People were tossing grenades, flash bangs, and anti-personnel bombs.

The noise was deafening, even where Vicky was. How anyone could think down there was beyond her.

Apparently, no one was thinking very well. Five squads on five different streets were now firing away with abandon. More intrepid souls danced out into the street to spray their weapons in either direction. More cries went out for medics.

A second copter had staggered in and been recharged. When it had enough power, it took a decoy over six blocks in the opposite direction, then up the street.

There, green troops had gone to ground, unsure of what to do next and very sure they didn't want to do it. The spy eye even found a few guys smoking and acting glad not to be up front.

The rotor copter skittered past them and into the block behind them.

A few seconds later, there was a shot fired. More single shots were soon answered with automatic weapons fire as those charged with checking the squads' rear started blasting away at the enemy trying to sneak up behind them.

The third copter had time to take a better charge when Maggie said, "They've called for reinforcements. There should be a couple of trucks coming up this way."

"Oh, I've always wanted to try a roadside bomb," the demolition sergeant said. He'd just joined them to look over his handiwork. The new copter got sent off with an oblong block hanging from its underside.

The winged drones orbiting high above them gave them a good picture of the five trucks hurrying their way toward the "firefight." The copter deposited the roadside bomb mid-block as the convoy headed up the road, fast.

The copter had just enough time to get out of the area before the lead truck gunned by. The bomb exploded, launching flechettes at the rear of the truck, shredding the wheels and many of the troopers riding in the stake bed above them.

Flattened wheels swung the truck into the explosion. Holes in the tanks had gas leaking all over the place.

The fire started somewhere around the wheels, but it spread almost as fast as if it had exploded. There were horrible screams as people ran, engulfed in flames. Some tried to render aid. Others just ran because people were running.

It took a while for the officers to manufacture some order out of the mess, but they did. Soon, squads were spreading out, eager to find who it was that did this to them.

Maybe too eager.

The second copter had finished charging up. The captain rushed it out. The troops were advancing from that burning truck with fury in their eyes. If something didn't slow them down, they'd make it to Vicky's position before the guys that were tied up killing each other only a few blocks away.

The copter settled on a rooftop to save power while Captain Blue used his eyes in the sky to study the different squads. He spotted an opening, finally, and had the copter swoop in and drop the noise maker between two of the most advanced squads.

They were three streets apart. Still, when a shot popped off between them, both of the guys dashing across the street and those standing by to provide cover fire, were on a hair trigger. One group fired right, the other left and soon they were heavily engaged and the squads around them moved out to flank the enemy.

The rattle of automatic weapons fire quickly rose to a crescendo as more poorly trained Red Shirts hopped out from cover to spray and pray. There were enough times that one shooter hit another to keep the entire firefight going long and loud.

"You think anyone has central command and control over these guys?" Vicky asked.

"Your guess is as good as mine," Captain Blue answered, without taking his eyes from his board. "I've got eight main drones overhead and I'm not catching anything that looks or sounds like drones up there. I'm thinking they're flying blind."

"Well, Captain," the demolition sergeant said, "I'd get some shooting going on over there on your far flank. They're getting way ahead of the other boys and might try to flank us."

They had to wait a few more minutes to respond to that. The quad copters were using up a lot of power diving and dodging. The main battery they charged from was also starting to run out of juice and was getting slower on the recharge.

Once a copter was powered up enough, they attached a noise maker and sent it off to the streets fifteen blocks up. There, the Red Shirt teams were almost even with the street Vicky's perch was on.

The captain and the tech sergeant studied the teams, spotted one that looked particularly jumpy, and dropped the noise maker into it and another squad.

The first shot from the decoy caught one guy about halfway across a street. He just about jumped out of his skin. He let off a blast of automatic fire and fled back to cover. As luck would have it, he winged a guy a street up from him, and dropped another guy three streets up.

Soon, seven or eight streets were gleefully shooting away at each other with the cries of "Medic!" growing more frequent.

The noise makers were programmed only to make noise when someone else wasn't. So, if the green troops were busy shooting each other, the decoy fell silent. Let the quiet grow on the battlefield, and a few shots would ring out, getting the gun-shy recruits firing again.

"We could keep this going all night," Vicky said, "but we came here to save the hostages. I need more nanos forward."

"The next two in are yours," the captain said. "Will that use up the last of your Smart Metal?"

"It should," Vicky agreed.

The next two did need a long charge before they were powered enough to make the run to the Park Blocks.

Then one of them had to be switched to lug a roadside bomb over to a convoy coming in on their right flank. Again, there were a few nails bit off in the seconds before they got the copter away. They got it there just in time.

The convoy was slowing to a halt when the lead truck tripped the bomb. The gas tank must have taken a major hit, because the truck exploded, sending wreckage and bodies flying into the air only to shower down on the trucks behind them.

The dismounting troops must have been met with a

grizzly sight. It took the officers a while to get their troops organized, spread out, and moving.

That was fortunate because, back on the top of the elevator shaft, Vicky and Captain Blue were eyeing the charging level on the only copter they had that was charging. It had been planned for the Park Blocks, but it was needed a lot closer to home.

It's battery finally showed enough of a charge that they could risk it on a mission that far away, so they slapped a noise maker on it and sent it out.

This crew were already close enough. The captain chose to drop the noise maker in their rear. The troops that were holding back found themselves drawn into a fire fight and the lead troops fell back to see if they could find the sniper.

Despite officers and NCOs shouting for a ceasefire, either the noise or the adrenaline was enough to keep the fight going for several minutes.

Still, it ended a whole lot sooner than Vicky would have preferred. However, even with the shooting stopped, the Red Shirts held in place while several squads patrolled their rear, hunting for the source of the shots that had killed and wounded their drinking buddies.

Meanwhile Vicky got the third copter that charged. The next one got sent out to cause trouble, so she had to wait for the fifth one to finish charging. She assigned the first load of nanos to the residence. She still hadn't found the central control.

Also, what with the noise of small arms fire in the distance, some of the party goers were getting a bit less cheery. Vicky kept a good eye on the duke. He was very happy with his bevvy of nearly-naked girls, but he had a really hard looking guy at his elbow with a scar down his face.

Given a choice of following one of them and only one, Vicky would bet Scarface would be the one who'd be most eager to push the button.

She kept a small cloud of nanos around the two of them.

People were starting to slip away. Most of them were in white tie or gorgeous dresses. Were they collaborators that had been invited in to party? They could also be junior members of some of the families locked up in cages and forced to show up. There was no way to tell just by looking at them. The temptation was strong to just laze the residence and let God sort them out, but the fear that someone out there at the concentration camps might have the authority to hit the murder switch kept Vicky from just jumping in.

She also would prefer not to kill the innocent along with the guilty.

As her second copter dropped off its load of Smart Metal and scattered them as nano scouts, Vicky decide to have some fun with the Red Shirts guarding the Duke.

"Captain, do you have any copters I could borrow for some fun? I've got two copters incoming that aren't bingo for power," she said. "You can have both of them if you can give me one that could carry a noise maker as far as the Park Blocks."

"I've got one juiced and another that has been juicing for a while," the captain allowed. "You can have them."

"I only need one," Vicky said.

The captain and the demolition sergeant gave her an evil grin. "Not if you want to pull off what we have in mind."

So, two more noise makers set out to do their duty at the duke's residence.

45

W hile the copters buzzed their way toward their destiny, Vicky did a quick review of the bidding. She didn't exactly have a grand slam, but most bridge players would have been happy with her hand.

Certainly, Mannie would be.

Around her, there was still sporadic fire as four or five groups of hostile forces tried to kill each other.

I suspect red-on-red is the new black this evening. How beautiful!

A bit farther out, the Red Shirts had set up a cordon around this battleground. A square, some twenty blocks on an edge, was blocked off with a lot of police cars, red pickup trucks, and anything else they could get their hands on.

The six troopers with Vicky were tying down a major force.

That was good, because with everyone facing in toward her, no one was looking to their rear. Things were definitely starting to happen there.

Muddy though they might be, the 1st Brigade, West

Column, was rolling into the outskirts of town, with 2nd Brigade not that far behind them. From the looks of the lack of mud on them, that bridge had finally gotten in place before the 2nd Brigade had to ford the creek.

From the East, the 3rd Brigade was almost to the suburbs with the 4th Brigade right behind them. Each brigade had two battalions of mechanized infantry with two battalions of light infantry riding along atop their wheeled carriers or in trailers behind them. Each of the brigades was intended to engage two hostage concentration camps.

However, there were now more targets than organized detachments. General Pemberton ordered 1st Brigade to shoot straight toward the center of town. The captain's drones, once he found out from Vicky that there might be as many as twenty hostage sites, had located twelve. The general was re-tasking companies on the fly.

Concentration camps might have to settle for a pair of companies liberating them rather than two battalions.

That could make for some bad situations if Vicky couldn't find the kill switch and disarm the explosives located around the hostages.

First Brigade shot down a road that Vicky had selected for them. They held to steady 60 kph arrowing right for the Park Blocks. Vicky had spotted them a clear route that would skirt where everyone was chasing their tail and hunting for Vicky.

It was into this situation that Vicky had a few nanos sacrifice themselves to trip the main breaker for the lights in the back of the residence. As total blackness fell over the back lawn of the duke's residence, a flash bang went off.

It was like kicking over an ant hill!

Red Shirts came streaming out of the back doors and from around the corners of the building, guns at the ready.

Then the noise maker popped off a round from the left side of the building.

At that point, the captain got to use a gizmo that had been loaded onto only two of his quad copters. It was a tiny, 3mm weapon. It wasn't very powerful, but then, when you were shooting a man in the face at 25 meters or less, it didn't have to be.

One man racing around the right corner of the residence crumbled. The guy behind him tumbled over him and released his weapon on full automatic into the dark. There were screams from wounded, and more automatic weapons fire from the left and the right. The center was taking fire from both flanks, so they fired in any direction they felt like.

Vicky, the captain, and the demolition sergeant were suppressing full belly laughs as the deadly comedy unfolded before their scouts.

Suddenly, the night air was rent by an explosion close to them. It was quickly followed by a short daisy chain of three more. After a brief pause filled with screams and calls for medics, a fifth explosion shattered the night.

Vicky had turned toward the sound, so she spotted the last explosion. It was in the next block up from them.

The cavalry hadn't arrived, but the bad guys sure had.

46

All three of them gazed as the night returned to inky black, but the moist air filled with screams of the wounded and yells for a medic. The smell of explosives spread until it filled their nostrils.

"Okaaay," the demolition sergeant said. "I guess I better get below and make sure we're ready to greet these bozos. The road approaches are covered. So is the basement. I'll check the first floor to make sure it's still to my liking, then I'll do up the second and third just as well. This will be a lovely work of art. I hope them poor dumb SOBs will be grateful for the show I'm about to give them."

"I'm sure they will be," Vicky said as the sergeant rolled over the edge of the elevator shaft's roof.

For five long minutes, the area around them stayed quiet, that is, if you defined quiet as the lack of further explosives. A corporal arrived from below; he tossed a sack up to the captain.

"That's the last of the whiz bangs, noise makers, and roadside bombs. The sergeant says to have fun with them."

The corporal then seemed to change his helmet, pulling

plates from his webbing gear until his head looked more like a box than a helmeted human head.

He moved around the rooftop, keeping his distance from the edge. He finally halted, sighted in on someone below, and fired. His rifle's sound was not like any Vicky had heard before. Now she spotted the flash and sound suppressor on the rifle. It was a big one.

The sniper was quickly moving to another side of the building, then another. He found a second target and fired. Again, he moved quickly away from where he'd shot. He went about that, move, fire, move, fire, again and again.

Meanwhile, back at the Duke's grand ball, things were getting confused. Lots of revelers were fleeing out the front door. A surprising number of them were nude. Not a few of the naked men had a very angry and fully dressed woman giving them all hell as a pretty young thing in her birthday suit tried to distance herself from the older couple while still fleeing the rattle of automatic gunfire from the south of the residence.

Maybe there was a reason why so many of the doors on the first floor were closed and locked.

Inside, the Duke and his scar-faced henchman were arguing. The Duke felt absolutely safe. "What are we paying all those Red Shirts you hired for if not to keep me safe in the middle of town?"

"Clearly, Your Grace, something is going on. You should at least go to the command center where you can be in a position to hear of developments."

"I thought you told me you would keep me appraised of any developments," the Duke snapped, while enjoying the ministrations of several of his bevy of willing girls while doing things to them that made them giggle.

Vicky shook her head. Where had the Bowlingames

found this outlier from Darwin's law of survival of the fittest?

While those two argued, in the Park Blocks between the residence and the hotel tower filled with doomed hostages, people milled about, continued their arguments, and tried to find someone willing to loan them something to cover their nakedness.

There weren't a lot of takers. Most were busy calling their chauffeurs to pick them up. However, there was no parking garage around the park block except the one under the hotel that was, presently, filled with explosives.

Most of the limos and their drivers lined the streets south of the residence. Between them and their employers, lots of bullets were still flying. Many talked among themselves, weighing this against that, before they finally concluded that they weren't paid enough to drive through gunfire.

They stayed put.

About the time that Vicky began to examine all the potentials for more fun around the residence, Admiral Bolesław interrupted her musings.

"Your Grace, I've waited patiently for you to tell me what's going on around you, and you've been very quiet. We did observe five explosives quite close to your position. Do you require any assistance, Your Grace?" sounded more like "Now can I do some hammering around your position, you dumb, suicidal Imperial?"

"We do have everything in hand," Vicky answered, checking to see if the captain had any copters she might borrow. He did. She was just about to ask him for the loan when there was an explosion off to her right not two blocks away.

The first was followed by a second, then, in slow succession, a third and a fourth. Finally, there were two more exploded so quickly as to sound more like one. After that, silence fell.

"Your Grace," Admiral Bolesław said on net, "you are now surrounded. Will you excuse me while I and General Pemberton try to save your ass?"

"Certainly, Admiral, and I'm very grateful, sir."

"You scared?" Captain Blue asked.

"I will admit to being worried," Vicky said through suddenly dry lips.

Behind them, their sniper fired again.

This time, his fire was met with return fire. Of course, all the rooftops around were being sprayed with automatic weapons fire as well, so it didn't seem like anything personal.

"Do you think we could drop some noise makers and a whiz bang behind one of these teams?" Vicky asked the captain.

"I'm willing to try, Your Grace, but we may have cried wolf once too often. I'm thinking that we've culled the herd of the dumb ones. Still, it's worth a try."

They tried spooking the rear of the column off to their right. It caused some distraction, and halted their advance for a few minutes as the officers and sergeants assessed the situation. Meanwhile, none of the gunners were up emptying their magazines with wild abandon. Most seemed to huddle down against the nearest wall, waiting for orders.

The captain was right; the stupid ones were already casualties.

"How about a roadside bomb for the ones to the west?" Vicky asked.

Two skitter copters, neither with a full charge, one with

a noise maker and the other with a roadside bomb, flitted off to deliver their loads.

The force to the west had pulled back after tripping the first daisy chain. Now, cautiously, they were advancing again. The captain had bent the bomb so it would send flechettes out in a full ninety-degree arch. It was left at the corner of the next building up, about where the first chain of explosives had sent the team fleeing.

The street there was still littered with dead and a few wounded that hadn't been picked up.

From both sides of the street, an officer ordered fire teams forward at a run.

Right as they were about halfway across the street, Captain Blue fired the claymore. The bomb was designed to destroy a truck. What it did to the fifteen people either moving or up, expecting orders to move, was a slaughter.

There were no cries from the street this time. More bone was visible than flesh.

The follow-up troops took one look at the blood and gore and broke for the rear. Their officers seemed to have been a part of the slaughter. There was no one to rally them, so they just kept running.

A street back, a noise maker went off. One of the armed drones was hovering quietly overhead. It shot the man leading the rout.

He went down. The man behind him stumbled and fell, his gun going off. The soldier behind those two sprayed his fire to his right where another team was running.

In a moment, the fratricidal battle was back on.

It would be a while before the west side troops would quit killing each other. It would be even longer before new and strange officers could reorganize the rabble into a fighting force.

That left Vicky with only the assault teams coming over from the east and the stalled team to the south.

Oh, and there were the Park Blocks to be tickled.

She had lifted one of the remaining noise makers up to the Park Blocks. She dropped it among the trees and bushes. There was a moment's pause, then a shot rang out.

Everyone in the two tree covered blocks froze. Then, some goon whipped out his gun and started looking around for someone to shoot. Of course, a lot of goons now had their guns out. More shots were fired. Some snob in white tie and tails pulled a pistol from the inside of his coat and started shooting at anyone with a gun.

He didn't last long, but he did bag three of the plug uglies before they got him, and a few others besides.

Now, shots were flying in every direction. No one was in charge here and no one had any idea who was doing what to whom.

Meanwhile, all the beautiful people or the naked people, or at least anyone without a gun, were running for their lives. People bolted in every direction, not looking back, not slowing down.

By the time the armed bodyguards realized that they were stalking each other through the bushes and killing each other, the deed was done. Most of those with any power on Dresden were busy racing away from where the levers of power were located.

Now, how to get at the Duke? Vicky thought.

"Your Grace," the captain said, "I think we've about run out of luck."

Vicky glanced at his board. She couldn't find anything wrong in his conclusion.

47

The feed from the overhead drones showed that someone had finally put his finger on the epicenter of their problems tonight. Troops all along the western edge of the battle that had previously been scattered over twenty blocks were now moving down from the north or up from the south to concentrate a few blocks back from her building.

"Even the stupid can only stay dumb for so long," Captain Blue observed.

"Yes. I remember Admiral Krätz warning me that hope is not a policy," Vicky agreed. "How many claymore mines do we have left?"

Captain Blue rummaged in the sack that had been tossed up on the roof of the elevator well. "Five, six, seven," he counted.

"Well, there is no benefit to dying with spare ammo," Vicky said, not remembering where she'd heard that.

They had two half-charged copters. From the gauges on the power source, these were likely to be the last they'd get.

Vicky and Captain Blue quickly bent a claymore into a

U, strapped them to the bottom of the quad copter, and dispatched one north and the other south.

As the copter struggled to lug their heavy cargo out, Vicky and the captain located two concentrations where the troops were clumping up under the watchful eyes of their officers, and moving quickly and purposefully. They were heading like a homing missile straight for the streets that surrounded Vicky's perch.

Both Vicky and Captain Blue had their copters come in fast and low from the west. They dropped off their loads right at the corner of a building across the street from the rally point. Then they skittered quickly away.

It looked like a Red Shirt spotted one copter. He shouted something and fired off a burst at the retreating copter, only to get slugged by the nearest NCO.

"No shooting until I tell you to shoot," rang out loud.

He was drowned out by two explosions, one right after the other.

The screams were horrible.

The Red Shirts had collected several hundred troopers, intent on storming forward toward Vicky's building redoubt. They hadn't been prepared for this.

Hundreds were down: dead, wounded, screaming. Those that weren't out of it knew that death was coming from the sky. Long bursts of automatic weapons fire streamed up into the night.

Of course, what goes up must come down.

There were more casualties, and more troops looking for the source of the rounds that killed and wounded their buddies.

It took the officers a good fifteen minutes to arrange a cease fire.

That was enough time for the captain to spot several of

the remaining officers and most effective NCOs. Before the last friendly fire fell silent, his two armed copters took out a quarter of the command structure.

Unfortunately, the officers had selected a few of their better troops to search the sky. One of the armed skitter copters fell to a fusillade of bullets as it shot down the senior-most officer of the task force coming in from the west.

"Your Grace," Maggie said, "The duke has gotten reports of armored vehicles in town. One of our companies charged into a movie theater and liberated the hostages. I think he's ready to blow everything up."

"Captain, try and keep them off my roof long enough for me to get this job done."

"Yes, Your Grace."

He turned to his board and Vicky stared off at the still brightly lit ducal palace. In her eye, Maggie was showing her the duke hurrying upstairs, and puffing as he reached the second floor. None of his bevy of girls were in evidence now.

"Tanks! What are they doing with tanks on the ground?" the Duke snapped. "You said their battleships were leaving! You said they couldn't land tanks without us knowing! You fool, I should have taken your head long ago."

"And I should have let you drown into your own shit years ago. I told you to keep the kill button in your pocket."

"And you don't think they would have shorted it out or jammed it?" the Duke snapped. "You are an idiot."

Can this marriage be saved? Vicky thought to herself as the supreme power on Dresden bickered with his chief henchman and boot licker.

Vicky shuddered as something exploded around her, but she kept her eyes on these two as she rallied every nano scout that she could lay her hands on to join them as one labored and the other half dragged the other up the marbled staircase.

If she could have, Vicky would have loved to have greased the stairs or done something to get these two flat on their backs with broken necks at the bottom of the staircase. She'd have to put some thought into how to do that when she had a few spare moments.

" Admiral Bolesław," Vicky whispered softly.

"Yes, Your Grace?"

"I may have a fire mission for you. On the west side of the cupola on the Duke's residence, there is a comm room. I think all communications may be cycled through that one room."

"I've got sensors and my fleet gunnery expert looking at it. Yes, Your Grace. We have the residence. Nice of him to light it up so brightly. We also see the cupola atop the roof. You say the comm center is right to the west of it?"

"It's the side closest to my direction. Can your sensors make anything off the place?"

"There's not a lot of radio traffic coming out of there."

"They're using landlines," Vicky said.

"We don't get anything off of landline."

"Okay. I want six 18-inch lasers targeted at eight meters west of the cupola. You do not have weapons release. I repeat, you do *not* have weapons release. I'm still trying to deactivate the damn bombs."

"Understood, Your Grace, we are to target eight meters to the west of the cupola, center of the building. We do not have weapons release. We will not take action until you give us weapons release."

"You got me right, now, Admiral Bolesław, I've got a hotel to keep from going boom."

"Good luck, Your Grace."

There was another explosion somewhere around Vicky, followed by a groan from the captain. "They got another rotor copter."

Vicky, however, spared the Navy captain no attention. She had left Maggie to observe the two idiots while she worked with most of her computer on the basement below the tower and the various ballrooms around the conference center.

Nanos were slipped in place, then converted into guillotines to snap the power lines in two. First, they sought out every one of the claymores stuck to the walls around the hostages. There were a lot of them.

In the parking garage under the convention center were more barrels of explosives. Someone wanted to make sure this place came tumbling down. Several nanos followed those lines up to a control room. There, an officer sat with one eye on a screen flipping through all the ballrooms and another eye on a porno.

It took Vicky a second glance before she realized it was not a 2D but rather an actual video take from one of the rooms in the tower. Some young and attractive hostage girl was being taken by a very overweight older man.

Vicky gritted her teeth. She did not have any time to chase that one tragedy down. Maybe later.

About that time, she did manage to locate the central control for the explosives under the tower. Two men sat there, also watching the same scene instead of paying much attention to the hall cameras. There wasn't much to see; everyone was locked down. The only ones stalking up and down the halls were a handful of guards.

Vicky got more nano guillotines in place to slice those wires.

She prayed that she had them all.

"Your Grace," Maggie said.

"Yes, Maggie."

"The Duke is within a few seconds of storming into the comm center."

"Admiral Bolesław, you have weapons release. Still, hold on my command."

"I have weapons release. I am holding on your command," the admiral repeated, his voice dead calm.

The same could not be said for the Duke. He charged into the comm center shouting, "Where is the control box? Where is the control box?"

"It's in the safe, Your Grace," the senior watch officer said as he shot to his feet.

"Well, get it out."

"Do you want us to send out a preliminary warning, Your Grace?" the junior watch officer asked. "There are a lot of people on guard duty."

"No time! No time! Get me that control box!"

The senior watch officer bobbled the combination and had to try it again. A few moments later, he again couldn't get it open."

"Damn it," Scar face screamed, "What's the number?"

The poor guy rattled it off.

The henchman snapped the safe's dial through the combination and yanked it open. In a moment, he held a small box with a single red button. He passed it to the Duke.

"Where do I plug it in?" the Duke demanded.

The junior watch officer stood aside, leaving his chair to the Duke and pointed at a standard large, male/female cable port.

The Duke sat as the henchman reached for the cable.

"Maggie, get as many nanos into that port as you can. Short it."

"On it, ma'am"

"Maggie, cut all the wires," Vicky ordered.

"Wires cut."

The Duke grinned out the window at the tower at the other end of the Park Block. The base was lost in the treetops, but the top twenty stories shown dimly above them.

The Duke pushed the button.

There were no flashes. No explosions. Nothing.

"Why's the tower still there?" the Duke demanded.

"Push the button again," the henchman shouted.

The Duke did. Several times he did. Nothing happened.

"Admiral Bolesław," Vicky whispered.

"Yes, Your Grace?"

"You may fire when ready."

Vicky didn't have time to take in a breath before a hellish light stabbed from the heavens into the brightly lit ducal residence. One moment, it shown gaudily into the night. The next second, it was blinding. Even a few seconds later, all Vicky could see were the flares of after-images in her blinded eyes.

"You could have at least warned me," Captain Blue groaned through his pain.

Vicky rolled over on the rooftop, blinking her eyes madly, trying to blink away the pain and the blindness. Finally, she applied the palms of her hands to both eyes. Nothing helped with either the pain or blindness.

"I've never been on the ground when you get lasered from orbit," Vicky admitted through teeth gritted against the pain. "I didn't know."

"No doubt, you'll remember the next time you call down hellfire," Captain Blue said drolly.

"Are we permanently blinded?" Vicky asked.

"I hope not," the captain said. "I think this will go away in a day, maybe less. No way to tell. But I can tell you we're going to have the worst headaches for the next month."

"Damn," was all that Vicky could say.

From the direction of the Park Blocks came the sound of walls collapsing and a fire burning. By the grace of God, there was nothing nearly as loud as a thirty-story tower coming down.

From behind them, there were several sharp explosions of a more normal proportion.

"Is that you blowing shit up?" Vicky asked, "or the sergeant?"

"I dropped a claymore off to the north just before you called endgame. That might have been it."

Blinded, there was little they could do but listen to the night's screams, shouts, automatic weapons fire and explosions, some close, some in the distance.

"I hope we saved all the hostages," Vicky muttered to herself.

Then things got rowdy around her position.

48

Vicky could only follow the developing battle with her ears; she found the limited information terrifying.

There were more explosions around her building, from just about all directions.

"I think they're starting their final assault," Captain Blue said.

"It sure sounds like that."

"I think I'll add a verbal option to my battle board in the future," he said.

"I think that might be a very good idea," Vicky agreed.

Matters continued to develop. There was more automatic weapons fire, more explosives.

"That doesn't sound good," the captain muttered.

"What doesn't sound good?"

"I think they're trying recon by fire. Shooting up the place and seeing if they can set off any explosives in the area before they trip them."

"That's not good, why?"

The captain did not answer her.

Vicky began to consider her options. She could try to fight and likely get shot for her effort. Besides being blind, her fighting wouldn't do much damage. She could surrender. Would she be allowed to survive as a prisoner for more than five minutes?

Whatever she did, it sounded like she'd be doing it very soon.

Then a deep throated sound was added to the rapid fire surrounding her.

"Is that what I think it is?" Vicky asked.

"You're damn right it is! A 30mm chain cannon is in the house," Captain Blue said, gleefully. "The cavalry has arrived!"

That the battle had changed became quickly apparent. Quickly, there was a lot less rapid fire. Where there was light arms fire, it was most often a single shot, or at most, two, in rapid succession.

"Your Grace, Captain, they're running!" gleefully shouted the corporal who'd been sniping from around their roof. "Oh, Lordy, are they running!"

"Very good, Corporal," Captain Blue said. "Have the command sergeant major advise the approaching task force that medical aid is needed on the roof."

"Are one of you hurt?" sounded shocked.

"No, Corporal," Vicky said, wryly. "We two were dumb enough to watch lasers from space blow apart a building. It was a really dumb move."

"Yes, Your Grace," from the corporal would fit nicely into the request for medical air . . . or the extent to which the two officers were dumb.

Vicky did not ask for clarification.

Blind as she was, she could hear the sound of the LAVs as they motored up to the building. She could even make out the sound of the aft ramp dropping down and the fast movement of boots as they slapped on the concrete of the street.

Two minutes later, medics were studying Vicky's eyes.

"Oh, ma'am, you did make a mess of things, didn't you?"

"Yes, I did," Vicky agreed.

With her eyes medicated and wrapped in bandages, and a shot of painkillers softening the pounding of ten thousand devils on her skull, Vicky was led down from the roof and down a flight of stairs.

It was no easy walk. Vicky was none too steady on her feet. Fortunately, some engineer had gotten the elevator running and they took her and the captain straight down to the basement. A moment later, Vicky was laying down, with the cool hands of a nurse holding what felt like a damp washcloth to her forehead.

Even with the painkillers in her blood, the feel of a woman's hand and a cool cloth made more of the pain go away.

Still, Vicky didn't want to lay there. "I've just conquered a planet. I've got to see that they corral up all the Red Shirts and the rest of the gutter snipes the Bowlingames had running this place. We need to get a government back up and see to the hostages."

"Your Grace," a gentle woman's voice said, "you have good people who have pledged you their loyalty. Trust me, they are tying up all those loose ends. You need to rest and let your eyes recover."

"I need to get this planet headed in some sort of a democratic direction," Vicky said, coming half up off the stretcher.

The woman pushed her back down, and Vicky found she really couldn't fight her. She was feeling rather sleepy.

"Trust me, Your Grace, your consort is already headed

down to meet with the locals and begin organizing a government that will represent all of the people, or so I've heard. It seems that you Peterwalds have changed your stripes a bit," the woman said with a chuckle.

"The other stripes weren't working all that well," Vicky mumbled.

The pain was getting more distant. That was nice. However, her body seemed to be getting more distant as well. At the moment, Vicky could not muster any opposition to that, either.

Vicky lay back in the stretcher and found she was listening to the nurse breathe. She was taking long, deep breaths. Vicky found herself doing the same.

In a few breaths, she'd fallen into a deep, drugged slumber.

49

Vicky came awake to find something over her eyes, as well as her entire head firmly wrapped. She reached for the bandages and found a soft hand blocking her effort to rip the covering from her eyes.

"The Grand Duchess is awake," came in a familiar, soft, feminine voice.

"Where am I?" Vicky demanded.

"You are in your own bed in your night quarters on the *Victorious*. Its name is very apropos. You have been quite victorious this week.

"This week? How long have I been out?" Suddenly, Vicky was filled with dread. How had things gone while she played sleeping beauty?

"You have been in an induced coma for two days," the nurse answered.

"How are things on Dresden? Have they got a government organized? Are there riots?"

"There are no riots," the soft feminine voice said with a chuckle. "You are quite renowned for your role in keeping the bloodshed to a minimum. Everyone is praying for your recovery."

"They are?"

"Yes, Your Grace. Suddenly it is fashionable to pray for a Peterwald, other than 'God bless and keep the Emperor far away from me'."

Now Vicky chuckled. "I imagine that was the Imperial prayer," she had to admit.

A male voice announced himself as a doctor. "How is your headache?" he asked.

"It's there," Vicky admitted through gritted teeth. His voice. Even her voice was like needles in her skull.

"Better or worse?"

Vicky lowered her voice to hardly a whisper. "Nothing could be worse, so let's call it better."

The doctor chuckled at Vicky's dry remark, but when he spoke next, his voice was softer, lower. "Now, please keep your eyes gently closed while I remove the bandages. We need to check on your progress."

"I'm not going to be permanently blind, am I?"

"It is very unlikely, but we need to see how long it will take you to fully recover."

Vicky held her tongue. Further questions would be worthless and even the whisper she was using caused a pain just behind her eyeballs. The doctor had told her what he knew and did not know. It was time to wait.

The pressure of the bandages around her head slowly lessened, and then seemed to fall away. Still, with her eyes closed, it seemed just as dark.

"I'm going to remove the plastic covers. Keep your eyes closed."

The last pressure around her eyes went away, one at a time. Now the darkness behind her eyelids lit up.

"Are things brighter?" the doctor asked.

"Yes."

"I'm going to put some drops in your eyes, tilt your head back."

Vicky did, and felt dampness along the seam of her eyelids. Without opening her eyes, she tried to blink a bit and move the liquid around.

"That's good. Now, slowly open your eyes. It may take several tries before you're comfortable with them open."

The doc was right about that. It took some serious effort to work one eyelid open a crack. When the first light streaming, the pain forced her to close it again. On the fifth or sixth try, she managed to work both eyes fully open, even if it was only to blink and blink again.

Vicky could tell that she was in her night quarters on the *Victorious*. However, if she tried to concentrate on anything, her eyes refused to focus on it.

"Look at my finger," the doctor said. "Can you see it?"

"Yes. Well, yes and no," Vicky said.

"It's hard to focus?"

"Yes."

"Try to follow my finger as I move it."

Vicky found herself blinking more, but not really following the finger.

"Try following my finger out of your peripheral vision."

This time, Vicky tried looking to the right or left of the finger. This time, she could follow it.

"Better," the doc said.

"Can I read something?" Vicky asked.

"That wouldn't be a good idea. I'm going to suggest that we put your bandages on and try some more of the eye regeneration serum."

Right, Vicky had several bags of IV's flowing into her arm.

Without being asked, she closed her eyes. Some of the pain quieted. In a moment, the world was dark, and she was bandaged again.

"I'll come by tomorrow and we'll see what we can do," the doc said.

"In the meantime, what can I do?" Vicky asked. She'd never liked doing nothing.

"Try listening to music."

"Can I have my computer read me reports?"

"I'd prefer that you try the music for a half hour, then read reports for a half hour. Then do it over again," the doctor said.

"I'd call you a slave driver, but you're ordering me to rest."

"My patients often accuse me of being a hindrance to progress."

Vicky listened to his footsteps as he left. Her nurse turned on some relaxing music.

"Thirty minutes," Vicky snapped. "No cheating on me."

"Thirty minutes. I'll set a timer," she said, her voice light, almost dancing with good humor.

"Maggie, don't let her cheat me."

"I won't, Your Grace."

Vicky adjusted her bed so that her back was up, and her legs were bent. She leaned back against her pillows and listened to the music.

She didn't notice when the timer went off.

50

Vicky came awake to the smell of food. Pancakes or waffles with syrup. Was there bacon as well?

"Is it time for breakfast?"

"No, Your Grace," another woman's voice answered. "Mannie suggested that you'd love us if your first meal was waffles with all the trimmings. You may not smell it, but there is some fruit here as well. We plan to have you eat that first."

"Is Mannie here?"

"No, Your Grace. He's down on the planet having himself a ball."

"I bet he is. Nothing like a planet to play with that is starting its government from scratch."

"Yes. I understand that he's trying to have the senate made up of people who get the votes of people. No geography. Just, if they have a community of interest and get enough votes, they're a senator. I don't fully understand all the numbers, but it's interesting."

"Any parties?" Vicky asked, and found she had to accept a spoonful of blueberries before she would get an answer.

As she chewed, the nurse said, "I don't think so. Not this vote, but I understand that he's making sure there are allowances for later."

Thus it went. Vicky would ask a question, accept a bite, and listen to how things were on the ground. Some of it was to be expected. The Red Shirts had tried to melt into the population. Most had been ratted out.

Many of them were quickly charged with rape, murder, and thievery. Some of those still on the loose when the charges began to stack up did not come in willingly, and there were several hostage situations.

This being Greenfeld, there was only one way for the standoff to end. The hostage taker surrendered or died. Several hostages died as well.

"We've got to get some of those sleepy dart guns from Wardhaven," Vicky muttered. "Maggie, fire off a request to Kris Longknife. Tell her I don't have a lot of hard currency, but if she can get me a couple of hundred of those rifles with ammo, we can save lives."

"The message is already on its way, Your Grace."

When it came to the three slices of bacon, Vicky didn't even bother waiting between bites. The nurse got out of the way and let Vicky eat them with her fingers and enjoy the moment.

"Any idea when I can get rid of these bandages?" Vicky asked in between bites.

She had to accept a delicious fork of syrup-covered waffle to get an answer to that question.

"The doctor will be with us later, Your Grace. It's fairly early in the morning."

Vicky was feeling very full and very happy by the time the meal was done.

Admiral Bolesław dropped in a bit after her meal. "How are you doing, my hero? Damn your eyes."

"You praise me and damn me in the same breath?"

He pulled up a chair; Vicky could hear it scraping across the floor to just beside her bed. "What you did was heroic. What you did was stupid. Had a young lieutenant done it, I would put him in for a medal. You, the leader of half of our Empire, and the half that's working, have no good reason for doing something like that."

"I had Maggie. With her, we stopped a blood bath. No lieutenant, no matter how brave, could have done that without a computer of Maggie's abilities."

There was a deep sigh after that. "Yes. Yes, I know. So, where do I send my recommendation for your *Pour la Mérite?*

"I don't deserve that. It's the highest honor, Alis."

"I'm putting the captain in, as well as the command sergeant major and your demolition tech sergeant."

"Only officers get the *Pour la Mérite*," Vicky hastened to point out.

"Both of them got spot promotions to captain. That should settle that."

"You're serious."

"Your Grace. What you and your team did was heroic, well done, outstanding, foolish on your part, but far above and beyond the call of duty. Sorry, gal. Oh, I'm sending all the recommendations to Admiral Waller to countersign. Then, who do we forward them to, you or your dad?"

"I can't sign my own," Vicky said, and cringed as the volume of her voice echoed within her skull.

"Well, do you want to have your dad review the commendation, considering that you are on his side of the demarcation line?"

"It would be a pain for him to see me risking my life to save people from the mess he's made."

"Kind of my thoughts, too."

"Tell Admiral Waller to create a board of senior and retired officers. They may pass on my recommendation. They can also compose a reprimand if they feel I was outside the performance expected of an admiral and Grand Duchess."

"Can they do both?" Admiral Bolesław asked.

Vicky had to suppress a giggle. Oh, it hurt to do anything sudden with her head.

"I imagine they'd love to have both options. I expect I'll get both."

"As you well deserve."

"Admiral, are you grinning from ear to ear?"

"Of course not, Your Grace."

"You definitely sound like someone enjoying himself," Vicky said, then changed gears.

"Okay, Maggie, a second message to Kris Longknife. 'Damn your eyes and the computer you walked in with. Something your Nelly did has caused my computer, Maggie, to contract something like her kids have'."

"Do you really find me offensive?" Maggie asked, her voice kind of trembling.

"No, Maggie, I could not have done what we did without you. It's just that Kris gets her nose into everyone's business. She should not have given me you without giving me some help bringing you up right."

"Oh."

Vicky continued. "I have found Maggie critical to saving lives and getting things done. For that, I thank you. I am being put in for the *Pour la Mérite* for what I alone could do, with Maggie, to save thousands of lives. I will also likely receive an official reprimand for the same. Admiral Bolesław, you remember him, he was the good-looking admiral, says I deserve both the award and the reprimand."

Vicky made a pouty face in the general direction she felt the admiral was sitting. She got a laugh from about the right place.

"I need to put together a command team like you did and I need to have all of them with something like Maggie so we can at least have more people making a ruckus. I am not suggesting that Kit or Kat get a smart computer. I would never trust them with one and I doubt Nelly would either. However, they will need some really smart dumb computers.

Vicky took a deep breath before launching into the part she hated. "Again, I don't have the money to pay the outrageous cost for Nelly's kids' computers. I'm still trying to figure out when you snuck the extra self-organizing matrix into my computer. Girl, I love you for it, like a sister, and hate you just as much. I hope I can see you again before too long. As you no doubt have learned from the news, we 've got a mess here. Have fun with your desk job."

Vicky couldn't help but laugh at that. Unfortunately, while the image of Kris behind a desk was hilarious, her skull felt like it was ready to split wide open.

"Admiral Bolesław, I've enjoyed talking to you, and I'm assuming that we don't have a hostile battle fleet heading our way, since you didn't mention it."

"Nope. Everything's going amazingly well."

"Well, I have a splitting headache. I'm going to ask the nice nurse for some more painkillers and I will likely go to sleep for a while."

"Understood, Your Grace. Get well. The people on Dresden are electing their first senate. They would really like for you to call it to order. I also understand they'd like a charter of some sort."

"Count on Mannie to come up with a charter of some sort," Vicky said, but she could feel the pain relief coursing through her veins. The restful music came up. Admiral Bolesław must have tiptoed out, because she didn't hear him leave.

As Vicky sank into the soft nothingness of sleep, her last thoughts were *How about that? A medal and a reprimand for the same ops. Not bad for a girl in the Greenfeld Empire. Maybe we can make it normal for us women.*

51

Vicky's eye recovery very quickly fell off the critical path. She would not be needed to address the new Senate any time soon. Mannie and the provisional congress couldn't decide how to elect a senate or who could be in one.

As she'd heard from her nurse, Mannie was trying something experimental. Negotiations had deadlocked over how to divide up the territory of each senatorial district. An ancient word called "gerrymandering" got dragged out and thrown about like a club. It quickly began to look like things would fall apart entirely.

However, trust Mannie to dig into his bag of tricks and come up with a batty idea. Why not allow Senatorial candidates to seek out the signatures of voters to endorse them? Let them get so many people to back them for the senate, and they got a seat. The limit was set so that if anyone got eighty percent of one five hundredth of the population of Dresden, they got a seat. They should get up to one five hundredths so there would be five hundred senators.

There were a lot of people running around seeking

signatures. Some made it quickly while others stalled out. After four days, everyone with less than thirty percent was taken out of the running.

A couple of platforms began to show up. The farmers elected their own thirty-two senators. The factory workers were divided, but the three groups they formed settled on ninety-eight senators between them. Other associations, no one wanted to say parties, included unmarried women, married women, several religious groups, and college students with a few professors admitted to their ranks among many others.

The oligarchs who had been running things under the Empire found themselves having trouble gathering many signatures. They got called out for offering money for signatures by one of the new independent medias that sprung up. Sure enough, quite a few people admitted they'd signed a wealthy man's enrollment for money, and the Business and Management Association took a major hit.

Vicky followed the developments dirtside, first by having Maggie read her the reports. Then, when the coverings finally came off her eyes, she watched them on the screen in her night quarters.

She still had to avoid focusing on anything, even a spoon of soup, but her vision was getting better.

So it was, that two weeks after being brought up the space elevator on a stretcher, Vicky was ready, under her own power, to go down to the surface to address the senate.

The day before she was due to address parliament, Admiral Bolesław showed up with Captain Blue and the newly promoted Army captains. Grinning from ear to ear the admiral said, "I have papers for you to sign, Your Grace."

With a flair, the admiral had a lieutenant following him present four very fancy Imperial warrants from a portfolio he was carrying. There, on imitation parchment, complete with fancy calligraphy were warrants very formally prepared for Vicky's signature.

Three of them awarded a *Pour la Mérite* to each of the three officers who had stood beside her and kept her alive for one eternally long night.

Vicky settled down at her desk and signed the three of them with delight.

That left a fourth one. She studied it long and hard. It was just like the other three, only it had her name on it. Did a Grand Duchess deserve a *Pour la Mérite?* By giving it to herself was she degrading the awards she had just signed off on for these other three brave men?

"Your Grace, don't hesitate," said the captain who'd been a tech sergeant handling explosives until a very few days ago. "You earned it. You kept that mission going time after time when anyone with good sense would have taken the excuse and run for the hills You stuck your neck out just as far as we did, and none of what we did could have been accomplished if you hadn't been there."

Vicky eyed the three men she'd almost gotten killed.

"So say we all," said the captain who'd been a sergeant major.

"Captain Blue?" Vicky asked. She'd known him the longest, and she'd trusted his sensor support through way too many battles to doubt his intelligence and street smarts.

"It's been a long time since a Peterwald has risked his neck for anyone, ma'am. Your dad awarded a *Pour la Mérite* to a certain Wardhaven Princess for what I would consider less. I would say that our Gracious Grand Duchess has earned her order at just as much risk to her life as that princess. Moreover, you rescued a more populous planet with your effort. If you didn't earn that cross around your neck, you should ask Kris Longknife for hers back."

Vicky chuckled at that. She could just see herself chasing down one Kris and trying to yank a decoration from around her neck.

With a warm, satisfied smile, Vicky signed her own warrant.

Admiral Bolesław handed her one more stack of papers. These were slightly less gaudy. They awarded the military cross to three corporals, who now were sergeants. Not being officers, the *Pour la Mérite* was beyond their reach.

Vicky signed their citations with pleasure.

"Now, my good admiral," Vicky said, leaning back in her station chair, "being blind has given me much time to think."

"Oh, God. We're in trouble now," Admiral Bolesław interrupted.

"Behave yourself, Admiral," Vicky interrupted right back. "Now, having thought much on this, I have concluded that the Empire would be well served by an Imperial Victorian Order. It would have several levels starting with Lord Knight Commander. That would be reserved for those who have personally saved the life of the Emperor or Heir. We'll come up with three or four lesser levels later, but I intend to induct you four as Lord Knight Commanders tomorrow.

"Your Grace," came in four soft breaths.

Vicky reached into the middle drawer of her desk. In it were five the Imperial Decrees that Maggie had arranged to produce for Vicky. The gold calligraphy on parchment was lovely. Each one had a gold seal with her coat of arms hanging from a blue ribbon. She picked up the five she'd ordered and . . .

Below the bottom one was another decree.

"Maggie, I ordered five of these."

"Yes, Your Grace, however, it is normal for the monarch to be a member of any order, so I had an extra one made for you."

"It *is* normal for the monarch to head each order," Admiral Bolesław put in, grinning.

Three of those before her looked startled and totally in the dark. One admiral did not. Not at all.

"Maggie, have Kris Longknife and Nelly given me a computer that no longer does what I tell her to do?"

"Your Grace, you did not tell me that I could not enlist the help of others to assist in this project. I needed help getting access to the 3D printers and the gold supply as well as being allowed to use artists and craftsmen from the fleet to design and produce the orders and seals. The same was true if I were to arrange for the red sashes and golden star-bursts that are the proper dress for this order."

"So, she brought me in on this," Admiral Bolesław admitted.

Vicky rolled her eyes and leaned back in her chair. It was clear that she'd been jobbed on this one. Of course, the admiral doing the jobbing was also the one that had saved her neck way too many times.

Okay, when you've been had, smile and act like you know what you're doing.

"Okay," Vicky said, slowly. "I'm going to sign these. All six of them. I'm also going to be dropping down to address the senate tomorrow. I can't think of a better time or place to award the recently earned *Pour la Mérite* and invest the first Lord Knight Commanders into the Imperial Victorian Order. Any complaints?" she said, eyeing the admiral.

"That sounds great by me. I have the four *Pour la Mérites* already printed out for you to hang around three necks, and the gaudy sashes and fancy gold starbursts for the new order. However, Your Grace, I would suggest that you have to wear yours to the investiture. You can't invest yourself."

"Suddenly, I've got a lot of men that think they can boss me around. Men and one wayward computer," Vicky growled.

"I am not bossing you around, Your Grace," Maggie interjected. "I am following your orders and improvising where your orders are vague."

"Yeah, right," Vicky said, dryly. "And you, Admiral?"

"I'm getting bossy," he admitted freely, "although in my defense, I will point out that most of what I've done was just to fill in the holes between what you want and how we got it done."

Vicky gave him a scowl, but knew she had too much up around the down of her mouth to make it stick.

"Okay, Admiral, will you help me figure out how to adapt my uniform to this new fruit salad?"

The admiral was immediately all business. They retired to her night quarters and soon had her dress whites spread out on the bed.

Admiral Bolesław eyed the orange sash of the Order of St. Christopher, Star Leaper and the blue of the Imperial Victoria Order. "Do you want to wear two sashes or is one order senior to the other?"

"Let's make the Imperial Victorian Order senior to this gaudy Star Leaper one," Vicky said.

So, the orange sash was put aside, and the red sash was laid across her dress whites, right shoulder to her left hip. The star of the Order of St. Christopher, Star Leaper was penned to Vicky's left breast to the left of the more stylish starburst of a Lord Knight Commander of the Imperial Victorian Order.

Above it, all she had was a good conduct medal.

"Your Grace," Admiral Bolesław said, "We've been awarding campaign medals to our sailors for battles fought and planet's taken. I notice that you haven't included yourself in any of these rewards."

"It didn't seem right," Vicky said. "Everyone else put their lives on the line for me. I just did what I had to do to stay alive."

"You put your life on the line for every man jack in the fleet, Your Grace, time after time. I disagree with you. Everyone who wears these campaign and battle medals will feel more honored to know that they share in the same award as you."

The admiral snapped his fingers, and the lieutenant who's carried the *Pour la Mérite* warrants stepped forward and pulled a long line of medals from his portfolio.

"I didn't earn all of those, did I?"

"You were at the First and Second battle of St. Petersburg, the Battle of Brunswick, that one at the unnamed system one jump out from St. Petersburg, and, of course the Battle of Cuzco. I put you in for the Space Combat medal with two stars for those little fights we got in. Remember when they damn near blew away my first command, the Attacker?"

"How could I forget?" Vicky said.

"We even borrowed one medal from Wardhaven, the Humanitarian Operations for Presov and Poznan."

"Good Lord, did I earn all of those?"

The admiral pointed at the chest of his own dress blues. "I'm wearing them, and I was standing just behind you on the bridge most of those times."

"You were in command, most of those times," Vicky pointed out.

"Let's not quibble."

Vicky motioned for the lieutenant to lay her medals down, along the chest of her dress whites. It did make for a rather imposing rank.

"Okay. Do I need to sign any paperwork?"

"Nope, as admiral commanding this fleet, I signed them."

"That can't be right, but as you said, let's not quibble," Vicky said, then had a second thought. "We also need to have some civilian medals for the people who stepped in and kept planets running during the change over from confusion and anarchy to something close to Mannie's democracy."

"We can do that, Your Grace. I'm sure Maggie can help us research successful uses of various orders to reward subjects for courageous innovative and selfless action."

"I never thought that being a good Imperial could be so difficult," Vicky muttered to herself.

"It's easy to be Imperial, Your Grace," Admiral Bolesław said, "just ask your father. It's a whole lot harder to be a regal king."

"As opposed to a pirate king?" Maggie asked.

"Oh, God. She's telling jokes," Vicky sighed.

"Was that not a good one?" Maggie asked.

"Yes, Maggie," Admiral Bolesław said, as one might say to a precocious ten-year-old, "that was a very good joke and spot-on for the situation."

"I know Nelly tends to tell bad jokes and that gets her in trouble. She told me to be more careful."

"You are doing very well, Maggie, very well," Vicky said while thinking, *Curse you, Kris Longknife*!

52

Admiral, Her Grace, the Imperial Grand Duchess, IVO, PM, stood outside the side door of the grand opera theatre that was serving as a temporary senate for the people of Dresden. She had her notes, and was ready to start.

In front of her, not quite blocking her way, was an older gentleman in archaic clothing: hose, knee pants, and a fancy coat, holding some sort of staff of office.

Unsure who was waiting on whom, Vicky said, "I'm ready."

"Yes, Your Grace," and the man did a smart about face, went to the door, and rather than opening it, rapped on the door with his staff.

"Who goes there?" a booming voice from inside demanded.

"Her Grace demands entrance to her parliament," the old fellow boomed back.

There was a brief pause, then the other voice answered, "The people of Dresden recognize no Imperial demands nor does this parliament of the people recognize her power over us."

Vicky's head whipped around. Mannie, a step behind her, was grinning.

"What have you done?" she demanded, in a whisper, but it was still a demand.

"Oh, that's just something someone discovered in the history books about how a parliament of the people works with a constitutional monarch."

"You constitutionalized me!"

"No, not yet. One planet can't make you a constitutional emperor for the entire empire. Still, it's a start."

Vicky considered seriously stomping away. Still, she had plans for recognizing some of the men who'd risked their lives to give these people back their lives and saved so many of them from the intended slaughter.

"What does a 'constitutional' monarch do next?" she grouched at Mannie.

"She begs leave to address the parliament of the people of Dresden."

"She does, does she?"

"Yep."

"And if she does, what sort of box is she walking into?"

"She's not walking into a box, good wife. The Grand Duchess is walking into the future for herself and her people."

Vicky knew that she had very little time to make one of the most momentous decisions in the Peterwald family history. Certainly, in the short history of the Greenfeld Empire.

Still, she'd had a lot of time to think, staring into the dark, or up at the ceiling. She knew Mannie. After all, she'd relied on him for so much of what had become her half of the Empire. She knew him well enough to marry him, even if he did have that hang-up on monogamy.

If she was honest with herself, she was not at all surprised by this bit of drama.

"Good man," she said to the welder of the staff. "Please pray permission from the parliament of the good people of Dresden for me to address a few well-chosen words to their hearts."

Again, he did an about face, and rapped on the door. "The Grand Duchess Victoria prays your permission to address a few well-chosen words to the hearts of the parliament of the people of Dresden."

The next voice just barely carried through the door. "Bid the Grand Duchess enter."

The two wooden doors creaked open. Vicky smiled; no doubt someone had sprayed fine dust onto the hinges until they made just the right noise. This was all pure political theater.

But it was political theater that drew people together for the hard work of making the compromises that let a diverse people rule themselves.

Vicky entered, Mannie and Admiral Bolesław two steps behind her. Behind them came the three officers followed by the three new sergeants. After them came several Navy lieutenants carrying the necessary paraphernalia of the awards and orders she would be bestowing today.

None of the uniformed personnel were under arms.

Only Vicky wore a ceremonial sword, and now she knew why Mannie had asked her to. The Provost officer of the parliament stood, blocking her way, his hand out.

Without a word, Vicky handed over her sword and scabbard.

Only then was she allowed to advance to the speaker's rostrum.

The room had been dead quiet as she entered. When she turned over her sword, the applause began. It grew as she approached the rostrum and went on and on. Mannie and the officers and sergeants took station below the rostrum. The other junior officers with the paraphernalia and panoplies of office she would award today stood off to the side.

Still the roar of approval went on.

The applause didn't come from just the floor of the opera house where the six hundred and twenty-two senators and their spouses and families sat. It turned out that 80% of one five hundredths of the population had become both the minimum and maximum for enrolling constituents.

That was no surprise. Mannie had always told Vicky that democracy was messy.

Four balconies rose above the main floor. They were filled to overflowing. Every person there, with the exception of some of the handicapped in the special boxes off to the sides, were on their feet, clapping, shouting, and whistling.

"Admiral, Mannie, get up here and bring the others," Vicky spoke, trying not to carry too far over the roar.

Mannie and the admiral led the six officers and sergeants up to stand behind her on the rostrum. Vicky presented each one of them to the crowd, and the clapping went even wilder.

"Do they even know who you are?" Vicky asked Mannie.

"The pictures of your six teammates has been circulating for the last two weeks. The admiral has been interviewed on the media about how the fleet was only too glad to help, and I, your humble servant, have been flitting about quite a bit."

Vicky went back down the row, now clapping herself

after she asked each of them to take a bow. That did nothing to reduce the applause.

Finally, Vicky leaned close to the microphone. "If you will grant me permission to say a few words, I have brought several awards for these brave men. I hope to award them if we don't run out of time."

Apparently, they did hear her over the clapping and cheering. The applause began to quiet down.

When it was low enough that Vicky thought she might be heard above it, she began.

"We are glad to stand before you today with your planet and people in much better health and cheer than the last time We passed this way. It is Our great joy to welcome all of you back into Our common realm. We invite you to rejoin Us in the search for fulfilling lives, responsible liberty, and the search for prosperity and happiness."

The applause began again, and Vicky listened to these, her people. She alone had not brought them their freedom. Many more had risked their lives to do that. She was just glad that she had done some part of it, and that she, as the personal embodiment of their Empire, could offer them a chance for a good future.

Mannie stepped forward and whispered in her ear, "You might want to raise both hands over your head, palms out, and kind of wave them back into their seats."

"Will that work?"

Mannie shrugged. "I've seen it work in historical videos. I've never had to try it myself."

"Thanks," Vicky said, then turned back to the people, raised her hands up, then motioned them down. After a few more gentle waves, the hall was quiet enough to go on.

"Here, before Us and you are your chosen representatives. You have raised them up to stand in your stead to establish a felicitous union for you all. That is not at all an easy job. Other planets have begun the long process of moving from the fiat rule that has been Our Empire's for far too long, to the difficult and messy business of rule by popular sovereignty."

There was a surprising break for applause at those words. If Vicky hadn't already arrived at the conclusion that her father and grandfather hadn't been tyrants, she might have gotten some suspicion from these cheers for her words.

Again, she waved the crowd back to quiet. It took a bit longer this time.

Lord, but we Peterwalds were not liked. Doubtlessly, the Empress and her family have not helped us burnish our crown.

When she could, she continued, "We enjoin you to pay close attention to how your future unrolls. We call upon you to work with your Senators to let them know what you like and do not like, what you need and will not brook. To join them in making your future one that you can be proud to hand off to your children and grandchildren."

Again, cheering and clapping filled the hall. Vicky stepped away from the mic. A man stepped up on the stage from the floor and ended up having to talk into her ear.

"Your Grace, I'm the Speaker, *pro tem*, of the Senate, at least until we organize ourselves seriously. Are you done with your speech? Do you have some awards you want to give?"

"Yes, if you can grant me the time. I'd like to award military medals for six of these men for participating with me in my effort to avoid massive slaughter when we took down the Duke. I also would like to induct these eight into an order for those who have risked their lives to save mine."

The Speaker nodded. "I think we can find time for that, Your Grace."

He took the rostrum and did the hand waving down thing to shorten the applause. Into the dull roar he announced.

"The Grand Duchess would now like to recognize the courage of some of the men who saved a lot of our lives from the Duke's plans to blow us to smithereens."

The hall fell silent, immediately.

Vicky stepped back to the rostrum. "I hope you can save your applause until I have recognized all three of these men for one award and then three more for another. Then, I will be inducting eight of them into a new Order I have just created."

She glanced over her shoulder. Mannie was whispering to Admiral Bolesław. He, in turn, was saying nothing, just grinning. The admiral was very good at grinning in a "no comment," way.

"The highest award that our Empire grants to those who have risked their lives in combat to achieve the mission and/ or save lives is the *Pour la Mérite*. We have before you three officers who volunteered without a word to follow me into the very heart of Dresden City, far ahead of the landing troops. Our goal was to find the controls that the Duke had for exploding all the mines he had scattered around town with the hostages."

Vicky paused to swallow, suddenly feeling that dark, damp night again.

"They got me in a position where I could do that, and then kept the Red Shirts from killing us all while I managed to deactivate the bombs and keep the Duke from the slaughter he intended. The courage they displayed was above and beyond the call of duty and in the best tradition of the uniformed services."

"Don't you deserve a *Pour la Mérite,* too?" a woman shouted from among the Senators.

"The Navy did award me one," Vicky said, pointing at the blue cross at her throat, "which I had to sign off on myself."

Vicky chuckled, then added. "The same senior officers who approved the award also wrote me a reprimand for sticking my nose in where senior officers are not supposed to mess around."

That brought the house down, this time with laughter and only a smattering of applause.

"So, now that I have been properly put in my place," Vicky said, to more laughter, as she turned to face the three captains. A lieutenant was suddenly at her side, three blue boxes in his hands.

One by one, Vicky went to Captain Blue, the former sergeant major and the tech sergeant. They bowed their heads, smartly, and Vicky put the lovely blue enameled Maltese cross around their necks. For now, they hung loose; later they would be tightened to dangle just below the collar.

That done, she offered the three for popular applause, and it went long.

After enough time had passed, Vicky called the next lieutenant up and went to stand beside the sergeants. The hall quieted of its own volition.

"These three sharpshooters kept the Red Shirts off Our neck at much risk to themselves. The Military Cross is usually reserved for officers, but it is very appropriate that they be recognized with it."

Vicky went up their line, pinning the ribbons with the dangling crosses on their breasts. Again, she offered them to the audience, and the hall filled with applause.

After a long minute, Vicky returned to the rostrum and the crowed quieted.

"Now, I would like to invest the first eight Lord Knight Commanders of the Imperial Victorian Order. All of these men have risked their lives to save mine. For that, I am eternally grateful.

She turned to them and said, "Admiral Bolesław, would you please step forward."

He did.

"As captain of the heavy cruiser *Attacker*, when it was set upon and seriously damaged in a sneak attack, you fought to save both your ship and my life. During the War of the Empress's Rebellion, he served at my side and many times, through advice and council, kept me from losing my head, both figuratively and actually. Admiral, it is most appropriate to induct you as the first Lord Knight Commander."

Vicky waved one of the lieutenants forward. He opened a large, flat, polished cherry wood box, and Vicky pulled forth a long red sash with a dazzling golden starburst holding the two ends together. She lifted up the other end, placed it over the admiral's head and settled the sash over his chest with the starburst on his hip.

"Thank you, Your Grace," he said with a bow of his head. Then he walked backwards to his place at the right of the line.

"Mannie," Vicky said, waving him forward.

"Are you sure, love?" he whispered softly.

"Must I command you?"

Mannie came forward to stand were Admiral Bolesław had been.

Vicky turned back to the microphone, "Most of you know Manuel Artemus as my loving consort. However, he has been at my side since well before I raised the flag of rebellion against the tyranny of the False Empress."

Vicky paused to take a deep breath. "The Empress had me kidnapped and staked out to die of thirst and hunger. As I had before, by luck and pluck, I managed to escape. Still, she had gunmen ready to give chase. I was barefoot."

Vicky paused to consider just how much bare she should share. "I had been stripped of all my clothing. Alone, defenseless, I fled ahead of my hired murderers."

Vicky turned to face Mannie. "Just when I thought I was only seconds from death, this man leapt from a helicopter to cover my body with his own. He put his own body between me and the gunmen. Manuel Artemus, you are the second Lord Commander of the Imperial Victorian Order.

Mannie looked at her, a soft smile on his slips. "I was terrified for you," he whispered.

"So was I," Vicky admitted.

A lieutenant with the large, shallow wooden box was immediately at her side. She pulled forth the bright red sash and medallion. The Navy and Army were all in dress uniforms. Mannie must have been intent in playing himself down.

He wore a blue herringbone tweed wool sports coat over gray trousers. His eggshell blue shirt was only slightly offset by a hand painted silk tied showing oceans and beaches. There was nothing there to draw the eye.

Across his understated clothing, Vicky laid the red sash of her new order with its gaudy golden starburst. She had promoted the self-effacing duckling into a peacock of the walk.

While applause rang out, he mouthed *I love you.*

I love you, too, she mouthed back.

She went down the line of the next six, seeing that each one got another round of applause.

When the room finally fell quiet for the last time, the Senate speaker *pro tem* stepped back up to the rostrum.

"We have a reception prepared in the ballroom next door. If you will all join us, we will be glad to spend some time together. Your Grace, will you be able to join us?"

"Of course," Vicky said. She expected this would be a long night.

"I have the Imperial Suite reserved for us tonight," Mannie whispered in her ear.

"Then it will be a wonderful night."

Vicky walked, with Mannie and Admiral Bolesław through a back passage to the ballroom. It was Mannie who asked the question that Vicky had left unsaid.

"I am assuming since we haven't heard anything bad from the fleet that the missing Bowlingame battle fleet is still missing?"

"They're out there somewhere," the admiral agreed. "We've set up enough outposts so that we'll know it immediately if they make a move on us. Still, if they stay far enough back in their territory, we don't have the means right now, what with all the jump buoys disabled, to know where they are."

"Where does the fleet go next?" Mannie asked, "I mean, if that's not a breach of operational security."

"Lublin is a couple of unoccupied systems from here," Admiral Bolesław. "It's a big system and I think Her Grace would love to cut it out of the Bowlingames' income stream. However, Oryol is also only three jumps, all of them occupied by colonies. If we showed ourselves in those systems, we might have a fleet ready to fight us."

"You'd like that, Admiral?" Mannie asked.

"I'd love that. I think that fleet is all that stands between us and the reduction of the Bowlingames to pauper prison."

"So," Vicky said, as they came to the end of the corridor, "Let's go encourage people in their own governance and then go find a fleet and kill it."

ABOUT THE AUTHOR

Mike Shepherd is the National best-selling author of the Kris Longknife saga. Mike Moscoe is the award-nominated short story writer who has also written several novels, most of which were, until recently, out of print. Though the two have never been seen in the same room at the same time, they are reported to be good friends.

Mike Shepherd grew up Navy. It taught him early about change and the chain of command. He's worked as a bartender and cab driver, personnel advisor and labor negotiator. Now retired from building databases about the endangered critters of the Northwest, he looks forward to some fun reading and writing.

Mike lives in Vancouver, Washington, with his wife Ellen, and not too far from his daughter and grandkids. He enjoys reading, writing, dreaming, watching grandchildren for story ideas and upgrading his computer – all are never ending.

For more information:
https://krislongknife.com
mikeshepherd@krislongknife.com

2018 RELEASES

In 2016, I amicably ended my twenty-year publishing relationship with Ace, part of Penguin Random House.

In 2017, I began publishing through my own independent press, KL & MM Books. We produced six e-books and a short story collection. We also brought the books out in paperback and audio.

In 2018, I intend to keep the novels coming.

We began the year with **Kris Longknife's Successor**. Grand Admiral Santiago still has problems. Granny Rita is on the rampage again, and the cats have gone on strike, refusing to send workers to support the human effort on Alwa. Solving that problem will be tough. The last thing Sandy needs is trouble with the murderous alien space raiders. So, of course, that is what she gets.

May 1 had **Kris Longknife: Commanding** published. Kris has won her first battle, but the way the Iteeche celebrate victory can be hard on the stomach. The rebellion won't quit and now Kris needs to raise a fleet, not only to defend the Iteeche Imperial capitol, but also take the war to the rebels.

On August 1, **Vicky Peterwald: Dominator** was published. Grand Duchess Vicky Peterwald has everything. A loving fiancé who's soon to be her husband, adoring crowds, and she gets to share her golden wedding carriage with Kris Longknife. What more could a girl want? Well, the Emperor, her father, could have showed up to walk her down the aisle, but she's not really bothered about that. It turns out that he didn't make the wedding because he's broke and living nearly homeless in an abandoned, half-built, palace. News isn't coming out of Dad's side of the Empire, so it looks like Vicky may need a battle fleet to go pay Daddy dear a visit with a few brigades of infantry and tanks. Somebody should have known better than piss Vicky Peterwald off. Now they have, and she won't let anything get in her way of being Vicky Peterwald: Dominator.

In the second half of 2018, you can look forward to the following:

Kris Longknife Implacable on November 1.

Stay in touch to follow developments by friending Kris Longknife and follow Mike Shepherd on Facebook or check in at my website http://krislongknife.com

MORE BOOKS BY MIKE SHEPHERD

If you enjoyed this book, here is a list of more books by Mike Shepherd, including some of his early works and short story collections. All have hyperlinks. Enjoy!

Published by KL & MM Books

Kris Longknife: Emissary

Kris Longknife: Admiral

Kris Longknife: Commanding

Kris Longknife's Relief

Kris Longknife's Replacement

Kris Longknife's Successor

Rita Longknife: Enemy Unknown

Rita Longknife: Enemy in Sight

Vicky Peterwald: Dominator

Short Stories from KL & MM Books

Kris Longknife's Maid Goes on Strike & Other Short Stories

Kris Longknife's Maid Goes On Strike

Kris Longknife's Bad Day

Ruth Longknife's First Christmas

Kris Longknife: Among the Kicking Birds

~

Ace Science Fiction Books by Mike Shepherd

Kris Longknife: Mutineer

Kris Longknife: Deserter

Kris Longknife: Defiant

Kris Longknife: Resolute

Kris Longknife: Audacious

Kris Longknife: Intrepid

Kris Longknife: Undaunted

Kris Longknife: Redoubtable

Kris Longknife: Daring

Kris Longknife: Furious

Kris Longknife: Defender

Kris Longknife: Tenacious

Kris Longknife: Unrelenting

Kris Longknife: Bold

Vicky Peterwald: Target

Vicky Peterwald: Survivor

Vicky Peterwald: Rebel

~

Mike Shepherd writing as Mike Moscoe in the Jump Point Universe

First Casualty

The Price of Peace

They Also Serve

Rita Longknife: To Do or Die

Ace Science Fiction Short Specials

Kris Longknife: Training Daze

Kris Longknife: Welcome Home, Go Away

Kris Longknife's Bloodhound

Kris Longknife's Assassin

The Lost Millennium Trilogy by Mike Shepherd, published by KL & MM Books

Lost Dawns: Prequel

First Dawn

Second Fire

Lost Days

Award-Nominated Short Story Collections by Mike Shepherd, published by KL & MM Books

A Day's Work on the Moon

The Job Interview

The Strange Redemption of Sister MaryAnn